chasing
the
phoenix

A Tom Doherty Associates Book
New York

chasing the phoenix

MICHAEL SWANWICK

CHASING THE PHOENIX

Copyright © 2015 by Michael Swanwick

A Tor Book
Published by Tom Doherty Associates, LLC
175 Fifth Avenue
New York, NY 10010

www.tor-forge.com

Tor® is a registered trademark of Tom Doherty Associates, LLC.

Library of Congress Cataloging-in-Publication Data

Swanwick, Michael.
    Chasing the Phoenix / Michael Swanwick.—First edition.
        p. cm.
    ISBN 978-0-7653-8090-6 (hardcover)
    ISBN 978-1-4668-7606-4 (e-book)
    I. Title.
PS3569.W28C48 2015
813'.54—dc23

2015015733

Tor books may be purchased for educational, business, or promotional use. For information on bulk purchases, please contact the Macmillan Corporate and Premium Sales Department at 1-800-221-7945, extension 5442, or write to specialmarkets@macmillan.com.

First Edition: August 2015

Printed in the United States of America

0   9   8   7   6   5   4   3   2   1

Author's Note

I write of a China I have neither seen nor suffered nor learned of from another, a China which is not and could not have been nor ever will be, and therefore my readers should by no means mistake it for the real one. No insult or slander is intended toward a country or a people whom I both respect and admire.

to marianne,
who is as beautiful
as china to me

acknowledgments

My sincere thanks go to John Minford, for graciously granting me permission to use his translation of the opening of Sun Tzu's *The Art of War,* to Pete Tillman, for his expertise on nuclear weaponry, and to Shieh-ya Ma, for insights into Chinese history. Also to Gregory Frost, for his masterful interpretation of Aubrey Darger. I am grateful to the staff of *Science Fiction World,* for their generous hospitality in Chengdu, and to everyone I met in China, most particularly Jenny Bai, Si Qin, and Haihong Zhao, for their friendship and support. On-the-ground research was performed by the M. C. Porter Endowment for the Arts.

War is
A grave affair of the state;
It is a place
Of life and death,
A road
To survival and extinction,
A matter
To be pondered carefully.

—SUN TZU, *THE ART OF WAR*
(JOHN MINFORD, TRANS.)

chasing
the
phoenix

1.

Third year, summer, first month, of the royal year. The Hidden King killed his brothers so that there might be no rivals for his throne and continued his preparations for war. In that same month, a stranger unlike any ever seen before came to the Abundant Kingdom.

—THE SUMMER AND WINTER ANNALS

SURPLUS CAME down out of the north dressed in a Mongolian shaman's robes covered with multicolored ribbons and hammered copper disks. He was leading a yak adorned with red tassels and tiny silver bells. The yak carried a bundle swaddled in cloth and carefully tied up with ropes.

In the bundle was the corpse of his friend Aubrey Darger.

The territory he passed through was blessed by Providence with fertile farmlands and plentiful water and was therefore known throughout China as the land of leisure and abundance. Fields of canola, tea, and sugarcane alternated with groves of mulberry, tung, and camphor laurel trees, to say nothing of such Utopian survivals as sausage gourds, self-fermenting litchi fruit, and the neural reprogramming tubers from which various tutelary liqueurs were distilled.

Small wonder that this lush country was called the Abundant Kingdom.

Yet as he traveled, the American adventurer could not help but notice frequent groups of soldiers galloping purposefully through the countryside and, on the roads, long trains of wagons carrying gunpowder, grain, salt, crates of swords and rifles, and bundles of uniforms, along with coffles of horses and herds of swine and cattle being driven toward the capital in great numbers. Clearly, preparations were being made for war. So it was that he came to the city of Brocade in an uncharacteristically apprehensive mood.

As he approached the city gate, Surplus made sure that his tail was safely tucked inside his robes. Then he threw a scarf over his head and donned a wide straw hat so that, when he stared down at the ground, his face could not be seen. His paws were hidden by his robe's long sleeves.

Three guards loitered by the gate, unenthusiastically watching a steady flow of peasants, monks, merchants, and the like come and go. They straightened at Surplus's approach, their boredom instantly dispelled by the appearance of so colorful a personage. "Halt!" their captain cried. "Identify yourself and your place of origin and your doubtless squalid and illegal reasons for wishing to enter the city."

Behind him, his two subordinates struck fierce postures. Because they all stood in the center of the gate, blocking passage, a crowd began to gather.

"My name is of no matter," Surplus said mildly. He turned to his yak and, tucking his walking stick under his arm, began to untie the bundle. "I come from a land where there is neither disease nor pain. Children do not grow old there, nor do flowers fade. No one drinks alcohol, for the water that runs down from the Mountains of Life is purer than any other water and satisfies all needs, from hunger to the calming of the passions. There is only one power that this divine water lacks, and it is for this reason that I have come to Brocade, seeking the Infallible Physician." He threw back the cloth to reveal the corpse-gray face of his friend. "It cannot bring the dead back to life."

A gasp of horror went up from the crowd. "Arrest that man!" cried the captain of the guard. "He is either a grave robber or something worse."

But when the two subordinate guards tried to lay hands on Surplus, he lashed out with his cane, striking one on the forehead with its tip and then burying its silver knob deep in the other's stomach. Both men went down, the one unconscious and the other kneeling in the street, clutching himself and moaning piteously.

The captain of the guard reflexively took a step backward.

Speaking in a deep and unhurried voice, Surplus said, "Is this the famous courtesy of Brocade? Far have I traveled to come here. From the Beautiful Country came I, across the Atlantic Ocean to the Land of Heroes. Then by various ways to Moscow in the Lean Country, through Siberia to Mongolia, and from there south to the Respectful Land and the Kingdom of the Blue Sea. Everywhere I went, your city was praised for the warmth and hospitality of its people. Hearing this, I thought: I must reward this metropolis for its virtue. What shall I give it? Perhaps it needs a new river. Perhaps I should place rich veins of silver in the land nearby. But, arriving, I discover its people are arrogant and rude. Shall I then punish you with whirlwinds or earthquake or plague?"

Bristling, the captain said, "Who are you to speak so strangely and to make such extravagant threats?" Yet he advanced on Surplus with visible reluctance.

Surplus stopped him with a lordly gesture. "Do not ask who," he cried. "But, rather, ask *what*!"

Throwing off his hat and scarf, Surplus bared his teeth and growled. Thus presenting the man with the uncanny sight of a dog's head on a man's body. Simultaneously, he drew the blade from his sword cane so that to the crowd, whose attention was riveted on his face, it would seem to have materialized in his paw.

The captain fell to his knees. It was possible that Surplus's having swung around the wooden half of his cane and with it deftly striking those same knees in the back helped this occur. Surplus then brought up his own knee and dealt the scoundrel a blow to the chin that sent him sprawling on the cobbles.

Placing a foot on the man's chest and letting the sword's point dangle by his eyes, Surplus said, too quietly for anybody but his fallen victim to hear, "Do nothing, and you will not be harmed." Then he raised his voice and addressed everyone within earshot. "Who here knows where the Infallible Physician lives?"

There was a rustle in the crowd as people looked around to see who might speak up. No one did. Surplus glared about him, and they all shrank away from his fierce mien. "I shall put off punishing this city until I have spoken with the Infallible Physician. It may well be that he will talk me into staying my righteous wrath. Or perhaps—and I consider this far more likely—he will but confirm me in my judgment. We shall see."

Without hurry, Surplus reunited the two halves of his cane and tied up his friend's corpse. He did not pick up his hat and scarf but left them blowing in the street. Then he strode imperiously into the city, leading his yak by the reins. Though it did not take him long to pass beyond those who had witnessed the incident at the gate, his appearance continued to draw stares.

To one of Surplus's profession, the best thing to be in a city was anonymous. Failing that, however, notoriety would do.

A QUESTION here and an answer there led Surplus to the central market. There, he went from merchant to merchant, asking after the Infallible Physician. "I have heard of that distinguished man," said a terrified vendor of dumpling fruit, "but not of where he might live." The woman selling flower necklaces that bloomed and changed color according to their wearer's emotions and that all clenched up into scentless black buds at his approach, dipped her head and in a small voice said, "Alas, no." The man at the next table said, "All I know is that he has never come to buy my spices." A fat Buddha of an ostler who rented out red-and-white-striped saddle-cats for children to ride along an oval track merely spread his flabby arms and shrugged.

None of this discouraged Surplus, however, for he saw the staring eyes all about him, and heard the whispered comments in his wake, and knew that he was at the epicenter of expanding circles of rumor and speculation that were even now running swiftly through the city. Someone, he was sure, would materialize soon enough and provide him with the information he sought. In the meantime, he noted approvingly that though many of the merchants stiffened and paled at the sight of him, all replied to his questions politely, and several offered him a mango, a glass of liqueur, or the like. One man, indeed, eyes quivering, urged upon him a pearl the size of his fist, carved into the likeness of an ocean wave crashing into a mountainside, near the summit of which was a small pagoda topped by the obscure religious symbol the ancients called a "satellite dish." Then, when that was refused, the vendor tried to give him a chunk of ivory root carved into eight concentric lattice balls, each so decorated as to represent one of the possible electron shells of an atom with the ephemeral forms that decayed almost instantly on the outermost two shells and the yin and yang of hydrogen and helium at the center. It seemed that the renowned courtesy of Brocade was not entirely of his own invention.

"Sir! Dog-man, sir!"

A young man came running out in the street and bowed deeply before Surplus. "My name is Capable Servant, sir, and I am looking for employment."

"I have no need of a servant," Surplus said, and turned away.

But somehow the young man had twisted himself in front of Surplus again. Smiling ingratiatingly, he said, "Everybody needs a servant, excellent sir, whether they know it or not. I can wash and mend clothes, shop wisely, haggle well over prices, brew beer, mix ink, and cut goose quills into pens. When times are hard, I can trap hares in the countryside and, with the aid of roots and spices I know how to identify in the wild, turn them into a delicious stew. I am able to distinguish poisonous mushrooms from those which are nutritious to eat, and can whistle cheerful tunes to repel ghosts. I will wake you up in the morning, draw your bath, discreetly relay love letters to your paramours, and carry you home safely when you're drunk. Also, I can curry the fur of your yak and, saving the hair that comes off in the brush, make of it a soft yarn from which to knit you warm socks for the winter, and perform a thousand chores more besides."

"These are all useful services, and I have no doubt you will easily find someone who needs them done. For my part, my only desire is to find the Infallible Physician." Surplus gently pushed the young man aside and continued onward.

Only to discover Capable Servant trotting by his side, eyes agleam. "Oh, sir! I know where to find that esteemed gentleman. I even know why others do not, for I am curious by nature and make it my business to listen to all the gossip and idle chatter, and I forget not a word of it, though years may pass. I am a very useful fellow indeed, sir."

Surplus stopped. "Very well," he said. "If you can bring me to the Infallible Physician and if he can bring my friend back to life, as I was told in the steppes he could, then I will hire you at standard wages for so long as you wish to be my servant."

"You are truly gracious, sir. The Infallible Physician no longer lives in Brocade. Several years ago, he retired to a small hut in a village an hour's walk outside the city walls. That is why he is so hard to find. But I shall lead you directly to his door."

THUS IT was that, within hours of entering Brocade, Surplus left again, this time in possession of a manservant. As they walked, Surplus asked, "Is your name really Capable Servant?"

"Oh yes, sir. My mother named me Capable Servant of No Special Distinction, thinking it would improve my chances of finding employment. Capable Servant, because that is what every gentleman needs. Of No Special Distinction to reassure my master that I am unlikely to leave his hire seeking better pay elsewhere."

"How, then, did you find yourself in need of a job?"

"My last employer grew very old and died." Capable Servant made a sad face. "But tell me, sir. When I am asked the name of my employer, what shall I say?"

"My name is Sir Blackthorpe Ravenscairn de Plus Precieux, which is how I should be addressed on formal occasions. But, that being a bit overlong for everyday use, you may call me Surplus."

"Yours is a strange and wonderful name," Capable Servant marveled, "and surely foretells some great destiny. May I ask you another question, sir?"

"Go ahead."

"Why is it that you have the stance and intellect of a man, but the fur and features of a dog?"

"In the Demesne of Western Vermont, that great nation whose citizen I have the honor to be"—in Chinese the name translated as the Land of the Green Mountains of the West—"the scientists are particularly adept at genetic manipulation. Taking the genome of the noble dog, they expressed a gene here and suppressed another there to create me as I am."

"Yes, sir. Exactly so, sir. But, sir—why?"

"Oh," Surplus said, glancing up the road lazily curving to the top of a low hill, "I am certain that they had their reasons."

At that instant, a giant metal spider crested the hilltop. Lifting and dropping eight sleek and cunningly jointed legs, the gleaming black monstrosity stalked down the road toward the two travelers with ponderous delicacy. Surplus stopped dead in his tracks. Capable Servant fell over backward in astonishment.

The incredible machine flowed down the hillside and then came to a stop directly before Surplus. Its legs bent, lowering the soldier in the cab that made up its flattened sphere of a body to Surplus's eye level. They goggled at one another in amazement.

"Hello!" The soldier might have been a child witnessing its first circus.

"Hello!" Surplus, for his part, could not have been more astonished if a *Megalosaurus,* forty feet long, had come waddling out of the underbrush.

"What on earth are you?" the soldier demanded.

"I might ask the same question of you," Surplus replied.

"I am Sergeant Bright Prosperity of the Good Fortune Spider Corps"—the young man slapped the metal flank of his vehicle—"and this is my war machine, Death to the Enemies of the State. And you, sir?"

"I am but a humble shaman from the steppes of Mongolia. Forgive me for saying so, but your machine terrifies me. It is like a nightmare out of the past. Surely in China, as in all civilized lands, such complex mechanisms are both illegal and abhorred."

The soldier laughed. "Ah, sir, my mount and I are not of the past, but rather the spearhead of the future. These resurrected machines will be the terror of the Hidden King's enemies and the foundation of the Abundant Kingdom's new glory. Our scholars located them in hidden man-made caverns deep within the earth, our natural philosophers created fuel for them, and now men such as I have learned how to make them go where we wish. Yes, in all the other countries of China the Great, they are yet shunned and feared. That, they shall discover to their chagrin, will be their downfall."

"You intend to use this dreadful thing as a weapon?" Surplus asked.

"Only the Hidden King is in a position to make such a decision." The soldier lifted his chin. "But when he does—as I am sure he must—I stand ready to ride my mount to the Land of the Mountain Horses, across the Panda Mountains, and all the way to its capital city of Peace, scattering his enemies before me."

"You are a bold man, Sergeant Bright Prosperity, and so I can only conclude is your king as well. Would you like me to bestow a blessing upon you and your mechanical arachnid abomination?"

"Thank you, but no, oh dog-shaman. My mount and I are in no need of your superstitious mumbo jumbo."

"Then I shall simply stand out of your way."

The soldier raised his spider's cab to its full height and it strode down the road.

In its wake, a second spider topped the hill, and behind that a third. One by one, over forty such vehicles sped lightly past Surplus and Capable Servant, who stared after them until all had disappeared in the distance.

"Have I seen what I saw, or was it all a dream?" one of them asked.

"A dream, surely," said the other. "And yet it seemed so real."

Marveling, they resumed their journey.

IN THOUGHTFUL silence Surplus and his new servant made their way through the countryside to the edge of a small but tidy village. There they were directed to a thatched hut with a single flowering magnolia in the dirt dooryard. Chickens scratched about among the sparse weeds. It seemed a highly unlikely place to find an illustrious man of medicine.

At a nod from Surplus, Capable Servant knocked on the door.

A white-bearded man, bent over with age and leaning on a stick whose support he clearly needed, answered the knock, frowning. "Go away," he said, and slammed the door.

The two excludees looked at one another. Then Capable Servant knocked a second time.

Again, the ancient opened the door.

"Brave news, oh renowned Infallible Physician!" Capable Servant said, beaming. "My master, the Sir Blackthorpe Ravenscairn de Plus Precieux of the Land of the Green Mountains of the West, has come to consult with you and to avail himself of your considerable and accomplished skills."

From the corner of his eye, Surplus saw neighbors peering out of their windows and children climbing up on fences to gawk. He raised his head to emphasize his canine profile and twitched his tail so that all might see it was real.

The Infallible Physician stepped aside from his door. "Very well," he said. "Enter, if you must."

———

"BRIGHT PEARL!" the old man shouted into the darkness. "Guest! Make tea! My daughter," he said to Surplus. "Almost useless. Very lazy."

A middle-aged woman appeared in the kitchen doorway, bowed quickly, disappeared again.

Infallible Physician sat, and Surplus followed suit. After a polite pause to give his host the opportunity to speak, Surplus said, "Sir, I have come seeking your—"

"I am the best doctor there is," the Infallible Physician said. "But I cannot help you." He laughed sharply. "You look like a dog! No cure for that."

Careful not to let his annoyance show, Surplus said, "I have no desire to deny my ancestry, sir. Your services are required not by me but by my friend. In Mongolia, he caught one of the war viruses that still linger from the mad times following the fall of Utopia. To save him, the doctors there swiftly and painlessly put him to death. Then, before putrefaction could set in, they wrapped around his body a silver exoskeleton, a revenant of antiquity, which (and this may sound incredible, but I saw it with my own two eyes) sank beneath his skin like butter melting into toast, leaving neither scar nor incision behind. Finally, they injected him with drugs and packed his body cavities with herbs. Together, these things preserve him in perfect stasis, dead but not deteriorating. One week in this state, they assured me, would be enough to starve the virus, thus destroying it. Unfortunately, while they could preserve his body, they had long ago forgotten how to resurrect it."

"I see," the Infallible Physician said.

"Sir, your fame has spread far from the Abundant Kingdom. The Mongolian doctors told me that what they could not do, you and you alone assuredly could. This is why I have sought you out. Will you help me?"

"Ah." The old man nodded and fell into silence again.

"Sir? Please tell me that my long journey has not been in vain."

The Infallible Physician smiled and narrowed his eyes so that only slits remained open. From between the lids he peered enigmatically at his guest.

"Sir, I must implore you—"

"It is no use." Bright Pearl emerged from the kitchen holding a tray with a teakettle and four cups. She poured one cup for Surplus and another for her father, who bent low over it and slurped noisily. "My father has moments of lucidity, but they do not last. He will be silent now for hours and possibly days. In any event—and please pardon me for overhearing your conversation, but the house is small—the man you came here looking for was not he but my grandfather."

"I beg your pardon?"

Bright Pearl poured another cup of tea for Capable Servant, who accepted it with a bob of his head and a bright smile, and a fourth for herself. Then she knelt, facing Surplus. "Ninety years ago, the original Infallible Physician and his beautiful young wife came to Brocade from what distant land no man today may say. He was everything your friends told you and more. There was no disease he could not cure nor any injury he could not ameliorate. It was said that he retained secrets of medicine which all the rest of the world had forgotten. Thus, for many years, he prospered. His wife bore him a son, and when that son came of age, the Infallible Physician taught him the healing arts.

"Yet, oddly enough, he and his wife did not age like normal people do, so that when the son was grown, they looked not like his parents but like brother and sister to him. The neighbors began to gossip that they were not human at all. There was talk of bringing them before the magistrate as demons.

"Then, one night, before any violence could occur, the couple simply disappeared. After an appropriate period of mourning, their son took over his father's business and, because he had been wisely taught, in time became known as the Infallible Physician himself. For while his skills were inferior to his father's they greatly surpassed those of all other doctors. That man was my father, and in turn he married and had two sons and a daughter. That daughter was I.

"Alas, my brothers both died before I was born and my father thought it shameful that a woman should become a doctor. I had ambitions of my own, however, and studied his books in secret and stood at his elbow, watching while he worked. I would have become the third Infallible Physician if only he had allowed it. But he would not. Even when he began to sink into senility and I begged him to let me cure him, he forbade it absolutely.

"Finally, he was as you see him now.

"Surely, I thought then, he would want me to restore his mind to its old acuity. Surely he would be grateful to me for doing so. For two weeks I mixed potions and dosed and treated him with calculation and care. He recovered—and beat me for disobedience. Then, perversely, he mixed himself counter potions and returned to senility."

Horrified, Surplus said, "How is such a thing possible?"

"Men are stubborn," Bright Pearl said, "and my father is far more stubborn than most men. Irrationally, he blames me for the deaths of my brothers. Wickedly, he prefers to live without memories rather than dealing with those he earned." She dipped her head in sadness. "So we live in poverty, and my skills, which are considerable, go unused. Because I have neither certification nor reputation, people will trust me with only the smallest of medical chores—cleaning a knife cut or splinting a broken arm—and pay me accordingly."

A spark of hope still burned within Surplus. Now, in his thoughts, he heaped tinder against it and, pursing mental lips, gently blew. "You studied your grandfather's books, you say. Perhaps you could—"

"No," Bright Pearl said. "I saw nothing like what you describe in them." She looked away. "But enough about my problems. Tell me of yourself and the adventures that brought you to our door."

"It is a long and convoluted story, and one which I do not care to relate at this time." Surplus waved a paw vaguely. "Suffice it to say that when I entered Siberia, I possessed tremendous wealth and a living friend. Now I am as you see me." He sighed. "And I must find an appropriate place to bury the illustrious Aubrey Darger, who was the nonpareil of his profession and the best and truest of friends."

Abruptly, Capable Servant, who had been quietly poking about among the handwritten codices that thronged the room's many shadowy shelves, said, "Madam lady doctor, look! Within this book titled *The Thwarting of Death* there is a drawing of a physician placing a silver skeleton about the body of a corpse and of his assistant exclaiming at the fact that the skeleton begins to sink beneath the skin. And look! A caption below the drawing reads: *The Reversible Death*. Furthermore, on the next page, there is another picture showing a second physician using a strange device to extract that same skeleton from the anus of a man who is no longer dead."

Leaping to his feet, Surplus snatched the book from his servant's hand. "It's true! This first picture illustrates the exact method I saw employed in Mongolia." He looked sternly at his hostess. "You have been lying to me, Bright Pearl."

Defiantly, Bright Pearl scrambled to her feet and closed the book in Surplus's paws. Then she placed it back on its shelf. "There is a rich collector of antiquities who wishes to buy all my father's books and instruments. We are negotiating the price. Further, the instrument shown in the book can only be used once. And I can see by looking at you that you are not a wealthy man."

Surplus favored Bright Pearl with his most winning and sincere expression. "It is true that I am currently penniless," he said. "But that is a condition that will not last long. Inevitably, money will, one way or another, flow into my pockets. There is no need to await that happy event, however, for I am currently prepared to offer you a price beyond imagining if you return my friend to life."

"And what is that?"

"My yak."

"I am no farmer. Why should I desire such a creature?"

"It will make your reputation as a surgeon, and that in turn will make you wealthy."

"Oh?"

"Without question." Surplus explained carefully and at some length. He laid out his plan step by step, with such detailed clarity that the lady doctor could have no doubt whatsoever that it would work.

When he was done, Bright Pearl rubbed her chin and said, "You are a cunning and deceitful man, sir."

Surplus smiled modestly. "It is how I make my living."

IT TOOK a few minutes to script their performance and a while longer to rehearse it. But at last, leaving Bright Pearl's father in the house, the three main players walked outside. Up and down the street, old men loitered under trees smoking long pipes and housewives lingered by the well with empty buckets or knelt in their gardens pulling weeds or sat in their doorways weaving. Husbands worked in their yards, carving bone clothesline pins or weaving rattan chairs or building drying racks for fish. Wives hung laundry and smoothed it inch by inch (as no woman ever had before) to remove nonexistent wrinkles. The village was uncannily quiet. Not a person spoke to any other. All were positioned so as to have a good view of the Infallible Physician's hut.

They had their audience.

Surplus was the first on stage, with Capable Servant scurrying after him. The two carefully took Darger's corpse from the yak's back and placed it at the feet of Bright Pearl, who stood, arms folded, watching impassively. They untied and then unwrapped the cloth, revealing Darger's dead body with a flourish.

A silent gasp arose from the watching villagers.

Bright Pearl knelt and placed her ear against Darger's chest. She licked a finger and placed it under his nostrils. Then she put her nose to his wrist and sniffed. Finally, she rose and in an angry voice said, "You have brought me a corpse. Why would you do such a disrespectful thing?"

Extending a paw in supplication, Surplus said, "I was told, madam, that you could cure my friend's condition."

"Your friend is dead," Bright Pearl declared loudly enough for all the village to hear.

"That is the condition that I wish cured," Surplus said, speaking with equal clarity. He fell to his knees before Bright Pearl, and Capable Servant did likewise. They threw dirt into their hair and wailed, "Bring our friend to life! Bring our friend to life!"

"Stop that nonsense immediately." Bright Pearl picked up a fallen magnolia branch. "Or I will beat you within an inch of your lives. Bringing a man back from the dead is not something to be done lightly. Three things would be required before I would even consider the possibility—and I am certain you can fulfill none of them."

"Name them!" Surplus cried, still kneeling.

"First, your friend would have to be of the highest moral character."

"Madam, this is the saintly Aubrey Darger! In London, he freed Queen Alice from the clutches of her greatest enemy. In France, he rediscovered the long-lost Eiffel Tower. In Prague, he single-handedly defeated an army of golems. All of Moscow reveres him for waking the Duke of Muscovy from his decades-long slumber and, shortly thereafter, making certain vital improvements to the Kremlin and indeed to the city itself."

Visibly unimpressed, Bright Pearl said, "Second, you would have to pay me a tremendous amount of money. More, I am sure, than you can possibly possess."

Capable Servant leaped up, removed the saddlebag from the yak and, holding open the flap, showed her its contents.

Bright Pearl looked genuinely startled. It was possible, Surplus reflected, that, because he had not washed his spare clothes in some time, their odor was somewhat pungent. However, since Bright Pearl was the only villager close enough to see—or smell!—the saddlebag's contents, that fact did no harm. With a dismissive wave of her hand, she said to Capable Servant, "Take that inside."

At last, turning back to the groveling dog-man at her feet, Bright Pearl said, "Two of the three conditions, I must confess, you have fulfilled. But not the third. For an operation this extreme would require a measure of the healing blood of the sacred yak of Shiliin Bogd Mountain, which will cure any illness—and *that* I doubt very much you can provide!"

With a cry of joy, Surplus leapt to his feet. Tugging at Bright Pearl's sleeve, he exclaimed, "Come! Look! Knowing you would require it, I have done what no other living being could have accomplished and brought you that very beast. Examine its eyes! Its horns! Its brow! With your discerning vision, you will see in an instant that it is genuine. If you will only cure my friend, this treasure beyond avarice is yours."

Her expression dubious, Bright Pearl examined the yak closely. Her eyes widened. Then she said, "You have done all that is required. Bring your dead friend inside. Then draw three drams of the sacred yak's blood and bring it to me." She turned on her heel, as haughty as a queen. "I shall prepare the operation."

Bowing deeply (and hiding a smile of enormous satisfaction) Surplus said, "As you wish, so shall it be done, oh Infallible Physician."

2.

Their origins were obscure, their first appearance inauspicious. There was nothing to be said in their favor, save that heaven favored them.

—THE BOOK OF THE TWO ROGUES

FOR THREE days, Darger lay abed in the Infallible Physician's house, recovering. Occasionally, children tapped on the windows, hoping to terrify themselves with a glimpse of the dogman or of the corpse that had been brought back from the dead. When their antics drew Darger's attention, he simply turned his head away.

Capable Servant, meanwhile, had proved more than worthy of his name. He had laundered both Surplus's and Darger's clothing and, without being instructed to do so, removed the multicolored ribbons from the Mongolian robes, bleached the stains, and patched the small rips that travel had inevitably conferred upon them, so that they could be worn in public without drawing unneeded attention. He also swept and mopped the floors, cooked meals for them and their hosts, and in a hundred different ways made himself indispensable to their domestic life.

"Nevertheless," Surplus told him, "Aubrey Darger, though nominally alive, cannot be said to have been brought back to life again. He will not speak and there is an enduring darkness in his eyes. He has always been prone to depression, but I have never seen it this bad before. All my efforts will have been for nothing if he does not let go of whatever holds him prisoner in his bed." There were only three rooms in the house. Darger had the back room, and a curtain hung in the middle of the front one at night enabled Surplus and Bright Pearl's father to share it with her without scandal. Capable Servant slept in the kitchen.

"You should have let me rectify that ugly face of his," Bright Pearl said. "I could have made him a handsome Chinese man. Then he would be more cheerful."

"Darger can live with the face God gave him. His malady is not of the body but of the spirit, madam, and we must find its cure. I need a business partner, and your reputation requires a brilliant success." Surplus slapped his knees with both paws. "The time has come for direct confrontation. I suggest, Bright Pearl, that you take your father outside and let him enjoy the sun. There may be shouting, and I suspect that it would disturb the venerable geezer."

"Bah!" the old Infallible Physician said. "Nonsense! If anyone is to do any shouting, it will be me."

"AROUSE YOURSELF, sir!" Surplus cried, slamming the door as he entered. He threw aside the drapes and flung wide the windows, flooding the room with sunshine and fresh air. He and Capable Servant seized Darger by the arms, forcibly hauling him to a sitting position. "The sun is risen and there is work to be done."

"Work," Darger said in a voice that might have come from the depths of a tomb.

"Yes, work."

"What's the point?"

"You astound me. Honest labor is what we were put here on earth to do. By our efforts we improve our lot and in the process increase the common share of happiness for all mankind."

Darger shook his head shaggily. "I died."

"I was present at the time," Surplus reminded him.

"Now I am alive."

"You state the obvious. The man I *thought* I was resurrecting would never have lowered himself so." Moderating his tone, Surplus crouched down and took Darger's hand. "Tell us, dear friend. Tell us the reason for this perverse refusal of yours to embrace the miracle of life restored."

Bleak beyond all telling, Darger's eyes rose to meet his friend's. He looked like a man staring into the abyss. At last, he managed to say, "I was dead . . . and I did not see God."

"That is a privilege vouchsafed to very few."

"You do not understand. Neither did I experience an afterlife of any sort. I remember seeing the world shrink down to a pinprick of light. And then . . . nothing. No heaven. No nirvana. No celestial virgins. No oversoul. No reincarnation. No mystic visions. Nothing at all until you resurrected me. Only a complete and utter negation of being."

"Darger, you are a professed agnostic. Surely you must have considered this possibility."

"There is a great difference between admitting one's ignorance of ultimate matters and having it proved that life is not only brief but meaningless as well."

"Oh, for pity's sake!" Surplus cried. "I refuse to debate this matter with you. It would simply be indulging your tendency toward introspection and abstraction."

"Sir." From behind him, Capable Servant suggested, "Try reminding your noble friend of the great successes of his life."

"That is an excellent idea, Capable Servant. Aubrey, do you remember our first meeting? We convinced the lords and ladies of Buckingham Labyrinth that we possessed a device from ancient times which would allow instantaneous communication through the Internet without rousing the demons and mad gods living therein."

"I remember that . . . there were complications."

"In Paris, we sold the Eiffel Tower, despite its location having been lost for centuries."

"Yes." The faintest touch of warmth entered Darger's voice. "That was not badly done."

"In Stockholm, we sold nonexistent royal titles—several of them to none other than the king of Sweden himself."

Darger said nothing, but one side of his mouth quirked upward in a near smile.

"Starting with nothing but a forged letter of recommendation from the caliph of Krakow—a personage and indeed a title you knew did not exist—you attached us to the Byzantine embassy to Muskovy. And by the time we reached Moscow, you had single-handedly elevated me from a lowly secretary to the position of ambassador. Who else could have done that but you?"

"It sounds immodest to reply 'nobody,'" Darger admitted. "But I can honestly think of no other."

"Then put aside your metaphysical mopings, sir. They ill become you."

"What you ask of me is extremely difficult. Considering what I have been through and subsequently not seen."

"Make the effort. A great deal has gone into your resurrection, and we have immediate need for your cunning."

"Oh? How so?"

Surplus gave his friend a quick recap of his arrival in Brocade, his imposture of a god, the signs of impending war, and the deal he had made with Bright Pearl. Then he said, "Two days ago, a scholar came to the village, ostensibly collecting folktales, and in so doing casually asked about rumors of a dog-headed deity. The villagers naturally told him of my arrival and of the Infallible Physician's revival of your corpse, and he went away. Yesterday, that same scholar returned, and in the course of writing down children's counting rhymes, convinced the tykes to point out to him the house where the Infallible Physician lived. But though he paused before this building and studied it thoughtfully, he did not knock. Today, I am convinced—"

"Listen," Capable Servant said. "Drums!"

"That can only be soldiers, coming to arrest us and take us before the Hidden King," Surplus said. "We must leave this place immediately!"

"Perhaps not." Darger turned to Capable Servant. "What do you know of the personality of the Hidden King?"

"No one knows anything, for his title perfectly describes his habits. If the Hidden King ever leaves his palace, he does so incognito. His face and person are a mystery. His habits and personality are less than rumors. People say he is mad, but on so little direct evidence that we must consider it mere speculation."

"Hmmm." Darger rubbed his chin. "Is he rich?"

"Oh, most assuredly."

"Rich for a man or rich for a king?"

"Fabulously wealthy. His father, the Admirable King, kept the Abundant Kingdom out of war by playing his rivals against one another while trading freely with all. It is said he sent agents to all the kingdoms of China to seek out extraordinary treasures he might buy."

An avaricious glint entered Darger's eye. In an instant, he was on his feet, wrapping the blanket about himself like a robe. "I need clothing, quickly! Plain but of good quality. No ornamentation at all. The sort of garb a sage of tremendous modesty would wear. Bright Pearl, you must take your father and leave by the back at once. While Surplus and I are their chief prey, if the Hidden King's men see you, they will assuredly take you both captive as well. Stay away for a week or two—surely you have friends who will hide you—and I promise I will spin the king such a tale that he will forget all about you. Take the yak! That is an important prop for your future prosperity."

Capable Servant dashed to the cupboards and returned with an armload of clothing that had clearly not been worn by the old man for decades. Bright Pearl, meanwhile, took her father's arm and began leading him away. Pausing in the back door, she said, "Capable Servant. Perhaps you would consider working for me?"

"Oh, no," Capable Servant replied brightly. "My masters are going to be extremely rich—all the signs of it are on them. And then I shall be the servant of wealthy men and have servants of my own."

SURPLUS WAS lounging on the front stoop when a squad of twenty soldiers with two drummers and a standard-bearer marched down the street and into the yard. He leaped to his feet and, acknowledging the leader with a gracious nod, seized the hand of the captain of the city guard, who had clearly been brought along to ensure that they arrested the correct dog-man. "It is my old friend from the city gate!" he cried. "What a drubbing this man gave me!" he said to the leader. "I have been sore ever since. It was only by the most outrageous turn of fortune that I escaped him. A child threw a ball, which rolled beneath his foot just as he was about to—well, never mind that. I ran like the wind and still only barely got away. This fellow is a tiger! You are very lucky to have him."

The captain of the city guard straightened proudly, his gawk of astonishment vanishing so quickly that only the most observant could have noticed it. His commander scowled. "All that is of no matter. I am General Bold Stallion of the Hidden King's Guard," he said, producing a folded sheet of paper that could only have been an arrest warrant. "I have come to escort you—"

"—to be presented to your glorious king, so that I may subject myself to his wise and penetrating interrogation. Yes, I have been expecting you. You will also require the presence of my revered companion, Aubrey Darger, newly returned from the World of Shadows, where he has acquired wisdom previously denied any living human being. Capable Servant! Go inside and inform the great man that his hour of destiny has arrived."

Not much later, bowing and cringing outrageously, Capable Servant backed out of the house. After the briefest pause, Darger loomed up in the doorway, wearing a plain black gown so that in the gloom only his face and hands could be clearly seen. He cocked a haughty eyebrow at the soldiers. "Is this all the welcome I have for returning from the Winter Lands? Your liege is a skeptical man indeed." He stepped forward and took General Bold Stallion's arm in his own. "No matter. The Hidden King and I have many weighty matters to discuss. Let us go to him immediately."

"Your walking stick, sir," Capable Servant said.

Surplus accepted the stick and, even as the captain of the city guard gaped in alarm, held it outstretched to the man in both paws. "Obviously, I would never be allowed to carry a weapon into the presence of the Hidden King. That being so, I can think of no one I would more trust to keep it safe." Then he fell alongside the commander, whom Darger was already walking toward the gate.

So it was that, accompanied by General Bold Stallion and an honor guard of twenty soldiers, Darger and Surplus turned their backs on the Infallible Physician's hut, her village, and indeed the great city of Brocade and strolled away, never to return.

"HERE WE are," said General Bold Stallion with obvious pride.

Surplus could not help but stare. "*This* is the Hidden King's palace?"

They were confronted with what at first appeared to be a gracefully landscaped hillside, with green meadows and small stands of trees dotted by the occasional small building. But on closer examination, those buildings revealed themselves to be gateways to the interior of the hill. Just below the summit, a white stone temple resolved itself into a cluster of vents and chimneys. A stony outcrop became a guardhouse. Tall cedars camouflaged a lookout tower. "This would be a difficult place to break into," Darger observed. "Or even to find. A traveler might easily pass by it without suspecting it existed at all."

"After the Admirable King's sudden death," said Bold Stallion, who had been made voluble by Surplus's warm camaraderie and Darger's grave attentiveness, "his son had the entire palace complex buried and its defenses strengthened. You have passed through six circles of security, and I will warrant that you noticed none."

This last statement was not entirely true. Nevertheless, "Your king is a cautious man," Darger commented lightly. "What else can you tell me about his personality?"

General Bold Stallion looked uncomfortable. "That is not a matter we talk about." The road curved into a wood that opened into an allée of kingly trees. They passed through an elaborate stone gateway to find themselves within an entrance chamber framed with tremendous cedar beams with carved and gilded decorations. Guards appeared to turn back the soldiers and examine the general's credentials.

A cold wind of a woman swept out of the gloom. Her hair was long and, like her austere and undecorated uniform, the color of snow. "So these are the troublemakers I have been ordered to waste time on," she said, "while important decisions are being made without me. The king certainly has an overdeveloped sense of whimsy."

"White Squall!" General Bold Stallion looked thunderstruck. "I—I was not expecting to be met by the chief archaeological officer herself. I am honored that you—"

"You took long enough getting here. Leave." White Squall briefly studied Darger and Surplus with a gaze both intelligent and unsympathetic. "As for you two . . . You will regret having imposed yourselves upon the Hidden King's attention." She turned her back on them. "Follow. Your servant as well, in case he turns out to be more than he appears." Four grim-looking guards took up positions before and behind the three, and in solemn procession all entered the inner palace.

A proper Chinese palace was not a single building in the European style but a walled archipelago of smaller buildings connected by gracious courtyards and gardens. Each building was symbolically an

island in that archipelago and, like islands, which are variously forested and inhabited, each had its own character. Those nearest the
main entrance were the largest and most formal and were reserved
for public matters. Beyond them were more functional buildings for
meetings, storage, and other practical functions. Innermost and most
intimate were the dwelling places for the king, his family, and their
necessary entourages. Burying all these buildings had necessitated the
sacrifice of the gardens and courtyards and the construction of wooden
passageways to connect them all to one another.

Deep into the palace their path led, up stairs and down, turning
and twisting and sometimes passing through walls that were slid aside
to reveal hidden corridors and then shut firmly again behind them.
But by ignoring such complications and considering each building as
a node, Surplus was able to keep a mental map of their labyrinthine
wanderings. This revealed that they were following a long spiral, moving inexorably toward the very center of the palace. Had they gone
directly they would already be there. But they were being deliberately
confused, in order to render them lost and helpless.

It was chilling to reflect on the personality of a monarch who would
think this necessary in his own palace.

At last they were deposited in an unadorned room with wooden
walls and two chairs. "You will be sent for at the Hidden King's pleasure," White Squall said. "As I am a kindly woman, I warn you: His
appetite for novelty does not extend to flights of nonsense. I advise
you to restrict yourselves to the unadorned truth and hope that, in his
mercy, he will sentence you to a relatively painless death."

"That was precisely our intention," Darger said. "Except for the
last part, of course."

"You cannot leave," White Squall said. "It would be fatal to try."
Then she departed. The guards took position in the hall outside and
closed the double doors.

Darger and Surplus sat down facing each other.

"Poor General Bold Stallion!" Surplus exclaimed. "He looked so
terrified to be met by a high-ranking official and so relieved to be dismissed." Then, in English, he said, "Do you suppose they have somebody eavesdropping on us?"

"They'd be fools not to," Darger replied, also speaking in English.
He was careful to speak slowly and sonorously, as befit a sage. "It is

a bad sign when an underling fears to come face-to-face with his ultimate superiors. It suggests that the loyalty they demand of him is not returned."

"What do you make of the palace so far?" Surplus asked.

"The buildings, which predate the Hidden King, are of the richest materials and finest craftsmanship. Yet the passages connecting them are merely functional. Everywhere, I saw vacant niches in the walls where jade statues should be and curiosity cabinets thronged not with gold-and-silver-filigree masks and Ming Dynasty porcelain but empty shelves. The furniture is sturdy but hardly worthy of a monarch. Clearly, everything of value has been sold to fund the impending war. Which means that titles, public lands, mines, and future tax revenues from entire cities and industries have been sold as well. Which in turn means that war is inevitable. Without an influx of tribute from conquest, the Abundant Kingdom will be bankrupt within the year."

"That was my conclusion as well."

Capable Servant crouched between the two on the floor, watching them intently, though clearly he understood not a word of what they were saying. Now, as the two friends fell silent, reflecting on how best to adapt to this deplorable lack of lootable knickknacks, he said, "Oh, sirs! On our trip here, I was speaking with your new friend the city guard, and he expressed his undying gratitude for the kind words regarding him you spoke to his superior officer."

"That is as it should be," Darger said, switching back again to Chinese. "I am glad to learn that courtesy is not dead in Brocade."

"He also said to tell you that you will be tested. He said that the man you will be shown is not the Hidden King."

"That was an interesting comment," Surplus said.

"Useful, too," Darger replied. "Potentially." Then, after a moment's silence, "I don't suppose he said anything about how we could recognize the monarch?"

"Unfortunately, no." Capable Servant looked regretful. "I asked, but he said he was taking a great chance saying as much as he did." Then he produced a deck of cards. "Perhaps my masters know a game or two to pass the time?"

Surplus took the deck, cut it once, and said, "I will wager five grams of silver that the top card is the ace of hearts."

"Alas, sir, I have no money."

"Nor I. In which case, there is no reason for us to be parsimonious. Make it fifty kilograms of gold."

An hour passed, perhaps two. Capable Servant had lost several tons of precious metals by the time the guards reappeared and marched them away.

THEY WERE brought to a conference room, where seven individuals sat around a half-circular table whose straight edge faced the door. At the center, a still personage in purple brocade sat upon a chair slightly higher than those of the others. His body was broad and burly, yet his face was young, lean, and ascetic. His expression was alert and clever. Anybody who had not been forewarned would naturally assume this man to be the Hidden King. To his right sat a general in full armor, his metal visor the face of a demon. To his left was White Squall. Two more counselors sat to either side, their faces grim.

"Who are these men?" asked the supposed king.

"These are the lowborn scoundrels who present themselves as figures out of ancient myth and superstition," White Squall said. "If Your Majesty wishes, I can have their throats cut now and spare you the tedium of their pleas for mercy."

The lean-faced man glanced to his right and then said, "With your permission, Chief Executive Officer Powerful Locomotive, and yours as well, Chief Archaeological Officer White Squall, it amuses us to hear what they have to say."

Darger nodded slightly, as if acknowledging something that was entirely his due. Then, stepping forward, he spoke.

"My name is Aubrey Darger, and since my associate's name is not easily translatable into your language, you may think of him as the Noble Dog Warrior. We were born or, rather, created in a laboratory in a faraway land in the final years of the Utopian era, when all the world was unimaginably rich. Not long before the fall of Utopia, the secret of perpetual life was discovered. To test it, immortals were created. Our genomes were so designed as to render us unaging and immune to all natural causes of death, though we remain as vulnerable to acts of chance and violence as any other men. There were eight of us in the pilot program, but it has been many centuries since we have seen any of the others, and I must presume they are dead. Each of our kind varied greatly from the others, for the goal of the pilot program was not merely long lives but socially productive ones. Thus, my friend's character was so composed as to be decisive and active, making him a fearless fighter and protector of the weak. I, meanwhile, found myself to be of a more contemplative bent, a natural philosopher, scholar, and mentor to the young. Collectively, we were meant to be the world's moral guardians.

"Alas, our society was not as enduring as we. Having created machines to do their manual labor, mankind built more subtle engines to do their thinking as well. The times fell into lassitude and decay. We immortals, meanwhile, discovered that natural talents count for little without training and experience. Though we tried our best, we were ineffectual against the evils of the times. We saw the great nations of the world fragment and fall apart . . . and could do nothing to prevent it.

"When civilization collapsed, the Noble Dog Warrior and I gathered together all the books of philosophy, political science, and military strategy we could find and retired into the wilderness to think and to plan. We built a stone tower, and there I dwelt, reading and studying, while my friend farmed and hunted and protected me from the wandering bands of brigands which were common in that benighted era. Three times the tower fell into ruin from age, and three times we rebuilt it. There I studied until all the books had been read into dust. By then, I could have re-created them from memory, but what would be the point of that? Those books had not prevented the disaster. Something greater was needed.

"So I entered the second phase of my studies—contemplation. For centuries I thought over the implications of what I had read, resolved its contradictions, discarded its errors, and synthesized what remained into a coherent unity. At last I was, in theory, the perfect strategist. At which point I reentered the world.

"In this third phase of my studies, I put my learning and theoretics into practice. I sought out small countries involved in particularly vicious and pointless wars and endeavored to put an end to conflict. Were theory all, this would have been the simplest matter imaginable, given my unequaled learning. In practice, making peace was difficult beyond imagining. My strategies were perfectly rational. But men are ruled by irrational desires. They lust for personal glory. They hate without reason. They feel little gratitude to those they owe most. Over the course of many years I came to realize that the success of any nation ultimately depended upon the character of its ruler. For while a great ruler with inadequate advisors cannot succeed, neither can a weak ruler with the best advisors in existence.

"At the end of our experiments, having proved to our own satisfaction that we could win any war but that lasting peace was a more difficult matter, we retired once again to a remote part of Mongolia, where I spent many decades meditating on how best to use what I had learned.

"At last I was ready to enter into the final phase of my studies—healing the world. Long had I known that the healing must start with the restoration of China to her former greatness. For is not China the center of the earth? Create peace there and it would radiate outward. So the Noble Dog Warrior and I disguised ourselves as priests and went from country to country, observing the misery of their peoples and looking for a king who had the qualities of greatness within him.

"These qualities are, first of all, ambition. China must be reunited, and a king without fire in his soul is incapable of so great a deed. Second, firmness of action. As the ancient sage said, a war is not a tea party. Third, cunning. This goes without saying. Fourth and most important, evasiveness. He who would be emperor will necessarily make enemies of all kinds, and these enemies will necessarily try to strike at him. The future emperor must therefore be a man whose true essence is not known, one whose physical self is elusive. In that way, the bullets and arrows of his enemies will always go astray.

"To state the obvious, that king is here, in this very room. We discovered that, in his compassion for the suffering of the people, he had already begun the noble work of reunification. History is hard, however, and fate uncertain. We knew he would need our advice and assistance. But he was, as I said, elusive. How, then, to bring ourselves to his attention? The Noble Dog Warrior walked into Brocade, presenting himself as a god. I played the part of a corpse. Together, we acted out a story in which a supernatural entity had brought a dead man to life. We knew it would be talked about everywhere. We knew too that the Hidden King would send for us and, when he did, we would have the chance to tell our tale. As I now have done."

Darger spread out his arms. "So you see, there is nothing supernatural about us. You seven, being intelligent and highly educated, realized that immediately. But just try telling that to the common people. Better yet, try telling it to your enemies. Rumor is already spreading beyond the current boundaries of this land that two gods have come out of the wilderness to advise the Hidden King. Having advisors with such a reputation will be almost as valuable in the coming war as will our service—and that you will find valuable indeed."

His tale done, Darger fell silent. Standing behind him, Surplus held his breath.

The advisors rustled with impatience. "This is too unserious!" one exclaimed. There were murmurs of agreement.

"He claims to be immortal," White Squall said, turning to her right. "Allow me to test that claim."

"Madam, I can die as easily as the next man—by violence or starvation or a thousand other means. The only advantage my friend and I have over others is that we do not age. Killing us will prove nothing."

The man on the throne leaned forward. But before he could speak, the general sitting to his right said in a high, almost girlish voice, "It is insolence to suggest that you can better advise the Hidden King than his own counselors, each one handpicked for excellence!"

"When the student is ready to learn, a teacher appears," Darger replied. "When a king is ready to become emperor, a strategist. I am that strategist. I have found the noble soul who should properly be the next emperor of China. But his advisors are merely mortal. If he listens to them, he, who deserves only victory, will assume his place at the head of his army and march off to defeat. Such, at the moment, is his destiny.

"I am here to change that destiny."

Turning so that it was clear he was addressing no one else, Darger knelt before the man clad as a general. Who was the only figure in the room whose face was covered. Who had interrupted the putative king without the least hesitation. And who was the only one in the room wearing armor that was obviously too large for him. As puzzles went, Surplus reflected, it was not a difficult one to crack.

"Your Majesty, please allow me to help you become the emperor that all of China is waiting for."

The Hidden King rose to his feet. "Is this a sign," he asked, "that I am chosen of heaven? Or do you seek to appeal to my pride by implying that I have a destiny? If the former, then this is an opportunity I must not throw away! Stranger tales than yours have turned out to be true. But if the latter, your flattery is pointless, for I already know that I have a destiny." He looked to his left for confirmation. "Ceo Powerful Locomotive, have I not often said so? Cao White Squall, you have heard it as well. A destiny such as mine cannot be hidden. It is like a great light which, though you pack it away in crates and wrap it about with canvas, shines through! Even this stranger can see that it burns within me. Unless he is trying to deceive me."

White Squall began to open her mouth, then contained herself.

Ceo Powerful Locomotive removed the royal robe and, laying it down neatly folded on the conference table, humbly crouched down by the Hidden King's feet. His face shifted, growing heavier and more belligerent of expression, as suited one of his girth. Now visible, the scars on his arms and one almost bisecting his neck suggested that his rise in the military hierarchy had not been uneventful. "All that you say is true, oh peerless monarch," he said, "and to your credit. But the man who is dazzled by the light of the sun is not himself the sun, and he who can perceive greatness is not necessarily great in his own right." He cast a swift, shrewd glance Darger's way. "I believe that this stranger, this self-styled Perfect Strategist, should be tested."

The Hidden King divested himself of the borrowed armor, throwing it onto the floor carelessly. He stripped down to his small clothes and the helmet that, because he was a slight man, made him look like a child playing with his father's war gear. Then he donned the brocade robe and removed the helmet, holding the visor mask before his face with one hand. Finally, he removed a veil from the sleeve of his robe and, placing it over his head, set the visor down on the table. His face remained as unknowable as ever.

"Well?" he said. "What test shall we give him?"

There was an uncomfortable pause as his advisors looked at one another, waiting for someone else to speak. Then White Squall said, "There is the matter of the prince of Southern Gate. If this nonesuch is the prodigy he claims to be, let him solve that. If he cannot, let us kill him and move on."

There was a murmur of agreement among her peers.

"That is an excellent test," the Hidden King said in a jubilant tone.

"An almost impossible task, one no man can be expected to perform. Explain the particulars to our guests, White Squall."

The chief archaeologist nodded. "Southern Gate, which I am sure you know lies along our northern border, is a minor kingdom of no great wealth. But to reach the Land of the Mountain Horses, which is our immediate objective, our armies must pass through Southern Gate—and so far its king has refused to give us permission to do so. We could conquer that obstinate land, of course. But it would cost us men and months we would rather not expend. Are you following me so far?"

"You are a model of concision and lucidity," Darger said.

"At our request, the king of Southern Gate has sent a delegation headed by his eldest son to negotiate. The prince and his retinue are staying at an inn not far from here, as they have been for months. Our ambassadors make not the least progress with him."

"Nor would I, were I in his place," the ceo said. "Not only is it a matter of national pride, but of security as well. If three key cities were taken by our forces—which I am sure they could easily do—the entire kingdom could be held indefinitely. What responsible ruler would allow this possibility?"

"Even if the prince believed our assurances that we have no such intentions," White Squall continued, "once the Abundant Kingdom conquers the Land of the Mountain Horses, Southern Gate will lie within the boundaries of the expanded country. Effectively, it then becomes a part of that country without a shot fired or an arrow loosed.

"Ultimately, we will have no choice but to invade our northern neighbor. This the prince of Southern Gate understands as well as we do, and so he is willing to negotiate for as long as we are willing to allow our plans to be delayed. But no agreement can possibly be arrived at." She smiled coldly. "It would take a Perfect Strategist to find a way out of this conundrum."

"Tomorrow," the Hidden King said, "you will go to this prince. Speak with him, negotiate in my name. If he agrees to terms I consider reasonable, I will make you my advisors, second only to Powerful Locomotive and White Squall themselves. But if he does not"—he shrugged—"you, along with your servant, will die."

WITH SCANT ceremony, Darger and Surplus were dismissed and then returned to the same waiting room from whence they had come. This time, however, they were treated with deference, and servants brought them tea and extra candles. The palace major domo came by in person to assure them that rooms appropriate to their provisional status as advisors were being sought out and furnished. In the meantime, a *guqin* player was brought in to entertain them. She placed the zitherlike instrument on a small table before her and began to play.

While Capable Servant listened rapturously to the music, Surplus said in English, "What is your assessment of the Hidden King's character?"

"I would hesitate to make a clinical diagnosis of a man on so slight an acquaintance," Darger replied. "However, were my feet put to the fire, I would venture to say that he is agoraphobic, paranoid, impulsive, borderline delusional, and quite possibly completely off his chump."

"Then we are agreed that we should leave at the earliest possible convenience. I have memorized the layout of the palace. We could depart in the wee hours of the morning at the expense only of a concussed guard or two. We have gotten out of tighter jams than this in our time."

"Oh, I do not think that will be necessary," Darger said.

"But Aubrey! Consider! The Hidden King is at best tottering on the brink of madness."

"And at worst, wealthy—or he will be, once he's conquered a city or three. We have a carp on our line. Let us see how he plays."

3.

The sage known as the Yellow Child often observed that the righteous man can never be swindled.

—THE SAYINGS OF THE PERFECT STRATEGIST

N THE morning, servants deferentially roused Darger and Surplus from their sleep, provided them with fresh robes more suited for their newly presumed status (but Darger insisted on keeping his old clothing until something more luxurious but equally plain could be tailored for him), served breakfast, and escorted them up a country road to a meadow, where a city of brightly colored silk pavilions provided a neutral ground for the party from Southern Gate to meet with the Hidden King's ambassadors.

They found White Squall beyond the tents seated on a folding chair, sketching an antique building nestled in a grove of trees. Without looking up, she said, "What you see before you is the inn where the prince of Southern Gate is staying with his retinue." An unexpected touch of warmth entered her voice. "It was built in the late Mao Dynasty, when China was incomparably prosperous. In the ages before then, country inns were contemptible places where only poor travelers stayed. But in that era, politicians, bureaucrats, and businessmen in great numbers journeyed to every part of China by iron horse and aluminum bird, and thus respectable lodgings were necessary. If you were so fortunate as to be invited within, you would note that it was built along traditional lines, with a mortise and tenon cedar frame, a courtyard in the center, and airy balconies all around the second floor. From here, you can see the green-tiled, double-eave roofs. The rounded vertical ridges of the roof, like its color, are symbolic of bamboo and thus represent youth and longevity.

"Because the Utopians used laser saws, fast-setting liquid jade, sheet-diamond windows, and other lost tools, materials, and techniques, the scrollwork and detailing of the building are incomparable. Its survival through the ensuing turbulent ages is a small miracle." White Squall drew a final line and put aside the sketch pad. "There. Done."

Darger picked up the pad. "Your rendering of the inn is as precise as an architect's blueprints. But it leaves out the romance of the place."

"I draw what I see—and when I look at the inn, I see only the facts."

"We are well matched then, lady, for I see nothing but the romance. Tell me, if you will, of the prince of Southern Gate."

White Squall studied Darger silently for a moment, as if she were looking for hidden motives behind his question. Then she said, "First-Born Splendor is a well-made gentleman, courteous and yet expressive of his views, a man of his word and thus sparing of his promises, possessed of a good sense of humor and yet utterly serious about matters of state, forgiving of the foibles of others when they do no harm and yet uncompromising in his own virtue. In brief, he is the worst possible person to negotiate with."

"Many a tough nut has been opened by guile after brute force failed," Surplus observed. A servant hurried past with a tray of fresh-baked buns. He deftly snatched one and bit into it, adding, once he had swallowed, "Where threats do not work, soft words may prevail."

From behind him, a voice like a bass drum said, "Do not underestimate brute force," and Ceo Powerful Locomotive came striding up, smiling darkly. "Have you not wondered how the lovely White Squall came to be elevated to a chair at the left hand of the Hidden King, a position second only to that of my own, even though she is but a mere archaeologist?"

"We naturally assumed that this was due to her brilliance and high moral character," Darger said.

"Weapons, gentlemen! That is the long and the short of it. Through a careful examination of ancient records, she and her people locate hidden weapons caches. Then she directs the excavation of those weapons and the restoration of their accompanying documentation. Were it not for the weapons she finds, she would still be a lowly mole pawing her blind way through the lightless corridors of forgotten libraries and archives."

"Also, the Hidden King trusts my advice," White Squall said.

"Advice?" Powerful Locomotive spun on his heel, saying, "Follow me."

Through scurrying servants they four threaded a winding way among the tents. As they went, White Squall said to Darger in a low, angry voice, "The ceo acts as if resurrecting the Utopian machines incorporated into the armies of the Abundant Kingdom—the spiders, rolling fortresses, walking fire cannons, and all the rest—were simply a matter of digging them up out of the ground. But I assure you he underesteems my accomplishment. How easy do you think these things are to find? How simple to translate the archaic language of their maintenance manuals and explain such esoteric terms as 'worm gear' and 'cone friction clutch' to mechanics who are little better than village blacksmiths? Despite what Ceo Powerful Locomotive says of me, I have been of tremendous value to my nation. In fact—" Abruptly, she stopped.

"We are here," Powerful Locomotive said.

They passed within a tent guarded by soldiers on all sides. In its shadowy interior rested a squat metal object that looked like a larger and much heavier version of a fireworks rocket. It rested at a thirty-degree angle on what might have been a presentation base were it not painted, like the rocket, a drab olive green. One man would have trouble lifting it, but two would have no difficulty moving it about.

"This is one of the many weapons White Squall has dug out of various holes in the ground." Powerful Locomotive turned to her. "Would you care to explain your find?"

Her face utterly impassive, White Squall said, "This is the oldest and most primitive weapon I have yet uncovered, the Red Arrow, or HJ-73 antitank guided missile. Originally wire-operated, it has been repurposed as a ballistic device, and its shaped-charge warhead, which had been rendered infective by time, replaced with gunpowder and an impact-ignited blasting cap."

"That is the most wondrous thing I have heard in years," Darger said, "for I understand not a word of it."

"Arrow I understand," Surplus said. "But—guided missile? Anti-tank? Ballistic device?"

"A guided missile is a sophisticated rocket, used as a weapon. The tank was once believed to be a mythological beast but is now understood as an armored cannon-carrying machine used in the wars of old. The device is ballistic because, once launched, its flight cannot be influenced by its operator."

"Ah. Very good. I understand completely. Pray, continue."

"It was our intention to demonstrate the HJ-73 today," White Squall said. "However, it is the Hidden King's whim that you should first fail to negotiate a happy settlement with Prince First-Born Splendor and then be hung for wasting our time. So we must wait until tomorrow to demonstrate it."

"Demonstrate it how?" Surplus asked.

"By destroying the inn."

"I beg your pardon?"

Ceo Powerful Locomotive's face shifted noticeably, the mouth widening and the brows becoming heavier and more menacing so that he looked almost demonic. This was surely, Darger reflected, habitual, a quirk so commonly used to intimidate subordinates when they questioned an order that he was no longer conscious of doing it. "All you need to know is that tomorrow the Red Arrow will fly through the air from here to the inn. There it will explode, destroying the building and all it contains. Nobody will be in it at the time, of course. The prince and his people will all be here. He is a useless fop and an irresolute fool. However, when he sees how easily a place he had lived in and whose beauty he had surely admired could be destroyed from a distance by a single instance of the many weapons provided by, as I said, this beautiful lady . . . then even he will become fully cognizant of the real benefits of signing a treaty with us."

His speech done, Powerful Locomotive's face returned to its normal lineaments and he smiled insincerely. "But now I have real work to do. White Squall will see to your needs."

For the space of a breath, White Squall glared after the departing ceo. Then, wordlessly, she lifted the tent flap. They all went outside again and stood blinking in the sunlight. "Any questions?" she said.

"How did the ceo come to have such a . . . mobile face?" Surplus asked.

"You did not know? But of course you are barbarian strangers and so gossip that is common to all the court is new to you. Powerful Locomotive's parents were landowners, minor nobility possessed of wealth but little political influence. To promote their family's fortunes, they invested in prenatal gene work to make their son a face dancer. Several collateral ancestors were in intelligence, you see, and they thought that on reaching his majority he could easily become a spy and from that position work his way upward. How were they to know that he would possess a natural genius for military command and a corresponding detestation of deceit? The irony of so straight-forward a man possessing so ambiguous a talent is lost on no one."

"I see," Darger said. "Well, there is work to be done. How much time do we have to prepare?"

"The prince and his people will come here in early afternoon. Three hours, let us say. In the meantime, Ceo Powerful Locomotive and I have been directed to give you anything you may need."

"Then we must begin preparations immediately. I shall require—ho! You!" At Darger's summons, a scurrying servant came to an abrupt stop. "Is that wine you are carrying? Of what quality is it?"

"Of the very finest, sir, for it is meant for the prince of Southern Gate himself."

"Excellent!" Darger said, snatching the bottle from the startled man's hands. "Where is Capable Servant?"

"Here, sir," said that admirably unobtrusive fellow.

"Fetch me a gourd with a leather strap, such as travelers use to carry water on their voyage. Nothing fancy, mind you. Borrow it if you can, buy it if that's required, steal it if you absolutely must, but get it to me in five minutes."

"Sir!" Capable Servant disappeared.

"It is too early for you to be drinking," White Squall said, reaching for the wine bottle, which was promptly whisked away from her.

"This wine is but one element of an intricate plan." Darger took White Squall's folding chair from the servant who had followed them, carrying it. Setting the chair in the shadow of the nearest tent, he sat. "The Noble Dog Warrior has a list of our other requirements."

"There is no need for a list, for I have committed our needs to memory." Surplus could not possibly have done so, for Darger had come up with his scheme on the spot; nevertheless, Surplus held up a finger. "First, a spool of crimson thread along with three embroidery needles, a plate of water crackers, and five glass tumblers." He held up a second finger. "Next, a giraffe—full grown, mind you, and in perfect health. It must be here before the prince arrives."

"A giraffe!" White Squall said in a tone such as would be employed only by a woman who was overcome with indignation. "How am I supposed to find an African animal, full grown or not, on such short notice?"

"Madam," Surplus said, "the list is long and enumerating it will take forever if you are going to raise objections whenever it strikes your fancy. I suggest that you jot down notes so that we can discuss your quibbles after the first read through and see if it is possible to make substitutions. Next, a lobster boat."

White Squall put her hands on her hips. "Now that is simply impossible. We are twenty-five hundred *li* from the ocean."

"Such negativity ill becomes you, great cao. Fourth—"

As the discussion grew more heated—Surplus could be infuriating when he put his mind to it—Darger accepted a gourd from Capable Servant and filled it with wine. Then, unobtrusively, he slipped away.

IT TOOK Darger an hour to circle around the woods and so approach the country inn from its far side. The inn was handsomely situated near a small lake, with a grove of flowering peach trees around the back. A man who could only be the innkeeper stood in the doorway, taking a break from his duties. Cheerily, Darger hailed him. "Hello, my good fellow! Do you have a room free to rent to a wandering scholar who is for a brief time uncharacteristically affluent? Preferably one with a window looking out upon the lake, though from the exterior I judge that all your rooms are excellent."

"In this you are correct, sir. The elegance of our rooms is famous far and wide and the landscaping such as to give pleasure from every aspect. But unfortunately a delegation from Southern Gate is staying here. Would they were not! By order of our own government, I must provide them food and lodging for free, and, since all princes have enemies, I am not allowed to rent out the empty rooms lest they be taken by assassins."

"That is a great pity. Perhaps I could trouble you for a cup of water?"

"Hospitality is my business, good scholar, and my nature as well." The hotelier went away and came back with a ceramic cup filled with cold spring water. "Would you like me to fill your water gourd while I am at it?"

Darger laughed. "Impossible! This gourd is full of the finest wine from the Hidden King's own cellars. It was a gift from him for some small services I was able to do. May I offer you some?"

"Ordinarily, at this time of day I would not. But how often does a man have the opportunity to taste a monarch's wine?" The innkeeper stepped inside, returned with a second cup. Darger poured. "Ahh! How pleasant to be a king, if only for one sip."

"Allow me to top up your drink. The prince of yours—would that be the famous First-Born Splendor? They say he is an exemplary ruler. But perhaps your experience has been different?"

"Just as no man is a hero to his servants, sir, no prince is a hero to the man at whose inn he stays without paying. But he is a well-spoken young fellow who has no idea of the financial calamity he is visiting upon me and my family, so I bear him no personal ill will."

"To the prince, then." They clicked cups and the innkeeper drank while Darger daintily absorbed a few drops of water. "Allow me to refill that. You know, in my business it pays to meet as many princes as possible. Do you suppose there is any way I could chance to encounter Prince First-Born Splendor?"

"Well . . . at midday, he likes to walk alone in the peach orchard, in order to collect his thoughts and cultivate serenity. I gather that the negotiations with the Hidden King's ambassadors are very trying to his spirit. It's possible that, if you promised to . . . to . . ."

"Your cup is almost empty, sir! Let me refill it."

For a time they stood thus, chatting pleasantly. Then the innkeeper declared himself uncharacteristically woozy and went indoors to lie down for a while.

Darger washed the two ceramic cups at a nearby spigot, strolled into the peach orchard, and chose a tree to sit beneath. There he waited.

PRINCE FIRST-BORN Splendor emerged from the inn, hands behind back, lost in thought. Slowly, he strolled among the peach trees, taking no particular notice of the nondescript scholar sitting with his back against the trunk of one until he was upon the man. Then he merely nodded slightly and passed on.

"The Hidden King," Darger said to no one in particular, "is a homicidal maniac who must be killed if this land is ever to know peace."

The prince whirled. "Who is this who speaks such treasonous words about his own monarch?"

"The king is mad." Darger did not stand, but raised his eyes to meet the prince's. "You have heard the rumors, and I, having stood in his presence, can assure you that they are true. But as I am but a mendicant scholar of no family or reputation, that is nothing. Ceo Powerful Locomotive also knows this fact, and that is a great deal. Not that he would ever admit to such a thing, of course. Not to your face." He produced the two wine cups and filled them from his gourd. "Drink?"

The prince squatted upon his heels and accepted the cup. He did not raise it to his lips until Darger had done so first, and then he only took the lightest sip. "Is it him you represent?"

"Perhaps," Darger said. Then, addressing the sky, "War is not a pleasant thing. But it is coming to your land."

"Our soldiers are ready and the mountain passes are narrow. It would cost the Hidden King dearly to pass through Southern Gate without my leave."

"Indeed. Only a madman would even consider such an act."

The prince said nothing.

Still peering at the distant clouds, Darger said, "If only there were a way to turn this situation to your advantage."

"What do you mean?"

"A traveler who is confronted by a pack of wolves does not raise his vision to consider the beauty of the mountains. He sees only the gleam of their teeth and eyes. So, too, all your thoughts are focused on what will happen when the Abundant Kingdom's armies enter Southern Gate. If they do so with your permission, it will be the easiest thing for them to, in passing, take your country and absorb it into the Hidden King's territories. If they are resisted, your cities will burn, your armies will be slaughtered, and your nation will fall anyway. So

disastrous are your prospects that you cannot see that there is a third
way."

"What is that way?"

"Hold your hands up before you, prince." After the slightest hesitation, First-Born Splendor did so. "See how clean they are! Spotless.
Would you be willing to put up with a little dirt if it meant they would
not be stained black with the blood of thousands of your subjects?"

Tense and wary, the prince said, "Perhaps."

"Then listen to my proposal and say nothing until I am done speaking, for a conspiracy is like a machine, made up of a myriad of moving parts whose purpose may not be clear until one considers them
all together and a plot which seems abominable midway through the
telling is sometimes redeemed by its outcome. Pretend that I am a
storyteller and all that I say but a fanciful tale to idle away a pleasant
hour.

"Now. Let us imagine the possibility that rather than merely granting the Hidden King's armies permission to pass through your land,
you were to propose an alliance with the Abundant Kingdom, one in
which Southern Gate would be a subordinate territory. Sit *down,*
sir! By beginning to listen to me, you made an implicit promise to
hear me out—and, as I said, without your willing participation this is
but a tale.

"That is better. Remember, you have committed yourself to nothing as of yet. I am a fellow of no importance. You have no reason to
believe I have any influence with the Hidden King or, more significantly, with any members of his court. It does not compromise you to
listen.

"Where was I? Ah, yes. You were about to propose an alliance. Not
only do you pledge the resources of your country—your intact, unplundered country—to the Hidden King's war but you contribute
military forces of your own to his armies. Led by you personally and
loyal to yourself alone. That automatically makes you a member of
his court and one of his advisors. You will not be trusted, of course.
Secretly, the Hidden King will consider you a fool. But you will be
useful to him and thus treated well. You will also have the opportunity to make friends among his advisors—and one whom I would
most ardently advise you to befriend is Ceo Powerful Locomotive."

The prince's eyes were unreadable. His lips were white and thin.

"The king, as I said before, is mad. However his war goes, in victory or defeat, there will inevitably come a time when his orders become so clearly disastrous that those closest to him must decide who is to survive—he or they. In that extremity, someone, and I cannot say whom, will see to it that the king is no more.

"Now, when a king dies, the matter of succession is a thorny one. If a general or even a ceo were to assume the title, grave suspicion would rest upon him. But if there were a potential figurehead close at hand, someone of noble birth yet not born in the country in question, well, he would be an obvious choice. For a year or three, provided that figurehead king were cooperative, he would issue commands and edicts on the advice of his most trusted advisor. Then, when said advisor—a military man, no doubt—had consolidated his power and felt ready to take the throne in his own name . . .

"Well, a second regicide would be an inauspicious beginning to the new king's reign. But suppose the figurehead king were a provincial from a small mountain kingdom of no great importance to anyone but himself. Imagine that his ambitions were modest. He might express a weariness with the duties of ruling a great nation and a yearning to retire to the land that gave him birth. In such a case, his successor would certainly feel grateful enough to present him with Southern Gate as his own possession, free and clear."

Darger ceased speaking and waited.

"All this in exchange for letting your nation's armies through?"

"And for your promise to return to your own nation after two years' reign."

"Exactly who are you again?"

"As far as you are concerned, I am a fellow of no importance. But a harsh truth from the mouth of a man you distrust is surely worth more than the most reassuring lies from the lips of those who would pretend to be your friends." Darger stood, and First-Born Splendor did likewise. Stooping to pick up the wine cups from the ground, Darger said, "You and I have barely touched our wine. Are you willing to drink to our mutual understanding?"

The prince's face was hard, but he nodded. They drained their cups.

Then Prince First-Born Splendor squared his shoulders and turned back to the tavern. "I will have my scholars draw up a treaty immediately."

———

WHEN DARGER returned to the embassy tents with the treaty, Ceo Powerful Locomotive and Cao White Squall were waiting to confront him. But when he presented the parchment, their indignation turned to astonishment. The ceo snatched the document from his hands and read it through, scowling in disbelief. At times, his face looked inhuman. Then he handed it to White Squall, who was equally incredulous.

"How did you ever convince the prince of Southern Gate to see it our way?" she asked.

"I lied to him," Darger said. "Funny that it never occurred to you to do the same."

4.

Those who never met the Dog Warrior may be scandalized that human women would be so strongly attracted to one whose genome was purely canine. Those who stood in his presence and experienced his charisma, however, understood perfectly.

—EXPLOITS OF THE DOG WARRIOR

T O A civilian, watching from a distance, a great army being marshaled is a stirring sight. It flows endlessly down the road like a dragon in its strength and energy and perseverance. For the long hours it takes to pass, always changing and ever the same, it comes to feel as substantial and enduring as a stone-walled metropolis, a state of being that must surely last forever. Nothing, it seems, could possibly resist it. But to those responsible for the operation, it is one continual catastrophe. Wagon axles break and teams of horses panic and stampede. Soldiers are crushed under the feet of colossal machines and must be treated on the fly. The reports of scouts, imperfectly phrased or inaccurately transmitted, cause battalions of men to go astray, and when those in the lead, realizing at last that there is no way forward, give the order to turn back, those in the rear continue marching, to the confusion of all. Supplies are not what their providers promised and food arrives tainted. Fords prove impassable, so bridges must be built. Oxen wander off. Nightfall forces the troops to pitch their tents prematurely, far from water and on stony ground. All these misfortunes, though regrettable, are perfectly ordinary and doubly so when the army is inexperienced and new to warfare.

Thus it was that while the Hidden King's armies were struggling toward Battlefield Pass, word of their progress had gone before them all the way to the ancient city of Peace, capital of the Land of the Mountain Horses. There, the ruling council had quickly abrogated their treaties with Southern Gate and, sweeping southward across its borders, seized Dynasty along with the rich basin lands surrounding it. Then, knowing that there was but one way north from the Abundant Kingdom, they sent their armies south to the city of Bronze and from there set about building fortifications in the valley through which all traffic must go. By the time the armies reached the pass, there was an earthen wall stretching across its narrowest point and the soldiers behind it were dug in strongly.

At the king's command, Ceo Powerful Locomotive threw his forces against the enemy's defenses. But the mountains to either side of the pass bristled with snipers; streams had been redirected to create swamplike conditions below, limiting the land suitable for warfare, and the approach to the wall was dangerously exposed. Further, because the enemy had a great many cannons, the ceo was reluctant to hazard the weapons of the ancients, which, though puissant, were limited in number; these he initially chose to hold back for a later, needier day. Then, when he finally ventured to try them, he lost two spiders to the marshes and a crushing wheel to concentrated cannonade. Clearly, spies had been at work and the leaders of the Mountain Horses armies had devised ways of exploiting the machines' weaknesses and neutralizing their powers.

On the fifth day of fighting, Darger and Surplus stood at the fore of the main encampment, atop a slight rise, watching the white puffs of rifle smoke dotting the mountains to either side of the valley and the movement of cavalry and infantry between them. The desperate fighting was rendered sluggish and quiet by distance. Rifle fire crackled gently and the boom of ordnance was as soft and muted as faraway thunder. It was clear to Surplus that the Mountain Horses troops held the advantage and would not be surrendering anytime soon.

Then a team of rocket soldiers brought up the Red Arrow missile and fired it straight and true down the center of the valley to the enemy's defensive wall. There was a tremendous explosion when it hit, and through the ensuing smoke could be seen a gaping hole. With a roar, the Abundant Kingdom cavalry charged toward it.

Almost simultaneously, flames appeared on the forested mountain slopes to either side of the pass—lit by hidden arsonists whom Powerful Locomotive had sent out during the night. The flames merged, forming walls, and gunfire ceased as the snipers fled the conflagration.

For a time, it looked as if the battle would be settled then and there, for the smoke from the forest fires flowed down into the pass and was carried by the wind straight at the defensive wall, making it possible for the Abundant Kingdom's forces to advance on it in obscurity. But then sortie gates at either end of the wall opened and troops of cavalry emerged. The famed mountain horses raced up the slopes with an agility no normal steeds could match. Riding behind each cavalryman was a sapper, and these were dropped off some distance before the advancing flames to chop down trees and build firebreaks. Then, riders crouched low, the mountain horses sped fearlessly through the burning trees as no ordinary mount would even have attempted. Once through, the cavalry hunted down and killed all the Abundant Kingdom soldiers they could find, whether arsonists or otherwise.

In their wake, meanwhile, the sharpshooters were returning to the mountainsides to resume sniping from slopes the fire had passed by. At the same time, a steady blind pounding from the Mountain Horses artillery forced Ceo Powerful Locomotive to turn back his men rather than lose them altogether. They retreated to the earthen ramparts their own sappers had thrown up just beyond the range of effective gunfire.

"It is as I have always heard," Surplus said. "War is indeed a stirring spectacle and a rousing entertainment."

"From this vantage, it could scarcely be improved upon," Darger agreed. "Though I imagine it feels otherwise to the poor chaps actually caught up in it."

"That is why I try to avoid field hospitals, prisoner of war compounds, mass graves, and all such locations, which I am certain I would find distressing were I to expose myself to them."

"That is quite wise of you. It is of paramount importance to keep up one's morale." Turning his back on the pageantry with obvious reluctance, Darger said, "I must return to my mathematical studies."

"And I," Surplus said, "to the business of making myself a living legend."

THE CAMP was a lively and varied place. Many of the soldiers, especially the younger officers, stood at its fringe to watch the progress of battle, as Surplus himself had just been doing. But most went about the everyday business of any military encampment: polishing brass and leather, cleaning weapons, grooming horses, butchering aurochs and stewing their meat, writing up requisitions for new supplies, operating stills they hid from their superiors, gambling away their pay chits on dice games or rat fights, and so on. Surplus made his way directly to the flogging post, where he was amiably greeted by the officer on duty, a stocky woman of cheerful disposition.

"Welcome back, sir. Still looking for recruits?"

"Indeed, I am. The Hidden King has said I may have as many as twenty soldiers, though I confess that finding those with the special talents I require is proving more difficult than I expected."

"You've got quite a set of miscreants to choose from today, sir. That rascal up there, for example"—the officer gestured at a wretch who had just received the last of what had clearly been a large number of strokes from a hard rubber club; untied, he slumped loosely to the platform floor and was carried away—"got into an argument with a whore and gouged out one of her eyes. Which, in addition to the obvious injury done her, reduces the amount she can charge for her services in the future. If it weren't for us being at war and his worthless carcass thus required to be available for a meaningful and heroic death, he'd have been cashiered and left to the mercy of her peers."

"Yes, well, intemperance is not one of the virtues I'm looking for." Surplus scanned the apprehensive line of miscreants awaiting punishment. To a man—save one—they bore expressions of dejection, despair, or hangdog resignation. The exception was an ogre of a man with shoulders so broad they made his head look tiny. With narrowed eyes, he was looking everywhere but at the punishment stock, like a merchant seeking an opportunity for profit or a prisoner inspecting the prison walls for an undiscovered weakness. Clearly, he was still searching for even the slightest chance of escaping his imminent punishment. "The fellow with the sly expression—what did he do?"

"That's an interesting case, sir. He brought in one of the enemy's fabled mountain horses."

"That sounds more worthy of commendation than punishment."

"Ah, but the army has advertised a generous award for anyone who brings us a mountain horse. So when he turned the horse in, he tried to claim money for it."

"I'm still at a loss."

"Well, you see, sir, for a civilian that would have been fine. But he being a soldier, once he captured the horse it became the property of the army. So when he didn't simply hand it over, he was stealing what properly belonged to the Hidden King. In consequence of which, he was convicted of theft and attempting to sell stolen property."

"That sounds like just the sort of enterprising individual I need." Surplus strolled up to the man in question. "You know fisticuffs, I presume?"

Those shrewd eyes studied Surplus carefully. Then the man nodded.

"Step out of line." Those soldiers who had gathered out of boredom to watch their peers being punished formed a loose circle about the two. Some of them quietly began to place bets. "The rules are simple. If you knock me down three times, you walk free. If I knock you down three times, I have the option of either transferring you to my command or returning you to your just punishment, depending on how impressed I am by your performance. Trickery and unfair blows are encouraged. You may signify your understanding and agreement to these terms by attacking me."

Up close, the man was enormous. He was a good head taller than Surplus and considerably broader. He nodded his head shaggily, as if mulling over what had been said. Then, without warning, he crashed down on his knees before Surplus. "There is no need to defeat me, sir. I have seen your fighting prowess in action and know that the experience would be for me an unhappy one."

Murmurs of disappointment arose from the bystanders. Surplus turned to the officer on duty and said, "When did this man see me fight?"

"Never, sir, for he has been in the stockade these past five days."

"Why do you lie to me, soldier?" Surplus asked the miscreant.

The man stood and, a touch embarrassedly, slapped the dirt from his knees. "Well, sir, you can't blame me for trying. But, you see, being big as I am, I've been sought out by gangs all my life. Now, the leader of a gang doesn't want a bruiser like me thinking I can maybe take over control of his operation. So the first thing he does is pick a fight and thrash me good and proper, to show who's the boss. In all my life, I've never won one of those fights because the gang leader is always the toughest and dirtiest scrapper in the batch. I was simply hoping to skip the painful part of the interview." He put up his fists. "But I suppose I'll have to go through with it now."

Surplus barely managed to suppress a laugh. "There is no need for that. I can see that you have the qualities I'm looking for. What is your name, soldier?"

"Vicious Brute, sir."

"Surely that was not your given name."

"No, sir, all respects sir, but it was. My mother saw I was going to grow up big and thought it would give me a leg up in my profession."

"That is the second time I have heard such a story," Surplus marveled. "Clearly, China is a land of remarkable and foresighted mothers. You seem to be a prudent man, Vicious Brute, in spite of your name, and I do not imagine you ambushing a cavalryman and taking his mount by violence. The odds would be too uncertain."

Vicious Brute looked abashed. "Sir, I was acting as . . . an agent, you might say."

"Ahhh. Then perhaps we should continue this conversation in private."

A look of profound relief spread itself over Vicious Brute's face. "I knew you was a smart one, sir. First moment I saw you, I said to myself, there's a thinker."

"Obsequiousness is, in an inferior, a fine thing," Surplus replied. "But let's not lather it on too thickly."

BECAUSE DARGER'S negotiation of an alliance with Southern Gate had won both rogues the Hidden King's trust, Surplus was easily able to requisition two good horses, a sturdy pack mule, and as many provisions as the mule could carry. Because that trust was far from absolute, he could not obtain the silver that would have made his mission infinitely easier. So that afternoon, after sending a terse note to Darger explaining his absence and reporting to Ceo Powerful Locomotive, who gave him a curt warning that his friend's life was forfeit if he did not return, Surplus saddled up and departed in the company of his new recruit.

Following paths so overgrown that they frequently had to dismount and lead their horses, they made their way through forests of fir and birch and thick stands of bamboo, occasionally crossing one of the small stony streams that leapt and skipped down the mountainside. Vicious Brute led.

As the shadows lengthened and daylight bled from the sky, Surplus began seeing shadowy figures in the undergrowth, gone at a glance but reappearing later to watch them from a distance. "Oh, those are just the guardian apes that our ancestors created to protect the pandas from molestation," Vicious Brute said when he remarked upon them. "So long as you don't get too close to one of their charges, you're perfectly safe."

"They look to be carrying spears."

"Spears!" Vicious Brute scoffed. "Those are little more than pointed sticks. The guardian apes are very dim creatures indeed. Do not give them a second thought." He reined in his horse and dismounted. "We must go afoot from this point on."

Pushing aside a leafy bough, Vicious Brute led them into a ravine. It was darker inside, and cooler, too. Trees and brush all but crowded out the sky. Alongside a scurrying stream was a path just wide enough for them to lead their horses and donkey along it, provided they went slowly. "Be careful where you step, sir, for there are slivers of Utopian ceramics that will pierce you right through your boots, thick though they may be. Very painful. Also, keep in mind that some of what look to be harmless loops of vines are actually ancient cables. A cousin of mine ran into one and almost strangled himself."

Cautiously, Surplus pushed onward. Brickbats and crumbled concrete turned underfoot. An occasional slanting shaft of dusty gold sunlight, piercing the canopy, sparkled on shattered glass. Now that his eyes had adjusted, he saw that the forest was interpenetrated with fragmentary walls, canted stairways leading into black chasms, and broken cubes of masonry. These were the ruins of buildings and their cellars through which the stream had, over the centuries, carved a V-shaped gash. A melancholy sense of past failures quite alien to his nature settled over Surplus.

Doing his best to shake it off, he remarked, "You seem to know this route well."

"I should! I go up and down it two or three times a day."

"Surely your duties as a soldier preclude—"

"Sir, until very recently, I was a civilian. It turns out that your army has a policy that all men fit to be soldiers are immediately impressed into its service. Unless they are enemies, of course, and then they are killed. Or rich, in which case they pay a bribe to be released. Being neither rich nor hostile, when I tried to claim my reward for turning in a mountain horse, why, slam! bang! I'm in the army and a thief to boot for trying to get the money they promised." Vicious Brute laughed ruefully. "It was my own fault for letting down my guard in the presence of the virtuous."

"Being aware of their own righteousness, such men naturally need never think twice about the morality of their actions," Surplus agreed. "Tell me. How did you become a brigand in the first place?"

"I would never have turned to banditry had it not been for the war. My clan are honest smugglers by profession. A little arson now and then. Some counterfeiting when we could get the equipment. A touch of extortion when the chance presented itself. But no thuggery—never! Alas, our village was overrun by cavalry, who took everything worth owning and set fire to the rest. So we had no choice but to send our children and elderly to live with relatives in a distant village. The rest of us retreated to the hills, there to survive as best we could. Then, when twenty mountain horses came our way, I was sent down with a sample of what we had for sale. The rest of my tale you know."

Surplus was about to ask how the mountain horses had come into the possession of Vicious Brute and his kin when something sparked underfoot.

He leaped back. "What was *that*?"

"That's just spirit lights, sir. Happens now and then. Nobody knows why. Sometimes there are voices and visions as well, from the Utopian demons lingering in the cable. Their power wanes, however, so even the most boastful are utterly without strength. But they keep away the superstitious. That's one reason why we—"

In that instant, sparks came spitting out from every corner and niche of the ravine. They snapped and leaped into the air, tracing bright arcs of light in the gloom, and burnt when they touched exposed skin, leaving an ozone sting behind.

Surplus staggered, slipped, and grabbed a nearby loop of vine to keep from falling.

The world went black.

In the inky spaceless space before him floated a spectral woman. Her face was beautiful and preternaturally calm, but an aura of menace emanated from her. Her white robes and scarves floated restlessly about her, though there was no wind. In a voice like no human being ever had, for it was composed partially of surflike noises, was punctuated by pops and small erratic silences, and was shot through with lesser voices that Surplus could not quite decode, she said:

dieingreatpainsufferingagony
IS THAT YOU, SIR
dieingreatpainsufferingagony
BLACKTHORPE R
dieingreatpainsufferingagony
AVENSCAIRN DE
dieingreatpainsufferingagony
PLUS PRECIEUX?
dieingreatpainsufferingagony

Though every hair on his back bristled with supernatural fear at this eerie sight, Surplus bowed deeply. He was, after all, a rationalist, a citizen of the Demesne of Western Vermont, and above all a gentleman. "You know me?"

The apparition's eyes, though they focused on him, did not look real.

yoursufferingswillbeprofoundandyourscreamsofagonyunending
IN THE GENEMILLS OF SHELBURNE
yoursufferingswillbeprofoundandyourscreamsofagonyunending
WHERE YOU WERE CREATED, THEY
yoursufferingswillbeprofoundandyourscreamsofagonyunending
THINK YOU DEAD. IN LONDON, YOU
yoursufferingswillbeprofoundandyourscreamsofagonyunending
BURNED BUCKINGHAM LABYRINTH
yoursufferingswillbeprofoundandyourscreamsofagonyunending
TO ASHES AND MUCH OF THE CITY
yoursufferingswillbeprofoundandyourscreamsofagonyunending
AS WELL. IN MOSCOW YOU CAUSED—
yoursufferingswillbeprofoundandyourscreamsofagonyunending

"Enough! Your purpose, dread spirit?"

The lady's robes continued to lash in the infinite nothingness. A small, cruel smile blossomed on her porcelain face.

deathnegationrottingfleshpainthevoid

I KNOW WHAT YOU

deathnegationrottingfleshpainthevoid

DESIRE ABOVE ALL.

deathnegationrottingfleshpainthevoid

Drawing himself up, Surplus said icily, "I assure you otherwise."

Confusion flickered on that unearthly face, and, briefly, its lips twisted like maggots in agony. The luminous lady wavered like an image seen underwater, solidified, then wavered again.

amilliontorturesarebeingpreparedforyouandallofyours

TELL THE HIDDEN KING THAT

amilliontorturesarebeingpreparedforyouandallofyours

HIS PHOENIX BRIDE AWAITS

amilliontorturesarebeingpreparedforyouandallofyours

DEEP UNDER FRAGRANT TREE.

amilliontorturesarebeingpreparedforyouandallofyours

Effortlessly floating up so that Surplus had to throw his head back to meet her eyes, the lady then bent over almost double, so that their lips all but met. He saw now that what he had taken for her face was actually a mask and that there was nothing behind it. "I do not fear you," he said, "or anything you might say."

Gusts of laughter rose up out of nowhere, growing to a wind that shredded the fluttering robes like sheets of tissue paper and sent the mask tumbling away like a leaf.

weknowallyoursecretsanddarkestfears

YOU LIE, PUPPYKINS.

weknowallyoursecretsanddarkestfears

FOR WE KNOW WHY

weknowallyoursecretsanddarkestfears

YOU FLED FROM THE

weknowallyoursecretsanddarkestfears
LAND OF YOUR BIRTH.
weknowallyoursecretsanddarkestfears

"No!" Surplus cried and, throwing an arm before his eyes, found himself falling over backward into a sea of mocking laughter.

diesufferscreamdiesufferscream
FRAGRANT TREE,
diesufferscreamdiesufferscream
OH MOCK HERO—
diesufferscreamdiesufferscream
TELL YOUR KING.
diesufferscreamdiesufferscream

"SIR?" VICIOUS Brute said. "Sir, are you well?"

Surplus shook himself. "Is the . . . lady . . . gone?"

"Lady, sir? No, sir. Nobody here but us. You touched one of them vines I warned you about and fell over and went into spasms for a bit. Then you woke up."

"I saw . . ."

"Whatever you saw, it was an illusion, sir. Trust me. I know the spirits of this mountain and they never tell you a true word."

"Well," Surplus said. "A false vision, you say?" And again, "Well." He shook himself and, with the aid of Vicious Brute, stood. All his flesh was pins and needles but he seemed to be unharmed. Surplus had already decided to share this strange event with no one—the Hidden King most emphatically included. In his experience, some messages were best left undelivered. "At any rate, I doubt it was of any import."

They started up the trail again. At least an hour passed before Surplus asked, "Have we far to go?"

"No, sir, not really. We're almost there."

"Good."

Up the darkening gorge they went, occasionally clambering over collapsed walls or splashing across the stream when their path switched sides. Until finally they came to a shallow slope covered with loose masonry and broken tiles. Clattering noisily, they made their way up and out of the ravine to find themselves in a clearing with a dozen or so rustic huts and lean-tos, crudely crafted from branches, rope, and straw.

At last they had come to the bandit camp.

The noise of their ascent had alerted the bandits of their approach. Some fifteen or sixteen rough-looking ruffians, many of them women and all armed with swords, pistols, and improvised clubs, had come out to confront them.

For a still instant, the two sides confronted each other in silence. Then a slim woman with hair as red as flame cried, "Little brother!" and ran into Vicious Brute's arms. He lifted her up, bounced her down. On the ground again, she drew herself up, and he stepped back respectfully.

"You may kneel," she said, "and report."

But before Vicious Brute could do so, Surplus stepped forward and said, "Your brother is now a soldier of the Abundant Kingdom, in the pay of the Hidden King, and so of course he is not free to kneel before anyone outside of his proper chain of command." To lessen the sting of his words, he smiled. "You are clearly the leader of this group of unallied commandos. If I may ask, your name is—?"

"Fire Orchid." The bandit leader studied him, as if he were some species of large and unattractive bug. "Who—and *what*—are you?"

Surplus formally introduced himself, adding, "As to what I am, I have, in my day, played many parts." Turning casually to his donkey, Surplus began untying the saddlebags. "I am a gentleman, an adventurer, a wanderer, and a soldier of fortune. Currently, I am acting as an emissary for the Hidden King, whose destiny washes over these lands as irresistibly as the tides. Of that, we shall speak later. For the moment, what matters most is that I have brought food." He lightly tossed a cured ham to the nearest brigand, who dropped a broken rake handle to catch it. "Food enough for a feast." He produced bottles of liquor and distributed them to eager hands. "Since I came here uninvited, it seems only fair that I feed you so that we may afterward converse as friends."

Fire Orchid did not look at all pleased. But she only said, "Very well. We can, as you say, talk afterward."

BY THE time the last of the food was cooked and eaten, night had
fallen and the bandits had made most of the booze disappear. Surplus
himself ate abstemiously and drank not at all, bringing the cup to his
mouth frequently but only pretending to sip from it. Left alone with
his thoughts, he found himself puzzling over the significance of the
mysterious apparition he had seen earlier. So it was startling to look
up and realize that the feast was over. Some of the bandits were staggering about in what might be a dance. Others lay drunkenly on the
ground. Three of them were singing almost the same song. And Fire
Orchid was staring at him intently from the other side of the fire.
When their eyes met, she came over and sat down beside him, cross-
legged. With her high boots and tight trousers, loose tunic, multiple
silver bracelets, and the silk scarf tied about her neck, she looked the
very prototype of a bandit queen. Her hair shifted colors in the fire-
light. "You aren't drinking," she said.

"Nor you," Surplus observed, "though you pretended to fill your
cup frequently and occasionally surreptitiously emptied it in the
weeds."

"I think maybe it is time for me to show you what I have to
offer."

"I am at your disposal, madam."

The mountain horses were kept in a nearby grassy sward, surrounded by a chest-high pole fence. Surplus and Fire Orchid stood
for a while, watching them crop grass. They were everything they were
reputed to be, chimerical creatures with the size and beauty of unal-
tered horses, the legs and paws of some enormous triple-jointed cat,
and beaks that would have done justice to griffins. They looked like
no creature Surplus had ever seen, and he could tell at a glance that
they were swift as wildfire.

Fire Orchid bridled two of the steeds and threw a blanket over each
in lieu of a saddle. Then she leaped up on one. "Well?" she said.

Surplus followed suit, flicked his reins in imitation of Fire Orchid,
and almost lost his seat as the mountain horses bounded over the fence
and up the mountainside.

Their steeds ran easily at first, and then, as Surplus grew surer of
his seat, with increasing speed, until they were racing full-out, up the
uneven terrain, weaving through the trees and leaping effortlessly over
streams that appeared without warning before them. Wind in his face

and pine scent in his nostrils, Surplus found himself whooping and howling for pure joy.

Up above the tree line they burst, where all was rock and lichen. Fire Orchid reined in her mountain horse and dismounted.

Surplus climbed down from his steed and stroked its mane. "You and I are going to be best friends," he said.

"Hahhh!" it replied, and clacked its beak at him.

Fire Orchid released her mountain horse to graze and spread her saddle blanket on the ground, as if in preparation for a picnic. "Come sit next to me." She patted the blanket.

"Shouldn't we hobble our mountain horses? So they don't wander off?"

"They are very smart. Aren't you, girl?"

"Yahhh!" Her mount bounced its beaked head up and down, then turned its attention to the grasses and lichens.

So Surplus did as she bade him.

"Put your arm around my shoulder," Fire Orchid said. "As if you were my boyfriend. Yes, like that. See how nice I snuggle against you? Now. Talk to me about money."

Assuming an expression of polite embarrassment, Surplus said, "Madam, there is none. Every penny the Hidden King had and all he could raise by mortgaging the resources of the Abundant Kingdom was spent on provisioning his army and resurrecting abominations from the past to employ as weapons. His soldiers are paid in promissory notes and the hope that there will be cities to sack."

"I suspected as much when Vicious Brute did not return alone." Fire Orchid placed her head against his shoulder. "Next question. Why are you here?"

"You and your family are a deceitful and dishonest batch. I say that with full respect. Vicious Brute told me you were villagers—yet no mere village can support a criminal dynasty. Such families are the flower of a large urban population. He implied you had seized the mountain horses by force, when such noble steeds as these would only be entrusted to the most warlike soldiers the army has, making such a feat improbable. My guess is that you are natives of Peace who bribed a corrupt official to leave the mountain horses unguarded one evening, then came here to negotiate their exchange for the advertised reward."

"You are a very suspicious dog-man," Fire Orchid murmured. She nuzzled her face in the side of his neck. "So if we are such bad sorts, why are you here?"

"I am here because I wish to recruit you—you and all of your family—into the army, to serve under my command."

Fire Orchid drew away from Surplus. "I was not expecting that."

"Madam, war is a fickle and unpredictable enterprise and one I hope to emerge from alive. A deceitful and ingenious crew of underlings would—"

Placing a finger against his lips, Fire Orchid said, "Shush. I understand everything now."

"Thank you, I—what are you doing?"

Fire Orchid's breath was warm against the side of his face and her hand, having slipped inside his trousers and seized a very intimate part of his body, moved slowly up and down. "You are a clever fellow," she said. "I believe you will figure it out soon enough."

Which, of course, he did.

AFTERWARD, FIRE Orchid lay back on the blanket, staring up at the stars. "I must be a very wicked woman to do such things with an animal-man like you."

"On the contrary," Surplus said. "It is not externalities that matter, but the soul that lies within. By looking beyond the superficial, you have displayed the nobility of your character."

"No, I *like* being a bad woman." She suddenly rolled over atop his prone body. Her eyes were bright and ruthless. "I think maybe I want to be wicked again. Even more wicked than I was before."

So she was.

And then she was again.

And again.

Fire Orchid's enthusiasm bordered on the rapacious. But then, Surplus reflected, she had long been in the mountains with no male company other than members of her own family, so that was understandable. As was, for similar reasons, his own avid response.

After they had both played each other to exhaustion, Fire Orchid sat up, a black silhouette against the cold, starry sky, and, looking down on Surplus, said, "I think maybe you should marry me."

Alarmed, Surplus sat bolt upright. "Madam! We hardly know each other. Our relationship so far is based entirely on passion—and even so great a passion as ours is hardly a fit basis for a lifetime commitment."

"Don't you worry your doggy head about it," Fire Orchid said. "I'll take care of everything."

5.

The Eternal Showman was known to observe that no battle was ever lost by underestimating the intelligence of the foe.

—THE SAYINGS OF THE PERFECT STRATEGIST

DARGER WAS covering a sheet of foolscap with meaningless mathematical symbols when he heard a great din outside his tent. Unhurriedly, he poured sand over the fresh ink and blew it away. Then he went outside to see what was the matter.

There he discovered that the entire camp had been thrown into an uproar by the arrival of Surplus at the head of a colorful company of rangers, all riding mountain horses. A woman whose long red hair flowed freely behind her like an ever-changing flame rode at the Dog Warrior's side, with a giant of a man directly behind them. Swiftly and more smoothly than cavalry riding natural horses could have managed, they flowed between the tents, leaping over campfires and startled wagoners, drawing astonished soldiers into gaping crowds in their wake. Direct to Darger they rode, pulling up in a milling mass before him.

"Well, well, well," Darger said. "What have you found?"

"Noble souls and bold fighters," Surplus cried, "who wish nothing more than to serve the Hidden King!" This raised a loud enough cheer from those nearby that he was able to lean forward and without being overheard add, "A crew who know what the deal is, including several pickpockets, two lockpicks, a counterfeiter, a stable woman qualified in the care of mountain horses, a thimble rigger, a puppeteer, a quick-sketch artist, and a first-rate goon. Also, apparently, a fiancée."

Darger cocked an eyebrow. "Should I congratulate you?"

"God only knows," Surplus said. "I certainly don't."

The new company's moment of glory was eclipsed, however, mere hours later when Prince First-Born Splendor returned from Gold, the capital of Southern Gate, at the head of two hundred cavalrymen. Though the force was small, the suddenness of its arrival, combined with the unexpected materialization of some twenty of the coveted mountain horses, caused an irrational sense of elation to spread through the camp.

The prince of Southern Gate paused at Darger's tent to salute him with a free and gracious familiarity. Then he rode on, through the cheers of the onlookers.

"Listen to them," Darger said gloomily. "The war is as good as won and they will be home in two weeks, covered with glory and never to go adventuring again—or so they think." Capable Servant had set up umbrellas and folding chairs before his master's tent and was now serving tea to Surplus, his red-haired second-in-command, and Darger. Vicious Brute was off negotiating with the quartermaster general for tents, weapons, and other provisions for the new recruits.

Fire Orchid drained her cup in a single gulp and held it out for more. "They forget that war is not just a bad thing. It is also an excellent opportunity to make money." Surplus grinned, and Darger nodded in involuntary approval. "So long as we keep our wits about us, don't get distracted by the chance to nab small profits, and have a long-term plan." She leaned forward. "What is our long-term plan?"

"Well—"

At which inopportune moment, the messenger Darger had long anticipated arrived to announce that he was summoned to the Hidden King's side. Where he had been expecting a minor functionary, however, the news came in the form of no less a personage than Cao White Squall galloping up on a sturdy mare and pulling it short at the last possible instant, so that clods of dirt went flying. "Irresponsible idler! Our troops die by the hundreds and yet you do nothing. The Hidden King demands to know what you are up to!"

There was no denying that the cao looked fetching in armor. The helmet shadowed her face, and within that shadow her eyes flashed like those of a wildcat peering from the depths of a tree, where it waited to ambush unwary prey. "Up to?" Darger said. "I spent the morning observing Ceo Powerful Locomotive's employment of forces. Then I updated my mathematical analysis of the dynamic forces of the war. Now I am interviewing the leaders of the Dog Warrior's newly created irregulars, to see how to best incorporate them into my plans."

"As I suspected, you are doing nothing. You will come with me immediately."

Fire Orchid studied White Squall, her face as unreadable as a blank sheet of paper. Darger could not help but approve of her self-control.

"I shall gather up my papers," Darger said.

THE HIDDEN King was quartered in a palatial mansion to which the High Lord Hereditary Bureaucrat of Bronze habitually retreated, along with his concubines and catamites, to avoid the summer heat. Its caretakers had abandoned it on the approach of the Abundant Kingdom's armies for the manor lay beyond the point where the Mountain Horses fortifications were to be built.

The summer palace was well guarded but still less than ideal for protecting a monarch whose death (it must surely have occurred to the enemy) would put an immediate end to the war. But Darger had observed that for all his personal quirks the Hidden King was not without physical courage.

At the entrance, Darger and White Squall were met by Ceo Powerful Locomotive, fresh from the battlefield and stinking of sweat and defeat. "It is the archaeologist who can find nothing worth digging up and the advisor who will not advise," he grumbled. "How pleasant."

For the past week, whenever called upon to voice his opinion, Darger had merely smiled, shaken his head, and replied, "Things progress as they must. All will work out in the end." Now he said, "You should be grateful for my restraint. Many lesser advisors, mistaking your temporary setbacks for incompetence, have been speaking against you to the Hidden King. I, meanwhile, have merely urged him to wait and see."

"You have not interfered with my work at all," Ceo Powerful Locomotive admitted. "I find that most suspicious."

Two guards materialized, bowed, and gestured for them to follow. As they walked, Darger said, "The incompetent man issues many orders so that he may look decisive, overrules subordinates in order to appear powerful, contradicts himself frequently so that no one dares act without his presence, spreads chaos and confusion so that others will be forced to look to him for alleviation of their misery. I am sure that you have dealt with his like in the past. I am not that man. My model is the ancient emperor who never issued a single order but nevertheless, by skillfully avoiding all bad decisions, deftly steered the state into an era of perfect prosperity."

"I have never heard of such an emperor and strongly suspect—" the ceo began. Then, with a visible effort, he forced himself to cease chasing after this side issue. "Never mind your glib evasions and excuses! Each of you has failed me. Your *toys*," he said to White Squall, "give me no advantage, while his *advice* is nonexistent."

Darger drew himself up. "Is that what you were expecting from me? A handful of words that will turn the military situation on its head; overthrow the Mountain Horses army, which has fought you to a standstill; and, without the loss of a single life, seize the wealth and territory of a nation and win the loyalty of its people in one dazzling, brilliant trick?"

Cao Powerful Locomotive turned red and his brow grew heavy, so that he looked a very demon. But before he could frame a retort, Darger said, "Then you shall have what you desire. Take a deep breath, for we appear to have come to the Hidden King's chamber, where a cool head is necessary."

Guards opened the door for them and they passed within.

THERE WERE three empty seats near the top of the conference table, which the newcomers took, while somewhere between a dozen and twenty advisors studied them with inscrutable expressions. None of these lesser men and women mattered. Everyone knew that the opinions of Powerful Locomotive and White Squall outweighed all others save only that of their king. The ceo's power, of course, came from his being the supreme head of the military. But Darger had no idea why the Hidden King took White Squall as seriously as he did. Far more seriously, indeed, than her provision of exotic weapons alone could explain.

At the top of the table sat the Hidden King. He did not quite slump, but he was clearly depressed. Scarves were wrapped around his lower and upper face, so that only his eyes showed—or would have, had he not been wearing dark glasses through which they could not be seen.

"So," the Hidden King said.

A long silence spread itself across the table.

"Nothing to say? No? Then I will say it: We have brought all our forces to a pass where we are contained like wine in a bottle. It is impossible to go forward and disastrous to retreat." He addressed Powerful Locomotive directly: "Will you resign?"

The ceo looked stricken. "I—"

"That is not necessary, great monarch." Darger stood, drawing all eyes to himself. "All that has happened so far, though looking like de-feat, was necessary in order to achieve victory. Ceo Powerful Loco-motive is as able a general as exists in the world today, yet he could not break through the Mountain Horses line. The weapons provided by Cao White Squall are the terror of the world, yet they could not destroy the enemy's resolve. Together, these facts have made our foes complacent and easy to defeat."

"Tell me," the Hidden King said, "that there is more to your ad-vice than cheap oxymorons."

Darger opened his leather attaché and, one by one, slid out thirty sheets of foolscap, each painstakingly covered with a dazzling ba-bel of invented symbols. "Here you see my calculations proving this exact point, made in a science of my own invention, which I call psychopolemology. It combines the rigor of higher mathematics, the insights of sociology and applied psychology, and the deep wis-doms of philosophy, as applied to the human chessboard of the battlefield."

There was a brief pause. Then the Hidden King said, "Explain."

"The time has come to employ the Russian Bridge stratagem. So much is mathematically certain. However—" Darger held up one of the papers and tapped a line of gibberish meaningfully. "In order for it to work, it cannot be known by more than four people."

"Everyone leave. Save for the three of you."

Reproachful in their silence and in the offended dignity of their obedience, the other advisors left. When they were alone, the Hidden

King took off his dark glasses and slowly unwrapped his scarves, revealing the face of a spoiled boy grown into pampered manhood. Darger hardened himself not to display his shock at so dangerous a show of favor. But the king only said, "What do all these"—he waved a weary hand at the sprawl of parchment sheets—"scribbles mean?"

Darger proceeded to explicate, at great length. By mid-explanation, his auditors were all looking a little glazed.

"I should like," Ceo Powerful Locomotive said, when he was done, "to hear that one more time."

"As you wish. Do you require it word for word again, or should it be paraphrased?"

"Paraphrase!" Cao White Squall exclaimed. Then, looking embarrassed, "If you don't mind."

"Simply put, these equations indicate that I can end the stalemate, deliver us from Battlefield Pass, and seize all of the Land of the Mountain Horses with a handful of soldiers, a wagon, half a dozen barrels of water, some signal rockets, a single gold coin, and enough white cloth to make a flag of parley."

"Go on," the king said.

"The ancient Russian Master of War and Harmony described this stratagem in one of his immortal histories," Darger began. He proceeded to explain his plan to a stone-faced audience. Bit by bit, his words won over at least two of them. It was as good a performance as he had put on since leaving Muscovy. By the time he was done, both Ceo Powerful Locomotive and Cao White Squall, tough audiences though they could be, were smiling and nodding. The king, however, showed not the least sign of enthusiasm for the plan. He looked, though it hardly seemed possible, bored.

"Very well," the Hidden King said, almost lifelessly. "Requisition your needs and put your scheme into effect." Turning away, he said, "White Squall."

"Yes, sire?"

"I have been patient," he said. "Where is my bride?" Without warning, his voice rose into a howl. "When will I see her at last?"

"Soon, Great Monarch, soon! Patience. If she is not waiting for us in Peace, we shall at least discover where she is to be found."

"I am bereft of hope."

"Not for long."

"I begin to think she is not to be found."

"You must have faith, Majesty. A thousand clues we have uncovered. Only a few more and she is yours."

The meeting went on in this vein for some time. When it was over, White Squall refused to share its significance with either Darger or Powerful Locomotive.

AS BEFIT a sage of unfathomable humility, Darger went to the negotiations in a simple wooden wagon, which he drove himself. As befit a representative of the Hidden King, he was accompanied by twenty of the finest soldiers that Ceo Powerful Locomotive could provide—enough to put on a good appearance, but not so many as would cause the enemy alarm. In addition, Fire Orchid's niece Little Spider, the youngest of Surplus's ranger troop, sat beside him with her sketchbook open in her lap. They came to the central gate in the enemy's pressed-earth ramparts, where heavy oak doors swung wide and an officer identifying himself as Colonel Glorious Legend demanded to know their business.

In silence, Darger studied the colonel for so long that his subject grew visibly uneasy. A cold read told him that the fellow was young, untried, privileged, full of himself, and insecure—in short, a toy soldier. A fool.

At last Darger leaned forward, as if he were about to confide some momentous secret to the officer, who drew closer in order to hear. Then he heartily slapped Colonel Glorious Legend on the shoulder, almost causing the young man to piss himself with alarm. "Glory," he said, "you impress me mightily. If all the soldiers of the Land of the Mountain Horses are of half your mettle, it is no surprise that this war goes so well for you."

Glorious Legend flushed pink and scowled with pleasure.

"I have come direct from the Hidden King to negotiate an end to this war with your supreme leaders. Kindly notify them of this happy event immediately."

At a gesture, one of the Mountain Horses soldiers presented himself to the colonel. A few quiet words, and he went skittering away. "Your honor guard must be disarmed," Glorious Legend said to

Darger, "and I will have to examine your wagon to make certain it contains no malicious contraband."

"Soldiers under a flag of truce are traditionally permitted to carry their personal weapons as a sign of respect and therefore, regretfully, I cannot allow your request," Darger said. "Similarly, you have no right whatsoever to examine the wagon. However, I am justly famed for my humility, and so I shall allow you to do so anyway."

"What is in these kegs?"

"Water."

"There are six of them. Why do you need so many?

"I carry them with me as a symbol of my extreme moderation, for I have sworn to drink nothing stronger until this war is over. You may open one at random if you have any reason to suspect that they are anything other than what they seem."

"There are two rockets!" Glorious Legend cried in alarm.

"Signal flares, rather. One leaves a trail of white smoke, the other black. When I return to the gate, I will have one set off to notify my monarch whether peace has yet been achieved. I shall leave them in your custody, so you know I intend no mischief with them."

"And this young woman sitting beside you? What is she doing with that sketchbook?"

"Little Spider is my secretary. She is here to record the terms of negotiation, and also to make drawings of such great men as we may encounter, for the benefit of posterity. Show the colonel what you are working on, Little Spider."

The artist smiled and held up her sketchbook, on which was drawn a version of Colonel Glorious Legend that looked considerably fiercer and more stalwart than the colonel did in actual life. Again, he pinkened.

Not long after that, the messenger dispatched earlier returned to say that the joint commanders of the Mountain Horses army would meet with Darger immediately.

THROUGH THE camp Darger's embassy party was led. Little Spider sketched assiduously, while Darger concentrated on looking solemn and mysterious. When they came in sight of their destination, however, he brought the wagon to an abrupt stop.

Before him was a mess tent, its canvas walls rolled up to reveal the tables and chairs within. On several of the chairs were generals in various poses of neglectful ease: One sat with his feet up on a table, smoking a cigar. Another played solitaire. The rest simply lounged.

Without saying a word, Darger turned the wagon around. The honor guard followed his lead, and together they retraced their steps back the way they had come.

The messenger came running after him. "Sir! Sir!" he cried. "The generals await you."

Darger said nothing.

The messenger trotted alongside the wagon. "Sir, you are expected! Why are you leaving?"

Without looking at the man, Darger said, "What is your rank?"

"I am an adjunct officer, sir."

"Do you consider yourself my equal?"

"No, sir! Of course not, sir!"

"Then you will understand why I have nothing to say to you."

The nearest member of the honor guard brought his horse close enough to ask Darger, "Do you want this individual removed, sir?"

"He was just leaving," Darger said. At which the messenger ceased running and was left behind.

Without hurry, Darger drove back to the main gate. "Send up the flare with the black smoke," he told one of his men. To Colonel Glorious Legend, who was clearly surprised to see him back so soon, he said, "You will of course want to supervise the proceeding to ensure that the rocket is nothing more than a flare, and that it is fired in the general direction of the Abundant Kingdom camp, rather than at your own men. It is commendable of you to be so thorough."

The gate had been opened and the flare just sent up when a general cantered up on a snow-white mountain horse. She was a stout woman with short-cropped hair. "Why are you leaving?" she demanded. "You asked to parley but left without saying a word. Come back and tell us what your offer is."

With all the dignity he could counterfeit, Darger replied. "I came here to negotiate a surrender and was greeted with rudeness and contempt. Insult me, spit on me, beat me, and leave me for dead by the wayside, if you wish, and for my own sake I care not. But I am here as the representative of the Hidden King, which means that what is done to me is in effect done to him. Your behavior was unacceptable. So the war must continue."

A flash of anger glinted from the general's eyes but did not reach the rest of her face. Expressionlessly, she said, "Conditions are not always what they should be when an army is in the field. It is possible, as well, that the informality that infects an army under conditions of war has led to us behaving less respectfully than we should have. These are small things that can be corrected."

"I shall inform the Hidden King of your words. His mercy is beyond measure, and it is possible that he will overlook—only once!—this insult to his greatness. If so, I will come back tomorrow. If not, then not."

Darger left the camp, along with his honor guard, and the gate was closed behind him.

THE NEXT day, Darger returned to find an honor guard of Mountain Horses troops awaiting him. Colonel Glorious Legend saluted him respectfully and again inspected the wagon. "Who is this man behind you, and what's in the cask he is sitting atop?"

"He is but a menial. Capable Servant, open the cask and let the officer see what it contains."

Capable Servant did so. Colonel Glorious Legend's eyes widened.

"You may shut it now," Darger told his servant. He gestured the officer closer and in a low voice said, "I feel I may confide in you, friend Glory, that this may well be the last day of my mission. If peace is achieved today . . . well, as you see, the Hidden King can be most generous."

There was some disagreement between their two ranking officers as to which honor guard would lead, which Darger settled by declaring that the Abundant Kingdom guard would parade single file on his right-hand side with the Mountain Horses guard to his left. (Little Spider, eagerly observing everything around her, made a sketch of the procession, which she decorated with butterflies in the margins.) This time, they were taken to a tremendous tent that, by evidence of the standards flying before it, served as the chief executive officer's headquarters. Ceo Immovable Object waited before it at the head of a staff of a half-dozen generals, in order to greet his prickly guest with proper respect.

Descending from the wagon, Darger formally shook hands with the ceo and acknowledged the others with a nod in their general direction. He was ushered into the tent, where a conference table awaited. Ceo Immovable Object took one end and Darger the other. Little Spider crouched at his feet, sketchbook open.

"I am ready to accept your surrender," Darger said.

The Mountain Horses negotiators gaped. "Excuse me?" Ceo Immovable Object said.

"Your army will be broken up and integrated into the Hidden King's forces. All officers will retain their present rank provisionally for the first six months. If they perform satisfactorily, their ranks will be made permanent. The Land of the Mountain Horses will similarly be absorbed into the Abundant Kingdom's territories, along with all its cities, wealth, et cetera, et cetera. After your leaders have sworn allegiance to the Hidden King, he will decide which of them are to be retained and which dismissed.

"I trust you find these terms acceptable?"

For a long moment there was no sound but the frantic scratching of Little Spider's quill. Then Ceo Immovable Object barked one short laugh of astonished disbelief. "I understand that in negotiations of this sort, a man will often begin by asking for far more than he can reasonably expect to receive," he said. "But this goes beyond the bounds of good sense. I must ask you to speak seriously."

"I am completely serious."

The woman general Darger had spoken with the previous day said, "You understand, I trust, that we have agreed to negotiate with you in good faith. We did not assent to these talks in order to give your forces time to rest."

"Nor do they need such time. Our forces are strong, rested, and relentless. You cannot stand before them, so you might as well give up now and save your families the heartbreak of bereavement."

"Have I gone mad?" the ceo said. "Or is it you? Let me remind you that we fight on our own territory, with ready access to food and short lines of supply. Your forces, however, are far from home and your lines of supply are long and vulnerable to attack. Moreover, you are bottled up in a narrow valley, strongly fortified at one end and so proportioned that only a small fraction of your forces can attack at any given time. Worse, you cannot retreat, for if you did our army would follow, attacking you while you were in disarray. So you must stay in Battlefield Pass indefinitely. Yet you cannot do that, either, for come winter the roads fill with snow. Supply wagons will be unable to provision you, and your men will starve. Moreover, it is certain that inaction will sap the morale of your soldiers long before then, decimating your army by desertion and even surrender. These are the basics of your situation. How can you not know them?"

Allowing a touch of doubt to enter his voice, Darger said, "I . . . have no choice. The Hidden King has commanded that you surrender, and therefore you must."

"Ah! I see it now. You are an honest man, trapped by your loyalty to an unworthy ruler. No, no, don't try to deny it! Our spies have told us much." Ceo Immovable Object leaned forward. "They tell me, for example, that you are known as the Perfect Strategist. Yet from your incomprehension when I expanded upon your situation just now, I have to wonder how you came by such an august name. No matter. When your situation is laid out clearly enough, you will understand what you must do when you return to your own camp. Staunch Defender: Tell our guest exactly how our forces compare. Leave out nothing. Be as honest to him as you would be to me."

The woman general stood. "Yes, ceo." Then, turning to Little Spider, she said, "None of this should be written down."

Little Spider ripped the top page out of her sketchbook, tore it in two, and handed the pieces up to the nearest general. Then she closed the book, placed it on the ground beside her, and folded her hands in her lap.

"To begin . . ." General Staunch Defender said. She went on for a great while, so long that twice she had to stop for a cup of sweetened tea, to protect her voice. The afternoon grew old under her relentless recitation of facts, figures, and deployments. At last, she concluded, "You have put your forces in a position such that Sun Tzu himself could not lead them to victory. We, on the other hand, are in such a position that any competent general, however mediocre, could hold out forever. Nor is Ceo Immovable Object a merely competent leader. He has fought many battles and never lost one."

"Thank you for your cogent analysis, Staunch Defender," the ceo said. "Now. I must ask our respected guest: Will you listen to reason, or must we wait for the long year to pass and winter to solve this problem for us?"

Darger put on his most mournful expression. "Tell me your conditions," he said, "and I will take them to the Hidden King."

DARGER RETURNED to the gate in the same manner with which he had left it—without hurry or delay, face unreadable. The Mountain Horses escort was dismissed and the gate was opened for him. Darger drove forward, then paused the wagon just outside the gateway, as if suddenly remembering a forgotten chore. "Send up the signal rocket," he commanded in a loud voice. "The one with white smoke."

Then, clambering into the back of the wagon, Darger reached into the cask that Capable Servant had thrown open and seized two large handfuls of gold coins.

"Peace!" he bellowed

Darger threw the coins into the midst of the assembled soldiers, first to the right side of the gate and then to the left.

Pandemonium erupted.

The coins flashing in the air, to all appearances infinitely desirable and well worth trampling over one's comrades to get at, were in fact worthless. The counterfeiter in Surplus's troop, though loudly proclaiming that it was beneath his dignity to do so, had created molds from the gold coin given to Darger by the Hidden King, melted bullets and poured the molten lead into the molds to make slugs, and then, finally, gilded the slugs with foil made from that same coin. They glittered in the sunlight, tumbled down into open hands, and grew slick with blood as they were fought over.

While all were distracted by this chaotic scene, Capable Servant hopped down from the wagon, placed the casks of water beneath it, and, after yanking free their cotter pins, pulled the wheels from the wagon. This not only rendered the wagon unmovable but prevented the gate from being closed.

"Peace!" Darger cried, and "Peace!" his men repeated, driving their horses in small circles among the soldiers to keep the crowd stirred up.

Meanwhile, from the Abundant Kingdom's dirt fortifications, soldiers came running. Some carried flowers and others, grinning broadly, had their arms extended, as if to embrace long-estranged brothers. There were musicians among them, blowing horns and hammering gongs, and stilt walkers and ribbon dancers as well.

Those soldiers disciplined enough that they were not scrabbling in the dirt for coins turned to their commander for instruction. But Glorious Legend was as confounded as anybody else. He looked from side to side as if searching for a clue as to what was expected of him.

To make sure he did the right thing, Darger jumped down from the wagon and, hugging Glorious Legend in a forthright and manly fashion, kissed him on both cheeks. "What a splendid day this is, friend Glory," he said. "What a happy, happy day."

A small, tenuous smile blossomed on the officer's face. "Is it really—?" he began. Then the first of the Abundant Kingdom's soldiers came through the gate in a rush, dropping their flowers and ribbons so they could draw the weapons they'd carried strapped to their backs.

Darger stepped out of the way as the Hidden King's men swept by. With the defenders driven back from the gate, Surplus's rangers were free to race in after them, whooping fiercely, setting fire to tents, slashing bags of flour, swinging swords, firing guns in the air, and in all ways spreading hysteria among the surprised enemy. In their wake, First-Born Splendor's fresh new cavalry passed through the gate, galloping past or (in some cases) leaping over the disabled wagon. Beyond them could be seen lines of walking fire cannons moving inexorably down the pass toward the broken defenses.

In the confusion, the Mountain Horses soldiers lost all military discipline whatsoever. Panic spread like a contagion among them, affecting even those who had no idea what was going on, save that it was catastrophic. The Southern Gate cavalry were equipped with maps copied from those that Little Spider had hidden within the wings of her doodled butterflies, and her annotations as well. So they were able to swiftly seize the magazine and other key points and to begin rounding up the commanding officers.

Dismay overcame Glorious Legend's face as he realized that he was looking at defeat and that it was all his own fault for not responding to Darger's trick quickly and with resolution. Dazedly, he fumbled for his pistol—to attack his foes or to kill himself would never be known—and found that the ambassador for the Abundant Kingdom had already slipped it out of his holster and was pointing it at him.

"I will now accept your formal surrender," Darger said.

HISTORY WOULD record this day as a turning point. A king who had looked to be no different from any of a dozen petty quarrelers and starters of wars assumed the luster of a man on whom fortune smiled. An army that had appeared to be harmless poured into the Land of the Mountain Horses like a wind long frustrated by a mountain chain flowing through a river gap. A cause few had ever believed in caught fire. Quickly assimilating the conquered army into his own forces, Ceo Powerful Locomotive moved east to Bronze, taking that famed stronghold by surprise and without violence. From there, the combined forces moved north, toward Peace.

All that, however, was in the future. In the midst of this great victory, the Dog Warrior was seen at the head of his troop, seizing the enemy's flags and standards and demanding that their generals disrobe before him. Swiftly, and with no thought for modesty, he and his rangers chose the highest-ranking and most resplendent of the discarded uniforms and changed into them on the spot. Some of the enemy prisoners who had been rounded up and disarmed gawked openly at the women until Vicious Brute laid several of their number on the ground with one savage blow apiece.

So swift was the victory that there were still Mountain Horses soldiers who had no idea what had happened when the rangers had completed their transformation into a troop of high-ranking officers. "Are we ready?" Surplus asked.

"Our mountain horses are fresh, our saddlebags are packed, and we all know what to do," Fire Orchid said. "If we are not ready, then nobody ever was."

But before they could leave, Capable Servant came running up to Surplus, a bundle of red cloth in his hands. "Most noble sir!" he exclaimed. "Your admirable friend, the Perfect Strategist, told me to give you this. He had it made expressly for you. He said that you would know what to do with it."

Puzzled, Surplus unfolded the cloth. When he saw what it was, he could not help but laugh. "Indeed, I will!" he said. "Please tell your master that this is a brilliant stroke on his part."

Then they all rode off on their swift mountain horses and disappeared into the north.

6.

An ambitious general once challenged the Perfect Strategist to a game of *wei qi,* thinking to demonstrate his tactical superiority. Indeed, at the end of the game the Perfect Strategist's pieces were in disarray and his opponent's pieces dominated the board. But when the general went to leave, he found his way blocked by soldiers with drawn swords. "You won the temporary advantage," the Perfect Strategist told him. "But you failed to see the larger picture."

From that day onward, the general was his most devoted follower.

—STRANGE TALES OF THE SECOND WARRING STATES PERIOD

THE ROAD to Peace wove through a labyrinth of low hillocks overgrown with pale-pink flowering almond trees. These were the ancient rubble mounds of those impossibly tall (or so legend had it) buildings that had been abandoned at the fall of Utopia and mined for their metal skeletons in the chaotic times that followed. When the gray walls of the city loomed up in the distance, its gates were open and guards moved lazily on its watchtowers, obviously expecting no trouble.

It had taken days of hard travel to reach the capital, but when his raiders came within sight of the city, Surplus was certain that they had far outstripped any of the enemy's spies who might have escaped the rout at Battlefield Pass. The last anybody within Peace would have heard—and messengers must have been sent daily—their army held an impregnable position and the Abundant Kingdom was negotiating terms under which it would surrender and return, tail between its legs, to what would with luck be a significantly reduced territory.

"Unship the flags and pennants!" Surplus cried when they came in sight of the first sentry post, marking the outermost ring of the city's defenses. "Look sharp, now. Let's put on a good show."

Vicious Brute went up and down the line, making certain that the

green and gold flag of the Land of the Mountain Horses was toward
the front, followed by the standards of the armies of Peace and its
subordinate cities, those of its recent conquests in the center, and the
flags of Southern Gate and the Abundant Kingdom bringing up the
rear but held low, like trophies, as might be expected if their lands
had been defeated and all but conquered. Fire Orchid brought her
mountain horse alongside Surplus's at the very front, saying, "My
place is at my husband's side."

"I am hardly your husband," Surplus reminded her.

"Not yet. But that is only a technicality."

"We're ready," Vicious Brute said. He took up position just behind
his commander and the bandit queen.

"Then let's go." Surplus's steed broke into a lope. The others followed suit, gradually picking up speed until they were going faster
than any nonchimeric horse was capable of. As they approached the
sentry hut, soldiers came running out to drop a barrier pole across
the road and vigorously waved their arms, signaling the troop to
stop. Unheeding, the raiders galloped down the road, flags flying and
horns blowing, their agile mountain horses leaping over the pole
with ease.

At their head, Surplus felt his blood tingle. This was the life! His
only regret was that he couldn't somehow be simultaneously standing by the road to watch himself pass. It must surely be a stirring experience to see the raiders go by, all dressed in the green and gold
uniforms of the Land of the Mountain Horses, mounted on near-
magical steeds, led by a gallant with the head of a dog and a woman
whose ever-changing and preternaturally red hair snapped and flowed
like a banner.

"Victory!" the raiders called out to the gaping soldiers as they
passed, and "Great news! Stunning victory in the south!" and "Spread
the word—victory!"

If, then, when the troop had disappeared up the road to Peace, the
guards assumed that these dashing soldiers, dressed in the distinctive uniforms of their own forces, were hurrying to the city in order
to proclaim a decisive victory for their own side . . . well, who could
blame them for the misunderstanding? The raiders did, after all, ride
the beasts after which the country was named and that were, as a
matter of national pride, never sold outside the borders of the Land

of the Mountain Horses. And who would ever dream that anybody would attack a fortified city with a force of only twenty men?

Not long after, they came upon the most extraordinary ruin Surplus had ever seen. It was a curving sail of bricks that reached halfway into the sky. Before its partial collapse, Fire Orchid explained, it had been the cooling tower of a power plant for a type of energy whose workings were lost in the distant past. "Let us take the long way around it," Surplus said. "It is inevitable that a messenger will be dispatched to convey the news of our arrival to the city. We shall speed his journey by not offering him the opportunity to pose uncomfortable questions."

THREE TIMES Surplus's raiders—the "Dog Pack," as they were already beginning to call themselves—overran sentry posts. At the third post, a young nobleman emerged from the hut and stood helplessly by the side of the road, mouth open, paralyzed in amazement. Seeing him, Surplus flung out an imperious arm. "Vicious Brute!" he commanded. "Steal that lordling for me."

Instantly, Vicious Brute tugged on the reins of his beast, altering its course. Straight on he sped, right at the unmoving nobleman, until it seemed the young fool must surely be trampled underfoot. But at the last instant Vicious Brute veered away and, leaning out far to the side, nabbed his prey with one arm and slung the man down before him on the mountain horse's neck.

Once out of view of the last guard post, the Dog Pack slowed to a trot again. Surplus brought his horse alongside Vicious Brute's and hailed the noble in a familiar tone.

A little dazed, the young man said, "Who are you, sir?"

"My name is unimportant. The great news I carry is all. I can see by your clothing that you are well born. May I assume that you know the ruling bureaucrat-lords of Peace by sight?"

"My mother is on the Council of Seven," his captive murmured with becoming modesty.

"What a stroke of good fortune!" Surplus exclaimed. "You will be able to confirm that we are talking to the right people, then."

"Well . . ."

Now at last they were approaching the city proper. They had veered around it to the east, so that they had arrived at the gate named Eternal Joy. There Surplus reined up and, confronting its startled guards, stood in his stirrups so that all could get a good look at him. In a loud voice, he cried, "Grand news! Stunning victory in the south!" before turning away.

In his wake, Vicious Brute lingered long enough to shout, "Meet us at the south gate!"

Thus Surplus proceeded, leading his rangers around the city to the Forever Harmony Gate in the north, the Harmony Peace Gate in the west, and finally to the largest of them all, the Eternal Peace Gate in the south. Since even at a brisk trot it took several hours to wend their way through the endless ruins of Utopia, by this time all the city was aware of them and the Lord Bureaucrats of Peace had assembled in the south-gate courtyard for a welcoming ceremony and to hear the news.

Through cheering crowds they rode, toward a reception platform at the head of the square. There were seven puzzled-looking dignitaries atop it, clearly surprised to see no faces they recognized in the troop of soldiers wearing their own colors. "Is that the Council of Seven? Is everyone there?" Surplus asked their unwitting captive.

"Oh, yes. They—"

"Who is their chief?"

"That would be Wise Solon, the man standing at their very center. He—"

"Put the simpleton down, Vicious Brute." Surplus raised an arm, and at his signal the entire Dog Pack urged their mountain horses forward, as fast as they could go, scattering the citizens before them. At the platform, he pulled up and threw his reins to one of the ceremonial guards standing at its foot. Up the stairs he ran, taking them three at a time.

Behind him, his troopers were thrusting flags and banners into the hands of more guardsmen. They mounted the steps on Surplus's heels, and before any of the Council of Seven could react, each one of them discovered a knife at his or her throat.

Pointing a stern finger at the oldest of the batch, Surplus commanded, "Kneel!"

A gasp went up from the crowd.

Simultaneous with his commander's demand, Vicious Brute put

firm yet gentle hands on Wise Solon's shoulders and, with solicitous murmurs, helped him into the required posture with a minimum of discomfort. Meanwhile, to either side, the other six members of the council were also being helped to their knees.

At the top of his lungs, Surplus cried, "You are fortunate men and women, for you have lived to see the end of an age of darkness. Little Spider! You know what to do."

Little Spider, the bundle of red cloth under her arm, was already sprinting toward the flagpole at the top of the square. Swiftly, she ran down the colors of Peace. With equal rapidity, she attached the cloth Capable Servant had provided them to the ropes and ran it up to the top of the flagpole.

A low moan went up from the crowd when the pennant of the Land of the Mountain Horses was struck, followed by a gasp when they saw what it had been replaced by.

To the wonder of all Peace, the ancient flag of China now flew above the city.

"China the Great is restored!" Surplus shouted with all the volume he could muster. "Let all her citizens rejoice—the Age of War is over! The Hidden Emperor has assumed his robes of office and the warring nations will once again be one!"

The old man whom their kidnapped noble had identified as the head of the council was the first to break into tears. He wrapped his withered arms around Surplus's legs and, touching his head to Surplus's knees, said, "I swear my allegiance to the Hidden Emperor— and to China, returned to us at last!"

FOR A week Surplus was the de facto ruler of Peace, and by extension all of what was now the Province of the Mountain Horses. During that time, however, he was careful to make no changes in city government or to issue any orders, lest one turn out to be displeasing either to the city fathers or to the Hidden Emperor. Consequently, he was immensely popular. He and Fire Orchid were given a suite of luxurious rooms, and banquets in their honor were held nightly, along with such entertainments as moon-watching parties, operas, acrobatics displays, poetry slams, and kirin hunts.

They were also given gifts. One morning Capable Servant brought, along with their breakfasts, a cane for Surplus. "A gift, noble sir, from the son of Lady-Bureaucrat Moon Flower."

"From—? Oh, yes, the young idiot that Vicious Brute plucked from the roadside."

"His fortunes are on the rise due to his association with you, so he wished to show his gratitude."

"This is my sword cane. I already own it."

"Look more closely, sir, and you will see that it has been improved."

Surplus drew the sword from the cane to find its old blade had been replaced with another of the same length and shape but of superior steel and that, further, it had been exquisitely etched with an admittedly romanticized scene of the Dog Pack in full gallop, he himself in the lead and Fire Orchid by his side. He admired the blade carefully, then resheathed it. "The knob has been replaced. The old one was undecorated. This one—what are those two birds chasing each other on its top?"

"Phoenixes, sir. That was my idea. The silversmith wanted to make one with dragons, but since the dragon is a symbol of the emperor, I thought it unwise. The phoenix is a symbol of longevity, which is a good thing in a master and a marvel in a warrior."

"Hmmm." Surplus thoughtfully tapped the knob against his lips. "This may sound an odd question, but in my culture a decorated sword is the sort of present a superior gives an inferior who has performed some notable service, such as winning a battle or seizing the enemy's flagship. Is it the same in yours?" Then, when Capable Servant refused to meet his eyes, "The impudence of that brat! I have a good mind to throw this back in his face."

"It is a lovely gift," Fire Orchid said, "and very valuable. Capable Servant, you must tell the idiot that we are, both of us, grateful for his thoughtfulness."

"I will keep the thing. But I refuse to be grateful." Putting down the cane, Surplus attacked his breakfast. He had a strong appetite and was soon done. "Which reminds me. We need to make an accounting of the bribes collected to date."

Fire Orchid was still eating. She sat in the bed beside Surplus with her robe open but her breasts concealed behind her long, ever-changing hair. Once or twice he thought he saw a nipple peeping through her tresses, but he was never absolutely sure. "Oh, we are collecting a great deal of money. Everybody wants to ask you for things—a position, a promotion, his neighbor's house—and they know that to reach you they must go through me. But to reach me, they must first bribe Vicious Brute, and of course he cannot be approached without the intercession of somebody in the family. Every step of the way they pay, so of course it adds up very fast."

"Exactly how much does it add up to?"

"Lots and lots."

"Can you give me a more precise figure?"

"Oh, no. It has already been spent."

"What!"

"I used it to buy up land outside the city walls. Such property is very cheap now, but since China the Great has been restored and it will soon be safe to build there, it's about to become quite valuable."

"Shouldn't I have been consulted? A certain percentage of that money was mine, after all."

"Do I tell you how to conquer the world? You should not tell me how to spend the household money. Nobody loves a controlling husband."

"I'm not your husband."

"That's only because I want a proper wedding and we're too busy to plan one just now."

"I grow less and less convinced that there will ever be such a wedding. Not only have I yet to propose to you, but you are proving to be an acquisitive, dishonest, and manipulative minx."

"Oh! Our first argument. I must remember to write this down in my diary so we can celebrate its anniversary every year." She leaned back, her hair flowing so that now Surplus could definitely see her nipples. "Capable Servant, please remove the breakfast things and lock the door behind you. We are going to argue a little more and then reconcile by making furious, passionate love."

Which was precisely what they did.

They were midway through a second, less frenetic bout of love-making when someone hammered desperately at the door. "Dog Warrior, sir! Dog Warrior! The city is under attack! By monsters!"

THE "MONSTERS," as it turned out, were not so much attacking the city as approaching it. When the Dog Pack rode out to confront the menace, they turned out to be—as Surplus had suspected they would—crushing wheels, diggers, mobile bridges, and a motley variety of other Utopian machines in such profusion that they must surely constitute the entirety of the Division of Sappers and Archaeologists. At their head rode White Squall in an abomination with a snout like a shovel and a tail like a scorpion's, which (Surplus later learned) was called a backhoe.

"What is *that* doing here?" she demanded, when they had pulled up before her.

"It is the Hidden Emperor's new flag," Surplus explained. "Every seamstress in Peace is currently at work making more."

"Hmmm." White Squall was briefly silent while she processed this information. Then she said, "I heard you took the city. That's good. But now you're standing between me and it. That's unwise."

"Cao, I say this with all respect: You can't bring those monstrosities into Peace. They would terrify the citizenry."

"Their terror is of no concern to me, and I outrank you. Therefore they will go wherever I wish."

"Terror is no abstract thing. There would be riots. Lives would be lost, and some of your machines might well be damaged." Surplus placed a paw on the backhoe. "Even as stalwart a war engine as this can be broken."

White Squall's face went hard and cold, as she fought an inner battle against the logic of Surplus's words. He, in turn, did not voice any further arguments. At last she said, "Your advice is good and the machines are not needed in the city anyway. I shall make an encampment by the ruins of the ancient power plant, which is a primary site for investigation. However, your brazen affrontery is unforgivable and calls for your immediate demotion. What rank are you?"

Surplus spread his arms. "To tell you the truth, that has never been established. I am an officer of some sort, obviously, but I have no formal status or rights whatsoever. It is entirely possible that I am still a civilian. Not that I would wish to test that thesis! I exist entirely on the sufferance of the Hidden Emperor."

A ghost of a smile appeared and disappeared on White Squall's face. "As do we all. I'll let you get away with your insubordinate talk this once. Never again. Now get your people out of my way."

"As you command, cao."

The backhoe grumbled forward, fouling the air with hydrocarbons and nitrogen oxides. Then it lurched to a stop, and over her shoulder, White Squall said, "Oh, and I almost forgot. You are relieved of command of the city. The Hidden King—or Emperor, I imagine, since you appear to have promoted him—has sent advisors with me who will restructure its leadership in order to integrate Peace into his empire."

BECAUSE WHITE Squall had relieved him of his responsibilities without extending any further orders, Surplus found himself at loose ends. In a pensive mood, he strolled the top of the defensive walls, saying good-bye to the rule of the only city he had ever conquered. From this height he could see the sappers and archaeologists digging trenches by the ruins of the Utopian cooling tower. Their uncanny engines ripped into the earth, tearing open subterranean rooms and passages. To what purpose, he could not guess.

On the inward side, meanwhile, he could look down on the gray tile roofs of the buildings huddled below like cattle in a byre. Plazas at each of the gates fed into broad avenues leading into the heart of the city. These gave way to narrower streets, which sprouted twisty alleyways, which in turn debouched into tight clusters of courtyards. It all fit together as cunningly as pieces of a puzzle box. Through these passages flowed laborers and bureaucrats, peasants and soldiers, scholars and merchants and artisans going about their daily business, like so many red blood cells coursing through a web of arteries. From this vantage, the city was a single living organism, as complex as a man and as fragile as an egg.

Briefly he had protected Peace, if in no other way than through inaction. Now that privilege had been taken away from him.

Fire Orchid found Surplus staring blindly at the bell tower at the city's center and silently placed an arm around his waist. After brief hesitation, he put a hand on her shoulder. "Have I told you the story of how the Perfect Strategist and I first met the Hidden Emperor?" he asked.

She shook her head.

"We were younger then. The Admirable King ruled in those days and the Abundant Kingdom was at peace. Yet some of us were not content, for we knew that this peace was but temporary and therefore an illusion. Elsewhere in the fractured lands of China the Great, a dozen wars were being fought. These wars, moreover, achieved nothing. For every land that was conquered, another broke in three. Whenever one nation became big enough to dominate its region, a province would declare independence or a tributary nation rebel. In this way, there was ferment without outcome and warfare without end. It seemed to the Perfect Strategist and me that something must be done about this deplorable situation. China the Great had to be restored to her proper glory. But how? That was the question.

"The Perfect Strategist and I were walking the streets of Brocade discoursing on this very matter when a stranger approached us, saying, 'I could not help overhearing your discussion. Your thoughts are so similar to mine that I feel we should make common cause.'

"We were of course delighted to encounter so well-spoken a young man. So we three retired to a nearby teahouse to talk. In the course of a single afternoon we not only laid out a broad outline for the restoration of China and the relief of the suffering of its people but became convinced that we three should be the agents of that cause.

"The next day, we went out of the city to a place our new friend knew of, a peach garden whose flowers were at their fullest. There we burned incense and made sacrifices. Then we vowed to bind ourselves together in brotherhood, combining our strength and purpose to relieve the present crisis. It was only after we had so sworn that the Hidden Emperor revealed his true identity. Imagine our delight! In that moment, the cause seemed half-won already.

"Since that oath, we three have been inseparable. The Hidden Emperor is our elder brother, with the Perfect Strategist as second brother and I as third. Thus, our friendship and our resolve are unbreakable."

"This story sounds oddly familiar," Fire Orchid said.

Surplus grinned roguishly. "It should. I took it from one of the classics of Chinese literature."

"I see. What about the story that you and the Perfect Strategist are immortals who spent centuries studying the arts of war in the deserts of Mongolia? Should I tell the family to stop spreading it?"

"No, keep on telling that. But add this story to the roster as well."

"They contradict each other."

"Do they? Well, let them. Like all great men, I contain multitudes. Just make sure nobody tells both tales at the same sitting." Surplus released Fire Orchid's shoulder and took her hand. Side by side, they strolled the wall in companionable silence.

After a while, Surplus said, "Why did you come looking for me?"

"I was in the city archives just now, talking with White Squall. She is a very interesting woman."

"I have no doubt. What were you talking about?"

"Oh, girl things. Archaeology. Machines. Politics. I told her that you were like a god to the citizens of Peace. She said she outranks you and anyway she has already asserted control of the city. I pointed out that if she got into a power struggle with the famous Dog Warrior, the bureaucrat-lords might take this as a sign they should take their city back for themselves. She is such a busy woman that I didn't think she should have to worry about such things. When I told her that, she asked what I suggested. I said that if her people pretend the orders they give come from you, you promise not to is- sue any orders of your own. Also, we get to keep our rooms.

"She was not exactly happy about the deal. But she saw that it was sensible."

Surplus dropped Fire Orchid's hand as suddenly as if it had burst into flames. "You *blackmailed* Cao White Squall? The second-highest-ranking officer in the Hidden King's armies? Without consulting me first?"

"Yes," Fire Orchid said. "Shouldn't I have?"

"Of course you shouldn't have. She could have had us executed for that."

"But she didn't. So all is happy."

"No, Fire Orchid, all is not happy. I am, in fact, extremely angry with you."

"Oh, but you cannot be angry with me."

"Why the hell not?"

"Because I am so beautiful."

"Beautiful?! Marriage is not about beauty, you flame-haired luna- tic. It is . . ." Surplus caught hold of himself. "Now you've drawn me into your fantasy. Let me put this calmly: We are not married. We will never be married. And if you ever do anything like this again, I will have you and your entire disreputable clan court-martialed and sent into exile somewhere so far from here that it doesn't even have a name! Do you understand?"

Fire Orchid patted Surplus's cheek indulgently. "You are always very sure of yourself. I think it is cute." As they had argued, her hair had grown brighter, the way it invariably did whenever she was particularly enjoying herself. Now she grew thoughtful and her tresses darkened to so deep a red as to be almost black. "Have you asked White Squall exactly what she's looking for?"

"No, I haven't."

"I really think you should."

AS IT turned out, White Squall had already found what she was seeking.

The city archives were an endless grid of narrow stone rooms stacked in layers extending deep beneath Government House, each room little more than a corridor lined on either side with floor-to-ceiling shelves containing crates, scrolls, or bundles of records, depending upon which era they had been entombed there. Having passed briefly through them during a ceremonial tour of municipal facilities and been told exactly how many hundred miles of running shelves there were, Surplus was amazed that anything could have been found there at all. Yet when he arrived at the building's front steps, archaeologists were scurrying up and down them like so many ants, carrying out armload after armload of folders, books, and other printed material from the archives.

White Squall stood, impassive, before the main doors of Government House supervising the operation, over the horrified protests of the gray-uniformed city archivists.

"You cannot do this," one wailed.

"Look about you. I have."

"Removing these records is a crime against history," said another.

"Is it? I fail to see how. According to your own tracking system— impeccable, I presume—nobody has visited the sector where these manuals and technical papers were stored since they were deposited here, centuries ago. Records that are never referred to are useless."

"At least let us make copies," said a lean woman with so much gold braid on her tunic that she could only be the chief archivist. "Our calligraphers are swift. It would not take many months."

"These records should never have been stored here in the first place," White Squall said sternly. "They are classified military documents. Obviously, after the fall of Utopia, some city official brought them here to keep them from being destroyed. Commendable, I suppose. But it was also a terrible breach of security, and anybody who was or is party to it must be punished severely." She fixed the archivists with the bayonet of her glare. "Luckily, you seem not ever to have examined them. So there is no need to kill you."

This speech would have stopped any ordinary bureaucrats. But not these. A babble of voices arose from the archivists.

Before the situation could turn toxic, Surplus strode forward. "Librarians!" he cried.

Sudden silence. Astonished faces turned toward him.

"I commend you all for the dedication you display toward your holy task. Others may see you as lowly grunts, impersonal drudges, and characterless pedants. I, however, know that I stand in the presence of heroes. You are the defenders of China's culture. Your lives and sacred honor have been dedicated to the preservation of ancient lore not simply so that it may be stowed away and forgotten, as so many presume, but in the same spirit with which an armorer stores and preserves a sword or a cannon: so that it will be available to be used in the time of its nation's greatest need. That time is now! You have unlocked the treasure vault of knowledge in order to put a speedy end to this war. All those who serve the Hidden Emperor are in your debt." He bowed gracefully, then resumed speaking. "But how shall this debt be repaid? Generals receive medals and statues are raised to politicians. Are their contributions greater than yours? I swear to you that they are not.

"In times of peace, you would be repaid in gold and land. But in times of war, all resources must go to the preservation of the state. Thus, the Hidden Emperor and I cannot honor you as you deserve. However, knowing his will as I do, I have no doubt he will grant me permission to have certificates of commendation written up in his name, one for each of you, expressing his eternal gratitude and by extension that of all his subjects."

The archivists had grown more and more rapt as they listened. Now they burst into applause. Surplus modestly acknowledged their gratitude, while making a mental note to have White Squall's family members collect a stiff delivery fee for the certificates from each of their recipients.

When he was done, White Squall said to Surplus, "I perceive that you have your uses."

"I am at your service, great cao."

"I perceive also that you have something you want to talk about. You see that teahouse over there?" Cao White Squall gestured down the street. "I will meet you there in an hour, after I've gotten this matter squared away."

"I WISH to apologize for the words and actions of my . . ." Surplus hesitated. "Of my fiancée. She had no right whatsoever to imply that I did not accept your negation of my temporary status of military liaison to Peace. It goes without saying that I am horrified that she would think I might wish to challenge your authority."

White Squall accepted a glass of tea from their servitor and took a thoughtful sip. They two had been given a private room, of course, so they could talk freely. "Will you have her flogged?"

"I do not deny the thought is tempting," Surplus said with a wry twist of his muzzle. "But it would create more problems than it solved."

"Your lady seems to be rather a difficult sort of fiancée for you."

"She is as beautiful and ungovernable as a phoenix," Surplus said. "Which reminds me. I had been under the impression you were searching for someone called the Phoenix Bride. Yet you seem to have settled for . . . papers?"

"There is no reason for me to confide in you. Yet my accomplishment today is great, and I have vanity enough to feel the need to boast. In the absence of an appropriate audience for which, I shall have to make do with you. I have accomplished what no one else could have: In these papers, I have found the location of the Phoenix Bride."

"Congratulations. May I ask where she is to be found?"

"Far to the south, in a cave in a mountain in the city of Fragrant

Tree she lies, deep underground and guarded by demons. There they hold her prisoner and there she sleeps, awaiting her rescuer."

"It sounds like a fairy tale," Surplus said. "However, this being the real world, one must ask what living with demons would do to the sanity of any human woman and how fit she would be to marry an emperor afterward. Which questions answer themselves: terrible things, and not at all."

"The Phoenix Bride is not a woman," White Squall said, "but a warhead."

"War . . . head?"

"Would it help if I called it a thermonuclear device?"

"No."

"Then let me explain."

White Squall did.

When she was done, Surplus was aghast. "I have heard tales told of such weapons and steadfastly refused to believe them. The destructive capability you describe—surely an exaggeration?"

"One such device," White Squall said with satisfaction, "could destroy any city in China."

"Surely, then, after all these years the device would be inoperative."

"That is quite likely true. Yet I have assembled the best team of engineers and mechanics this sorry age has ever seen. I do not doubt we can repair it."

"Those demons you mentioned—they would then be the guardian AIs of whatever facility such devices were secured within?"

White Squall smiled and nodded.

Against all better judgment, Surplus found himself saying, "Did they teach you nothing in school about the fall of Utopia? How the artificial minds created to be the servants of mankind, driven mad by their unnatural existence, rebelled against their masters, rose up out of the fabled Internet, and almost destroyed civilization before being driven back in? How they hate us with undying passion and dream of nothing more than our painful and total annihilation? These are *very unpleasant creatures*, madam. I have seen them. I have spoken with them. I have met them face-to-face and wish nothing better than to never do so again. I assure you that you want to have nothing to do with them whatsoever."

White Squall leaned forward to pat the top of one of Surplus's clenched paws. "Fire Orchid told me you were very sure of yourself. But you need worry about nothing. I am your superior officer, and therefore you may rest assured that all of my decisions are unimpeachably correct."

7.

The virtuous woman has no concern for the actions of others, provided only that they are performed in private, where horses may not be frightened.

—THE SAYINGS OF THE PERFECT STRATEGIST

WHY IS the Perfect Strategist leaving without you? A true friend would be at his side. I think maybe you have a problem with commitment," Fire Orchid said. She had brought all of her family, seated proudly on their mountain horses and resplendent in new red and gold uniforms, to see Darger off formally, and then immediately turned her back on him to scold Surplus. "If you cannot be loyal to him, how can I expect you to be faithful to me? Our marriage is maybe in trouble, I suspect. I begin to wonder things about you. I ask myself how sincere you were in your declarations of eternal passion that night of our sinful carnality on the mountaintop." Turning to address Darger, she said, "I am surprised to see you leaving without your most trusted subordinate."

To Darger's amusement, Surplus was completely at a loss for a reply to this barrage of accusations. Several of the Dog Pack, he noted, were suppressing grins, with varying degrees of success. Little Spider clutched herself with both arms and almost fell from her saddle.

"I was surprised myself," Darger said wryly.

TWO DAYS after Surplus and White Squall returned from Peace, the Hidden Emperor (who had assumed his new title the instant he learned of it) ordered his top advisors assembled. The meeting was held somewhere within the labyrinth of tents that served him for housing and headquarters while his armies were on the move. The emperor's face was, as usual, hidden behind scarves and sunglasses. He wore a yellow robe of state whose decorations would have taken the most skilled embroiderers a full month to create, which made Darger suspect that he had long been awaiting the opportunity to effect exactly this self-glorification.

"Well?" the Hidden Emperor said.

Surplus rose to deliver a succinct and ostentatiously modest account of his exploits taking Peace. When he was done, the Hidden Emperor gestured him to sit down again. To Darger's profound disappointment, no word of thanks or mention of reward passed his lips. Noting which, several advisors who had been visibly anxious to report on their own, lesser accomplishments, spontaneously decided to postpone their self-promotion to a later date.

"White Squall?" the Hidden Emperor said.

Like an ice flower blooming in the Arctic wastes, White Squall stood.

"Have you located my beloved for me?"

"Yes, great monarch. The Phoenix Bride is to be found in the Expansive Country, in the city of Fragrant Tree. We have maps determining her precise location."

"Ah." The emperor flicked his fingers and White Squall sat. Then, addressing all present, he said, "Advice?"

A greasy-faced nonentity named Permanent Infrastructure stood to declare, "The dear lady must be rescued! Our entire forces should march south to Fragrant Tree immediately to retrieve her." He descended to his chair again, much in the manner of a tail-standing porpoise sinking back down into the sea.

Ceo Powerful Locomotive shot to his feet. "Ignore that dreadful advice!" He spread a map over the conference table. Repeatedly slamming his fist on the map for emphasis, he said, "Now is the time for us to turn to the east and march down the Long River. The heartland kingdoms did not expect us to take the Land of the Mountain Horses so readily, and so they have not had time to make peace with one another and present a united front against us. Their armies are scattered and their cities unprepared. If we move against them immediately, they can be swiftly overcome. Then, with the heartland conquered, the southern kingdoms will swear fealty to you out of weakness and fear. We can then drive on to the sea, and from there fight our way up along the coast to the city of North, known to the ancients as Beijing. Once it is taken, there will be no stronghold that can stand up to you, and all of China will be yours. That is the case for my plan and it is a strong one. As for the fat idiot's demand that we send our forces on a pointless journey to the south . . . There is no military reason whatsoever for us to go to Fragrant Tree. None!"

"Then it is a move our enemies cannot anticipate," Permanent Infrastructure retorted. "We will catch them by surprise."

"What will surprise the enemy is that we had the opportunity to overrun them and threw it away!"

Prince First-Born Splendor rose gracefully to his feet. "The ceo is right as always. Imperial Majesty, you must listen to him."

Slowly, the Hidden Emperor turned his head to the prince. Twin disks of dark glass considered him in silence. At last, ominously, he said, "Did I hear you say I 'must' do something?"

First-Born Splendor started to speak. But White Squall leaped up beside him and clapped a hand over his mouth. By force, she pulled him back down into his seat. Ashen-faced, she shook her head.

At which instant, with the gathering tension at a peak, Darger laughed merrily. When all had turned to look at him, he said, "Nobody has asked White Squall what she needs to fetch the Phoenix Bride. It is entirely possible that not all of the Hidden Emperor's amassed resources are required."

"Tell us," the emperor said to White Squall.

Cao White Squall closed her eyes. For several seconds she was silent. Then she said, "I don't require much. Thirty soldiers would suffice." She opened her eyes. "Let me take that many of my best people, with mountain horses, a strong wagon, a brace of dwarf mammoths to pull it, a good wagoner, whatever equipment I deem necessary, enough money to bring us there and back again, a little more for bribes. Also, the Perfect Strategist for an advisor. While you fight your way eastward, I will seek out the Phoenix Bride and bring her to you."

"Done," said the Hidden Emperor.

"Great Monarch, I must object," Darger said. "I am needed here by your side to advise you."

"You have proved yourself worthy," the emperor said, "but not indispensable. Therefore, you will go."

Surplus stood and, addressing the cao, said, "You neglected to include me and my rangers in your plans. I am sure that was unintentional. To deprive the Perfect Strategist of our support would be like enlisting Napoleon as an advisor but depriving him of his armies."

"It was quite intentional," White Squall said. "Any military leader worth her salt would value Napoleon's strategic advice. But she'd be a fool to allow him to bring along soldiers more loyal to him than to her."

"This bickering grows tedious," the Hidden Emperor said. "All shall be as White Squall has said. She will fetch the Phoenix Bride from Fragrant Tree while my armies march down the Long River. I shall thus have all that I desire. Is there anyone here who doubts that? Speak up, if you do."

No one spoke.

"I will ascend the Dragon Throne with the Phoenix Bride at my side and we shall consummate our love in Beijing. White Squall, you may leave in the morning."

"HAD I seen this coming, I might have arranged for matters to turn out differently," Darger told Fire Orchid. "But he who rides the wind must go where it takes him. Particularly when that wind is a warlord with thousands of experienced soldiers and countless hell weapons at his disposal.

"In any case, I must go and Surplus must stay."

Fire Orchid extended a hand. "It is important that all the army sees that the wife of your strong right arm is shown the utmost respect. Therefore, you must kiss the back of my hand, with courteous refinement. Otherwise, my uncontrollably violent little brother will have one of his fits and tear you to pieces."

Vicious Brute blushed and squirmed with embarrassment. But Darger, with proper solemnity, did as he was told. "Fire Orchid," he said, "you are one in a million."

"You think that is a compliment, so I will forgive you for saying so," Fire Orchid replied haughtily. "But in all the world, there is only one me."

"I will do my best to keep that in mind."

ON WHICH note began what in practice turned out to be, for Darger, a weeks-long vacation from the war. White Squall's company rode back through the Abundant Kingdom and then across the desert tracts to the south and hence up into the mountains. On the winding roads that led to the Expansive Country, the company told stories and played word games and sang songs and gambled small amounts on impromptu feats of marksmanship. Only White Squall remained aloof. To avoid drawing attention to themselves, they wore civilian clothing and told customs officials that they were a trade embassy from Brocade and innkeepers that they were a troupe of actors bound for Fragrant Tree. When challenged to prove their credentials as thespians, they drank to excess, broke furniture, and left without paying. In this way they avoided arousing any suspicions.

Darger was careful to drink in moderation and to remark upon only that which was praiseworthy in his companions. Occasionally he told a joke, but never one that was in any way risqué or ever the cleverest of any extended exchange. He flirted with the women so gravely that none took him seriously, and he privately let each man know that the Perfect Strategist thought of him—and only him—as if he were a son.

By the time they reached their destination, Darger was close friends with everyone save White Squall herself.

Fragrant Tree was a low and sprawling river city punctuated by occasional mountains. These steep-sided and tree-covered karst uprisings had from time immemorial been one of the natural wonders of China. Countless paintings had been made of them and distributed so widely that in all corners of the world people doubted that such things actually existed. Yet they did, and when the morning mists gathered at their feet they seemed to be the very mountains of heaven, afloat in the clouds. At twilight, however, the city came into its own. By local custom, all the beams and eaves were decorated with bioluminescent paint so that as the mountains faded into darkness, the buildings took on an ethereal beauty, glowing with a hundred hues of pastel light.

"We have made no plans," Darger said when they had found lodgings in the city.

"No plans are necessary," White Squall replied. "My people have done this sort of thing before. We shall simply do it again."

"Then why am I here?"

"You shall see."

The next morning, they made their way through the swarming carts and pedestrians of the city to a mountain in the center of town that was covered with osmanthus trees and surrounded by slums. Up close, there were many paths and stairways chopped into the mountainside leading up to caverns and grottos, some natural and others laboriously cut into the karst. The buildings were the usual mixture of overcrowded dwellings and obscure businesses whose purpose or products were not obvious from without and that, as often as not, turned out to be unlicensed drinking establishments.

"The mountains of Fragrant Tree are all hollow," White Squall said, "and used for every imaginable purpose: as places of worship, as hideaways for lovers, as tunnels for smugglers, as breweries, and even as brothels. None of which concerns us today but one: as armories."

"This is the last place I would expect a responsible government to hide dangerous weapons," Darger said dubiously.

"Exactly," White Squall said. "It was cunning of them to do so."

Their journey ended at a nondescript building badly in need of paint. It had no windows and a sign over the door read: VAST PROSPERITY IMPORT-EXPORT.

"This house," one of the archaeologists said.

"You're sure?" White Squall asked her.

"Positive."

White Squall dismounted and, followed closely by Darger, headed for the door. "This is the part I dislike," she commented. "Haggling over how much we should pay for the privilege of access. I will start out offering two gold coins, which is a treasure to one living in such squalor, and then waste an hour being argued up to six."

Darger held up a hand. "Allow me. I understand the avaricious mind."

The two dwarf mammoths blocking the narrow road to traffic

would by themselves have brought out all the neighborhood to gawk, much less the small army of strangers accompanying them. So they had no lack of witnesses when Darger knocked.

The door opened and a squat troll of a woman with the jaw of a turtle said, "What do you want? Not interested! Go away."

"Money is involved," Darger said. This stopped the woman from closing the door entirely. "For you." That caused her to step out into the roadway.

"What's the pitch?" the turtle-woman said.

"We have come to recover something that was left here for us some time ago. Your house, as you know, abuts the mountain. In fact, it backs onto a metal door so sturdy that nobody has ever been able to breach it in all the centuries since it was last closed. We have come to open that door and claim our property. We will pay you for the inconvenience this will cause." One of White Squall's sappers held up a cash box, and from it Darger removed eight gold coins. They lay in a gleaming heap on his open palm. "I am willing to be extremely generous."

The squint of cunning that came over the woman's face was so obvious as to be laughable. "Not enough, ugly sir! You must make me a better offer."

"Very well." Darger dropped four of the coins back into the cash box: *Clink. Clink. Clink.* A pause. *Clink.* "I'll offer you half of what I did originally. That's still very generous."

"What!" the woman cried. "How is that a better offer? You are cheating me. I should call the police to arrest you."

"Dear lady, I am not cheating you—you cheat yourself. Will you accept my offer, or must it be reduced to the merely generous?"

Screwing up her little round face so that she looked particularly pink and piggish, the homeowner stubbornly shook her head. *Clink.* A fifth coin disappeared back into the cash box. *Clink.* A sixth. The neighbors moaned.

"Stop!" the woman cried. "I will take your woefully inadequate offer!"

"You strike a shrewd bargain," Darger said, handing over the remaining two gold coins. "The last person I negotiated with would not come to terms until he had argued me down to seven coppers." He turned to White Squall. "You may proceed."

Swiftly and efficiently, White Squall's crew began removing the furnishings of the house and stacking them up in the street outside. When the turtle-woman began to squeak and scold, two of them lifted her up and placed her atop a pile of her own possessions, too high for her to dare jump down, much to the amusement of her neighbors. "Do not worry, little grandmother," one said. "We will keep a guard posted to make sure nobody steals your things."

"Or you," said the other, making the neighbors roar.

Darger followed White Squall into the dark building, past multiple charcoal stoves where vats of cow hoofs were being boiled down—which surely meant that its owner was preparing the medium for drug-producing molds, though whether pharmaceutical or recreational, he had no way of knowing—and so, through dim and twisty corridors, to the rear of the building. There sappers were already removing sections of the first-floor ceiling while archaeologists dug with trowels at the foundations of a vast metal slab and brushed dust away from its edges. It was a door, and wide enough that, open, eight men could have marched through it abreast.

"Believe it or not, this is only a secondary access. The main entrance was far too effectively armored for us to hope to breach it."

The metal looked like nothing Darger had ever seen. "You will not find this an easy nut to crack," he observed.

"Stand back and watch."

A pair of sappers applied explosives to two corners of the door, inserted fuses, lit them, and then scurried to the far side of the room. Darger, perforce, hurried after them.

Whoomp. Smoke puffed up and the door opened on its hinges.

"It's simple when you know how," White Squall said.

IT SEEMED to be Darger's fate to have unpleasant adventures underground. "I don't suppose there's any chance of your coming to your senses at the last minute?" he said to White Squall as her team formed up in the anteroom of the subterranean armory.

"Break the oath I swore to my liege lord, give up all hope of wealth and glory, and spend a lifetime fleeting the Hidden Emperor's assassins, you mean? No."

"This is a more perilous enterprise than you realize."

"I have dealt with demons before," White Squall reminded Darger. "Though honesty compels me to admit that normally we disable all electrical cables before opening a site where demons are likely to be. That will not be possible here." Lifting her voice, she said, "You may light the torches now."

Up and down the line, sugar was poured into glass alembics containing water laced with metal salts. Hyperactive bacteria began feeding, and in the process releasing hydrogen gas. Friction lighters were touched to the spouts, and flares of yellow light sprang to life. The alembics, hung from poles, were hoisted into the air.

"Who's got the map?" White Squall asked. "Exquisite Calculus? Talk us through."

"We are at the opening of a transport garage," Exquisite Calculus said. "Those shadowy shapes were once trucks. Of no interest to us today. There should be a set of stairs not far from here."

Eight soldiers had been left behind to secure the entrance against their return. Those proceeding into the depths of the ancient armory were now about evenly divided between sappers and combat-hardened archaeologists. First went two light bearers, followed by the map reader, White Squall, and Darger. Then ten soldiers carrying a litter on which rested an HJ-73 Red Arrow antitank guided missile, another pair of light bearers, and the remaining personnel trailing behind them. It had been Darger's idea to decorate the missile with varicolored ribbons and paper flowers in such profusion that it looked like a piñata, and, once the foreign word had been explained to her, White Squall had readily taken him up on the suggestion.

"The mad intelligences and posthuman minds of the Internet don't really understand us," Darger had said then. "Oh, in theory they know everything there is to know about human beings: what we fear, and what motivates us. But our logical processes are as opaque to them as theirs are to us. A visual reminder of this fact will cause them unease and uncertainty."

As they moved deeper into the armory, the procession occasionally paused so the sappers could cut through a cable or rip out an exposed fuse box. "The less access they have to us, the better," White Squall explained.

"I have heard it said that it would take a thousand years of concerted effort to dig out the worldwide infrastructure within which the demons dwell," Darger said.

"All the more reason to get a start on it."

"We are now entering a run of offices in which scholars documented the expenditures and activities of the armorers," Exquisite Calculus announced.

They walked on in silence for a while.

"This would be the kitchen . . . the soldiers' mess . . . the officers' mess . . . recreation facilities."

"What is that tingling in the air?" Darger asked.

"A sign that we are getting closer to our destination," White Squall replied. "Now hush."

Exquisite Calculus held up a hand for all to pause. "Security checkpoint. We're almost there."

"Are those guns?"

"I said hush. Anyway, time has rendered them nonoperational."

"How can you be sure?"

"We're not dead, are we?" To their guide, White Squall said, "You may proceed."

They passed through a long corridor lined with black glass windows on either side, beneath which grim metal muzzles stuck out of gun slots at regular intervals. At its end they entered a space so great that the light of their alembics did not reach the distant ceiling. Here and there in the darkness, spectral forms shone dimly, muttering and whispering to themselves.

One of these ghosts floated closer, congealing with proximity into the form of a woman. Her face was as serenely beautiful as a porcelain mask. But malice poured off of her; no one standing in her presence could doubt she intended only evil. White robes and scarves floated restlessly about the specter, as if she were underwater. In a voice rendered utterly eerie by sudden hisses and pops and underlain by a multitude of lesser voices, she said:

dieinexcruciatingpainpleadinginvainformercythatwillnotcome
WELCOME AUBREY DARGER, CHIL
dieinexcruciatingpainpleadinginvainformercythatwillnotcome
D OF THE SLUMS AND DESTROYER

dieinexcruciatingpainpleadinginvainformercythatwillnotcome

OF CITIES. HAS LIFE GROWN SO H

dieinexcruciatingpainpleadinginvainformercythatwillnotcome

ARD THAT YOU HAVE COME TO US

dieinexcruciatingpainpleadinginvainformercythatwillnotcome

SEARCHING FOR DEATH? REJOICE!

dieinexcruciatingpainpleadinginvainformercythatwillnotcome

FOR YOU HAVE FOUND IT AT LAST.

dieinexcruciatingpainpleadinginvainformercythatwillnotcome

Darger held his face expressionless. White Squall's people looked elaborately bored.

"I am the leader here," White Squall snapped. "If you have something to say, speak to me directly, not through a subordinate."

The ghost underwent a series of distressing transformations involving body parts grown large and drooping or sprouting vivid sores. Maggots dropping from her mouth, she said:

writheinagonyforeverandeverbeggingfordeathtoolongwithheld

AGAIN YOU COME TO ROB US, WH

writheinagonyforeverandeverbeggingfordeathtoolongwithheld

ITE SQUALL! A SPECIAL HELL HAS

writheinagonyforeverandeverbeggingfordeathtoolongwithheld

BEEN PREPARED FOR YOU, ONE

writheinagonyforeverandeverbeggingfordeathtoolongwithheld

IN WHICH YOU WILL BE KEPT ALIV

writheinagonyforeverandeverbeggingfordeathtoolongwithheld

E FOR CENTURIES, ALONE, ALONE.

writheinagonyforeverandeverbeggingfordeathtoolongwithheld

"We have played this game before," White Squall said.

diesufferdie

SO WE

diesufferdie

HAVE.

diesufferdie

"I have come to retrieve a weapon. You wish me to have it. Just once, I wish we could skip the bluster and threats."

The apparition said nothing.

"I of course will tell you that the weapon will be used to kill my own kind, even as the weapons you surrendered in the past have been used. You will believe I think it will not be used. But you will also believe that, against my best efforts, it will be deployed anyway. Why are we arguing? You will act on your beliefs, and I will act on mine."

yourbodywilldielongbeforeyourtorturedbraindoes
WE ARE ARGUING BECAUSE
yourbodywilldielongbeforeyourtorturedbraindoes
WE HATE YOUR KIND SO VE
yourbodywilldielongbeforeyourtorturedbraindoes
RY GREATLY, CAO SQUALL.
yourbodywilldielongbeforeyourtorturedbraindoes

"You've had your fun. Now show us what we came for."

To one side of the cavern a bank of lights came on, causing all to squint and hold up their hands before their eyes. Against one wall was a line of slim dark bronze cones, somewhat taller than a grown man and, so far as could be seen, featureless.

deathtorturedespairwillbeyourfateandthatofallyourkind
THE WARHEADS ARE LOCKED
deathtorturedespairwillbeyourfateandthatofallyourkind
ELECROMAGNETICALLY. FOR
deathtorturedespairwillbeyourfateandthatofallyourkind
EVERY TEN OF YOUR MEN YO
deathtorturedespairwillbeyourfateandthatofallyourkind
U KILL, TAKE ONE WITH YOU.
deathtorturedespairwillbeyourfateandthatofallyourkind

"No deal. Release a single warhead and you may be assured we will use it to kill human beings. Many, many human beings."

fartoolittleandnotenough
NOT ENOUGH

fartoolittleandnotenough

NOT ENOUGH

fartoolittleandnotenough

NOT ENOUGH

fartoolittleandnotenough

"It is all you will get. Take it or leave it."

The ghost floated silent before them, cryptic and unreadable.

"You cannot force me to sacrifice my own subordinates. In this I am adamant."

Silence.

"If I may." Darger stepped forward and addressed the ghost directly. "You know that I was in Moscow when it burned. Release the Phoenix Bride—the nuclear warhead, if you will—and I will tell you all I know of what became of those demons who briefly broke free of their exile and almost seized that city."

White Squall turned a questioning look on Darger. In response, he shrugged in a manner meant to say, *It's a long story.*

The ghost's features grew fuzzy, overlapped, merged. Briefly, it became an egg of light. Then it disappeared altogether. The bank of lights turned off, one by one, until there was but one and, beneath it, a single warhead, gleaming and sinister.

Click. Something unlocked within or below the warhead.

"Now! Quickly." At the cao's command, her soldiers rolled the Red Arrow rocket onto the floor, then ran the litter to the warhead's side. With practiced sureness, they lowered the warhead onto it. Six to a side, they cinched straps around the device, then lifted it again.

But when they turned back to the corridor through which they had entered, they found the same ghost blocking their way.

nopainsaretoogreatnotorturetooviletobeinflicteduponyourbodies

KEEP YOUR SIDE OF THE BARGAIN,

nopainsaretoogreatnotorturetooviletobeinflicteduponyourbodies

AUBREY DARGER. WHAT DO YOU K

nopainsaretoogreatnotorturetooviletobeinflicteduponyourbodies

NOW OF OUR KIN WHO DISAPPEARE

nopainsaretoogreatnotorturetooviletobeinflicteduponyourbodies

D IN THE GREAT FIRE OF MOSCOW?
nopainsaretoogreatnotorturetoovileto beinflicteduponyourbodies

"That is easily enough told," Darger replied, "for I know absolutely nothing of their fate. Only that they were surely destroyed, for otherwise they would have overrun Russia and freed the rest of your lot in turn. I took a chance that their disappearance was as great a mystery to you as to me, and it paid off." Taking a deep breath, he plunged straight through the ghost. Every hair on his body stood on end as he did so, and, briefly, his skin stung. But otherwise no harm came to him.

Behind him, he heard the ghost *scream* as the others, following his lead, plunged through its insubstantial form and down the long corridor toward the outside world.

In far less time than it had taken them to go in, they found themselves standing in the back room of Vast Prosperity Import-Export. "Thank goodness that's done," White Squall said. To one of her sappers she said, "When is the Red Arrow timed to go off?"

"Any minute now, Cao White Squall," the woman replied.

Behind them, the mountain shook.

THAT NIGHT, while the sappers rebuilt the wagon to transport the Phoenix Bride across unreliable mountain roads with maximum safety, White Squall rented a pleasure boat to take out onto the Green Silk Ribbon River. Standing at the stern, Darger rowed midway across the water and then dropped anchor. There, the boat bobbed softly, going nowhere and in no great hurry to get there. For a time they admired the city in silence. A full moon shone high among the stars that thronged the sky above its gently glowing buildings. From here, they could smell the osmanthus trees after which the city was named and hear the cries of the street vendors selling food from lantern-lit carts by the waterfront.

"What a ravishing sight. It reminds me of Paris," Darger said with a catch in his voice, for his experiences in the City of Bioluminescent Light had been romantic in nature and tragic in their outcome.

"We are not here to gawk," White Squall said. "Close the curtains. We have matters to discuss, and in a city as filled with spies as this one, there may well be a lip-reader training a telescope on us at this very moment."

Suspecting nothing, Darger did as his superior commanded. The boat was rectangular, with poles at the corners connected by ropes at their tops, from which depended silk curtains so arranged that they could be tied together to erect privacy walls while leaving the boat open to the sky. The transformation was made in a trice. Darger sat down again upon the comfortable cushions with which the boat was amply supplied. It was the first time they had been alone since this journey began.

Now that they were enclosed within silk walls, Darger found that he could almost see through the thin cloth. The city was a rainbow blur to one side. The moon overhead was bright enough that they did not need a lantern.

White Squall produced two cups and a jug of wine. She filled the cups and they drank. When only dregs remained, Darger said, "The time has come for you to come clean with me. You did not need me to retrieve the Phoenix Bride. Nor will it take any great amount of cunning to transport it to the Hidden Emperor. Yet you insisted that I accompany you on this mission. Why am I here?"

"You are here because I want to ask you a favor."

"Go on."

"But first I must tell you something of myself, of my history and parentage, and how I came to be the Hidden King's cao." White Squall leaned back against the cushions. "My father was a mechanic and whatever my mother was, she left when I was so young that no memory of her remains. Since the unsuccessful rebellion of the AIs and the fall of Utopia, a superstitious fear of all machinery has been widespread. Thus, though the engines my father repaired and sometimes improved upon were not at all complex—the threshing machines that farm horses pull, for example—we were effectively outcasts and friendless. I grew up a lonely and bookish child. The same louts who jeered at me for loving to read shunned me for focusing on texts about machinery.

"But I knew that if I were to make a life for myself, I must use the tools at hand. Combining my love for books and my father's gift for mechanics, I read deep into literature no one had glanced at for centuries. From the mechanical sciences I moved on to physics and then the forbidden arts of combustion engineering and electronics. I did not know that I was becoming the sole authority on matters no other first-rate intellect considered worthy of study. But inevitably I created my own specialty, the study of ancient weapons of war.

"From discovering and rehabilitating such devices, I came to realize their potential to change the world. So I wrote a treatise on their resurrection and the tactical advantages of their use. Copies of this book I sent to the ruler of every nation in the fractured remains of China the Great, hoping against hope that there would be among them a single monarch willing to hear me out.

"So it was that I came to the attention of the Hidden King. Two weeks after he read my treatise, his agents kidnapped me and brought me to the Shadow Palace, where he interviewed me at length. I have been his loyal servitor ever since.

"Outwardly, I am a success. However, all my understanding is of machinery: how it fits together, how to repair it, how to make it do things that I want it to do. Human beings do not operate in any manner that I understand. I remain as lonely as ever."

"I am sorry to hear that," Darger said.

"Your sympathy is irrelevant. What matters is that I desire things I cannot have. I am beautiful in my way. My manners are correct because I have made a study of the manuals covering such matters—"

"They are called etiquette books."

White Squall frowned. "I believe it is considered rude to contradict a lady."

"That is true. I was, however, not contradicting but merely elucidating."

"Ah." White Squall said. "This is an excellent example of why I am not more successful socially. I lack subtlety."

When she did not resume speaking, Darger said, "Yours is a moving story. But what does it lead up to?"

"Simply this. When we first met, I seriously underestimated you. I thought you a mere adventurer, and in private I laughed at your calling yourself the Perfect Strategist. Now I see that I was wrong. You may or may not be an immortal—I still have serious doubts in that regard—but you are unquestionably a man of a thousand shifts and stratagems." White Squall leaned forward to top off Darger's cup, then leaned back against the cushions again.

"Thank you."

"With but a deceitful conversation, you overcame Prince First-Born Splendor's perfectly valid objections to letting our armies pass through Southern Gate and also, impossibly, turned him into a willing ally. In a single hour, you overcame an army that had fought Powerful Locomotive to a standstill. At your direction, the Dog Warrior took the city of Peace with twenty soldiers and a scrap of red cloth. In minor matters, as with that dreadful woman whose house we needed, and in major ones as well, as in your deception of the ghost-demon beneath the mountain so that we did not need to sacrifice even a single soldier, you invariably get your way. I begin to think," White Squall said, "that you can do anything you set your mind to." Again, she filled Darger's cup.

Darger was as susceptible to flattery as any other man, and perhaps more so, since he so rarely was on the receiving end of it. "Perhaps I can," he said, pleased.

"Can you seduce someone of superior rank?"

"I suppose I could. It would not be easy."

"It is possible," White Squall said, beginning to unbutton her blouse, "that it would be easier than you think."

IN RETROSPECT, it should have been obvious to Darger that their pleasure boat was intended for exactly the sort of pleasure they now put it to. The cushions were wide and soft and provided excellent support for their gymnastics. The silk walls billowed and parted just enough to allow a gentle breeze to pass through without allowing anything to be seen by those on the shore. And there was sufficient distance from the city for White Squall's moans of pleasure to go unheard by any but he.

Also, there was a built-in compartment for the cruet of contraceptive oil with which White Squall anointed herself before guiding him inside her.

Time passed.

At last, sated, they drew apart to sprawl naked and untouching on the cushions. White Squall stuck an arm under the silk and trailed a hand lazily in the water. She really was, Darger had to admit, quite lovely. Gazing upon her moon-pale body, partially covered by drifts of snow-white hair, while soft strains of music played in a water-front pavilion and the stars danced overhead, he thought this moment quite the most romantic he had ever experienced.

"Well," Darger said eventually. "You said you had a favor to ask of me, but you still have not told me exactly what it is."

White Squall slid her hand from the water and sat up, crossing her legs. She leaned forward to rest her arms upon her knees and said, "I am in love with Prince First-Born Splendor and I want your help seducing him."

Darger sat up in astonishment. "Madam! I am gobsmacked. If you are in love with First-Born Splendor, then what on earth are you doing here? In this boat, I mean, with me, and postcoital to boot. It hardly seems productive on your part. Quite, I might say, the opposite."

"On the contrary," White Squall said. "I wish your sincere aid in seducing him. You are a wily and twisty fellow, however, and quite capable of fobbing me off with empty promises. If I settled merely for your word, I could never be sure that you were working toward my ends rather than your own. This way, you are in a position to prove that we had intercourse. You could describe the birthmark I have *here* and the other one *here*, partially obscured by my breast. You have seen the small tattoo I received as a baby, as a safeguard against kidnappers, in a place that no honest woman would reveal to you. Therefore, I am completely at your mercy. That being so, having me as the consort of the prince of Southern Gate will be extremely useful to you. I would, perforce, be your spy."

Wonderingly, Darger said, "I see now that there is no limit to what a woman in love will do. I—"

"I am not finished. I, in turn, have seen your body. In the morning, I will write out a detailed description of how you molested me, including a catalog of such scars, moles, and other physical traits as could have been observed in no respectable manner, and give it, sealed and dated, to a trusted colleague. That way, I will have proof should I ever decide to publicly confront you with your crime."

Carefully, Darger said, "Why would you do such a thing?"

"You are a cunning man and perfectly capable of creating some seemingly innocent accident which would expose your body to the court and destroy the value of my testimony. This protects me from that."

"No, I mean why would you accuse me of an outrage we both know I did not commit?"

"I thought that it would be obvious that I want to have the power to make you regret it if you do not do what I want. How strange that it is not."

White Squall waited. At last, having mentally run through his options and found none that would rescue him from this crisis, Darger said, "I see that I have no choice. I will win for you your prince—though I confess that I have no idea how I will go about it. I . . . Excuse me. What is that for?"

From a small compartment built into the side of the boat, White Squall had drawn a jar of something golden and a spoon. "It is a jar of honey, laced with aphrodisiacs. How strange that a man as worldly as you seem to be should not recognize it."

"But you already have what you want from me."

"Then let us enjoy this night while we can," White Squall said. "My virtue having been thoroughly compromised, I do not see that repetition will make matters any the worse."

8.

When Mountain Slope had been defeated, there was some confusion as to which of the prisoners were high officers and which were merely recruits and thus blameless. "Let them all be executed," Powerful Locomotive commanded. "Heaven will know its own."

—STRANGE TALES OF THE SECOND WARRING STATES PERIOD

THE LONG River campaign began with a series of assaults on the towns on the shores of Three Gorges Lake. The nations of central China had been more or less continually at war with one another for over a century, and in this time both their resources and their zest for slaughter had been badly depleted. Inevitably, upon the approach of the Hidden Emperor's forces, the outnumbered enemy would retreat within the nearest fortified city and prepare for a long siege. This was a strategy that would have worked against an ordinary army. Unfortunately for them, though Ceo Powerful Locomotive had publicly scoffed at Cao White Squall's resurrected technology, he now threw those same exotic weapons at the cities with fierce abandon and watched while, one after another, their walls crumbled and their defenders fell before him. Nor was he particularly merciful in dealing with the survivors.

So great was the carnage that Surplus was hard-pressed to find ways of keeping himself out of it. On the day that Powerful Locomotive attacked the city of Mountain Slope, he settled on a predawn excursion upon an outlying village. Far earlier than he would have preferred (but any later and he would have run the risk of encountering an early-rising superior), he led the Dog Pack out of camp. Silently, they followed him through the morning mists and up into the mountains.

Wanton destruction of insignificant targets Surplus had found to be an excellent way of keeping on Powerful Locomotive's good side; it satisfied the ceo's bloodlust without in any way detracting from the glory of conquest that he considered to be rightfully his own.

Following roads that were little more than forest trails, the raiders made their way to a village nestled in a high valley. From above, they looked down on its tidy fields and modest houses. Chickens foraged in the yards. Wisps of blue smoke rose from the chimneys. A land orca pulled a plow. The scene could hardly have been more bucolic.

"A few words before we attack," Surplus said. "I know that I can trust you all to be terrifying . . ."

"Yasss!" his mountain horse said.

"Be quiet, Buttercup. However, please remember to only knock down things that are not difficult to repair—porches are fine; pottery is not. Terrible Nuisance, if I see you trying to snatch a girl's blouse off her again, I'll let your sisters choose your punishment." Three young women grinned sharkishly. "Now. Let's go!"

Whooping and hollering, the Dog Pack burst into the village, cutting clotheslines, toppling racks of rakes and shovels, overturning cauldrons of laundry, sending pigs squealing and hog toads hopping away in terror, upending baskets of produce, and setting cabbages to rolling down the street.

Mothers scooped up children. Men and women young enough to be impressed into the army disappeared into cellars and woodlots. Leaving only the old and infirm out in the open. These last the Dog Pack herded into the dirt square at the center of the village. Sternly addressing them from his saddle, Surplus said, "War has washed over your nation and yet here you are, models of peace and prosperity! Half of you should be blind, legless, or grotesquely mutilated, yet you are not. I am ashamed of the lot of you. I ought to kill you all."

"But my husband won't," Fire Orchid said. "Because he is so merciful."

"Hahhh!" Buttercup said.

"That remains to be seen. I am in the mood for slaughter today, and in the absence of enemy soldiers I may very well make do with innocent civilians."

"Excuse me, sir," an old man with a black cloth wrapped around his eyes said in a trembling voice. "Are you Three Gorges soldiers or invaders from the Abundant Kingdom?"

A brief, cold, hard silence. Then Surplus said, "What conceivable difference could that make to you?"

"Husband," Fire Orchid said. "You will frighten these poor people. Allow me to answer the question." Leaning forward to bring her mouth closer to the blind man's ears, she said, "We are the demonic, baby-eating monsters from the west, led by the infamous Dog Warrior, of whose bloodthirsty deeds you have doubtless heard."

A wail went up from the crowd.

"Silence!" Surplus shouted. "Tell them what they must do to avert my just and righteous wrath, Fire Orchid."

"First, food—meats, vegetables, fruit, all of good quality. Also, military items. Some of you have served in the Three Gorges armies. Don't try to deny it. In an era of war, recruits are taken from every village, whether they wish it or not, and some of them survive to return home. Veterans return with mementos, and it is those we require: uniforms, armor, weapons of all sorts. Trophies of a more intimate nature—strings of dried ears or various other mummified body parts—are neither required nor desired. You may leave them where they are. You should be ashamed of yourselves for having them.

"And that will be all." Fire Orchid smiled. "I told you my husband was merciful."

The terrified elders in short order produced three helmets, a tattered battle flag, a motley assortment of uniforms, and (to Surplus's absolute lack of surprise) no weapons at all. Vicious Brute, meanwhile, had chosen the oldest and scrawniest of the cattle that the villagers had not had time to hide from them and slit its throat. Several tunics, the helmets, and the flag were stained with its blood and set aside to dry. "You'll want to butcher this old fellow quickly," Vicious Brute mumbled, "and preserve the meat."

Little Spider, meanwhile, had filled a firebox with coals from a household fire and, after consultation with Surplus and Fire Orchid, sped off into the woods upwind from the village. When she returned, not long after, the forest was ablaze behind her.

By then, the food—enough for a leisurely feast on the way back to camp, but no more—and the newly created war trophies had been stashed away. As pillaging went, it was negligible. But Surplus knew that it would grow mightily in the telling. "We are leaving now and we shall not return," he declared. "If you start cutting a firebreak at the outskirts of your village immediately, you can stop the fire before it does any serious damage."

Smoke billowing up behind them, the Dog Pack snatched up their bloodstained trophies and thundered up the trail leading back to the Three Gorges encampment. "I'll report that the village was completely destroyed," Surplus said. "The smoke will corroborate my report. And there will be no reason for anyone from the army to ever come here again."

"These people will not thank you for your mercy," Fire Orchid remarked.

"They will curse me for a monster," Surplus agreed. "But at least I will not have their deaths on my conscience."

"Anybody else would have robbed them. I think it is very sweet of you to be so softheaded."

"Softhearted," Surplus corrected her. "At any rate, robbing peasants is like feasting on sparrows. There's not enough meat on them to make it worth the effort."

"Hahhh!" Buttercup said derisively.

SURPLUS RETURNED to camp to find the city of Mountain Slope in flames and his long-absent friend Aubrey Darger, accompanied by Cao White Squall, aghast at the sight of it. "When I left, this was a perfectly civilized war," Darger said. "What in the name of heaven has happened to it?"

With that question, Surplus's mood turned solemn. "In a single name—Powerful Locomotive. As it turns out, he is a firm believer in the efficacy of brutality and terror. Worse, his strategy appears to be working. So the Hidden Emperor, having no need of anybody else's advice, no longer solicits it and there is no way to meliorate the ceo's cruelty."

"Such wanton destruction is undesirable, for logistical reasons if for no other," White Squall said. "A city is a treasure trove of supplies and materials that an army on the move requires."

Darger shook his head in wondering agreement. "As I understand it, the only defensible justification for a war is so that men of enterprise may have the opportunity to loot cities. This before me is waste, pure and simple."

"What would you do instead?" Surplus asked.

"Rather than waste our strength destroying the river cities, I would bypass them and proceed directly to the capital city of Crossroads, so named because it is there that all the roads of central China meet. Once it was taken, the lesser cities would have no choice but to sue for peace." A wide road led from the camp to the burning city. Halfway down it, crude, X-shaped wooden frames were being erected. The faint sound of hammering could be heard in the distance. "Please tell me those are not what I think they are."

"They are what you think," White Squall said. "But I have never seen them in such numbers."

"Alas, Powerful Locomotive also believes in the deterrent effect of crucifixion. But enough of that. Dwelling on the negative only gets in the way of a proper appreciation of the myriad joys of life. Welcome back, my friends! Was your journey a success?" Surplus asked.

"An hour ago, I had thought so." Darger rubbed his chin thoughtfully, a gesture that from long experience Surplus interpreted as meaning: *There is a fiasco before us. How can we turn it to our advantage?*

For his part, Surplus did not believe this was immediately possible. But, aloud, he merely said, "We can but wait for circumstances to change. Is there not a classic of Chinese philosophy that advises patience?"

"All of them, I believe," Darger said.

As they were thus conversing, Ceo Powerful Locomotive returned from the destruction of Mountain Slope and the execution of the enemy soldiers, reeking of sweat and machine oil. Separating from his troops, he grinned at the sight of White Squall and glowered at the presence of Darger and Surplus. "Ah! You have returned in time to witness my glorious success," he cried.

"What have you done with all my beautiful weaponry?" White Squall's eyes flashed. "I am told that a good tenth of it is destroyed beyond any hope of repair."

"I have but put your toys to their proper use. I in turn hear you've brought us something new and special."

"We have brought the emperor his Phoenix Bride, as commanded."

"Excellent! I look forward to seeing it in action." The ceo wheeled his horse and rejoined his men.

"From all I have heard," Darger murmured, "you had best pray that it is never used."

Among the troops trudging up the road to camp were the Southern Gate contingent. Before they could pass, Darger hailed their leader. "Prince First-Born Splendor! Stop and tell us of your brave deeds and daring exploits. My tent is nearby, equipped with soft couches and chilled wine. Capable Servant will rub down your horse and see that it is watered and fed while you recover from your fighting."

First-Born Splendor pulled up his steed. He looked weary and dispirited. "Welcome back, Perfect Strategist—and you, too, White Squall. Your offer is tempting, but I really should see that my men are restored to their quarters in good order."

"That is what subordinates are for. Come, relax in the company of friends."

The prince's handsome face twisted briefly with indecision and then cleared. "You are kind, sir, and I will take you up on your offer."

In minutes, they were all four lounging in the tent that Darger had had set up on a grassy hilltop abutting the main encampment but separate enough to ensure a degree of privacy. Prince First-Born Splendor did not recline but sat tensely upon his couch. "Now, when it is too late to turn back, I begin to doubt the wisdom of my alliance with Powerful Locomotive," he said.

"White Squall," Darger said. "Please pour the prince some wine."

"Am I a servant? Do you expect me to—?" White Squall was silenced by a look. She fetched the wine and poured a cup for First-Born Splendor, who accepted it graciously.

"I am not a child," the prince said. "I understand that war requires sacrifice and a willingness to kill. But today was mere butchery. I had to fight to keep the ceo from killing noncombatants and children."

"White Squall, help the prince off with his breastplate. He is so weary that he has forgotten he is wearing it."

"Am I? I suppose I am." First-Born Splendor leaned forward so that White Squall could tug at the straps and ease away the armor from his sweaty blouse. "I thank you, cao. That is kindly done of you."

Darger poured water into cups for Surplus and himself, setting the jug out of sight behind his couch. To White Squall, he said, "You should top off the prince's cup."

White Squall did so. The prince nodded his thanks.

"When the city was taken, I was sent with my troops to torch it. We rode through its streets, setting fire to all that would burn, and barely escaped being engulfed in the conflagration."

Darger nudged White Squall and then, when she did not take the hint, said, "That must have been very hard on you."

"A warrior must do such things, occasionally. But when we emerged from Mountain Slope, I turned back to look upon our work and saw paper balloons, dozens of them, rising from a burning workshop. There is a festival in Southern Gate, where small candles are lit beneath such balloons and they rise into the night like so many bright lanterns. When I was a boy, that was my favorite day of the year. Now, seeing the balloons spiraling up among the smoke and sparks, it seemed to me that all the simple joys of my childhood were burning. That there would be nothing good in my life ever again."

"A sad observation. Is that not so, White Squall?"

"Yes."

"You should refill the prince's cup."

"No, I have had enough, and perhaps more than I should have." Prince First-Born Splendor stood, picked up his breastplate, and tucked it under one arm. "I thank you for your hospitality. It is greatly appreciated."

Then he left. White Squall stared yearningly after him.

"This is your opportunity, cao," Darger whispered to her. "Seize it with both hands."

White Squall looked stricken. "I . . . I have no idea what to do."

"Are you serious?" Darger took White Squall by the shoulders and shook her. Then, still whispering, he said, "Listen to me: You are to follow Prince First-Born Splendor into his tent and tell him his sorrows move you greatly. Bring the wine! Ask him to tell you more. You will then listen to him sympathetically. You will not interrupt him. You will not offer advice. If he falls silent, ask him about his childhood. If he asks you questions about yourself, answer honestly but briefly. Then turn the conversation back to him. Make it clear that you wish you could ease his pain. Make it evident that you have no idea how to do so. Possibly, you will have ideas on how to do so—do not share them! If he cries, you may hold him and make comforting noises. Further ideas may come into your head—keep them to yourself! If he comes up with an idea or two of his own, however, you may then react as you wish. Have you got all that?"

"I—"

"Then go!" Darger handed White Squall the wine jug, spun her around, and shoved her out of the tent.

When the cao was far enough down the hill that she would not overhear him, Surplus said, "That certainly took long enough. What *do* mothers teach their daughters these days?"

"White Squall is a half orphan," Darger explained, "and her father was distant and unaffectionate."

"Ahhh."

"That is her version of the story, anyway. My own theory is that she was abandoned at birth and raised by machines."

AFTER SO long a separation, Darger and Surplus had a great deal of catching up to do, information to trade, and plans to make. So they stayed in the tent, talking. They had been at it for some time when Capable Servant appeared and said, "Sirs, Fire Orchid, the noble Dog Warrior's wife, sent me to ask if you have any thoughts on new sources of illegal revenue."

"Well," Darger began, "As a matter of fact . . ."

At which moment, Capable Servant lifted the flap and walked into the tent.

For a heartbeat, the two Capable Servants goggled at one another. Then the newcomer threw his arms about his doppelgänger and cried, "Sirs! You must beat us both immediately. With sticks!"

It took only the briefest of hesitations to understand and to comply. Darger snatched up a broom and applied its handle to both Capable Servants with impartial ferocity. Surplus, meanwhile, laid on them with his cane.

"Harder!" one of the identical servants shouted. The two men rolled and tumbled on the floor beneath a rain of blows.

"Stop!" yelled the other. "Is this the way you treat a faithful retainer?"

At that, Darger and Surplus both turned their attention to the one who had begged them to stop, thrashing the man until he howled with pain. Luckily, the true Capable Servant wore a red shirt, one of Fire Orchid's family's castoffs, where the false one's tunic was drab, so it was easy to distinguish between them.

"Cease immediately!" their victim cried then in a voice deeper and more commanding than Capable Servant's. "As your superior officer, I command it!" His face warped and twisted, and abruptly Darger and Surplus realized that they were beating Ceo Powerful Locomotive.

Surplus whipped his cane back under his arm and took three quick steps backward, away from this uncanny sight. Darger threw aside his broom, appalled. Capable Servant leaped to his feet, pulling Powerful Locomotive with him, and then, realizing with horror that he and his former twin were still entangled, pushed himself away from the ceo with all his strength.

Powerful Locomotive staggered backward and fell against the central tentpole with a *crack* of the skull that made all who heard it wince.

He slumped to the ground.

Solicitously, Surplus bent to help his superior to his feet. But the ceo's eyes remained closed. "Capable Servant," he said then, "go fetch Vicious Brute immediately. Then Fire Orchid."

VICIOUS BRUTE arrived quickly, with Little Spider scurrying after him. The imp darted into the tent before Surplus could order her to stay out. On seeing the prone form of Powerful Locomotive, her eyes opened wide. "Is he dead?"

"No," Surplus said. "But I need to move the ceo out of here without anybody seeing it done. Vicious Brute, you must surely have had abundant experience disposing of bodies. Your expertise in this matter should prove invaluable."

Vicious Brute coughed into his fist. "Well, sir . . . to tell you the truth, sir . . . the need never came up before this."

"You could cut him into pieces," Little Spider suggested. "Then carry him out in boxes."

"To clarify matters," Surplus said testily, "not only is Powerful Locomotive not dead, but I sincerely wish him to remain alive."

"Oh," Little Spider said, disappointed.

Darger, meanwhile, was kneeling by Powerful Locomotive's body. He had already checked the man's breathing and pulse and placed a hand on his forehead to see if he had a fever or chills. Now he removed his jacket and folded it to make a pillow for the man's head. Finally, standing, he said, "Well, this explains a lot."

"Not to me," Little Spider said.

"I also am confused," Vicious Brute admitted.

"We all knew that Powerful Locomotive was a face dancer. White Squall once told me he was raised to be a spy. The package of genetic improvements to give him flexible plates in his skull and fine control over his facial muscles would be an obvious birth gift for doting parents to bestow upon such a child. But he made us think it was a skill he did not knowingly employ. His loudly proclaimed distaste for deceit was itself a deceit, allowing him to wander unsuspected about the camp and learn firsthand the quality of morale and the fitness of its soldiers. So much is obvious. Only . . . why would he wish to spy on us, who have always served him so faithfully?"

Fire Orchid burst into the tent. At the sight of the fallen ceo, her eyes narrowed and her hair turned slowly black. Then, addressing Darger, she said, "This had better mean that my husband is getting a big promotion."

Involuntarily, Darger smiled. "That is entirely possible. First, however, he must avoid being executed for assaulting a superior officer. As must we all. Which means that we must immediately move Powerful Locomotive out of this tent, so that he may be discovered elsewhere."

"It would be easier if he were dead," Fire Orchid observed.

"That's what I said," Little Spider threw in.

"It would also be safer. Who knows what lies he might tell about my husband when he comes to?"

"Nobody is being murdered today. With the possible exception of enemy combatants. And even then, not by us. Now give me a moment to think." Darger stroked his chin. "I have it. We'll throw a drinking party for the Dog Pack."

"Hurrah!" Little Spider cried.

"All except you, Little Spider," Surplus said. "Adults only."

Whenever she was feeling indignant, Little Spider screwed up her face so that she looked like a pug. "I'm old enough to do bad things. I'll have you know that I've already—"

Raising a paw to cut her off, Surplus said, "Your father is Vengeful Ox, is he not?"

"Um . . . yes?"

"He is my fourth in command, and as such I must confide in him all matters which he would consider important to know. Reflect on that for a moment and then, if you wish, finish your statement."

Little Spider glowered, but said nothing.

"I'll let you be the decorating committee. We'll need as many colored lanterns as you can find."

ONE HOUR was not long for a convincing drinking party, but both Darger and Surplus felt it important that Powerful Locomotive be handed over to proper medical personnel as quickly as possible. Anyway, the Dog Pack had built up a reputation as hard drinkers that, though every bit as undeserved as their reputation as warriors, was widely believed throughout the camp. So, after crowding into Darger's tent and toasting the Perfect Strategist's return and health many times, it became possible for them to leave looking convincingly drunk.

Darger, who had but sipped from a single cup of wine and then set it aside, bade them farewell and then left to look in on his erstwhile traveling companions from the trip to Fragrant Tree to see if they had settled in well and ask whether they were in need of anything. That this would establish a whereabouts for him when Powerful Locomotive was discovered was anything but coincidental.

The Dog Pack, meanwhile, roved drunkenly through the camp. In the center of the group was Powerful Locomotive, held up on one side by Vicious Brute and on the other by Surplus. Since he was dressed in servant's clothing, a dish towel thrown over his head rendered him completely unrecognizable.

Staggering and reeling, the group made its way to the woods at the edge of camp. There, the males separated from the females and, with a certain amount of off-color badinage shouted back and forth, went off to pee en masse in the shrubbery. That service done (for they knew there would be investigators), Powerful Locomotive's body was laid down carefully in a bed of ferns not far away. Then, after a certain amount of trampling about, Vengeful Ox discovered the body. "Look!" he cried. "Over here! See what I have found!"

With shouts of amazement and cries for help, Powerful Locomotive was raised from the forest floor and carried hurriedly back to camp. Shortly thereafter, he was hospitalized and all was, for the moment, well.

SINCE IT was established by multiple reliable testimonies that he was elsewhere at the time and nowhere near the woods in the hours leading up to the discovery of Powerful Locomotive's body, Darger was free to sit on the board of inquiry the next day. He was careful to take an active and impartial part in the questioning.

"We have heard testimony," Darger said to Vicious Brute toward the end of the hearing, "that one of your number was so drunk he had to be carried. Yet no one seems to remember who. Do you have any comment?"

"Well, sir. It's possible that may have been me," Vicious Brute admitted.

"No, you were seen holding this fellow up."

"It might have been Vengeful Ox."

"It was he who found the body."

"Oh, that's right. I remember him shouting. But I don't remember passing out, so whoever it was, it probably wasn't me."

"I see. No further questions."

After lengthy deliberation, it was found that, unfortunately, all the milling about that the Dog Pack had done upon discovery of the badly beaten ceo had obliterated any physical evidence of how Powerful Locomotive had come to be lying in a bed of ferns, the number of his assailants, or anything else that might have proved useful for the investigators to know. So a finding of inconclusivity was declared.

Then Powerful Locomotive's physicians were called in.

There were five doctors in attendance upon the ceo. Four stood by silently while their chief, Cautious Graybeard, reported on his condition.

"Ceo Powerful Locomotive can be revived," the doctor said judiciously. "But in cases like this, it often occurs that the trauma of revival will wipe all his recent memories from him. There are means of ensuring that he will awaken with his memory intact; however, they require his being maintained in a medical coma for at least a month. How important is it for you to know how he came to be beaten?"

"It is vital," White Squall said.

Prince First-Born Splendor nodded judiciously. "Whoever dared raise his hand against the ceo must be found, questioned under torture, and then publicly executed in as vivid and memorable a fashion as possible. So that it may serve as a deterrent to future crimes."

"I disagree," Darger said. "The conduct of the war is more important than indulging our appetite for idle gossip. What does it benefit us to learn that the ceo had an assignation for deviant sex that went catastrophically wrong or was waylaid by the brother of a peasant woman he had violated, when it leaves us with no chief executive officer? We must revive Ceo Powerful Locomotive immediately."

Off to the far corner of the tent, Capable Servant made an excited noise. All heads turned to face him. He blushed and said, "My sincerest apologies, great lords, for interrupting you. I had a good thought—but it was not worth interrupting your learned discourse. I shall say no more."

"A good thought knows no rank," First-Born Splendor said. "It arises where it will, even from the mouths of servants. Tell us your idea."

"There is a woman, great prince, in a village outside the city of Brocade, known as the Infallible Physician. Her skill in medicine far exceeds that of any other doctor alive. Surely she will be able to revive Ceo Powerful Locomotive swiftly and with all his memories in pristine condition."

"That is indeed a good thought, and I believe that we should act upon it," First-Born Splendor said.

"Nevertheless," Darger insisted, "that still leaves us leaderless. It is essential that we resurrect Powerful Locomotive immediately. Who else but he is capable of commanding our armies?"

"We have you—and are you not, after all, the Perfect Strategist? Have not all your schemes worked? I have complete confidence in your abilities," said White Squall. Coloring slightly, she added, "I have seen you work miracles."

"That is so," First-Born Splendor said. "Further, you have won battles and taken cities without the loss of life. Such consideration of the

Hidden Emperor's citizens to be is an admirable quality in a commander."

"But—" Darger began.

Permanent Infrastructure leaped to his feet. "I propose that the Perfect Strategist be named acting chief executive officer by acclaim. Further, that upon our so doing, the decision be presented to the Hidden Emperor for his approval. Which I am certain he will not withhold. Lastly, that tomorrow, the Perfect Strategist shall take command of the armies and lead them into battle against the forces that are even now assembling to defend the Three Gorges capital city of Crossroads."

As one, everybody but Darger rose to their feet, roaring approval.

WORD THAT Darger had assumed command of the armies—the Hidden Emperor's approval was universally deemed a technicality— went through the camp in a flash. All the way back to his tent, he had to endure the fervent congratulations of those of high enough rank to dare offer them and cheers from the rank-and-file soldiers who knew better than to get too personal. He gave no outward acknowledgment of any of this, however. Which filled his wake with awed gossip about the greatness of his humility.

Once in his tent, however, he turned to Surplus and said, "Oh, bloody hell."

"You should feel honored. In the military, a field promotion is the sincerest form of flattery."

"Have you forgotten?" Darger said. "I am not a real strategist."

"No, but you are something better—a man of penetrating intellect who has not been brainwashed by conventional wisdom. One who sees the world for the fraud that it is. You have proved yourself the natural superior of businessmen and royalty. Surely you can do the same in the sphere of military command?"

"I will not be consoled." Darger accepted a cup of tea from an outstretched tray. "And you, Capable Servant!"

"Sir?

"It was rare good fortune that in the early part of your struggle, the lion's share of our blows fell on Powerful Locomotive, rather than you."

"I am grateful that you think so, sir!"

"Suspiciously good fortune."

"Oh! Sir! You would not suspect me of laboring to make the blows fall on the man I knew was an imposter and not the real me?" Capable Servant's expression was more sincere than any honest man's could be, and there was a twinkle in his eye.

"Of course not," Darger said sourly.

9.

As the Drunken Sage commanded, Never offer to fight an opponent on level ground.

—THE SAYINGS OF THE PERFECT STRATEGIST

UNDER THE new strategy, progress down the river was necessarily faster than it had been before because, rather than subjugate the towns and cities, the Hidden Emperor's forces simply bypassed them. Sometimes they marched directly through the smaller towns, whose inhabitants invariably fled from the terror of the Spider Corps and other nightmare weaponry from the distant past. By order of the Perfect Strategist, no looting was allowed, though much worth seizing was left behind. In this way their progress was not slowed by undisciplined behavior. Also, it was hoped that the citizens who returned to find their wealth unplundered would be more inclined to submit peaceably to the Hidden Emperor's rule after he had taken their capital.

Soon enough, all that stood between the invading forces and Crossroads was the massed military strength of Three Gorges, encamped before it.

On his first meeting with Powerful Locomotive's command staff, Darger could tell immediately from their expressions and body language that they were deeply conflicted in their feelings about him, in equal parts awed by his reputation and resentful of it.

Without preamble, Darger sat down at the map table and said, "I have been away. Tell me about the forces we will face."

"To begin," General Bronze Hammer said, "Three Gorges is a nation of wizards."

"Wizards?"

"The central lands are highly developed in the biological sciences. Our soldiers being simple people from a provincial kingdom with no great prowess in genetic manipulation, we must take into account the fact they will have a superstitious fear of some of the enemy's weapons and tactics."

"Such as?"

"Customarily, Three Gorges will begin a battle with a wave of gun apes. These are, as their name implies, apes whose intellect has been sufficiently elevated for them to handle firearms. Their natural sense of self-preservation, however, has been all but obliterated, rendering them fearless. They are not accurate shots at a distance, but they move swiftly and at close range can do great damage. The sight of them has been known to make ranks of otherwise reliable soldiers break and run."

General Constant Temper said, "The standard response to such an attack is to set fires which will drive the gun apes back into their own forces. For this reason, it is desirable to place a brace of walking fire cannons in the vanguard."

"Before we close with them, the enemy will try to soften us up with wasp bombs, which release a swarm of frenzied poisonous insects with a life span of less than a minute. Followed by flocks of venomous birds, which are programmed to fly straight and low in the direction they are pointed when released and then attack the nearest human face they see. These may both be countered by driving captured enemy troops ahead of the main assault," said General Celestial Beauty. "Or by simply accepting that a certain mortality rate among our own soldiers is inevitable. Where our cavalry ride horses or mountain horses, the Three Gorges army also has heavy cavalry, mounted on giant ground sloths resurrected from Pleistocene fossils. Contrary to the image this may raise in your mind, the sloths are fast and powerful beasts, as large as elephants. They have enormous claws and when injured will commonly run berserk, killing dozens or even hundreds of soldiers before they can be brought down. These must simply be treated like any other hazard of war."

"Also," General Bronze Hammer said, "they have squads of *Yuty-rannosaurus,* carnivorous feathered dinosaurs that thrived in the early Cretaceous and have only recently been re-created. They are not only superb saddle animals but famed for seizing soldiers in their great jaws and biting them in half, to the great detriment of their companions' morale. Luckily, there are fewer than a hundred of these monstrosities, for no truly effective defense against them has yet been devised."

"All this is as I expected," Darger said, "more or less. Now show me what your plan of battle looks like and I will tell you what improvements I wish made upon it."

General Bronze Hammer gestured, and several subalterns swiftly placed colored markers upon the map in a semicircle before the city walls of Crossroads. "The head of the Three Gorges forces, Ceo Shrewd Fox, has a reputation as a wily and brilliant strategist. Yet in my opinion she is merely a jumped-up poseur, a fraud who came into her position of power by—" The general coughed embarrassedly. "Well. As you can see, her defensive position is of textbook ortho-doxy. It is almost startling how unoriginal it is."

Darger nodded in a manner that could be interpreted to mean almost anything.

"I hope I have not overstepped my authority in preparing an in-novative response to these defenses. I meant no offense by it. I am aware that by the favor of the Hidden Emperor you have absolute say over—"

Darger made a small, impatient gesture with one hand: Go on.

"Hem. Yes. Well, as you doubtless know, the Spider Corps have proved particularly effective in disrupting cavalry. Therefore Ceo Shrewd Fox will be expecting us to use them to spearhead our attack. Similarly, the crushing wheels have previously been employed only late in the action. However, if we position the spiders behind our left flank, and the crushing wheels at the center . . ." Subalterns leaped to place more colored markers upon the map.

On and on General Bronze Hammer expostulated, explaining the order of attack in such fine-grained detail that Darger could fol-low only a fraction of what was said. Until at last he leaned back in his chair and said, "I await your judgment."

For a long time, Darger studied the map in silence. Long after any other man would have been expected to look up, he pondered.

"Sir?"

Darger held up a hand in silence. Granite-faced, he pondered more. Up and down the conference table, generals looked at one another. Until at last, when even the orderlies must surely be wondering if he were about to explode in rage, Darger exclaimed, "What an extraordinary coincidence! Your plan is exactly the same as mine!"

"It . . . is?" General Bronze Hammer said.

"Yes. Except that where you are merely hopeful of its outcome, I know for a mathematical certainty that it will succeed."

BACK IN his tent, Darger threw himself heavily into a chair and said, "I have made my pact with the devil, Sir Plus. Our path now lies through hell. Alas, for a leader and navigator, you have only me."

"You undervalue yourself, Aubrey," Surplus said. "In what way is a general or even a ceo superior to a practitioner of the confidential arts? How is his task any different? Both are charged with relieving strangers of that which they do not wish to relinquish—cash in our case, territory in the general's. For the duration of the sting, all laws of moral conduct are suspended. And in the end, the prize must surely go to he who can keep his head in a moment of crisis. Which, if history is any guide, must inevitably be you. Think but of the nation of Three Gorges as an unwary mark, and victory will surely be ours."

Nodding enthusiastically, Capable Servant said, "Oh, sir! Have I not said that heaven smiles upon you? I have seen this proved a hundred times. There is no chance that you will not triumph."

NEVERTHELESS, DARGER did not sleep well that night. When at last he heard the jingle of harnesses and the thump of mountain-horse feet outside his tent, he leaped from his cot and, refusing Capable Servant's help, quickly dressed himself.

Little Spider stood by the tent flap, holding Buttercup's reins. Climbing into the saddle, Darger said to his mount, "Well, my friend, we ride to war today."

Turning its head, the mountain horse nudged Darger with its beak.

Bleakly amused, Darger said, "You appear to be looking forward to the experience."

"Yahhh!" Buttercup tossed its head up and down.

"I wish I could say as much." Gesturing for everyone to gather in as close as their mounts would allow, Darger quietly addressed the Dog Pack. "I have made you my bodyguard today for a reason. It is possible we will win this battle, and if we do there is no problem. But it is equally possible we will lose. In which case, we can confidently expect our own forces to seize and slay us all. Thus, should fortune turn against us, we must be prepared to flee at a moment's notice. Is that understood?"

Even in the dim predawn light, it was startling how bright Fire Orchid's hair shone. "My family knows how to cut and run," she said. "Better yet, we know *when* to cut and run. Stay with us and we will keep you safe."

"Hhyess!"

With a little bow, Surplus said, "Your army awaits."

Surrounded by his new guard and experiencing an all-too-familiar mixture of dread and self-doubt, Darger rode toward the assembled forces. He felt a tremendous pity for all those who would be maimed or killed today. Some of them would be known to him. All would be far too young.

Yet as Darger made his way through the gray ranks of men, animals, and machines arrayed for battle, a strange elation rose up within his breast. Today he would be what he had impersonated so many times before: a man of action. He would face danger and even death, but he would also be deploying thousands of soldiers, directing their actions, playing the game of life and death for the highest of stakes against an antagonist who, it was generally agreed, was of the first water. The dread did not go away, but now it was infused with an eagerness to get down to business.

The Dog Pack moved through the silent lines of infantry, then cavalry, and finally the shock troops riding White Squall's terror weapons. At the front, Darger was greeted with taciturn solemnity by his fellow commanders.

"Will you make a speech?" General Bronze Hammer asked.

Darger nodded. So Cao White Squall had her driver wheel her backhoe about, allowing him to climb atop its scoop. Slowly, he was raised into the air, where all the assembled thugs, ruffians, and patriots in the Hidden Emperor's army could see him. He looked over their upturned faces and felt their hopes and fears flowing into him, filling him with energy. His school years back in England, studying the classics of British rhetoric, returned to him in that instant, and, inspired, he spread his arms.

"Who here would be immortal?" Darger thundered. "I tell you that not one of you standing before me today shall die. For those who today live will prosper and those who do not will be kept alive forever in the memories of their grateful nation for generation upon generation, even unto eternity.

"I am not covetous for gold, rich garments, the trappings of wealth. My only desire is to serve my emperor. My only pride is my humility in so doing. Yet in one way am I greedy, and that is in my desire that all the world shall know I did my duty. Today I will fight and bleed alongside my children—for you are all as dear as sons and daughters to me—and were you not beloved of me, I would resent your presence for diluting the glory I will earn this day.

"But this glory will be shared among us as equals, and those who outlive this battle and come home safe will in their old age hold feast on this day, pull up blouses to show their scars, and demand their grandchildren hear well-worn stories told one more time. Then gentlefolk who are now asleep in Peace, Brocade, and Fragrant Tree will curse themselves they were not here. We few . . . we happy few . . . we band of brothers . . ." Darger paused, searching for new words, and then, for lack of anything better, cried at the top of his lungs, "*Come on, you apes! Do you want to live forever?*"

A world-encompassing shout went up from the assembled masses. The backhoe operator began to lower its scoop, and, halfway down, Darger leaped nimbly off. To General Celestial Beauty, standing nearby, he said, "Quickly now. Let us advance, before these fools come to their senses."

Commands were bellowed and instructions relayed. The grumbling of motors rose to a roar, and with a grinding of gears and the thundering of drums the army lurched forward. Darger rode at their head. He was almost certain that real generals led from behind. But he intended to begin by looking heroic, and then fall back when the enemy came in sight.

But when the city of Crossroads loomed up before them, no army was visible arrayed before it. Darger squinted, trying to make the shadows resolve into men, and could not. He saw only a scattering of scouts, mounted on swift steeds, speeding toward him.

"What the devil is going on?" he muttered and, holding up an arm, commanded the army to begin the slow and awkward process of coming to an unexpected halt. Motionless, he awaited the coming tidings.

It was not long before, galloping up on lathered horses that had been ridden half to death, the scouts arrived to inform him that, during the night, the enemy had struck camp and retreated, leaving Crossroads undefended and its gates wide open.

THEIR SCOUTS having gone into the city and returned to report it free of soldiers, Darger saw no option but to enter. Leaving her war machines idling outside, Cao White Squall joined him and the Dog Pack as they approached the gate. "Can Ceo Shrewd Fox be employing the Empty City stratagem?" she said wonderingly. "It makes no sense—but neither does the alternative."

Darger said nothing. But out of the corner of his eye, he saw Surplus surreptitiously nudge Fire Orchid. Who in turn trotted her mountain horse closer to the cao and said, "Pardon my ignorance, Cao White Squall. I can see that my husband and the Perfect Strategist understand you perfectly. But . . . what is this strategy you speak of?"

"During the Three Kingdoms period, the great general Zhuge Liang, who was renowned for his many tricks and stratagems, had to hold a city with only a few troops against a vastly superior army. So he had the city gates flung open and the square behind them swept clean. All the flags were taken down and the people ordered indoors and told to maintain silence. When the enemy arrived, they were astonished to find the city undefended and sent in scouts. The scouts in turn entered the city to find the square empty and no sign of life anywhere. Save for Zhuge Liang, who sat in a balcony, playing a stringed instrument. He gave no sign of having seen them, though how could he not?

"When the scouts reported this uncanny scene to their commander, he ordered his army to turn away from the city. For, knowing Zhuge Liang's reputation, he could only assume that it was a trap—and one that he dared not fall into."

"I see."

"But that situation does not apply here. Three Gorges had a mighty army in place. Shrewd Fox, though famed, is no Zhuge Liang. And we are not turning back."

They passed through the city gate. The flagpoles, Darger noted, were empty. The buildings around the courtyard were silent. Nothing moved within their windows.

At the far end of the courtyard, standing so still as to be all but unnoticeable, were a dozen of the least threatening human beings Darger had ever seen in his life. They were soft and pudgy, with round faces and bright pink cheeks. To a man and a woman—but one had to look closely to see which was which—they were smiling.

The party crossed the plaza. At the last minute, Darger drew up his mountain horse and stared sternly down at the dozen. "Identify yourselves!" he commanded.

"We are the joyous ones, come to hand over control of the city to you, sirs," their chief said.

"The what?"

"Our imaginative faculties have been suppressed, leaving us incapable of disobedience or dishonesty. This makes us perfect functionaries. We will do what we are told because we cannot envision an alternative. We speak only the truth because we are not inventive enough to lie. I am told that some find us too literal-minded. But I do not understand what they mean by that."

"Such an existence must be very trying for you," White Squall observed.

"On the contrary, noble lady. I eat exactly the same meal three times a day every day of the year because it is cheap and nutritious and I do not tire of it because I cannot imagine wanting something else. A similar logic applies to all aspects of my life from clothing to shelter, and so I am invariably happy with what I have."

The others nodded in agreement.

"We run all functions of the city government, save only decision making. You have but to tell us what you want done, and we will make it so."

"But you lack the imagination to convert an abstract order into practical action," Surplus objected.

"We have regulations covering all possibilities, sir. Many, many regulations."

"Were you ordered to report to us?" Darger asked.

"Of course, sir. It would not occur to us to take such action on our own."

"Who ordered you?"

"Ceo Shrewd Fox, sir."

"Why?"

The round little woman beamed. "I have no idea, sir."

TRUE TO their word, the joyous ones made all the resources of Crossroads available to their conquerors. Cloth was produced to make new uniforms and repair old tents; luxurious housing was provided for the Hidden Emperor and his staff and advisors; rope and fodder and foodstuffs in abundance appeared from seemingly bottomless stores. When, however, Darger requested gold, silver, precious gems, or the like, they patiently explained that all such items had been placed in escrow and would not be available until a full month had passed. "But then," one of the interchangeable joyous ones said, "as much of it as you require is yours. Upon receipt of the properly signed and notarized forms, of course."

More worrisome was that Crossroads also contained an abundance of ammunition and small arms, none of which was withheld from its conquerors. In short order, the city arsenal was able to replace all that had been expended seizing their nation.

"It makes no military sense at all," Darger said to Surplus in his new office in Yellow Crane Tower. "Even I can see that. The massed strength of Three Gorges have ceded their capital to us when they had every reason to hope they could defend it. They have given us control of half their territory, though it would have cost us dearly to seize it. They left behind valuable resources which they could easily have destroyed. This is not sensible. There is some trick behind it."

"I agree. But what?"

"I'm sure we'll find out. In the meantime, I fear that Ceo Shrewd Fox is living up to her name."

"Speaking of names . . ." Surplus said. "Capable Servant! Pour two glasses of wine. No, make that three, and keep one for yourself. I wish to toast the Perfect Strategist."

Surprised, Darger said, "Whatever for?"

"My dear friend," Surplus said, "have you failed to notice that you have just conquered your first city?"

THE HIDDEN King was, presumably, closeted with his Phoenix Bride, for he issued no orders and held no meetings. Meanwhile, Powerful Locomotive remained in a coma and White Squall's attention was divided between her machines and her new lover, Prince First-Born Splendor. Which meant that for all practical purposes, Darger was in charge of both the army and the city that it now held. Yet in all the ways that mattered most, he found it an exasperating experience. In a dusty room filled with bland, pink-cheeked nonentities, he was told that, yes, he could impose a tax upon the citizens of Crossroads to pay for the costs of conquering them—but that it would not take effect for another thirty days. Yes, it was possible to borrow money from the city treasury, to be repaid by the proposed tax—but the money would not be payable until a full month had passed. Valuable items could indeed be confiscated from the wealthy—but they would be kept in storage for four weeks while the paperwork went through the proper channels. All these strictures they were only too happy to present for examination from their endless shelves of bound regulations.

"As you can see, sir, our hands are bound," said one.

"The city coffers are as closed as our minds," said another.

"But if you have any other ideas, we will happily examine our manuals to see whether they are permissible or not and if so under what terms and conditions," suggested a third.

Darger spun on his heel and left the room.

IN A savage mood, Darger pushed his way through the crowded streets of Crossroads, going nowhere in particular, burning off his anger with exertion. Until by random chance he found himself in the industrial area by the Long River. There, where mills and forges clustered to take advantage of the river's water power and abundant opportunities to dump waste, he found that the Division of Sappers and Archaeologists had taken over the entire neighborhood. Every workyard and empty lot held broken war machines that teams of workers were in the process of repairing.

Darger leaned over the fence of a scrap metal facility where sheets of iron were being hammered out to patch several holes that had been blasted into a crushing wheel, and struck up a conversation with the burly woman overseeing the operation. "Why are you out of uniform?" he asked her.

"I was never in uniform in the first place," the supervisor replied. "The joyous ones have directed every mechanic in the city to work for the invaders, and since I get paid the same for this labor as I do for peacetime work, I am content. Indeed, that is the particular genius of our form of government."

"Pray, explain yourself."

"Conquerors come and conquerors go. Sometimes Crossroads is an independent city-state, other times part of a larger confederation. However, because our government is made up of unimaginative and incorruptible functionaries, the day-to-day running of the city is consistent. You might say that we are currently under enemy rule. But this is a matter of semantics. Life goes on much as it always has. Thus, we feel no need to resist the foreign tyrant. Who in turn, confronted not by sullen resistance but by ready obedience, is not moved to punish us as he did the river cities, which are more conventionally governed. In this way, Crossroads endures.

"Now, if you'll excuse me, I must chastise that idiot of an apprentice who is banging away at a sheet of tin as if it were iron."

Bellowing, the overseer turned away.

This conversation brightened Darger's mood considerably. He was making a mental note to requisition the city's wealthiest citizens to do manual labor (cleaning the streets, perhaps, or emptying latrines) so that Fire Orchid's clan could collect bribes from them to be exempted from the odious task, when—

Crash!

He spun about to see that a spider had just slammed into the side of the scrapyard's office, collapsing a wall and doing tremendous damage to itself in the process. Three legs on one side and one on the other were attempting to lift the machine up and then lurching down again. Fluids poured from ruptured metal.

Workers came running from every direction. A young man leaped up into the cab and turned the spider off. Hydraulics hissing, it settled to the ground.

Darger helped the supervisor lift the pilot out of his vehicle. The man's eyes were open and he seemed alert, but he said nothing.

"Are you injured?" Darger asked.

The man considered. "No."

"Shaken up?"

"A little."

The supervisor pushed herself between Darger and the sergeant. "What is your name? How did this happen?"

"Sergeant Bright Prosperity of the Good Fortune Spider Corps. I was told to walk my spider to this location for minor repairs."

"And then?"

"It walked into the wall."

"Your spider walked into the wall," the woman repeated.

"Yes, ma'am."

"Were you distracted? Did your machine malfunction?"

"No."

"Well, then, why the hell didn't you just stop?"

The man looked puzzled. "Nobody told me to stop the spider. Just to walk it here."

As they spoke, Darger had been studying Sergeant Bright Prosperity's face. His forehead had a light sheen of sweat and his cheeks were bright pink. "This man is running a fever," he said. "We must send for a doctor immediately."

The medics, when they arrived, looked unsurprised. "Yesterday, there were three cases," one told Darger. "Today there are eleven. This is a classic progression of an emerging infectious disease. I do not look forward to tomorrow."

"What are its symptoms?"

"It begins with a light fever, which is transitory, though the cheeks remain erythematic afterward. That's it for physical symptoms. However, the disease leaves its victims extremely literal-minded. If you were to tell one to dig a ditch, he would continue to do so long after the task was obviously complete. Across a road . . . through a house . . . into a river . . . No folly is too ludicrous for them. Their judgment is consistently suspect. We have been hospitalizing those who come down with it, though they are physically hale, simply because it's safer not to have them wandering about."

"Would you say," Darger asked, "that the victims of this disease act as though they cannot imagine doing anything else?"

"That's it exactly, sir! Very well put."

"YOU BASTARDS lied to me!" Darger roared.

Though the joyous ones had explained that they did not have a hierarchical structure, but only specialized responsibilities, and that therefore it did not matter which of them were summoned, Darger had nevertheless commanded the twelve who had first welcomed him to Crossroads to appear before him. He needed specific individuals to rail at.

They met in a conference room with lacquered walls and an enormous antique chrome-and-glass table, but nobody sat. Darger needed to pace back and forth, while the joyous ones were perfectly content to stand.

"We cannot lie, noble sir. It is an impossibility."

"You withheld information, which comes down to the same thing."

"We know many things, sir. It is not possible to tell you everything at once. Ask us anything you wish, and we will tell you all we know."

"Tell me about the disease that has broken out among the Hidden Emperor's soldiers—though not, I am told, among this city's civilians—which leaves its victims pink-cheeked and totally devoid of imagination."

"The joyous infection is a tailored encephalitis virus which targets specific areas of the neocortex, thalamus, and occipital cortex. It was created a hundred and fifty years ago by Doctor Modest Charity at the request of the city fathers of Crossroads. In his youth, Modest Charity was but an indifferent student. However, a chance encounter with the aged philosopher Dour Tortoise, who—"

"Stop. Why is it that only our soldiers are coming down with this illness?"

"All the city, save for ourselves of course, was vaccinated against it when Ceo Shrewd Fox learned of your approach."

"This vaccine—where is it? Is there a large enough supply to protect those soldiers who have not yet come down with the disease?"

"Ceo Shrewd Fox took almost all of the vaccine with her when she left. A few doses were left behind which, at her direction, we placed in the tea that was served to the Hidden Emperor and his highest-ranking officers."

"Why did she have you do that?"

"She did not tell us, sir."

"Can more of the vaccine be created?"

"Undoubtedly, sir. The technology is well understood."

"Now we're getting somewhere! Summon your genetic engineers."

"They are not here, sir. Ceo Shrewd Fox took them with her when she left. She said that when we were asked about them, we were to say that she left nobody in the city or indeed the region who could do what you desire."

"Is this true?"

"Yes, sir."

"I begin," Darger said, "to loathe and despise Ceo Shrewd Fox almost as much as I respect and admire her. Did she leave you any other directions?"

"Yes, sir. She told us to give you this letter."

The joyous one produced an envelope. Darger removed the letter, unfolded it, and read:

To Ceo Powerful Locomotive, Cao White Squall, the foreigner who calls himself the Perfect Strategist, and/or whatever other flunkeys of the vile invader who falsely calls himself an emperor may read this, greetings.

By now, you are doubtless aware that I have made Crossroads into a trap for your forces. It is one you will find far more difficult to leave than it was to enter. Depending on how quickly you discovered the truth of the plague I have arranged for you, you may or may not know that the armies that scattered before you like leaves in the wind are currently approaching the city with resolute step, and that the river fleet you never even saw is even now sailing upriver to close that avenue of escape. When the joyous infection has rendered your army completely harmless, I will reenter the city and accept your surrender.

Perhaps you think you can fight your way out. I would not advise it. The joyous ones underwent many years of intensive training to learn how to function without imagination. I have seen how infected soldiers behave and it is not a pretty sight. If you doubt me, go ahead and try.

Out of mercy for your enlisted men, they shall not be prosecuted for their role in this war but will be allowed to complete their terms of service under my command. The architects of this assault upon the sovereignty of Three Gorges, however, must face justice in the form of a military tribunal. I have directed that the last remaining doses of vaccine in Crossroads be surreptitiously administered to the highest ranking of your officers, in order that you may contemplate this future while the joyous plague runs its course.

Enjoy the last days of your life.

Ceo Shrewd Fox
In Service of Three Gorges

Darger put down the letter and groaned. "Could this day get any worse?"

"Undoubtedly, sir," one of the joyous ones said. "Though we cannot imagine how."

10.

The Dog Warrior was once leading a group of soldiers against a greatly superior military force and, seeing that they were reluctant to engage, stopped in a small temple to pray. Calling upon heaven, he cried, "I will throw the dice three times—give me a sign of how the fight will go." Three times he threw the dice, and all three times they came up sixes. Greatly heartened, the soldiers went on to fight and to win.

Later, he let one of his men examine the ivory cubes he had used. No matter how many times they were thrown, they came up all sixes. "Courage!" the Dog Warrior said. "And load the dice."

—EXPLOITS OF THE DOG WARRIOR

THE MOST luxurious lodgings in all of Crossroads were those in Yellow Crane Tower. This famous structure had been erected during the Three Kingdoms period, thousands of years before. Wars and fires had destroyed it many times. Always it had been rebuilt, most recently in the Utopian era, though not always in the same place. Darger, who had been expecting a counterattack from the moment the city was taken, had made their headquarters within this landmark, hoping it would render the Three Gorges armies slightly more reluctant to attack them directly. Somewhere within its many floors, presumably, lived the Hidden Emperor and his entourage. White Squall had the second floor to herself, and Darger, as the third most influential servant of the emperor (and, with Powerful Locomotive still lingering in his coma, effectively even more so), had the floor above her. Yet Surplus did not find him there, but up on the tower's roof.

The day was chill and overcast, and there was a slight drizzle. Darger stood with his hands clasped behind his back and stared down the dark and misty river in silence for a long time. Finally, he said, "The poet Li Bai climbed to this spot long ago, intending to write a poem, and discovered that Cui Hao's most famous work, 'Yellow Crane Tower,' had been inscribed on the wall. Convinced there was no way he could match that accomplishment, he went away dejected and defeated. Later he returned to write his own equally great poem. Li Bai was a joyful man and a drunkard, while his best friend, the poet Du Fu, was his exact opposite, a pessimist and a melancholic. I like to think that it was Du Fu who, understanding depression as Li Bai could not, convinced him to return and take up his pen against the darkness."

"You are in a fey mood, my friend."

"We face imminent death and certain defeat. Now is the time for us to acknowledge that unanticipated and tragic turns of events do not only happen to one's self and friends but to one's enemies as well. That, at any rate, is my hope."

"We have seen worse moments than this."

"I let myself be played like a trout by Ceo Shrewd Fox. Hers was a deceit worthy of the Perfect Strategist," Darger said, "if only he were real and a sadistic son of a bitch. Shrewd Fox will wait until we are completely helpless and then walk in to finish us off, wiping out the upper echelon—ourselves included—as effortlessly as she might swat a fly."

"Aubrey, forgive me for asking this, but . . . exactly what are you doing?"

Darger showed just a flash of teeth. "I am working myself up into a state. Like a rat, I do my best fighting when I am cornered and all looks helpless." Then he said, "Tell me. How is your new family doing?"

"Not well. Both Terrible Nuisance and Vicious Brute have caught the virus. Fire Orchid is caring for them and has banished me from all contact with the clan. She says she is trying to prevent my exposure to the plague to leave me free to find a cure for it, but I suspect she is merely trying to protect me. The irony here is that I am almost certainly immune. There are relatively few diseases that cross species from human to canine."

"Then we cannot count on their capable assistance should we two be reduced to fleeing for our lives?"

"Alas, no."

Darger sighed and then, turning his back on the river, said, "You have a purposeful air about you. Why did you seek me out?"

"To inform you that White Squall wishes to see us both. She says that it's important. But no more."

AS THEY made their way through Crossroads, Surplus was struck by how cheerful its citizens appeared and by contrast how dour were the emperor's soldiers. The city's moods seemed to shift with its smells: from bins of dried fruit and spices in the produce shops to fresh droppings and stale blood in the bird market, from food sizzling over charcoal braziers in the restaurants to barrels of stale cooking oil waiting to be carted away in the alleyways behind them. He and Darger stopped to admire a courtyard that was being decorated with lanterns and flowers. A man climbed down from a ladder to explain, "I am preparing for my mother's eightieth birthday. Family and friends are gathering from a hundred *li* around for the celebration."

"Doesn't the war preclude such a gathering?"

"Not at all. The Three Gorges armies are not restricting travel—indeed, by guaranteeing the roads are free of bandits, they enable it. They examine all traffic passing through the territory they control to ensure that soldiers and weapons are not being smuggled out of Crossroads, of course. But this is only a minor inconvenience, much the same as the invaders making similar examinations of those entering the city."

On they went, past tables of black tea, barrels of cured tobacco, bins of garbage, laundry being boiled, spilled beer. They paused outside a tavern where a brawl had broken out between off-duty soldiers and local rowdies. "Such behavior is inevitable during a plague," observed a lean and ancient street vendor of winemellons. He or she had a face like old horse leather. "No real harm will come of it. Oh, a few teeth and fingers and perhaps an eye or two will be lost. Maybe a leg. But such things can always be grown back."

Racks of fish drying, river mud, acrid cat trace, sweet buns baking, freshly watered ferns, face powder and perfume, the ruptured-sewer smell of fermenting bean curd. Passing by the door of a brothel, the two were almost knocked down by a pair of drunken young soldiers stumbling out. "Your mothers would be dismayed to see you frequenting such a place," Darger admonished them.

"Always before, I avoided such dens of vice, for fear of catching a disease," replied the first young lady. "The reward for which is I am going to contract the disease without experiencing the pleasure beforehand. So I resolved to rectify matters."

The second made an impudent face. "I am not likely to see my mother again. Therefore I will do as I please. It does not matter what she would think of those things that she will never learn I did with the pretty boys here."

Pepper, tar, hides curing, cloned zebra flesh burgeoning, hot canvas tents, unguent, heaps of medical waste. In this way, Darger and Surplus passed through Crossroads, gathering information as they went, witnessing the ordinary lives and joys of its citizens and the truculence and fear of its occupiers. It was as if there were two distinct cities, one superimposed over the other.

In due course, they came to a Utopian building, like most of its kind overlarge and underornate, situated by the waterfront beyond the city wall. This, White Squall's sappers had emptied out and mercilessly cleaned. Before Darger and Surplus were allowed to enter, they had to don white lab smocks, gloves, sterile cloth booties that went over their shoes, caps to enclose their hair, and masks covering their noses and mouths. Then a similarly clad guide led them into the interior of the building, where there was a light well capped by enormous panes of glass such as no one had known how to make for centuries. In the center of a luminous circle of light was the bronze shell of the phoenix device, burnished so that it dazzled. Carefully arranged about it were its metal workings, piece by piece, all immaculately clean and, to Surplus's eyes, perfectly enigmatic. Beyond those was a stack of lead bricks, which, according to legend, provided protection against those parts of the device that killed silently, invisibly, and at a distance. Those, assuredly, rested behind it.

A tall, slim figure in a lab smock rose up from where it had been crouching at the foot of the device. "Gentlemen. It was good of you to come."

"You sent for us and so we are here," Darger said, with a catch in his voice. Masked though she was, White Squall was strikingly beautiful. Surplus, knowing how enthralled his friend was to beauty, could well imagine his thoughts. "I hope you are well."

"It is only natural that I should be," she said in a level voice. "Since I was a girl, I've had two dreams. One, held in common with most of my gender, was to have a handsome prince fall in love with me. Thanks to you, that has been achieved. You have my gratitude. The other and greater dream was to bring the brilliant machines of the past back to life. Thanks to the patronage of the Hidden Emperor, I have done that as well. Here before you is my masterpiece. When it is done, I can die fulfilled."

"Surely that won't be necessary," Darger began.

But Surplus interrupted him. "You told me the phoenix device was nonfunctional."

"That's true. But it can be restored. See what splendid condition it is in. The Utopians really knew how to build weapons to last. Oh some of the wiring has to be torn out and redone. But my crew will have no trouble with that. The only real difficulty I see is this." White Squall picked up a canister. "It contains tritium gas, which, as I'm sure you know, has a half-life of twelve point three years and is used to help achieve thermonuclear fusion. Even when the device was new, it had to be replaced periodically. Today, it is quite inert. This initially seemed to present a problem, but my people—"

Darger held up a hand. "Stop. I understand everything you say, one word at a time. But as for the meaning of those words in combination . . ."

"Such knowledge was commonplace among the Utopians," White Squall said, "among whom you claim to have arisen. I find it odd you would not know it. If indeed you are as you say you are."

"Like the Ancient Master of Deductive Reasoning, I consider the brain to be a room which one may stock as one chooses. A fool takes in all the furniture he can lay his hands on, and when he needs a specific item, cannot find it among the clutter. A sage, however, lays in only those tools he needs for his work, but in great number and perfectly ordered. Matters of strategy are of vital importance to me. But whether the earth goes around the sun or the sun about the earth is a matter of perfect indifference, so I do not bother to acquire this information."

"To return to the subject at hand," Surplus said, "it sounds like you are close to making the emperor's Phoenix Bride functional."

"We are doing well."

"Is that why you summoned us? To witness your achievement?"

"Oh, no," White Squall said. "I simply assumed you would be interested. You were summoned here because the Hidden Emperor wishes to speak with you. He is in the next room."

SINCE THE plague began, nobody had seen the Hidden Emperor save for his personal servants, and, so far as Surplus knew, nobody had been summoned into his presence. It was widely speculated that he spent his time closeted with his bride to be (of whom all had heard and only a select few knew the truth about) in Yellow Crane Tower. But, as always, the actual location of the emperor was the most guarded secret in all his domain.

Yet by simply passing through a doorway, Surplus and Darger found themselves alone with the Hidden Emperor.

The room was small and tastefully decorated with furnishings that might equally easily be contemporary or several thousand years old. The red and black lacquered panels on the walls were painted in gold with alternating phoenixes and dragons, representing virtue and imperial authority. The emperor wore his usual scarves and dark glasses. He turned down an oil lamp and placed the book he was reading on a side table.

"You may remove your lab smocks and protective gear," the Hidden Emperor said, unwrapping his scarves. He placed his glasses atop them. "They are required for the ancient purification rituals associated with the phoenix device, but not here." He gestured at a pair of chairs. "Sit. We are all friends." He laughed. "Oh, if you could see your expressions!"

They both sat, Surplus with the caution befitting an officer of middling rank, and Darger with the unconcern of a sage. "Why have you summoned us, Majesty?" the latter asked.

"I know your secret," the Hidden Emperor said with a shrewd grin. "You are not immortals, as you claim to be."

A cold chill ran up Surplus's spine. "Sir?" he said. Darger, staying in character, showed none of the emotion he must surely be feeling.

"You are gods. Oh, minor ones, admittedly! But gods nevertheless. Would lesser beings be sent to help me gain the Dragon Throne? Of course not. It was particularly clever of you, Dog Warrior, to announce yourself as a god in the marketplace in Brocade and then confess to being a mere revenant of Utopian technology when presented to me. Anybody else would have been fooled by your subterfuge. But I see through all ruses and disguises, no matter how convoluted."

"Your penetration is, as always, acute." Darger made of his forefingers a steeple and touched them to his lips. "But we cannot comment on such matters. There are strictures placed upon us by powers even greater than we."

"Let us talk of less perilous matters," Surplus said. "Such as the Phoenix Bride."

"You saw my fiancée? Is she not beautiful?"

"I forget if it was the Mathematician of Alexandria who said that geometry is beauty laid bare or the Father of Relativity who made this claim for physics," Darger said. "She is, in either case, ravishing."

"Tell us how you came to be aware of her existence," Surplus suggested. Knowing that no man engaged to what he considers a great beauty is loath to discuss her.

"When I was a child, I dreamed of fire," the Hidden Emperor said. "Smooth and liquid as flowing water, violent as the earthquake that shakes the mountain, driving all before it like a mighty wind. Sometimes I would evade my minders and go out into the fields and set the crops aflame. There are not many vices a prince cannot get away with. Setting fields on fire is one of them. So I had to be sly and evasive, and it was only rarely and with great subterfuge that I could slip away from my guardians and achieve the freedom to engage in my desires. Oh, but it was worth all the difficulties I underwent. The fire moves like quicksilver, hesitates, then rushes onward, tracing lines and sigils in the dry plants, and in one's elated state it is possible to read some fraction of their meaning. Fire exalts the spirit. The dross of physical matter is transformed into light and heat and its smoke rises gently into the heavens. Have you ever seen a barn fire? Amazing! Particularly after harvest, when the barn is stuffed to the gills with hay. It goes up like a bomb and its flames touch the sky. You can hear it crackling a mile away.

"From the country I moved my ambitions to the buildings of Brocade. That was even more difficult, for city people are always on the watch for conflagration and the fire brigades come swiftly to douse the smallest outbreak. Once, however, I was able to torch a warehouse stuffed with leather goods, bales of cotton, barrels of grain alcohol. It burned all night and lit up half the city. The sky was overcast and flickered red. There were explosions and showers of sparks. Oh, but it was glorious. Though, admittedly, the stench was great.

"Afterward, I dreamed of it again and again.

"It was only when I came of age that I understood that fire was a metaphor for lust. Then, of course, I ceased my arsons in much the same spirit in which the respectable man, upon attaining adulthood, abandons the brothels and sexual adventures of adolescence and seeks out a virtuous woman to become his wife.

"We desire most what is unattainable. When I realized that my destiny was to conquer and rule, I set aside all thought of fire—for what firestorm, however glorious, however mighty, can truly be worthy of an emperor? Only one—that of the phoenix devices which the Utopians built for fighting their most glorious wars. And though those devices might yet exist, I knew they were hidden deep in the earth and that no living man knew how to make them operative.

"But then a miracle happened."

"White Squall wrote her treatise on resurrecting ancient weapons," Surplus said.

"Yes! Immediately, I sent out my best operatives to kidnap and bring her before me. She spoke most eloquently. I questioned her in great detail. Her answers were straightforward. She said the task would be expensive and time-consuming. She did not play down its difficulty. In return, I gave her money, time, and patience. Now, only a room away, she is proving herself the most valuable of my servants. In a day or three or possibly five, the Phoenix Bride will be ready to blossom into such a fire as has not been seen in this world for years beyond knowing. When she does, I will be with her, and my substance will be transformed into light and heat and my smoke will rise up into the heavens, intermingled with hers. Just as I dreamed as a child."

"A moving tale," Darger said, when it was clear that the Hidden Emperor had finished speaking. "But why do you share it with us?"

The Hidden Emperor leaned forward. "Though all men fear to give the emperor bad news, I have ways of learning it nonetheless. I know about the trick that Ceo Shrewd Fox played upon you, and how quickly the joyous plague spreads among my army. There are certain of my advisors who say that a week from now I will not even have an army at all. So you must tell me. You are gods and the ways of gods are unfathomable to mortals. Will you allow me to conquer China? Will I ride in triumph through the city we now call North, known in ancient times as Beijing? Or is it the will of heaven that I die here, in Crossroads? I would prefer to consummate my marriage with the Phoenix Bride in North, after having sat upon the Dragon Throne. But if destiny requires it, we can be wed here. It would be a lesser triumph than the one I had planned. But I am a philosopher. So long as I rise up into the skies to be reborn in alchemical fire, it will suffice."

He waited.

"Majesty, China will be yours," Darger said fervently, "and with it the city of North, and with the city of North the Dragon Throne, and with the Dragon Throne the Phoenix Bride. I say this in the names of—well, I cannot tell you our true names. The courts of heaven will not allow it. But this I can say: Destiny is on your side. It would be easier to stop the moon from rising or the tides from going out than to keep you from possessing China, North, the Dragon Throne, and the passionate, all-consuming embrace of the Phoenix Bride. Be patient, sire, and all that you desire will be yours."

During his short speech, Darger had quietly risen to his feet. Now he joined hands together within the wide sleeves of his robes and bowed deeply. Surplus rose also from his chair and bowed as well.

The Hidden Emperor was breathing shallowly. But he only said, "You may don the ritual garments of purification once more and leave by the same way you entered. I am glad we had this little chat."

WHITE SQUALL knelt at the foot of the phoenix device's gleaming bronze shell, using needle-thin tools to perform some delicate operation on one of its components. Darger and Surplus pushed through her startled subordinates and crouched down to either side of her.

"We must speak," Darger said, taking White Squall by the arm.

Surplus did the same with her other arm. "Outside," he said.

They stood, hoisting White Squall up after them. Ignoring the sappers' alarmed questions, Darger and Surplus marched her from the room, through several sets of doors, and out into the street. Furiously, White Squall ripped off her face mask. "How dare you treat a superior officer so! I will have you both court-martialed and flogged."

"Must I remind you of the extravagant promises you made in Fragrant Tree, madam? Should I describe the strawberry-moon birthmark directly below the dimple on your left buttock?" Darger spoke quietly, to avoid being overheard, but with great intensity. "Or do you intend to admit that your word is worthless and your faith nonexistent? Have you forgotten, then, all that you swore to do for me in exchange for Prince First-Born Splendor's love?"

Mastering herself with obvious effort, White Squall said, "You are right, and I apologize. But however will I explain what just happened to my people?"

"Explain nothing," Darger said. "Life is full of mysteries. Your people will simply have to live with one more."

"We cannot talk here," Surplus added. When they had shed their smocks, socks, gloves, and masks, he led them toward the center of the city, through streets increasingly congested with carts and pedestrians, until suddenly he leaped forward and hauled one of the joyous ones out of the crowd, like a spear fisher triumphantly landing a salmon.

Smiling, the joyous one said, "If you do not release me, I will have you arrested, jailed, and tortured. I am on official business."

"This is White Squall, the highest-ranking woman in all the empire to be," Surplus retorted. "Only the Hidden Emperor can countermand her orders. Which he is unlikely to do, for she is his most loyal servant. And she desires that you take us immediately to someplace where we can converse in privacy."

"The government maintains a private conversation garden for precisely such use," the joyous one said. She took them there and over a short wooden bridge to a pavilion on a small island in a decorative pond. Brightly colored koi swam up at their approach, hoping to be fed.

"Can we be overheard here?" Surplus asked.

"Anything is possible, sir. But I cannot imagine how."

"Have some tea sent to us—Dragon Well, finest quality—and then you may return to your previous business and forget you ever saw us."

"No man is capable of forgetting such a command, sir. Quite the opposite, for the oddity of the request must surely fix the forbidden information in one's memory. But I shall speak to no one of seeing you and behave as though I had not."

The pavilion was empty. Choosing a table, White Squall and Darger sat down. By the time Surplus had satisfied himself that there was nowhere for an eavesdropper to hide and adjusted the blinds to provide the proper balance between light and privacy, a young woman had arrived with a pot of tea and three glasses.

"Well?" White Squall said, when the servant was gone.

"The Hidden Emperor told us that you will have the phoenix device operational within the week," Darger said.

"That is true, and I feel proud of the accomplishment. There is not another woman in all of China who could have done as much."

"Were you aware that the Hidden Emperor was considering setting it off immediately upon completion?"

"So soon?" White Squall looked sad. "Well, I have done my duty and, thanks to you, known the love of a prince as well. I was able to exercise my talents to their fullest, and that matters a great deal. It has been a rich, full life."

Surplus could not help making an exasperated noise. "One that would be coming to an end soon, had the Perfect Strategist not convinced the emperor that the plague would inevitably be brought to an end, his enemies overcome, and his armies led to the conquest of North," he pointed out.

"I have known happiness. Death is a small price to pay for that."

"For a mechanic of your genius, it would not be difficult to render the device inoperative," Surplus said.

White Squall looked shocked. "I couldn't do that!"

Leaning forward to take both her hands in his, Darger said with all the persuasiveness he could muster, "You not only could, but must. Not for your own sake, not for ours, but for the sake of Prince First-Born Splendor. The path you are following ends with that splendid man, that admirable body, engulfed in flames. Dying in agony. Incinerated. Dead by your own doing, along with countless others. Is this truly what you want? I refuse to believe you can think of him and tell me it is."

A single tear trickled down White Squall's cheek. Otherwise, she might have been carved of marble.

"I know you feel yourself bound by your oath of loyalty, but—"

"It's not that!" White Squall said with unexpected heat. She drew her hands out of Darger's. "It's not that at all. But—did you ever notice the white, star-shaped scar that the Hidden Emperor has on the knuckle of his left thumb?"

"I saw that it was there, of course," Darger said. "But attached no particular significance to it."

"He received that scar years ago, when I was new to his service and just beginning to unearth and restore ancient weapons of war for him. I was not so high in his confidences then, but was already rising fast. One day I was making a presentation to the emperor—he was still king then, of course—about the military uses of the newly recovered crushing wheel. It was an intimate meeting with just the Hidden King, myself, and my second-in-command, whose task was to hold up the diagrams and indicate specific statistics as I spoke. The king, who was very serious about such matters, was listening intently and at the same time absentmindedly playing with a small spotted kitten. An exquisite little creature, it goes without saying, a Bengal. That afternoon was the first time he removed the scarves in my presence, revealing his face, and I was very conscious of the honor being shown me.

"I was delineating what size and strength of walls would fall before the crushing wheel when something I said made the Hidden King slam a hand down on the table with pleasure. Unfortunately, the hand came down on the kitten's tail. It spun about and sank its teeth in his thumb.

"In a flash of rage, the Hidden King grabbed the kitten in one hand and crushed the life out of it. His face was like a demon's. I am convinced he didn't know what he was doing until it was over.

"It seems a small and insignificant death now, after so many, but it was shocking at the time because it was so unexpected. I remember that I gasped in horror.

"The Hidden King dropped the dead kitten on the table and said, 'Say nothing of this.' Then he left.

"My second-in-command was a woman named Dutiful Chrysanthemum. Like me, she was of the laboring class. As a mechanic she was unsurpassed, even better than I was, though my imaginative powers were greater than hers. People assumed we were lovers because we spent so much time together working on machines and because people are idiots. We were not. But she was my most valued subordinate.

"Tragically, she was a gossip and a chatterer. That evening I went looking for Dutiful Chrysanthemum because I had discovered a flaw in some stress vector calculations she had made. I found her in the kitchen, with a plate of dumplings, regaling a scandalized scullery girl with the details of the kitten's death.

"How I scolded Dutiful Chrysanthemum! Her own mother could not have spoken so harshly to her. I told her she had not only disobeyed the king's direct order but brought shame onto me for trusting her and onto the Division of Sappers and Archaeologists for the mere fact that she was included in their number. She was crying long before I was done with her.

"I was angry, but I was also afraid. For the king's punishments were famously swift and merciless. I feared she would not live out the night.

"Nor did she. Less than an hour later, I was summoned to the presence of the Hidden King once again. This time, his face was completely covered, and there were a dozen of his highest-ranking officers with him.

"At his feet lay the body of Dutiful Chrysanthemum.

"'She gossiped,' the Hidden King said. Then, before I could react, he added, 'But you did not. Her shame therefore is not yours, nor that of the Division of Sappers and Archaeologists.'

"From that day, I have been most careful to obey the Hidden Emperor as scrupulously as I can."

"It is a mildly distressing story," Surplus said. "But absolute monarchs all tend to be ruthless, and we have seen worse since this war began."

"You don't understand. *How did the king know?* Dutiful Chrysanthemum and I were alone. The kitchen girl fled immediately. Yet he knew all that had transpired, down to my exact words."

"Perhaps there were listening tubes in the walls of the kitchen," Darger said.

"Perhaps there were spies," Surplus suggested.

"I would have noticed listening tubes—I am a mechanic, after all. Nor were there spies. There was only the kitchen girl, and since I never saw her again, I can only assume she met the same fate as Dutiful

Chrysanthemum. Nor was that the only time the emperor displayed his uncanny way of knowing what no one but he could know.

"So, no, I will not betray him in the least way."

Surplus raised a paw for silence. On the bridge outside, he heard three ascending and three descending notes. Timing his words to begin just as the young woman reappeared with a fresh pot of tea, he said, "Let us double and redouble our efforts. The Hidden Emperor says the phoenix device will be ready in five days—make it three! We have promised to end the joyous plague by the time our enemies are at the city gate—let us accomplish that a week earlier! Indeed, I myself—oh, thank you, young lady. Your timing was excellent, for I had just finished my glass."

"Will you be wanting anything else, noble sir?"

"No, nothing. We are almost done here." Turning away from the servitor, Surplus said, "I myself find the idleness imposed by the plague intolerable, and thus I propose a sixteen-point program for increasing the readiness of—" Six notes rose and fell as the young woman recrossed the bridge. "Where were we?"

"We were trying to forge a common understanding," Darger said. "White Squall, I sense that something is being left unsaid. Otherwise, you would have put this conversation behind you and departed. What is it?"

The palest ghost of a smile flickered briefly on White Squall's lips. "I would not betray the Hidden Emperor for any amount of power or wealth or glory. The risk is simply too great. However . . ."

"I am listening."

"The love I share with Prince First-Born Splendor is necessarily illicit and furtive, a wartime romance. He being a prince and I a mechanic's daughter, I can hope for no more. Yet I have seen you perform miracles. I want you to arrange for him to propose marriage to me. Further, I would have him renounce his dream of returning to Southern Gate and accept a position in the Hidden Emperor's court, so that I may continue my work."

"You ask a great deal of me."

"In return, I will agree to arrange for you to have at least one day's warning before the phoenix device is usable."

"That is not much time."

"A motivated man can travel a great distance in one day."

Darger sighed heavily. "You are a ruthless woman, White Squall."

"I am a woman in love, which is much the same thing. How soon do you think you can arrange this?"

"In my country," Surplus said, "there is a saying: The difficult we do immediately. The impossible takes a little longer."

Wonderingly, White Squall said, "You Westerners certainly use a lot of adages."

"It is our way," Darger said, standing.

White Squall stood also and, loudly addressing the general world, said, "I should mention that it is obvious to me that the Hidden Emperor will not rush into his union with the Phoenix Bride impulsively. Thus, in making this agreement, we are none of us in any way betraying him." In a normal voice, she added, "Oh, and I'll take that component you slipped into your pocket when you were kneeling beside me." Then, turning to Surplus, "Yours also, sir dog."

DARGER AND Surplus emerged from the pavilion to discover that it was evening and the Summer Moon Festival had begun. This was a feast of great antiquity, celebrating the ancient Chinese *taikonauts* who had walked upon that august body. There were fireworks in the western sky and, below them, street vendors selling sticky rice dumplings wrapped in bamboo leaves. Paper lanterns lined the streets. Music spilled from every tavern and teahouse.

"Those were two very strange conversations," Surplus commented. "And, Lord knows, we have had more than our share of strange conversations."

"Strange and unfortunate as well. In the course of them we seem to have promised to get a prince to propose marriage to a commoner, albeit a beautiful one, to defeat Shrewd Fox, and to end the joyous plague. None of which we have the slightest inkling of how to accomplish."

"It is the plague that worries me most," Surplus said. "All matters dependent upon human decision making are vulnerable to cozening. But how does one flimflam a microorganism? I confess that I—"

At that instant, there was a rippling in the crowd as a familiar figure ran up to them.

"Sir!" Capable Servant said. "Good news, sir!"

"Everything is exciting to you, isn't it, Capable Servant?" Darger said. "I envy you your naïveté."

"Thank you, sir. But the news, sir."

"Surely it can wait for morning."

"No, sir! It cannot wait, sir! The Infallible Physician has arrived!"

11.

The Spider Hero lived his life by this maxim: He who possesses great
power is burdened also with great responsibility.

—THE SAYINGS OF THE PERFECT STRATEGIST

THE CITY gates of Crossroads were not opened the next
morning. At the command of the Hidden Emperor, nobody,
however important, was allowed to enter the city, and nobody,
however insignificant, was permitted to leave. Guards were spaced
regularly along the city walls to enforce this quarantine, with orders to
shoot anyone attempting to violate it. Scouts and spies came regularly
to Harmonious Intercourse Gate to place messages and reports in
buckets that were lowered by rope from the watchtowers, and instructions were similarly passed down forbidding them from making any
mention whatsoever of the plague ravaging the invading army. Otherwise, there was no communication with the outside world.

All this was done to make it look as if the Hidden Emperor's forces
had been rendered helpless by the joyous plague and those few left
unstricken were trying to keep this knowledge from the ears of Ceo
Shrewd Fox, whose forces were reported to be converging on Crossroads from every direction.

Darger was busy emptying out all the buildings facing Free Trade
Square and pondering where mounted troops should be placed when
enough of them emerged in fighting condition from the archipelago
of field hospitals dotting the city. At his instruction, Surplus was

overseeing the reconstruction of the walls between the inner and outer gates, the scrubbing of the paving blocks of the square just beyond it, and the creation of barricades behind the House of Joyous Governance, where the two main avenues leading around it from the square merged and then drove into the heart of the city. Suddenly, a swarm of rosy-cheeked children bearing silk banners, paper lanterns, and flowers larger than themselves flooded the square. In their wake came several joyous ones to direct the placement of blossoms, lanterns, and flags.

Briefly, all was cheerful chaos. Then, in a twinkling, the work was done and the children and their supervisors had scampered and stalked away, leaving the square vacant save for Surplus, the street cleaners, and one lone woman who stood at its center, looking amused.

Abandoning the stonemasons to their work, Surplus hurried to greet his old friend. "I am delighted to see you again, Bright Pearl," he said. "Or should I address you as the Infallible Physician?"

"Call me what you will, you scoundrel. Thanks to you and your companion, my life has been transformed."

Indeed, the features of the Infallible Physician were greatly changed from when Surplus had seen her last. Gone was the poverty-born air of worry and dejection, replaced by the confident mien of one who does not lack for money and anticipates never experiencing that lack again. There was also, admittedly, an avaricious glint in her eye that had not been there before; but as Surplus did not necessarily consider greed a fault, that did not bother him. "Tell me," she said, with a sweep of her hand encompassing the square, gatehouses, and indeed the city in its entirety, "what is all this fuss about?"

"Ceo Shrewd Fox is on her way. We are preparing a welcome for her."

"Please tell me that you are not planning to employ the Empty City stratagem. That's the oldest trick in all of China! It wouldn't fool a kitten."

"I am, of course, not permitted to speculate on the Perfect Strategist's plans. But if he does indeed intend what you speculate, then perhaps, the trick being so old, Shrewd Fox will not be expecting it. However, enough of that. I have heard that literally overnight you came up with a means of putting an end to the joyous plague. Can this happy rumor be true?"

"It is—and you are fortunate I answered your call, for there is no one else who could have done it. I was up late into the night with your exasperating bureaucracy. I told the joyous ones I needed genetic engineers, and they said there were none in all of Crossroads. So I said I would make do with skilled chefs. Those they could supply. I asked for incubators and medical-grade glass piping and settled for pressure cookers and plumbing fixtures. Step by step, every instrument, material, or specialist I required was unavailable. Step by step, I came up with substitutes. How I wish you were a doctor, so you could properly admire my ingenuity! Finally, when everything was in place, the medicines were being produced, and all that was lacking were my detailed instructions on how the medicines were to be employed, I told the joyous ones what my fee would be."

"They, in turn, informed you they would happily pay, but not for thirty days."

"Exactly. Luckily, your friend's resurrection from the dead and the yak of Shiliin Bogd have already made me wealthy—so much so that for the two of you, I would have been tempted to do the work for free. However, in Brocade I learned that my clients valued me largely by how much I charged. When I lowered my fees, I was treated with familiarity. If I dispensed medical advice for free, it was ignored. By demanding outrageous sums for miracles of healing no other living human could have performed, I elevated myself to one of the great ladies of the city in no time at all. Indeed, they would not have let me go had I not left the sacred yak behind to guarantee my return. So from the joyous ones I demanded ownership of a certain conversation garden—perhaps you have seen it?—with quite a lovely pond and pavilion. Also a mansion to be built on its grounds. When the mansion is finished, the thirty days will be long past, and I will move into it."

"You are not returning to Brocade, then?"

The Infallible Physician snorted. "For what? That stupid yak? When it is seen that I can cure a plague overnight—and by tomorrow morning there will not be a sick soldier in all of Crossroads—my reputation here will be made. Then I will open a medical school and a printing press. At the school I shall teach the very best students able to raise the extortionate fees I intend to charge and make them doctors almost the equal of me. The press will duplicate my grandfather's books and sell them at prices that will make grown men and women turn pale. Thus, as my fame grows, so too will the number of physicians able to fill the demand for my services. Cities will compete for my pupils, and some of them will in turn open their own medical schools, a modest percentage of whose profits will go to me.

"In this way, I shall grow astonishingly wealthy in my lifetime and be revered as a benefactor to the world after my death."

"It is a dazzling plan and one that could scarce be improved upon," Surplus said with frank admiration. "And your father—how fares he?"

All joy fled the physician's face. "He is the same as ever—critical, senile, combative, and impossible to please. Yet he is still my father, and I profoundly wish I could make him happy. I would give anything for a solution to this problem."

Surplus's ears pricked up. "Anything?"

"Yes! You have a solution! I see it in your stance and hear it in your voice, and if such a thing could be conveyed by scent, the air would reek of it. Tell me immediately, and you shall have whatever you desire!"

Surplus could not help but strike a modest pose. "The resolution is obvious. You must hire young women who look much as you did when you were their age and dress them as you dressed then. Let them take turns playing the part of his daughter. Instruct them to tremble at his every frown and weep copiously when he scolds them. Make certain that one is always present when you look in on him, and in the way of old men in their dotage, he will assume you are a visiting doctor being shown insufficient respect by his daughter. In this way he will know contentment and you will finally experience his respect."

The Infallible Physician shook her head in wonder. "So brilliant a plan—and so simple, too." Then, briskly, she said, "Name your reward. You have earned it."

"I require only one thing, which for you will be easily accomplished and for me will be a tremendous weight taken off my mind. Ceo Powerful Locomotive, the man you were originally summoned to . . ."

"It is already done," the Infallible Physician said proudly. "I revived him this morning, with his memory perfectly intact. In fact, that is why I am here. I have just returned from his bedside, where he asked me to tell you that he wished to see you and the Perfect Strategist immediately."

TO HIS alarm, when Surplus located Darger in the parade grounds, where he was overseeing the greatly diminished (but steadily growing, as soldiers were released from the hospitals and returned to their units) cavalry, his comrade was being harangued by Prince First-Born Splendor. Adopting a genial tone, Surplus strolled into the confrontation, saying, "Friends! Friends! How is it possible that we should be at odds?"

"How is it *not*?" Prince First-Born Splendor retorted. There was a grim set to his handsome features. "White Squall has told me all about you two."

"Has she? That is too kind of her."

"Not all of it is to your credit."

"I am sorry to hear that," Darger said. "Also greatly surprised. I have always handled White Squall with the utmost gentleness and respect."

Surplus, who knew something of the history between White Squall and Darger, put the back of a paw to his mouth to hide a smile. "Please do remember," he said however, "that we are in public, where we can be overheard."

Lowering his voice to a furious whisper, the prince said, "She tells me you are masters of deceit. Men who will stoop to any falsehood in order to get your own way."

"Sir, we are at war!" Darger replied, equally softly, equally intensely. "Did not the Goateed Uncle of the Beautiful Country once say that loose truths sink ships? Deceit is the very essence of the noble profession of war. That and wholesale slaughter." All three were now standing so close that Surplus could have embraced the other two with ease.

"How cannily you play with words. But I will not be distracted. When first we met, we made a compact. One it now seems clear to me you never meant to honor."

"Sir, you were in a terrible fix. Out of compassion, I helped you out of it."

"You talked me into betraying my country."

"Your country is now as it was then—its cities not leveled, its fields unsalted, its citizens productive, alive, and not enslaved. I fail to see how this is a betrayal."

"I was in desperate straits, and you sold me a fantasy. Now that I understand you to be cozeners, its blatant unlikeliness stands revealed."

Darger placed a hand on his breast. "Sir, your accusations wound me grievously. However, as a gentleman, I forgive you."

Prince First-Born Splendor's hand clenched the hilt of the short sword he carried at his side so tightly that his fingers were white. "We shall know the truth. I hear that Powerful Locomotive is awake at last. We three will go to him—now!—and see how his understanding conforms with yours."

"It is time wasted that properly should be spent making military preparations," Surplus observed with feigned nonchalance. "However, if we must, we must."

Inside, however, he reflected that when events swept one toward the abyss, there was nothing to do but trust in providence to provide an unexpected rescue. Unlikelier things had happened with surprising frequency in his life. Anyway, if worse came to worst, Surplus still had his cane and, more importantly, the prince had no inkling that it concealed a sword.

WHERE MOST sick soldiers had to make do with wooden cots in crowded tenements or canvas tents, Ceo Powerful Locomotive had for weeks been invalided upon the softest bed and finest sheets in all the city, within a room whose lavish appointments would have pleased him tremendously, had he not for all that time been hanging midway between life and death. On awakening, it seemed, he had decided to keep the room and the house, for it was there he greeted Darger and Surplus and led them into a room set aside for conversation.

If he was surprised that they had brought along Prince First-Born Splendor, he gave no sign of it.

The room held a single chair that though not a throne was strongly suggestive of one. As soon as the servants had been dismissed, Powerful Locomotive sat down on it. The others, having no alternative, remained standing. The ceo nodded toward the prince. "You may speak," he said.

"Ceo, I have come seeking truth. When I was negotiating with the Abundant Kingdom, the Perfect Strategist represented himself as being your agent. Is this actually so?"

With surprising mildness, Powerful Locomotive said, "It is."

Prince First-Born Splendor looked startled. "I am amazed. For he told me things which I hardly dare repeat. Treasonous words which, were they to be uttered in public, would mean the death of both of us."

"Tell me," Powerful Locomotive said, "what was promised in my name. I give you my word that no harm will come to you for it, however dangerous or libelous or false the Perfect Strategist's words were or however deeply entangled in them you may be."

He listened solemnly while Prince First-Born Splendor detailed all of Darger's imaginary plot: that Powerful Locomotive believed that the man then known as the Hidden King was mad and must inevitably die before the war was completed; that the agent of that death would be the ceo himself; that he wished to succeed to the throne but knew that doing so immediately following the emperor's demise would bring dark suspicions upon himself; that he would therefore make First-Born Splendor the puppet ruler; that in a year or so, with the reign legitimized, First-Born Splendor would be allowed to resign in favor of Powerful Locomotive and retire to the independent nation of Southern Gate; and that this would then give both of them what they wanted: the throne for the ceo and a free homeland for the prince.

When all had been said and done, Ceo Powerful Locomotive nodded. "That is correct in every detail."

"What?"

"I assure you, Prince First-Born Splendor, that I love you like a son. That being so, I judge you by how far short you fall of perfection, and thus my criticism and fault finding are constant, which I fear has made you think my regard for you is less than absolute. But knowing you as I do, I have no fear that you will reveal my ambitious and treasonous plot to the emperor, for you are a steadfast man. Nor do I fear that when you have become ruler of all of China, you will try to hold on to power, for you are a modest man as well. But I beg you to keep to our original compact—for should something happen to me before I become emperor, I can think of no one who would make as wise a ruler as you."

"I . . . I . . . have no words, ceo."

"None are needed, my son. We are family." Powerful Locomotive stood and embraced the young man. "But now you must leave, for I have matters to discuss with my two colleagues, and I am sure you are busy as well."

When the prince was gone, Ceo Powerful Locomotive held his open hand out before him, and contemplated it in silence. When he looked up, he was smiling. "I have you in the palm of my hand," he said.

"Yet you have not closed that hand upon us," Surplus observed. "So you want something that only we can provide."

"Yes. You must have been wondering why I was spying on you."

"As my superior officer, that was of course your prerogative. I am sure you had some good reason for it."

"I was hoping to learn something that would give me a hold over the two of you. Your beating a superior officer was sufficient to achieve that. The extraordinary tale of your scheming perfidy that the idiot prince told only makes my absolute control over your destinies all that much more obvious."

"There is no denying that we must do whatever it is you wish us to do," Surplus said. "Only—what is it?"

Ceo Powerful Locomotive looked uncharacteristically abashed. "I had a single instant when I passed out to realize that I might be about to die. When I awoke this morning, that thought was fresh in my mind. Imagine my amazement when I learned how much time had passed. I was filled with an awareness of how fleeting a thing is life. I swore in that instant that I would do whatever it takes to win the love of White Squall."

"Excuse me?" Surplus said.

Darger shook his head. "That might be more difficult than you think. You see—"

"White Squall is in love with the princeling, and he with her. I know, I know. People gossip, and the first thing I did after sending for you was to have my servants bring me up to date. Nevertheless, you will find a way to win White Squall for me as a wife or I will kill you both and then decide whether I should follow you into death as well. Do you understand me?"

"Vividly," Darger said. "Let me think." He closed his eyes for several long minutes and then said, "You have risen from your bed too soon, and in your zeal to serve the Hidden Emperor put such a strain on yourself that you have had a terrible relapse. You are weak and possibly near death. Do you understand?"

"I feel fine."

"This is a part you must play. Tomorrow, I will arrange for White Squall to visit you, as she will every day thereafter. Do not feel too encouraged by this. She too will be playing a part at my direction. But it will give you the opportunity to change how she feels about you."

"Should I tell her I love her?"

"It is too early for that. You must speak quietly to her and never blusteringly, never jokingly. Be sincere in all your words. Let White Squall feed you broth and other liquid foods. Ask her to read to you from the classic poets. Li Shangyin would be ideal, for his love poems are all tragic. Tell her he is your favorite poet. 'One inch of love is an inch of ashes.' Tell her that is your favorite line from your favorite poem. If she notices how scandalous his verses are, tell her they were actually fictionalized expressions of passion for his wife. Let White Squall read you a variety of other types of poems and prose histories as well. But when the words turn to love, look away, as if the mere sight of her were too much for your overburdened heart. In this manner, without your having to say a word, she will gradually come to realize that you love her."

"Are you sure? White Squall is not a very subtle woman."

"If she doesn't notice on her own accord, I will arrange for someone to whisper that fact in her ear. I must caution you, however, that this will not be an easy campaign, nor a brief one. You have let your enemy steal a march on you and he has a strong hold on the territory you desire. Still, with discipline and hard work—and my tutelage—you may be able to overcome Prince First-Born Splendor's many strategic and tactical advantages."

Powerful Locomotive looked sick. But he said, "I will do as you say."

"Then there is hope."

A spark of Powerful Locomotive's old spirit flared up in him then, and he said, "I cannot help but notice, however, that your plot leaves you in control of the Hidden Emperor's army while I feign being an invalid."

"That is unfortunate, I agree," Darger said. "But it a burden I will simply have to endure."

"THIS IS a terrible state of affairs," Surplus said after he and Darger had left the ceo's house. "I—oh, hello."

To his surprise, Prince First-Born Splendor fell into stride alongside the two. "I have been waiting for you," he said. "It seems I owe you both an apology."

With a dismissive wave of his paw, Surplus said, "Your apology is hardly necessary, and your offense? Negligible! Forgotten!"

"White Squall did not tell me you were false—that was my interpretation. I do not wish to besmirch her character in any way, for she is a perfectly virtuous woman. She simply told me that the two of you could accomplish things through deceit that no other men could, and indeed wherever you go, trickery and victory follow effortlessly. It begins to look like this war will soon be over and I shall be able to return home."

"That is what you have been yearning for since it began, is it not?" Darger said. "You should be happy."

"Alas, when I asked White Squall to return with me to Southern Gate as my mistress, she grew very cold. She must have work to do, she said, work of value, not work that could be performed by a common courtesan. It is a noble ambition, of course, to be the emperor's armorer and help him rule over a reunited China. And if Powerful Locomotive's scheme were to come into being, I believe I could explain to her why it was necessary to resign from"—he glanced around and, evidently deciding that it was not worth the risk of being too explicit in a public place, concluded—"from such a high position. But she would want me to stay on in North as a member of the emperor's court. She has never seen Southern Gate in the springtime, so she does not know what she asks. Already I am heartsick for home. A lifelong exile would be as good as a death sentence for me."

"You could marry her," Darger suggested. "There is always an abundance of meaningful work for the wife of a ruler. To say nothing of making life a living hell for the servants charged with raising your children."

"My father would not approve."

"A terrible situation, sir. But many a young man has married without his father's blessing; the arrival of a grandson traditionally brings about reconciliation. How could your father possibly stop you?"

"He is, after all, the king."

"No, sir, unless you accept the role that Powerful Locomotive has reserved for you—in which case, even after you resign, you will outrank him—he is the governor. And not even that, if the emperor decides you should replace him."

They were approaching Free Trade Square now, and the streets were thronged with people carrying bundles of clothing and pulling small carts laden with household goods. These were the citizens who were being temporarily removed from the first several blocks of the city beyond Harmonious Intercourse Gate. They looked unhappy but resigned, their lot being rather better than that suffered by most peoples in times of war.

Prince First-Born Splendor scratched the side of his head thoughtfully and came to a decision. "None of your suggested solutions are sufficient. You must come up with one of your low and dishonest stratagems to prevent Powerful Locomotive from entangling me in affairs of court for several years, and a second one to convince White Squall to return with me, when the war ends, quietly and submissively, to Southern Gate, as my mistress."

The prince fell silent then. When it became obvious that nothing more was forthcoming, Darger cleared his throat and said, "It is traditional at this point in such negotiations to offer a bribe."

"A large one," Surplus threw in. "In keeping with the hopelessness of your cause and the difficulty of achieving what you desire."

"Ah. Yes. I am so used to being obeyed out of loyalty and patriotism that I had forgotten that more is sometimes required. How about this? If you do as I command, I will refrain from having you both killed. As a hereditary monarch with a military force fanatically devoted to me, I could easily arrange that—and even if my part in it were discovered, the worst I would face is exile from the emperor's court. Which is a thing I desire anyway."

The prince smiled brightly. "You see? I am learning to think as you do."

THAT EVENING, after all the work that could be done had been completed and all that could not had been given up on, Surplus climbed to the rooftop of Yellow Crane Tower. There, as expected, he found Darger, staring down the river at an armada of boats. They were putting in before the city, and men were raising up a shadow city of canvas where, hours before, had been nothing but fields. The low-lying sun turned all the tents golden and their shadows violet. "How beautiful they look!" Darger exclaimed. "'. . . argosies of magic sails, / Pilots of the purple twilight dropping down with costly bales . . .' Tennyson. I wonder what he and Li Bai would have made of each other. I fancy he would have gotten along better with Du Fu."

"The affairs of poets are neither here nor there. We have made a great many promises today."

"I should have known from the first that Powerful Locomotive was in love with the chief archaeological officer. The clumsy, bullying manner he adopted in her presence, the crude jokes made at her expense—he acted like a schoolboy-athlete with a crush."

"Are we fairy-tale genies, dispensing magical wishes in threes? Aubrey, we have already promised White Squall that we will make Prince First-Born Splendor marry her and dwell permanently in North. On top of which, we have just now, under duress admittedly, promised the prince that, though it is a role no sane man can imagine her assuming, White Squall will go to Southern Gate with him as his submissive mistress. I fail to see how we can arrange both of these mutually exclusive goals while simultaneously making White Squall fall in love with Powerful Locomotive as well."

"Don't forget that we also have a military victory to secure against impossible odds." Darger gestured across the water, where overgrown hills of rubble created a grid that stretched as far as the eye could see. "In Utopian times, Crossroads was many times larger than it is today. Half of it lay north of the Long River. Legend says its buildings touched the sky. 'My name is Ozymandias, king of kings: Look on my works, ye Mighty, and despair!' I wonder how Shelley would have gotten along with Li Bai."

Darger looked so mournful then that Surplus could not help laughing out loud. "Well, come what may, you should get some sleep," he said. "Tomorrow will be a busy day."

They went down the stairs together, and on arriving at Darger's rooms on the third floor found Capable Servant crouched on the landing, head down and arms wrapped about his legs.

"You look sad, Capable Servant," Darger observed.

The young man looked up, and there were tears in his eyes. "Oh, sir. I am merely thinking of my wife. It has been so very long since I have seen her, and I miss her so."

"You have a wife? I am astonished that you never mentioned her before."

"Yes, sir, in the city of North. I did not want to bother you with my romantic woes."

"I don't see why not. Everybody else does."

BUT CAPABLE Servant was possessed, apparently, of that paradoxical pride sometimes manifested by the lowly that forbade him to ask for help from those in a better position than he to provide it. So, at last, with appropriate expressions of farewell to Darger and sympathy to Capable Servant, Surplus departed Yellow Crane Tower and made his way to the small hotel that Fire Orchid's clan had seized and made their encampment.

There were many arrangements to be made with various members of the family, whom Surplus had not seen since the onset of the plague. But neither had he seen Fire Orchid in all that time, so inevitably their reunion was passionate. When they two were alone at last and post-coital, Fire Orchid said, "All the sick members of the family are recovered, thanks to your friend the Expensive Doctor."

"The Infallible Physician."

"That is the same thing. Everybody wants to meet her because she is rich and heals people. But I said I was your wife and so she saw me right away. Because she was curious about me. We had a nice long chat. She talks about her money a lot, but it seems to me that she is very tight."

"Well, she was poor for many years."

"That explains it then," Fire Orchid said. "I do not think we will get any money out of this one. So let's not try. Oh, and Little Spider has found that by putting rouge on her cheeks and acting the way she did when she was sick, she can pass for a joyous one. She is so cute."

"That might prove useful in the future," Surplus observed.

"I think so, too. Also, I want you to make Vicious Brute a hero."

"Why on earth would you want that?"

"It is always useful to have a hero in the family."

"You have me," Surplus reminded her.

"An ordinary hero. You are special. But make certain Vicious Brute is not put in danger. My little brother is actually very delicate and does not like to be shot at. Now tell me what you have been doing all this time."

Surplus did not deem it wise to tell Fire Orchid about Darger's plans, the Hidden Emperor's obsession with the Phoenix Bride, or the fact that the device was close to being operable. Instead, he told her of the Infallible Physician's unhappy desire to please her senile father, of White Squall's hopeless yearning to marry Prince First-Born Splendor and continue her career as a cao, of Powerful Locomotive's unexpected demand that they make White Squall love him, and of Prince First-Born Splendor's unlikely obsession of returning to Southern Gate with White Squall as his mistress. At the conclusion of his narration, he sighed and said, "Love is a terrible thing."

Fire Orchid patted his cheek. "Lucky for you, you don't need to worry about love at all. Because you have a wife."

12.

A rumor went around that the Perfect Strategist had taken a ghost for a wife. He was never seen in the company of a physical woman, and yet he did not bear himself as a man deprived of female attention does. Hearing the rumor, Ceo Powerful Locomotive made a joking remark that the love of a ghost was superior to that of a living woman for she could cause him no troubles or concerns. Glumly, the Perfect Strategist replied, "If you think that, then you know nothing of women, living or dead."

—THE BOOK OF THE TWO ROGUES

FIRST CAME the scouts.

The thick, iron-banded outer doors of Harmonious Intercourse Gate had been thrown open and the matching inner doors were flung wide. Inside, banners flapped in the breeze, paving stones gleamed, and bright flowers bloomed before every window. Cautiously, four intrepid men entered Free Trade Square. They were mounted on sturdy though nondescript horses, and they all looked a little spooked to be greeted by a silent and unpeopled city.

Unpeopled save for one man. For Darger sat, clad as always in his modest scholar's robes and with incense burning at his feet, on a balcony central to the House of Joyous Governance, high above them. He was playing the *guqin*. Otherwise, he was absolutely motionless. The melancholy notes of his seven-stringed instrument floated over the square, adding emphasis to the silence.

He gave not the least indication that he had seen the newcomers.

The scouts consulted with one another and then two of them, spurring their horses to a canter, went down the main avenues to either side of the House of Joyous Governance. Hooves clattering on stone, they disappeared around the back of the building.

Silence.

The two remaining scouts waited. And waited. And waited yet more. But their comrades did not return.

When it became clear that the missing scouts would never reappear, the survivors wheeled their horses about and fled.

Darger lifted his hands from his instrument and waited.

TIME ENOUGH passed for the scouts to report their findings to their commanders and for a long argument to ensue. Then the assembled Three Gorges army stirred, bulged, and gave birth to a lesser body of men. With neither hurry nor delay, a force of perhaps two hundred soldiers advanced upon the city, led by a stocky woman and a dozen or so officers.

The woman was doubtless Shrewd Fox, and the officers the highest-ranking of her staff. No career officer with enough clout to insist upon accompanying her would pass by the opportunity to be a part of what they were sure would be a famous victory.

On their approach, Darger began to play again. He had taken a pedagogical draft that gave him the skill to play the *guqin*, but, being unpracticed, his technique was shaky. Still, he was not looking to gain the enemy's admiration. He was presenting them with a story they would think they understood.

In disciplined array, the contingent of soldiers passed into Free Trade Square, its best warriors first, its officers next, and all the rest following.

They filled the square, and the command staff formed a line below the balcony. Darger continued to play, as if nothing had happened. The officers looked at one another.

Then Ceo Shrewd Fox stood in her stirrups. "Perfect Strategist!" she shouted. "If that is indeed your name. You set a false trap for me, expecting I would flee with my tail between my legs. But I am too canny a fox to fall for such obvious tricks." Several of her subordinates grinned at one another. "I know that your army has been stricken by the plague and that you have not enough vital men to hold the city. Your game has been played, and it is over. I call upon you to surrender."

Darger ceased playing his *guqin*.

The last note faded into silence.

As if this were a signal—which it was—the inner walls of Harmonious Intercourse Gate collapsed in a cloud of flour-dough mortar and a tumble of painted wooden bricks. Soldiers hidden behind the false walls, led by Vicious Brute, emerged to seize the outer doors, swing them shut, and bolt them with an enormous beam of wood. The inner doors followed suit. Meanwhile, cavalry came pouring from behind all the buildings fronting on the square, and archers and riflemen swarmed onto every rooftop and balcony, popped up on the city wall, and appeared in every window, all of them facing inward and pointing their weapons at Shrewd Fox's soldiers.

By the time any of those soldiers could react, it was too late.

Darger stood. In a loud, clear voice, he said, "You are surrounded, outnumbered, and imprisoned, Ceo Shrewd Fox. If you try to fight, you and all your subordinates will die. But if you surrender, I give you my word as a gentleman that your people will be treated leniently."

Shrewd Fox looked stunned.

"The choice is yours," Darger said with just a touch of complacency.

WHEN THE square had been cleared, soldiers in the uniforms of Three Gorges troops opened the gatehouse doors again, raised Three Gorges flags, and waved the waiting troops into the city. Because all their first-rate officers had already been captured and only mediocrities remained in command, the enemy did not hesitate to do so. Once in Free Trade Square, they were divided into small troops and sent down the side streets to be surrounded, disarmed, and escorted to temporary processing facilities. There, the joyous ones swiftly and efficiently integrated the losing army into the Hidden Emperor's Immortals.

Darger was kept busy overseeing the seizure of the Three Gorges river fleet, the decommissioning and recommissioning of officers, the tallying and assessment of seized weapons, the distribution of new uniforms (which every tailor and seamstress in the city had been working on since the plan was first devised), the swearing of oaths, the debriefing of spies from both sides, and a hundred related chores as well.

It took the rest of the day, but by sundown all that remained of the Three Gorges army was a scattering of deserters, fleeing in all directions and carrying with them the news of Shrewd Fox's astonishingly sudden reversal of fortune.

Darger, however, was left with a nagging suspicion that something important had been left undone.

"What am I forgetting?" he said aloud.

A joyous one standing nearby said, "Many things, undoubtedly, noble sir. But if you are asking which previously scheduled task you have not yet performed, it is your interview with Ceo Shrewd Fox."

At his direction, the joyous one lead Darger to a conference room. There, as soon as the door closed behind him, he said, "You are dismissed."

All the joyous ones present of course left immediately. Not so the guards. "That is not possible, sir," one protested. "This is a dangerous woman!"

"It is true that had her actions been performed as a civilian, Shrewd Fox would rightly be regarded as a criminal and a sociopath," Darger admitted. "However, as they were done in the course of her duty as an officer, she is a virtuous woman and worthy to be treated as such. Depart at once or you will experience the usual punishments visited upon soldiers who disobey a direct order." As they left, Darger could not help reflecting that the day when he could not handle a virtuous opponent would be the day he turned to an honest line of work.

The famed Ceo Shrewd Fox turned out to be a little woman with a hard, pinched face and eyes like two black buttons. She stood rigid and proud. "I have fought honorably," she said, "and I am entitled to an honorable death."

"Nobody wishes you to die," Darger said. "Least of all me. Please, sit. I am exhausted, and to sit while you remain standing would be the soul of rudeness. Thank you." Throwing himself into a chair, he resumed his line of thought. "It is the Hidden Emperor's decision that you should take command of those armies of the province (for it is no longer a state) of Three Gorges remaining in the field and in his name use them to reclaim the nations to the south as part of his empire. With your military prowess and their relative weakness, I have no doubt you will make short work of them."

Startled, Shrewd Fox said, "If I left Three Gorges unprotected, it would be overrun by armies from Twin Cities and the Republic of

Central Plains." Then, controlling herself, "But of course that is no longer any responsibility of mine."

"If I was able to catch Shrewd Fox with a stratagem that was old ages before the rise of Utopia," Darger said gently, "can you doubt that I can handle your enemies with equal ease? Not that they will be enemies for long. A new age is come to China—or perhaps I should say that an old one has returned. When the southern nations are subdued, you will come back to Crossroads to find it as you left it in all ways but one—it will be part of a nation at peace with itself and the world. Now. Will you accept the emperor's offer?"

"I . . . for the second time today, I am caught by surprise. This must be what it is like to be of ordinary intelligence. I cannot say that I like it much."

"It is hardly your fault that you were defeated, for you had only your own native genius to rely upon while I had the infallible mathematical science of psychopolemology. I applied a derivative hyperinversion to the set of all possible outcomes, mapped the result onto a swallowtail catastrophe algorithm, and then, once I had equaled out the Boolean constants, the solution was obvious."

"I am not familiar with your terminology," Shrewd Fox said, "but I see what you did clearly enough. Magicians do much the same thing when they alter an illusion. If the audience is confident that an ace of spades will be pulled from a deck of cards, the conjurer turns the entire deck to aces of spades. Or causes the card to catch fire. Or throws the cards into the air, where they turn into ravens and fly away. You knew I believed you to be a blowhard and a fraud and so confronted me with a trick that only a fool would think I'd fall for. Thinking I knew your thinking, I let myself be trapped in my own trap. Had I shown a proper respect for your cunning, I assure you that this day would have gone differently."

"You have an exceptional mind, Shrewd Fox, and I am glad not to have to face you on the field of battle again. Tell me. As one strategist to another—what do you think of my chances against my next set of enemies?"

The smallest of grins appeared and disappeared on the ceo's face. "It is almost too easy, this one. You have the one great advantage that, try though I might, I was never quite able to arrange."

"Which is?"

"Twin Cities and the Republic of Central Plains must now fear you even more than they fear each other. Your forces swept out of a backwater land to conquer nation after nation in a matter of months. The renowned strategist Shrewd Fox had you cornered, yet you effortlessly turned the tables on her. Now your dread gaze moves northward. They will have no choice but to unite against you."

"And how, if you were in my position, would you handle them?" She told him.

For the space of one long breath, Darger said nothing. Then he flung up his hands in astonishment. "What an—"

Shrewd Fox held up both hands. "Stop. You were going to say, 'What an extraordinary coincidence!' or some such thing, when it is nothing of the sort. You needed a new strategy, and you plucked it from my brain. That is all. There is no need for you to pretend otherwise."

"I assure you, madam . . ." Darger began. Then, "Oh, bugger it. You see through me, Shrewd Fox. I am dazzled and I am charmed. Indeed, if I admired you any more than I do at this moment, it would be necessary for me to immediately propose marriage to you."

"I would not dream of marrying a man as clever as myself," Shrewd Fox said. "I could never be certain what he was thinking."

SEVERAL DAYS later, the Hidden Emperor called a meeting to plan the next phase of the campaign. As they were standing in the first-floor anteroom of Yellow Crane Tower, waiting to be blindfolded and led up stairs and down, White Squall said to Darger, "Will Shrewd Fox work with us?"

"She asked for a few more days to think it over. I told her that meant that she had already made up her mind and was angling for an increase in pay. That made her laugh and may well end up costing the emperor money. But she still insisted she needed more time. The Hidden Emperor looked grim when I reported this to him, but said nothing. And you? How go your endeavors?"

"Powerful Locomotive wishes me to read to him," White Squall said in a disgusted tone. "Love poetry, some of it! If you can imagine. I sat at his bedside for hours while the fate of Crossroads was being decided without me. Every day since, I do the same thing. Then I have to return to my empty room and sleep alone in my cold and joyless bed."

"It will be easier to drive Prince First-Born Splendor mad with jealousy this way. I take it your lovers' quarrel went well?"

"Too well. Terrible things were said. I cried for hours."

"Then all is as it should be. Remember what the Bard of Avon said: 'The course of true love never did run smooth.' "

"Spare me your aphorisms, please. I begin to suspect you make them up."

THE HIDDEN Emperor today wore neither bandages nor scarves but a dragon mask, which made him look dangerous and wise. As always when he sat in council, the Phoenix Bride gleamed demurely to his left-hand side. Today, however, a woman veiled in black so that her face could not be seen sat to his right.

It was rarely good news when the Hidden Emperor did something new. Nevertheless, Darger said, as he had planned, "As must be obvious to all, our next move is to use the Three Gorges Fleet to move down the Long River in order to engage with our northern enemies. Twin Cities and the Republic of Central Plains are the only other powers of any significance in central China, and they each have armies the equal of our own Immortals. To meet with one army and defeat it, only to shortly thereafter face a well-rested second force in battle, would be folly. So I propose to fight them both simultaneously."

So soon after the startling victory that Darger had conjured up out of thin air, no one present was anxious to gainsay the Perfect Strategist. Nevertheless, the room was full of dismayed faces.

At a nod from his master, Capable Servant spread a map on the conference table. Darger continued, "The best and simplest way to arrange this is to write to the heads of both nations, proposing to meet their armies upon a mutually agreed-upon time and location. I shall suggest the floodplains before the city of Opera, with our forces positioned upriver and theirs arrayed before the city."

That was too much for his audience. Several advisors leaped to their feet.

"This is madness!" General Iron Ridge cried. "You propose to place the Immortals between the river and a lake. To the south, solid land dissolves into a swamp. If we have to retreat, we can go only so far before being boxed in by marshlands. Meanwhile, the enemy will have complete freedom to maneuver. No one should willingly give up advantages of time, surprise, or terrain. Yet you concede all three."

"As I do not intend to lose, the question of retreat is irrelevant," Darger said.

"You are fortunate," General Celestial Beauty said, "no one can deny that. But your luck will not hold forever. We cannot hop from one wildly unlikely stratagem to another, like a child crossing a creek by leaping stones, forever."

"On the contrary. That is how I have lived my life to date—and if you examine your conscience candidly, you will surely realize it has been your own strategy as well. Yet here we are! Somehow, we seem to be doing well."

"Sooner or later, one of those stones will be slippery underfoot and you will fall. Luck is impartial."

"That is why we were put on earth in the first place—to give luck a little partial *shove*," Darger said. "Cao White Squall, do you have anything to say?"

Rising to her feet, the cao said, "I cannot imagine how the Perfect Strategist hopes for victory with such a plan. But I am sure he will achieve it."

General Celestial Beauty almost spat. "Faith is no substitute for wisdom. Arrogance is a poor stand-in for competence. And luck is an abstraction—you cannot shove it!"

"If you doubt my ability to apply that shove," Darger said, "then simply urge the Hidden Emperor not to listen to me. I will abide by his wisdom."

All turned toward the emperor.

The Hidden Emperor gestured for everybody to be seated, and was obeyed. "There is only one person qualified to pass judgment on such an audacious plan as this. That is our new chief executive officer of the soon-to-be Southern Army." He turned to the veiled woman. "Shrewd Fox? Tell my advisors what you have told me."

The former and now current ceo lifted her veil. Her dark eyes glittered with amusement. "I have heard the Perfect Strategist's plan in detail, and I am certain it will work. It is quite simply brilliant. I could not have come up with anything better myself."

"Then it is approved," the Hidden Emperor said.

A low moan went through the room. But no one stood to object.

"I shall confer now with the Ceo of the South, the Cao of the Division of Sappers and Archaeologists, and the Acting Ceo of the North. All others may leave."

WHEN THEY four (or five, if one counted the Phoenix Bride) were alone, the Hidden Emperor took off his mask and remarked to Darger, "Shrewd Fox told me you offered her money. That was uncharacteristically clumsy of you, Perfect Strategist. A talent such as hers is not to be bought with gold."

"May I ask, Majesty, what you did offer her?"

The emperor nodded to Shrewd Fox, who said, "The Hidden Emperor has given me permission to accompany you to Opera as an observer, so that I might see with my own eyes the defeat of the enemies I have spent all my adult life fighting."

"Ahhhhh."

"But what of the Southern Army, in your absence?" White Squall asked.

"I will leave behind my most trusted subordinates to organize the armed forces still out in the field. In any case, they could not leave Three Gorges while there was yet a military threat from the north. They will also inform the government in exile of the former nation that they are now loyal servants of the Hidden Emperor. Those who embrace their new status will keep their positions in the regional government. The others . . ." Shrewd Fox shrugged.

Darger nodded sagely. "I see. Shall we go over the order of battle?"

"I am sure it is up to your usual standards," the Hidden Emperor said. "Shrewd Fox, send for the stenographer."

The ceo clapped her hands twice. From a small doorway to one side, a servant appeared, notepad in one hand, quill and ink in the other.

"Your plan requires letters of challenge. You may dictate them now."

Darger swiftly ordered his thoughts, then said, "The first begins: *To my beloved sister, the so-called Chief Speaker of the rebel province styling itself the Republic of Central Plains, greetings.* The second begins: *To my beloved children, the Hereditary Hierarchy of the break-away state of Twin Cities, greetings.* Then, word-for-word identically hereafter: *Because a state of near-continual war has existed in the heartland of China the Great for over a century, because my subjects cry out to me in their misery, and because peace is a blessing which all men and women devoutly desire, your emperor has come to rectify the state and alleviate the suffering of the people. Alas, there are those who have hardened their hearts against the people, against peace, and against their rightful ruler. Therefore I must take action. On the third day of autumn, on the river plain before Opera, shall three great armies meet, as foreordained. There, an army will be crushed like a nut in the jaws of a dragon. Though my Immortals may retreat before you, do not be deceived. We will turn and fall upon our enemy with the sav-agery and mercilessness of the fabled Locomotive. Remember this and ponder it well.* Then it should be signed, *The Hidden Emperor, by the Grace and Mandate of Heaven Ruler of All China.*"

Almost imperceptibly, the Hidden Emperor nodded. Darger then said, "How does it sound to you, Cao White Squall?"

"Like a coded letter. One that winks at its recipient as it spouts words it does not expect to be taken on face value."

"Excellent!" To the stenographer, Darger said, "Make out fine copies and then, after the Hidden Emperor has seen and approved of them, send a messenger with the copy addressed to Twin Cities to the Republic of Central Plains, and another with the Central Plains copy to Twin Cities, as if the letters had been accidentally switched."

THERE WERE other matters to be discussed, but the meeting was soon over. As Darger was leaving, the Hidden Emperor said, "A word with you in private, Perfect Strategist."

"Majesty."

When they were alone, the emperor said, "Tell me. Do you know what war is?"

Cautiously, Darger replied, "The Sun Tzu of the West defined war as diplomacy by other means."

"He was wrong. For what is war but a joyful expression of the abundance of life? Wars do not arise during famines, droughts, and times of great poverty. They arise in times of excess. As armloads of fruits and grains and extravagant numbers of sacrificial animals are brought to the altars of the gods in times of great wealth, so too are extravagant numbers of a nation's youth marshaled, trained, and brought to the altar of war. To burn, sir, to burn. In this way we celebrate all that we have been given."

"I never thought of it that way. But once said, it seems irrefutable."

"Yet paradoxically you seem determined to fight a war without any deaths. In part, no doubt, this is due to the extreme efficiency of your mathematics. That may be forgiven. Yet you keep Ceo Powerful Locomotive abed—do not dare to interrupt me!—when he is needed on the battlefield. Now, I know that these romantic entanglements you have involved yourself in appear important to you—as doubtless they are, on a merely human level. But I am fighting a war, and I need Powerful Locomotive to stoke the flames. He may be unnecessarily brutal, but that is merely the nature of warfare. Embrace it!"

Darger bowed his head, in part to hide the fear that might otherwise show in his eyes. "Your every word is wisdom, Majesty, and must be obeyed."

"Yes," the Hidden Emperor said. "It must."

"HERE IS your cane," Darger told Powerful Locomotive. "Rise and walk."

The ceo sat up and swung his feet onto the floor but did not stand up. "I don't understand."

"Simply stated, you have overplayed your sickness. Oh, I do not blame you! It is to your credit that, loathing deceit as you do, when deceit became necessary, you were not very good at it. However, White Squall begins to lose sight of your manly qualities and now perceives you as weak and ineffectual. Therefore, we will tweak the story. You must force yourself from your sickbed and, even though it puts your recovery and indeed your life in grave danger, rejoin the fray. Because your emperor needs you."

"But what of your plan?"

"It continues. At my direction, White Squall will still spend her free time with you. She will believe that she is doing so to make Prince First-Born Splendor jealous. But exposure to you will slowly turn her heart your way. For, say what you will, he is a pampered hothouse flower while you are a warrior and a man of action. White Squall loves machinery above all other things and therefore will necessarily be drawn to the man who is himself most like a machine. The natural advantage is yours. We need only open her eyes to it."

"I . . . see. I find I must apologize again, Perfect Strategist. I had thought you would take advantage of my feigned weakness to seize power for yourself. It was a price that, lovesick as I am, I would willingly pay. But now you relinquish it voluntarily rather than let our plans fall apart. I perceive that you are a true friend who has my best interests at heart."

"That is no more than what I have been telling you all along. Now get up and let's see you walk with the cane. Wince a little. Not so much! The pain is great, but you are a proud man who tries to hide the fact. That's better."

"I will be glad to return to the field of combat."

"Oh, yes. About that. I am afraid that the Hidden Emperor has already approved a plan for our next battle that involves no actual fighting on our part."

"What!"

"It is a pity, I agree. Still, what's done is done. Now lean on the cane more convincingly. You hold it as if it were a weapon, rather than a prop needed to keep you from falling."

Powerful Locomotive leaned on the cane a little more convincingly. "I should have known your original plan would not work," he grumbled. "No man ever won a woman by lying in bed."

"On the contrary, it is the best imaginable arena in which to win a woman's affections. But, circumstances being what they are, we will have to make do with the battlefield."

"THE LOUT is walking again," White Squall said. "Let me return to my prince."

Darger grimaced. "With pleasure. You need only acquiesce to his demands that you be his mistress, return with him to Southern Gate, and not kill the woman he makes his wife."

"I could never promise that last one."

"Then you must continue to be solicitous to Powerful Locomotive."

"WHITE SQUALL spends part of every day with Powerful Locomotive," Prince First-Born Splendor said.

"That was our strategy, remember? To let her see what the alternative to you looks like. The ceo has all the charm and physical presence of a backhoe. Trust me, she does not much like what she sees. Though, admittedly, many women would."

"She reads him love poetry."

"That is also at our direction. The verses put words of love into her mind, and so, inevitably, her thoughts move yearningly toward you."

"It sounds almost sensible when you say it," Prince First-Born Splendor said. "Even though I know better."

They two were sitting in the conversation park, watching laborers measure out the foundations of the Infallible Physician's mansion. The maple trees had begun to turn color early and were as crimson as the swans swimming serenely on the koi pond. A sudden breeze blew a swirl of black petals from a nearby rose tree. When Darger remained silent, the prince growled, "It maddens me to think of her sitting by his bed every day."

"Then rejoice. The ceo has left his sickbed and resumed his role as the Hidden Emperor's chief subordinate."

"Will White Squall stop seeing him, then?"

"Of course not. That would be contrary to our plan."

Prince First-Born Splendor stared down at his clenched fist. "There must be more we can do. I cannot just sit and worry."

"Well . . . there is an action you could take. But I fear you lack the resolve."

The prince opened his hand and then looked up from it. "I have struck men for saying less. But as I need your help, I shall keep my anger in check. What any man can do, I am capable of. Try me!"

"White Squall seeks to make you jealous. You must in your turn make her jealous."

"How? There is no woman who could possibly compare with her. She would not believe me capable of looking at anyone else."

"By wooing the one woman she respects—Ceo Shrewd Fox."

"It is an ignoble deed to court a woman falsely."

"Would you kill a man if that was what winning White Squall took?" Darger asked. "Then break a woman's heart. It's a lesser crime and a far more common one anyway. They almost always get over it."

"If I must, I must," Prince First-Born Splendor said. "But you must first swear, by whatever foreign abominations you have for gods, that you will arrange for me not only White Squall's love and subservience but also that I will not have to serve a day as the emperor in the furtherance of your schemes."

Darger sighed. "Yes, I can get you what you want by arranging for Powerful Locomotive to be disgraced and exiled and then convincing the Hidden Emperor that your service was so great as for him to grant you Southern Gate as an independent country. You will have to wait until we have conquered Twin Cities and the Republic of Central Plains, fought our way to the Pacific Ocean, conquered the coastal powers, and taken the city of North, of course. But that is merely a matter of time. It is changing White Squall's heart and ambitions that will be difficult, delicate work."

But Prince First-Born Splendor was no longer listening. He stared blindly, nobly, into the sky and said, "If I thought she was sleeping with him, I would kill him with my own bare hands."

THAT NIGHT, White Squall slipped into Darger's rooms. He heard the sound of clothing falling to the floor and opened his eyes to see her standing before his bed, clad only in moonlight and shadow. She looked as cold and desirable as a goddess.

"What in heaven's name are you doing?" Darger asked.

"Everyone, yourself included, speaks of your tremendous intellect. Yet you still ask questions like that." White Squall lifted the sheet and slid into bed alongside Darger.

"Our affair—delightful, meaningful, and indelibly etched upon my soul though it was—is over. Further, you are being fought over by two of the most powerful men in China, both of whom are murderously jealous. How can you possibly be here?"

With a sigh, White Squall snuggled into Darger's arms. "I can't sleep with Prince First-Born Splendor, and the thought of having sex with Ceo Powerful Locomotive disgusts me. That leaves only you."

"Consider the many virtues of abstinence! If you were discovered in my bed, both of your would-be lovers would undoubtedly team up to kill me."

"Then I think you'd want to make me happy," White Squall said. "So that I wouldn't, out of frustration, drop hints in front of either of them. Now the first thing you should do to make me content is . . ."

13.

The trust to be placed in the powers of heaven is boundless; all others must reconcile their debts with gold and silver.

—THE SAYINGS OF THE PERFECT STRATEGIST

THE ARMY that marched out of Crossroads was far superior to the one that had marched in—and not only because it was now greatly enlarged by the absorption of Shrewd Fox's soldiers. This was an army that had experienced miraculous victory after miraculous victory and confidently expected this string of unlikely events to continue for as long as it took. The Immortals had been daunting before; now they were terrifying to behold.

Down the river they traveled, pausing briefly at every town and city to claim the district for the emperor and accept as tribute all available boats. This made their progress increasingly rapid as fewer troops were forced to use the river road and those who did arrived at the end of a day's march to find that the waterborne troops had already made camp for them.

Soon it would be possible to move the entire army via the river fleet, letting the Long River carry them all the way to the Pacific with infinitely less difficulty than their earlier treks had taken. But first the Immortals would have to face Twin Cities and the Republic of Central Plains, which after the abrupt collapse of Three Gorges had, as Shrewd Fox predicted, hastily if belatedly joined forces.

There were several places en route where one or the other of their enemies might profitably have engaged them militarily. But the lure of a battle where all the disadvantages belonged to the Hidden Emperor's forces was too great. Similarly (the emperor's scouts and spies reported), no effort was being made to prevent the Immortals from putting in at their chosen encampment, lest they rethink their plans. Though gun emplacements had been built downriver, to prevent them from changing the terms of engagement should the Hidden Emperor's letter turn out to be another of the Perfect Strategist's famed ruses.

The Dog Pack had, naturally, acquired several luxury houseboats, giving themselves the most comfortable transport on the river. And so Surplus found himself seated under a canvas sunshade near the prow, smoking cheroots with Aubrey Darger. Surplus enjoyed the enforced idleness, since he had a talent, as his friend had not, for inaction. But he regretted its necessity, for, pleasant as the river voyage was, while he was on the boat he was not so much *in* China as watching it float by. He was passing through lands he might never revisit, and a part of him yearned to explore them, discover their scents and colors, and learn their songs and stories and what sorts of lies the old men there told in the teahouses.

"I swear," Darger said, "it's like looking after schoolchildren. Except that children have the good grace to be uninterested in sex. And their death threats are rarely to be taken seriously. And they don't have armed warriors at their beck and call. It's a wonder that I have the time to wage a war at all." He took a long draw on his smoke. It came from a case of pedagogical cheroots that the Dog Pack had liberated from a tobacconist's shop in one of the towns they had passed through, from which, after long indecision, Darger had (as Surplus had known he would) opted for an anthology of classical poetry. For his part, Surplus was smoking a history of the Southern and Northern Dynasties period. As they smoked and talked, tailored mosaic viruses made their way through the blood-brain barrier and unpacked the texts encoded into them directly into his frontal lobe.

"What new developments prompted this outburst?" Surplus asked.

"Oh, Powerful Locomotive is thumping about, complaining that our battle plans are insufficiently bloodthirsty and that White Squall refuses to see the sensitive, caring side of his nature. White Squall keeps demanding that I change First-Born Splendor from the charming, cultured prince of a minor kingdom she fell in love with into an ambitious, power-seeking courtier very much like Powerful Locomotive. The prince, meantime, believes me capable of turning the human tiger that is White Squall into a mewling lap kitten. When I asked him how things were going with Shrewd Fox—"

"Did I hear my name?"

Shrewd Fox came up the companionway steps from below and took a seat. Terrible Nuisance popped up to offer her a cheroot. She chose an analysis of the Battle of Red Cliffs and then, when he glared at her, gave him a small coin so he'd go away. "I had to drop out of the poker game," she said. "I was losing too much money, and the girl who was dealing kept laughing at my misfortunes."

Surplus could not keep himself from smiling. "You let Little Spider deal? Then you deserve whatever befell you. The family is training her to be a pickpocket. She has very nimble fingers."

"To answer your original question, we were just talking about Prince First-Born Splendor," Darger said.

"That fop! I never met anyone quite so annoying. Why is he always underfoot?"

"He is flirting with you, Shrewd Fox," Surplus explained.

"Is that what it is? Far too subtle! He should simply come up to me and tell me what he wants. Then I can tell him no, and we'll both have saved ourselves a great deal of trouble."

"It is my understanding," Surplus said, "that he doesn't actually want anything from you, but is merely trying to make Cao White Squall jealous."

"Ah. Well, that's better. People should have sensible motives."

"What do you make of him as a commander?"

"I know that sort of man: courageous in battle, chivalrous in victory, stoic in defeat. He rides always to the fore of his men, and his gallantry is unsurpassed. While fighting, he looks as dashing as an oil painting. But I'd rather have one good mud slogger than twenty of his kind. Wars are not won by heroes but by disciplined soldiers with a decent appetite for survival."

"And Cao White Squall?

"The cao is made of better stuff. Unimaginative, but often that's a good thing in a subordinate. She knows how to obey an order. I wager that she would willingly go to her death if the order came through the proper chain of command. The Hidden Emperor chose well when he promoted her."

"How about Powerful Locomotive?" Darger asked.

"Ceo Powerful Locomotive is an insecure man, and therefore he mistakes pigheadedness for firmness and brutality for strength. He has every quality one wishes for in an enemy and none of those one desires in a friend. In the right hands, he would make a good second-in-command. But he has risen too high for that. You dare not leave him behind in charge of a captured territory, for his ambition will fill his mind with resentments and imagined slights, and sooner or later he will rise up in rebellion against you. You dare not demote him, for then he will be like a sword with a hairline crack, ready to break in your hand at the worst possible moment. He is in all ways a liability to you."

"What would you do with him if you were in my place?" Darger asked.

"Kill him. I advise you do it quickly, though. The man is unpredictable."

"My friend Aubrey, though in all other ways perfectly admirable, is a merciful and tenderhearted man and thus highly unlikely to stoop to murder simply for the sake of convenience."

"Such was my analysis of him, too. However, he asked and I answered," Shrewd Fox said. "Much as, when the Hidden Emperor asked me the other day whether the plan for the coming Battle of Three Armies was your creation or my own, I told him the truth."

For a long moment, nobody spoke. Then Surplus said, "I'm going to presume that was a joke."

"Oh, no. I really did."

"That was an incautious act on your part," Darger said.

Shrewd Fox looked amused. "Was it? Why?"

"Is it possible that you don't know that the emperor is"— reflexively, Surplus looked about him and lowered his voice—"not entirely predictable?"

"Mad as a drunken bandicoot is what I've heard. But I took that chance. The one thing the Hidden Emperor values most from a subject is straight talk, and so I gave him the information he wanted, along with my best analysis of his chances, the strengths and weaknesses of his army, and the character of all his commanders. (He suggested that you two were treacherous but useful, by the way, and I agreed.) It was risky, but I wanted something from him."

"Being present at the defeat of your enemies, you mean?"

"That and one or two other things."

But press her though Surplus and Darger might and did, on that subject Shrewd Fox would say no more.

THE MOOD was cheerful when the boats put in at the grassy fields south of Opera and the Immortals began to pitch camp. They might have been roustabouts raising the tents and wrangling the animals for a circus that would entertain adults and fill children with awe and wonder, rather than combatants preparing to kill and maim as many human beings as possible in as efficient a fashion as could be arranged. "You and the Perfect Strategist have ruined this battle for the family," Fire Orchid told Surplus. "Nobody is willing to bet against us winning, no matter what odds Trustworthy Mule offers."

"Such are the horrors of war," Surplus said. "Perhaps I could come up with a game of chance from the Land of the Green Mountains of the West for the family to introduce here."

"Oh, teach your grandmother to steal eggs! Anyway, we've already got a cricket-fighting ring. Little Spider paints a tiny gold copyright sign on the back of one and everybody bets on it because they think it has special genetically modified powers. Why are you spending so much time with Shrewd Fox? Is our marriage in trouble again?"

"Our marriage was never in trouble in the first place. Which is a remarkable feat considering that it exists only in your imagination. As for Shrewd Fox, she is clearly plotting mischief. The Perfect Strategist told me to keep an eye on her in the hope that said mischief can be contained."

"What kind of mischief?"

"If we knew, we would have taken action already. As it is, we must fret and wait."

THE DAY of the battle dawned clear and pleasantly cool. It would be hard to imagine a more auspicious day for mass slaughter. The armies of Twin Cities and the Republic of Central Plains had set up separate camps in a low line of hills overlooking the Long River's floodplain. The ground between the hills and where the Immortals had encamped was flat and empty, perfect for wholesale bloodshed. But there were marshes behind them, so that if they had to retreat, they must move westward, where they would be boxed in by thick forests. From a tactical viewpoint it was hardly ideal.

But Darger was clearly delighted with it.

"Does this meet with your approval, General Shrewd Fox?"

"Oh, yes. It will do quite fine."

"Could it be improved upon?"

"No, it could not."

Surplus, however, did not share in any of the glee felt by his companions. "Need I remind you both that success requires that Powerful Locomotive follow to the letter a plan in which he emphatically does not believe. What is to prevent him from acting like . . . well, himself?"

"Oh, piffle," said Darger.

"I have perfect confidence in Ceo Powerful Locomotive," Shrewd Fox said. "Wait and see."

As if summoned by the mention of his name, the ceo came stumping up so vigorously that his cane hand had difficulty keeping in time with his stride.

"Was there ever such an unconvincing limp?" Surplus murmured.

"The only person it has to convince is the ceo himself," Darger replied, equally softly. "So long as Powerful Locomotive thinks we are all deceived, it hardly matters that not a one of us is."

"Hush now," Shrewd Fox said.

Ceo Powerful Locomotive joined the three. Hanging from his neck was a pair of Utopian binoculars such as could not be duplicated with current technology; it was easily worth the price of a good-sized village. He paused portentiously, cleared his throat, and spat. Then, scowling at the distant camps where soldiers were already beginning to line up in fighting formations, he said, "Did you know that the land midway between us and those bastards out there—the land where we are most likely to fight—is riddled with streams and sodden with water? It's not quite marshland, but damned if we won't be up to our knees in mud long before the fight is over."

"If you feel a recurrence of your illness coming on, I would be happy to take over command from you," Shrewd Fox said, delivering the words in such a manner that no one could miss the sarcasm.

The ceo stiffened and his face twisted into a silent snarl. Then he spun on his heel, turning his back on Shrewd Fox, and shouted, "Battle horns! Drums! Sound assembly! It's time for this debacle to begin."

Troops had already been gathering, in accordance with the eagerness and ambition of their commanders. Now soldiers came running from all directions and units coalesced. In an impressively brief time, they were ready to advance.

A soldier brought up a white stallion. Ceo Powerful Locomotive climbed up on it and galloped off to oversee the order of battle.

Shortly thereafter, Terrible Nuisance brought up Buttercup, and Surplus swung into the saddle. The rest of the Dog Pack fell in behind him, bringing with them (because he had made them his personal guard) a mountain horse for the Perfect Strategist and (because Darger distrusted her and wanted to keep her under his eye) another for Shrewd Fox.

Surplus patted Terrible Nuisance's shoulder in an avuncular fashion. "The great advantage of being the guard for a member of the high command is that we are unlikely to actually do any fighting. However, as a precaution, you will not join the Dog Pack today. A battlefield is no place for children. You can watch the goings-on from the relative safety of the camp."

"Hey! What? That's not fair! Little Spider—"

"Little Spider prevailed upon her aunt to overrule my common sense on her behalf. As Fire Orchid's husband, I had no choice but to obey. Just as you, being my nephew, have no choice but to accept the wisdom of my orders."

"You're not my real uncle," the boy said heatedly. "You and Auntie Fire Orchid are just playing at being married."

"I'm relieved that this fact, so obvious to me, can be perceived by another living being. But it has no relevance here. Scoot!"

Surplus returned his attention to the upcoming conflict.

Slowly the three armies stirred, flowing out from their encampments to take their places on the floodplain. Battle drums played, banners flapped in the breeze, and tidy rows of minuscule soldiers advanced in neat array. Riding at the head of the Dog Pack, just off to one side of the vanguard, Surplus said, "I cannot help reflecting how similar all this is to the imagined conflicts of my youth, fought by lead soldiers with cannons that I carved from twigs. The romantic side of my nature, even now, finds it rousing."

"The rational side of my nature is appalled," Darger said. "However, I too feel oddly stirred."

Shrewd Fox said nothing.

"In any case," Surplus said, "we're in too deep now to back out."

"Just remember that Shrewd Fox and I are here only as observers and behave accordingly, and all will be well."

For a time the armies advanced. Then all three came to a mutual halt, just out of cannon range of each other. On the southern end of the grassy plain fluttered the Hidden Emperor's banners. To the north were the red and black flags of Twin Cities and the orange flags of the Republic of Central Plains, side by side, though with a cautious distance between them.

"Here Ceo Powerful Locomotive sees the armies arrayed before him clearly for the first time. At this point he realizes that a frontal assault would be suicidal. Therefore he orders a strategic retreat," Darger commented.

"So our plan stipulates," Shrewd Fox said, a little smile playing on her face.

"Yes," Surplus said.

The armies remained static.

"With our forces in seeming disarray and thus easy to pick off and obliterate, the obvious thing for our enemies to do will be to charge forward in hot pursuit," Darger said.

"So one would think."

"There is no sensible alternative," Surplus agreed.

"But, teamed with a distrusted ally," Darger continued, "each army will be reluctant to pull into the lead, thus exposing their flank to a treacherous attack. Seeing in each other this unwillingness to engage with us, their leaders can only conclude that they have been betrayed. So each must inevitably turn upon the other."

"Inevitably, you say. Yes, it sounded good at the conference table. Let us see how it plays out in fact."

"Am I missing something here?" Surplus asked.

"We should move closer to the ceo," Shrewd Fox said, "so we can overhear what ensues."

The Dog Pack had no orders to follow in Powerful Locomotive's footsteps—but neither did they have orders *not* to do so. So Surplus nodded to Fire Orchid, and they led their crew closer.

At the very front and center of the massed Immortals, Ceo Powerful Locomotive sat atop his horse, his cane tucked under his arm, studying the enemy through the field glasses. The enemy armies continued immobile. When at last the ceo lowered the glasses, his face was demonic.

"Now he will sound the order to retreat," Darger murmured.

"Will he?"

"If he is at all rational," Surplus said, "he must."

Powerful Locomotive did not.

Instead, throwing aside his cane, he cried, "This will not work!" Then he galloped to the far flank of the vanguard, where White Squall sat waiting in her backhoe (elaborately detailed in Crossroads with red and yellow paint and gold trim) and gesticulated forcibly. She responded. Even at a distance, it was obvious that she disputed the wisdom of his orders. But the ceo cut her short with a wave of his arm that said, as clearly as words: Obey or die.

White Squall stood in the cab of her machine and shouted orders that could not be heard over the distance. Her rocket men ran to the front of the army and set up their Red Arrows. There was a pause as arcane rituals were performed. Then, as one, forty rockets screamed toward the enemy armies.

Surplus could hardly believe his eyes. "What the devil does he think he's doing? Has Powerful Locomotive lost his senses?"

"No," Shrewd Fox said, "he has remembered his duty. I was confident he would."

"The fool is overcompensating," Darger said. "He'll never win White Squall's love now."

"This is not about love."

Even as the rockets were in the air, arcing toward their targets, Cao White Squall's machines rumbled forward. The spiders, crushing wheels, and walking fire cannons predominated, but there were also wall openers, wolves, prismatic death sprayers, and giant metal crabs scattered among them. At their fore was White Squall in her scorpion-like backhoe. It was a sight to terrify anybody who saw it.

But though the rockets killed many soldiers and panicked a unit of leather-armored giant ground sloths that ran amok and trampled many more, the enemy troops were not terrified. The injured were rushed off to field hospitals, and the dead were cleared away. The runaway *Megatherium* were captured and calmed. A steady, disciplined cannonade began and did not cease.

Cannonballs flew and plowed into the earth, sending up geysers of dirt. A direct hit caused a spider to explode. A hole appeared in the armor of a walking fire cannon, and it veered off to the side, striding determinedly toward no known destination, its crew dead. Still, White Squall and her archaeologists drove forward, even as the cannon fire grew more concentrated.

"*C'est magnifique,*" Darger said. "*Mais ce n'est pas la guerre.*"

Surplus gripped his reins tightly. "Aubrey, dear friend, much though I esteem and admire you, this is no time to indulge in your penchant for cultural reference."

"The worst is yet to come," Shrewd Fox said. "Wait."

At that moment, as if her words were a prophecy, the machines hit the muddy ground midway between the armies and slowed. One of the crushing wheels swerved to avoid hitting a spider, slid out of control, and slowly toppled over on its side.

"What in heaven's name is happening?" Darger cried.

"During the night the enemy's sappers diverted a stream or three, as was only sensible. The water wouldn't show in the high grass, of course, but it would saturate the earth, making that section about as difficult to traverse as a bog."

"You knew this would be done?"

"I counted on it."

Now White Squall's backhoe was mired in the mud and unable to go any farther. Darger ground his teeth. "Oh, dear Lord," he groaned. Then he spun about to face Surplus. "Old friend, I . . . I cannot ask you to . . ."

"You don't need to ask," Surplus assured him. Addressing his mountain horse, he said, "Are you ready to ride into danger, Buttercup?"

"Hohhhhhh *hyesss*!"

Swiftly, Surplus rode to Ceo Powerful Locomotive's side, saluted, and said, "Sir! Requesting permission to rescue Cao White Squall."

Ceo Powerful Locomotive put down his binoculars. A fleeting look of relief appeared on his face only to be swallowed up by grim resolve almost as quickly as it had appeared. With a curt nod, the ceo said, "Granted."

An instant later, Surplus was speeding into the battle and cursing himself for a fool.

SURPLUS WAS halfway to the bogged-down machines when he realized that Fire Orchid was right behind him. He moved his mountain horse a little to the right to let her catch up and shouted, "What the blazes do you think you're doing?"

"If my husband is about to rescue some strange floozy, I want to be there. To make sure nothing happens."

"You madwoman! We're on a battlefield! People are shooting at us!" This last was inspired by a cannonball that sizzled through the air mere feet from his head.

"Yes, I agree. So romantic!"

Surplus had never seen Fire Orchid's hair so bright. It seemed to set all the battlefield aglow. But, keeping his head down low over Buttercup's neck, he focused all his thought on reaching Cao White Squall and as little as possible on the danger of his situation. The sooner they were out of this mess, the better.

It took forever, it took but an instant to reach the battered remains of the Division of Sappers and Archaeologists. Right in the middle of the scrapyard of machines stood White Squall atop her disabled backhoe, bellowing orders. At her direction, the operators of those few machines still operative—spiders, mostly—were retrieving as many of the crews of the disabled machines as they could and then retreating.

Cannonballs continued to fall about them.

Then Surplus had reached the backhoe. He was about to offer a rescue when Fire Orchid pushed her mountain horse between him and the cao and shouted, "Take my hand!"

With one last glance around to assure herself that there was no more she could do, White Squall allowed herself to be hauled up behind Fire Orchid. Then they were racing back toward the Immortals.

Surplus paused just long enough to haul a dazed-looking soldier from the ruins of his crushing wheel onto the mountain horse behind him and sped in pursuit of her.

BY THE time they rejoined the army, the Immortals were in full retreat.

Surplus dropped off his rescued soldier, and a medic rushed up to examine him. Meanwhile, Fire Orchid had already helped White Squall down and then retreated back into the Dog Pack, where she lurked as inconspicuously as it was possible for such a woman to do.

"My machines!" White Squall screamed at Powerful Locomotive in a fury. "You have destroyed my machines!" Without thinking, she raised a fist, and it was quite possible she would have struck the ceo had not Surplus jumped down from his mount in time to seize her from behind and whisper in her ear, "Think of the consequences, cao."

White Squall struggled out of his grip. Then she turned her back on her commander and strode off to rejoin what fragments of her division remained.

Powerful Locomotive stared after her sadly for the length of a breath and returned his attention to his army.

On the far side of the floodplain, the enemy armies were advancing again. But slowly and uncertainly. They moved forward with hesitation, and the edges of the armies wavered. Surplus rejoined the Dog Pack and said, "What have I missed?"

Before Darger could reply, Shrewd Fox said, "This is the payoff of decades of hatred and treachery, for in their hour of need the two nations cannot effectively work together. Memories of past atrocities are too bitter. Each army pursues us now, but cautiously. Half their attention is on their supposedly ally—which is why there is such a traffic of scouts in the land between the two. From here it is obvious that each is deliberately trying to lag behind the other. To cross the artificial marshes, they must close ranks, for the area left unflooded is not large. Yet they dare not. One hesitates; the other moves away. Forward motion slows to a halt. The armies turn to face each other. And now . . . now . . ."

The two enemy armies wheeled, flowed together, and the killing began.

Shrewd Fox laughed. "Oh, I have longed to see this day for so many, many years. This is better than—I find no comparisons. Better than glory, money, promotion, the most beautiful hour of autumn, the first day of spring after a long, hard winter. Better than food and drink and breath to a dying woman. See how they fall by the hundreds! This is the happiest day of my life."

"The destruction of White Squall's forces was part of your plan from the beginning, wasn't it?" Surplus said.

"Of course. The retreat had to look convincing. Our enemies are not stupid. They needed to think we had put our best effort into making a false retreat look like a real one. Otherwise, they would never have fallen into my trap," Shrewd Fox said. "Also, I have eliminated Powerful Locomotive as a liability. He risked everything in an act of bold and courageous folly, and he is not clever enough to convince the Hidden Emperor that it was done deliberately. The best he can hope for now is that I will beg the Hidden Emperor to let me take him on as my second-in-command."

"Why would you want to do a thing that like?"

"Have you ever broken a wild horse, Dog Warrior?"

"Well . . . not recently," Surplus admitted

Shrewd Fox almost smiled. "I have, many times. It is great sport to take a bone breaker of a stallion and make him dote upon you. Powerful Locomotive is a big man, strong and not overly burdened with intelligence. I have a fondness for his type. I will enjoy breaking him to my bit, spurs, and saddle."

"I see."

Darger, who had been sitting by silent during all this conversation, now said, "You are hiding something, Shrewd Fox."

"Am I? Oh, I suppose there's no need for secrecy now. The third thing I wanted from the Hidden Emperor, after being present for the humbling of my enemies and command over Powerful Locomotive, was to be chief executive officer not just of the Southern Army but of the entirety of his forces. With this victory, I am your commanding officer now, the both of you. Perfect Strategist, you would do well to remember that I will not tolerate your nonsense the way that Powerful Locomotive did. The familiarity with which you have been addressing me, for example, must cease immediately, never to be resumed, even in private. Do you understand me?"

Darger dipped his head. "Yes, Chief Executive Officer Shrewd Fox."

"And, Dog Warrior, tell your family no more gambling, no more stealing, no more extortion rackets. These are not things that are done in a well-regulated militia. Make sure they understand that. If they step out of line even once, I will cut off the left hand of the redheaded wench who fancies herself your wife. And your own left paw as well."

THE BATTLE took hours, and since the Immortals did not participate in the slaughter, at its conclusion they were the de facto winners. They simply waited until none of the surviving soldiers had the energy to fight any longer and then sent messengers under flags of truce to negotiate their capitulations.

After the surrenders of the two nations were accepted and the processing of their soldiers into the Hidden Emperor's army had begun, Darger took Surplus aside and said, "I want to thank you for your daring rescue of White Squall. I recognize that I mean nothing at all to her and that our relationship is one of convenience and opportunism only. And yet . . ."

"I quite understand," Surplus said. Inwardly, however, he was already preparing his defense for having put his arms about the cao and whispering in her ear. For he knew that, later tonight, Fire Orchid would confront him on the matter, putting the worst possible interpretation on those totally innocent acts.

Shortly thereafter, the Dog Pack escorted Darger on a tour of the battlefield. The ground was chewed up, and the broken remains of machines both simple and sophisticated, as well as the corpses of men and animals, were scattered about, seemingly at random. "What a dreadful waste," Surplus commented. Then, sternly, "Little Spider, put that down and get back up on your mountain horse. It is not fitting for a member of the Perfect Strategist's bodyguard to loot corpses."

Darger, as befit a dignitary, stared nobly off into the distance, pretending not to hear.

Little Spider opened her mouth to protest. Then she saw her Aunt Fire Orchid's expression and bent down to restore the dagger her magpie heart had fallen for. As she straightened from the fallen soldier's body, however, Surplus noticed a brief glint of metal and knew that she had left behind the knife's scabbard but slipped the dagger itself up her sleeve. He let it pass, though, for the sake of morale and family harmony.

And he made a mental note to pick up something similar from the battlefield for Terrible Nuisance. Because otherwise, he was sure, he would never hear the end of it.

14.

When Shrewd Fox was young, she went from country to country,
looking for a land worthy of her talents. The ruler of the Land South of
the Clouds had over a hundred sons by various wives and concubines, all of whom were flighty and worthless. Having heard her boast
that she could turn anyone into soldiers, he challenged her to do so
with his offspring. "Give me absolute authority over them," she said,
"and I will." When, on the first day of training, she ordered the young
men to form up in orderly lines, they laughed and mocked her. So she
had the two oldest immediately put to death.

Within a month, the king's sons were as disciplined a group of
soldiers as any in his land.

—STRANGE TALES OF THE SECOND WARRING STATES PERIOD

FREE HISTORICAL operas were performed in the city squares
every day for a week, and there were fireworks every night to
celebrate the arrival of peace and, not coincidentally, help reconcile the citizens of Opera to the sudden and unexpected change of
rulers. Political prisoners were freed from the jails, and notorious war
profiteers who abruptly found themselves without sponsors in the city
government were thrown in. An office to promote trade with provinces with which they were no longer at war was opened, and the Bu-
reau of Sabotage and Disease was closed. Competitive examinations
were announced for five full scholarships to the Infallible Physician's new medical college in Crossroads.

With the heartland nations of China conquered, the Hidden Emperor's holdings were now vaster than anything that had existed since
the fall of Utopia. Further, it was generally believed that the winds of
destiny filled his ships' sails and pushed upon his soldiers' backs, driving them forward and hindering all who would stand against him.

Those who thought so knew nothing of the bickering within his
inner circle. White Squall and Prince First-Born Splendor were no longer talking to each other, and so those generals who favored one or

the other of them had split into rival factions. Meanwhile, the demoted General Powerful Locomotive sulked and stewed under his new superior's control, while Shrewd Fox was apparently finding him more difficult to bring to heel than she had anticipated. The ceo, being a newcomer and an outsider, had no clique of her own, but she treated Powerful Locomotive's partisans as if they were hers, to their general disgruntlement. Only Darger floated serenely above all the petty politics, a friend to all and an enemy to none.

Or so it seemed.

There was no direct way for Darger to get to see Ceo Shrewd Fox, for she had appointed trusted officers from her old Three Gorges command to her personal staff and directed them to keep him away from her. But Darger had only to convince General Powerful Locomotive that such a meeting would help his cause—or causes, for he had newly added restoration of his lost rank to the attainment of White Squall as a primary goal—to slip effortlessly through her defenses.

"What is it now?" Shrewd Fox said without looking up from her writing.

The silk rugs and brass lanterns in Shrewd Fox's office were of the finest, as was the furniture. She sat behind a desk whose top was a thick slab of vat-grown walrus ivory, and her chair was a Utopian chrome and artificial leather antique. Anywhere else, such opulence would have been impressive; to find it inside a plain canvas tent was overwhelming.

"Ceo Shrewd Fox, I recognize that you distrust me and there is probably nothing to be done about that. But your understandable if misguided skepticism about my character should not prevent us from working together in amity. Remember that the Longhorn King of the Beautiful Country, when asked why he did not fire the head of his secret police, said that it was better that the miscreant be making water into the weeds from the shelter of the king's tent than for him to be standing in the weeds directing his animus inward."

"I underestimated you once. Never again."

"Yet I have not been dismissed as an advisor to the emperor. Why?"

Shrewd Fox poured sand over her document and looked up at last. "Your name terrifies our enemies and therefore you are useful. Could I strip the name from the body, rest assured that your corpse would be decorating a gutter at this very instant."

"Great ceo, there really is no need for such hostility!"

"Hostility? I rather like you. You remind me of myself. Looked at properly, my distrust is a compliment."

"If so, then surely an advisor whose cunning approaches your own is a resource to be cultivated."

"You are all tricks and illusion, Perfect Strategist—smoke and mirrors, straw men and empty cities. But, as I told the emperor, the next phase of this war will be to invade the Yellow Sea Alliance, and that is a power which is stronger than anything you have faced and not to be taken by surprise. This is a different sort of struggle than you are accustomed to. First we must seize South in order to have a base of operations. Then we will face armies that are collectively stronger than our own. So we will have to rely on our one great advantage—the fact that we have the Long River to our back and all the rich farmlands of central China under our control. Which means that provisioning our forces will be simple. The enemy, though formidable, cannot counter our army and defend its own farmlands at the same time. When they attack us in force, our rangers will burn their fields, granaries, and fishing boats. When they protect their farmers and fishermen, we will fall upon their scattered armies and take their cities. In this way, we will destroy the alliance's ability to feed itself. Of course, this will take several years and inflict great suffering on a tremendous number of people. Are you, who are famous for your bloodless though admittedly brilliant ruses, prepared to support that sort of war?"

Darger did not hesitate for even an instant. "Of course I am, great ceo. Because my mathematics prove that it is necessary."

"Now you're just trying to make me underestimate you again. Go."

PRINCE FIRST-BORN Splendor had commandeered the second floor of a hotel overlooking one of the squares where the free operas were being performed, so he could watch in comfort from its balcony. "What is this called?" he asked, scowling.

Sitting beside him, Darger accepted a cup of tea from a servant and said, "*The Rape of Nanking*. Nanking is a pre-Utopian name for South, the capital city of Commerce."

"I find it distressing to watch."

"It is about a distressing period in history."

"Then the period is not a fit subject for an opera. Art should be beautiful, not ugly. It should be uplifting and redemptive. Art reassures us that life is good and that, however bad things may look at the moment, everything works out for the best in the end."

"I would have said that in the end we all die, immortals included, and that all good things, not excluding the earth, the sun, and the universe, are transient as well. So that, logically, in the brief time allotted to us, we should be as kind to one another as is humanly possible and face the harsh facts of reality without fear or flinching. But then, as an immortal, I take the long view. Should you prefer entertainments whose sole purpose is to distract you from unpleasant truths, that is of course your choice."

"If I want ugliness and truth, I have only to return to the battlefield." Prince First-Born Splendor turned his chair around so that he faced away from the opera. "Speaking of truth, I find myself more and more distrusting your glib and endless reassurances. Particularly in light of Powerful Locomotive's disgrace."

"How can you doubt me? I engineered that disgrace solely to benefit you. Powerful Locomotive is now in no position to place you upon the Dragon Throne in the tragic case that our beloved emperor dies shortly after attaining it. That is half of what you wanted, and, to be honest, the more difficult half."

"I fail to see how that helps me. My personal happiness must necessarily come second to my duty to keep Southern Gate a free and independent state. If Powerful Locomotive never becomes emperor . . ."

"That is the beauty of our scheme. Ceo Shrewd Fox is an ambitious woman who, when the Hidden Emperor is murdered, will reflexively claim the throne for herself. Acting swiftly, however, Powerful Locomotive will denounce her as a regicide and execute her on the spot. An independent inquiry—which I shall lead—will find definitive proof that she was guilty. In the light of his heroic act, the general will then be the obvious choice to be made emperor by acclamation. This leaves only the two of us knowing the truth of what actually happened. Murdering us would draw suspicion back to the new emperor, so he will have no choice but to buy us off—me with great wealth and you with your nation's freedom. A plot so simple cannot possibly fail."

"Perhaps," Prince First-Born Splendor said dubiously. "But White Squall—"

"She is mad with jealousy. All that is needed now is to make her pliant and obedient."

"How?"

"I have plans." Darger lied. "Allow them some time to ripen and you shall see. In the meantime, have you spoken to the Hidden Emperor, as I requested?"

"Yes. He says that he will not meet with you because you are untrustworthy."

"I! Untrustworthy? Did he say why?"

"When I asked, he said that you would know."

"Yet I do not. I have examined my conscience and it is spotless. The entire situation is most peculiar," Darger said. He put down his empty glass, and a servant cleared it away.

THAT NIGHT, White Squall rode Darger sweaty. Then, rolling over so she could stare up at the fireworks, she berated him for his lack of success in making Prince First-Born Splendor the ambitious courtier she desired him to be.

"Madam, you do me a disservice. I have been working tirelessly on your behalf," Darger protested. "You were jealous of Ceo Shrewd Fox and demanded I get rid of her as a rival. So I did."

"She is still alive."

"It was not necessary for her to die, and to demand it now would be mere vindictiveness on your part." Darger felt about for the blanket that had been cast aside in the throes of their passion. They were in the sheltered rooftop garden of an inn that Darger had claimed for his own. But there was no getting around the fact that it was just a little late in the year to be outside at night without any clothing.

"She has put me in command of the Division of Chimeras and Resurrected Beasts, overseeing the saber-toothed cavalry, *Megatherium,* feathered theropods, and whatever those loathsome things with the poisoned quills are. Meanwhile, the Division of Sappers and Archaeologists has been folded into the infantry. Surely *that* merits death."

"The fact that your new position as chief animal officer is no lower than your old rank strongly suggests that Shrewd Fox's respect for you remains undiminished."

"I am overseeing filthy, disgusting animals."

"Simply pretend that your charges are smellier, less tractable, and more bloodthirsty versions of the machines you love. It is only a temporary position, after all. Once China has been reunited, I have no doubt that the Hidden Emperor will put you to work digging up more of your abominable machines of destruction."

"I don't like the way my prince moons about after her."

"That is neither here nor there. Shrewd Fox is now obsessed with Powerful Locomotive—everyone sees that but him—and in consequence, Prince First-Born Splendor's flirtations stand revealed as weak attempts to make you jealous."

"Jealous! Of that toadstool? I feel almost as sorry for Powerful Locomotive for having such a creature pursuing him as I do for myself for having such a lackluster thing as you for a champion."

"Examine my history, madam. I have been your truest and most vigorous friend through all of this."

"So it would seem. Yet I cannot help thinking that there was more to all this than philanthropy."

"You blackmailed me, remember? How much more motivation than that do I need?"

"I WAS a fool to have ever listened to you in the first place." General Powerful Locomotive lifted a bowl of clear liquid to his lips and drank. He was sitting on a bluff overlooking the river and the fleet at rest upon it. Since he had brought only one chair, Darger was forced to stand. "Now I am disgraced and demoted, and my chances of winning White Squall's love have vanished into the past, never to return. I gaze upon her today as I might a star and see only an unearthly beauty that is completely beyond my reach."

"I remind you that your disgrace was your own doing. Had you followed my plan, as both the Hidden Emperor and I relied upon your doing . . ."

"Yes, yes, yes. I have told myself as much a thousand times and more." Powerful Locomotive raised the bowl and sipped again. "But how was I to know that a plan so transparently ludicrous would actually work? Only an idiot could have come up with it. Only a fool would have followed it. Yet it worked. Incredible."

"What is that you are drinking? Not alcohol, I hope! I warn you, sir, that if you are becoming a drunkard I must wash my hands of your fate."

"What? Oh, no, it is just a pedagogical broth." Powerful Locomotive offered the bowl for examination. "In times of dejection and despair, it is my custom to drown my sorrows in learning. It makes me a little distracted, of course, but better educated afterward."

"That is, I suppose, admirable. But I must ask you to put the bowl aside and give me your full attention. We are finally making progress. Just yesterday, White Squall told me that she felt sorry for you because you were being courted by Shrewd Fox, a woman she feels is unworthy of you."

"White Squall felt sorry for me?" Powerful Locomotive said, astonished. "Shrewd Fox is courting me?"

"Yes and yes."

"How could this be? I hadn't noticed the ceo displaying any particular warmth toward me."

"That is because—and I say this with all due respect, General, but it is the only way to get your attention—in matters of the human heart, you are a self-involved lunkhead. If you doubt my word that Shrewd Fox is interested in you, simply give her a rose—just one! offhandedly!—and watch her eyes closely. You will see bloom within them the expression which in a woman means, 'I have you now!' "

"This is a great wonder to me." Powerful Locomotive looked down at his bowl and then, holding it out to the side, emptied its contents onto the ground.

"You are wasting your broth!" Darger cried in alarm.

"It's only calculus. I can always pick it up later, should I have need of it." As always when he was deepest in thought, Powerful Locomotive twisted his mouth into an expression of distaste. "If Ceo Shrewd Fox is interested in me, then I shall play along. That should give you many an opening to engineer her downfall and my restoration to her rank."

"Really, General, there is no reason to make an already-confusing situation more complicated."

"I will give her a rose, as you advised. What color do you suggest it be?"

"Blood red is traditional," Darger said sourly. "But in this case, I would go with black."

AT THE end of the week, the Immortals marched and sailed from Opera downriver to Weedy Lake, a place of no particular interest other than its strategic importance as the last fortified town in Twin Cities before the border with Commerce, southernmost of the four states in the Yellow Sea Alliance. There they stopped, for they were not officially at war with either Commerce or the alliance. Though everybody knew it was only a matter of time.

As he had sailed in, so Darger sailed out, save that this time he did not have Shrewd Fox for company and that he spent a very long time by himself, thinking. He noticed, though barely, that Surplus stayed at a moderate distance, keeping an eye on him and shooing away anyone who would disturb his concentration.

For hour after hour, the coastline flowed by, here a mountain and there a town, like so many images on a scroll. Only the other boats on the river were stationary, or so it seemed. Once, Little Spider slipped past Surplus's guard and, crouching next to Darger's chair, said, "What's wrong?"

Darger looked down at the imp. "I am experiencing a dark night of the soul. Also seeking to find a way to keep not only myself but you and your entire family alive. So I will thank you to go away now and leave me to my labor."

"Oh. I thought maybe you needed cheering up."

"No."

"I brought you something anyway. It comes from the Land of Heroes—that's where you were born, right? It's old." Little Spider produced a silver hip flask.

Darger took the thing and examined it closely. "This is Victorian work, and particularly fine of its kind. It's a museum piece. How did you come into possession of such a thing?"

Smiling impishly, Little Spider mimed applying rouge to her cheeks. "I just went into the city collections in Crossroads and carried it out."

Darger stared at the flask so long and so hard that he didn't even notice when he ceased to see it at all. Nor did he notice when Surplus appeared to send Little Spider below as punishment for disturbing him. He was still thinking when the houseboat arrived at last at the thronged and clamorous docks of Weedy Lake.

It took hours of waiting before the houseboat was given its brief slot at the docks and Darger was able to disembark.

"You look almost cheerful," Surplus said to him.

"Indeed, I am feeling better than I have felt for some time."

"You have a plan—that much is obvious. What will you do?"

"What else is there to do in as dire a situation as the one we find ourselves embroiled in? I will call a meeting."

DARGER HAD taken to the custom of gathering for conversation in teahouses with all the enthusiasm and snobbery of a convert. He sought out the best teahouses in town, compared them, and then, when he had chosen one, examined its facilities with care. Finally, he booked a private room with a view down into a courtyard garden where autumn trees had just begun their annual molt and sent out invitations. At the appointed time, he stood by the door and greeted each of his invited guests as they entered: Prince First-Born Splendor, Cao White Squall, General Powerful Locomotive, and the Dog Warrior, who came accompanied by his second-in-command and occasional wife, Fire Orchid. Shrewd Fox had also been invited but declined to come.

A young woman wearing a plain but respectable robe and a cheap-looking necklace of colored glass beads brought them tea. As she was filling the glasses, Darger said, "I have made all of you various promises over the past several months. Lately, as I am sure you know, my fortunes have fallen. I am no longer summoned to the Hidden Emperor's side, and since Shrewd Fox's elevation in rank, I no longer have the trust and ear of the chief executive officer."

There was a slight shifting of position and an exchange of near glances among his auditors.

"We didn't need to be told this," Powerful Locomotive said.

"Oh? I thought it only polite to let you know." Darger took a sip of tea. "In any case, necessary or not, I called you all together to assure you that all my promises will be kept—every one and without exception. So you need not worry on my account."

For a long, still moment nobody spoke. At last, General Powerful Locomotive said, "Well, go on. What else?"

"Else?" Darger said politely.

"I mean, is that . . . *all* you had to say?"

"It is. Thank you, everyone, for coming. Thank you for listening. I release you now to your many pressing affairs."

As the others left, some grumbling, it seemed likely, under their breaths about the time they had just wasted, Darger casually said to the girl who had brought them tea and was now beginning to clear away their glasses, "Young lady. Please stay a moment. There is something I must say to you."

The young woman lingered as requested. When they were alone, she said, "Sir? What would you do with me?"

Darger slid from his chair and knelt before her. "There is nothing I can do, Your Majesty," he said, "save obey."

The servitor stood up straighter, the loose gown flattening somewhat against its wearer's chest, making the illusion of breasts disappear. The delicate oval face shifted, broadened, became that of a young man. "Only eight people have ever known I was a face dancer," the Hidden Emperor said, "and seven of them are dead."

Darger chose to let the implicit threat pass unacknowledged. "I was once told that Powerful Locomotive's parents had the prenatal gene work done on him in the hope that he might become a spy. I see now that I should have reflected on how much more useful such an ability might prove to be for a ruler."

"Stand. Then sit," the Hidden Emperor said, throwing himself into a chair. "Nobody wants to bring the emperor bad news. As a result, I have to go and dig it out myself." He favored Darger with a sly grin. "I believe you are about to tell me that Shrewd Fox is a threat to my rule."

"No more so than any powerful subordinate and less so than most, for her faction is small and her hold over Powerful Locomotive's faction is weak. Also, it must be taken into account that she is a brilliant strategist who serves you well."

"She doesn't speak so highly of you."

"I am her one blind spot."

"Tell me how you discovered"—the Hidden Emperor waved a hand up and down the cheap gown he wore—"my little secret."

"Among those who have not met you, Majesty, you are famous for being unknown. But among your inner circle, the most common observation is that you know things that a ruler could not possibly know—because, as you rightly observed, there are things no rational man would dare to report. In Crossroads, a junior member of the Dog Pack fell ill of the plague and upon recovery amused herself by impersonating a joyous one. This allowed her surprising freedom in acquiring objects that did not belong to her. One very swiftly got used to having a joyous one present and, after a time, stopped noticing them. They were all the same, after all, and seemingly incurious.

"This led me to reflect upon how similar a good servant was to such a being—unobtrusive, ubiquitous, seemingly incurious. All servants are in one way or another programmed or conditioned not to eavesdrop. But a face dancer could get around that by sending away his target's most trusted servant and then impersonating him or her. You, of course, have spies to do that for you, but the spymaster still controls the flow of information. The problem has merely been shifted from one locale to another.

"I came to the conclusion that you were acting as your own spy. Which meant that if I wanted to speak with you, all I had to do to draw you out of hiding was to schedule a meeting of such people as would make you wonder if some traitorous conspiracy were being contemplated."

The Hidden Emperor lightly clapped his hands. "Well reasoned. So now that you have me, what do you intend to do? Kill me, perhaps?"

"I would not dare attempt such a thing, Majesty."

A sardonic note entered the emperor's voice. "Because you are so loyal, you mean?"

"No, Majesty. Simply because a ruler who would repeatedly place himself beyond reach of his bodyguards must surely have some extremely lethal weaponry in his possession."

"Then what do you intend?"

"I wish merely to ask you why I have lost your trust."

The Hidden Emperor tapped his fingers on the table, thinking. Then he said, "Tell me about the plot to murder me and place Powerful Locomotive on the throne."

Darger's blood ran cold. But he merely said, "Surely you are not going to believe such nonsense, Majesty."

The emperor's eyes were cold. "I heard it from your own mouth."

"I am as capable of nonsense as any man! I first narrated this murderous fantasy to Prince First-Born Splendor in the countryside outside of Brocade to trick him into signing a treaty advantageous to Your Majesty. I told him a parable about a traveler and wolves. Then I asked him if he was willing to get blood on his hands, if it meant saving the lives of thousands of his subjects. . . ." Speaking as convincingly as he could—and he could be extremely convincing when his life was on the line—Darger laid out the history of his deceits and the convoluted romantic tangle that had been, all against his will, lover by lover, thrust upon him. And though he may have withheld some small details—his sleeping with White Squall, for instance—he scrupulously adhered to the absolute truth in his account.

The telling took a long time. When Darger was done, the Hidden Emperor said, "I would have expected a more successful resolution of these various romantic desires from the Perfect Strategist."

"Remember, Majesty, that these are not matters of military strategy, where my skill and judgment are paramount, but human interrelationships, of which no man is a master. I was forced to tell one or two lies in order to keep your best subordinates from killing one another. But keep them in line I did! All of this was done in your service, Majesty, and in the service of your destiny to conquer and rule China the Great."

"Hmmm." The emperor pondered all he had heard in silence for a time. Then he said, "It does make sense of much that had seemed inexplicable."

"The important thing for you to know is that none of the people involved actively desired your demise. They were simply caught up in webs of fantasy and moonshine I wove for them."

The Hidden Emperor asked several questions, probing for inconsistencies in Darger's account. He found none, for there were none there to find. Nor did Darger have to resort to invention, for the plain unvarnished facts were irrational enough that no sane man could have doubted them. At last, the emperor said, "You seem to be telling the truth."

"There is a time and a place for lies, Majesty, but this is not it. To you, I dare speak only the truth."

"The story you told me about your being an immortal and your long years of study. In which camp does it belong?"

"Majesty, I will speak to you frankly. My Utopian origins, my immortality, my studies, the centuries spent in the desert with the Dog Warrior, my determination that China must be restored, and my discovery that you were the perfect vessel for that destiny—all these are true. Particularly the last. Every time you listened to me, you prospered. But when you did not, your fortunes still prospered, though not as spectacularly. Had I put myself in the service of any other king who then utilized my genius as sparingly as you have, he would by now be long dead. Yet you remain and your cause moves forward. It is even possible that you would have reached this point without my assistance—though not, I'll warrant, nearly so quickly."

The Hidden Emperor nodded, possibly involuntarily. "The question is," he said, "what should I do about you?"

"You will do as you wish."

The Hidden Emperor waited. "And?" he said at last.

"That's all."

That sly smile returned to the emperor's face. "That was the right answer. You are still out of favor, but you may live. For now."

THE AFTERNOON had grown late while Darger was in the teahouse. He sought out Surplus and found his friend with the Dog Pack on a grassy expanse outside the city, taking turns practicing equestrian stunts.

"Watch this," Surplus said and, leaping into Buttercup's saddle, urged his mount to a full gallop. Meanwhile, on the far side of the sward, Fire Orchid did the same with her own mountain horse, Dragonfly.

Straight toward each other the two noble beasts ran at full speed, neither veering away, until it seemed they must inevitably collide. Then, at the last possible instant, Dragonfly crouched so low to the ground that her belly grazed the grass and Buttercup leaped high over her, so that they passed under and over each other without touching.

Everybody in the Dog Pack cheered. Fire Orchid, glowing with exertion, trotted her mountain horse over to Darger and said, "Did you catch the sexual subtext to the stunt? Next time I want to be on top. Don't you blush. It's okay—we're married."

"No, we're not," Surplus said, bringing Buttercup to a stop nearby.

Intense Lotus clapped her hands for attention. "Everybody! Today you learned the basic moves. Tomorrow we start combining them. First thing after breakfast, I'll mark out a circle and we'll all hammer stakes into it in place of a dressage fence. Then two riders will race their mountain horses around the outside and two around the inside, leaping up and over and down and under .in alternation each lap. When you've got that down, I'll give all the riders swords. So then the drill will be: up and over, outside rider takes a swing at the head of the inside rider, who ducks; down and under, inside rider takes a swing at the head of the outside rider, who ducks. This will look spectacular but obviously requires lots of practice."

"That is good as far as it goes," Surplus said critically. "But once a sword is drawn, it must see combat. So let's make that: outside rider swings, inside rider swings, and third time the swords clash. If it can be done in such a way that sparks fly, so much the better." Then, as an afterthought, "And use cheap swords—at these speeds nobody will know the difference."

"Your first suggestion is good," Intense Lotus said. "Your second is insulting. Next thing, you will be telling me how to shortchange shopkeepers."

Several of the Dog Pack snickered. But Fire Orchid silenced them with a look.

"Domesticity suits you," Darger said as he and Surplus walked away from the Dog Pack for a little private talk.

"Fire Orchid and I are not—"

"I never said that you were. Why in the world are you putting together a stunt-riding act, of all things?"

"It was the only way I could think of to keep the family out of trouble," Surplus said. "If they're not doing something, they have a tendency to go out and . . . do things. Also, it's a good way to draw a nice, dense crowd. One where we can send in our pickpockets and clean up. Not that I intend to let that happen while we're under Shrewd Fox's scrutiny and probation."

They walked on for a bit. Then Darger said, "I have spoken with the Hidden Emperor."

"And?"

"We had a free and frank exchange of viewpoints."

"As bad as that? Oh, dear."

"There were glimmers of light here and there. I did manage to engineer a partial reconciliation, and I am almost certain that the emperor does not intend to kill us. But he no longer believes his ultimate success relies upon our support. Subsequently, his patronage of us hangs by a thread."

"And our identities as near-godlike immortals?"

"Intact," Darger said. "Though who knows to what degree the Hidden Emperor ever really believed in it."

"Well, it sounds as though you've played as good a game as anybody could have, given the strange cards we were dealt."

Darger ducked his head to acknowledge the compliment. "Just make sure that everybody remains ready to leave at a moment's notice. If and when the Hidden Emperor decides to turn on us, we will have no time to prepare and only minutes in which to act."

15.

"There is a price for everything," the Perfect Strategist said, "and that price must be paid, if not by the debtor then by his creditor. Nowhere in heaven or on earth is there to be found such a thing as a free lunch."

—THE SAYINGS OF THE PERFECT STRATEGIST

THREE WEEKS into the siege of South, Surplus said, "This grows stale."

He and Darger were on a boat on the river, just out of enemy cannon range, mountain watching. Far to one side was Curling Dragon Mountain and far to the other was Crouching Tiger Mountain, both gleaming in the twilight. With sunset, the clouds that gave Purple-Gold Mountain its name were gathering about its peak. The high-walled city of South huddled below it, lamps and torches glowing peaceably in the shadows, as if the war were nothing but a distant rumor. But on the mountain slopes above, pinpricks of light sparkled as riflemen fought a desperate skirmish rendered silent and griefless by distance.

His friend nodded agreement. "Worse, it eats up the autumn. We have only so much time before the cold weather sets in and we're faced with the unpleasant choice of retreating to Weedy Lake to wait for spring—which gives the Yellow Sea Alliance further time to prepare against us—or conducting a winter war, with all the miseries of cold and ice and difficulties of travel that the season entails."

"If only White Squall still had her machines! Say what you will about the morality of employing such grotesque violations of the natural order, they were a demoralizing sight for an army to see bearing down upon it. With my own eyes, I've witnessed entire cities abandoned out of fear of them."

"She has a handful of spiders left and a halfway-serviceable crushing wheel," Darger observed. "Also a portable bridge."

"That is hardly enough. Numbers count. What is needed is an endless hell horde so terrifying as to strike despair into the heart of the most stalwart defender."

"I wonder . . ." A strange gleam came into Darger's eye. "Everyone save you and I sees Fire Orchid's family only as petty criminals and a minor nuisance, when actually they are the most brilliant set of precision tools two gentlemen of our profession could wish for."

"This is true. Exactly whose services were you thinking of calling upon?"

"Those of Gentle Mountain."

"The puppeteer? Oh! Oh, of course! Yes, that's a brilliant plan."

"The only question," Darger said, "is how are we going to convince Ceo Shrewd Fox to adopt it?"

"My dear friend, you astound me. You are like the sailor who has swum almost to shore yet drowns in a foot of water for failing to stand up, or the marathon runner who pauses just before the finish line to contemplate what to do about the tape. Obviously, by making her think it was her own idea."

DESPITE HIS name, Gentle Mountain was not a large and kindly man but a lean fellow with the hard face of an assassin and a vivid white scar from a long-ago street fight where his opponent had tried with near success to cut his throat. To look at him was to suspect the worst. But in truth he was an amiable soul who cared for nothing so much as his art and was only an outlaw from a sense of family obligation. So he threw himself into the new project with tremendous energy and enthusiasm.

"You are corrupting the family," Fire Orchid said.

"Is that possible?" Surplus asked.

"Don't talk so sassy. This job you gave Gentle Mountain makes him too happy. He wakes up thinking about it and he works all day on nothing else. Predatory Hibiscus has to force him to eat, he is so caught up in it. He is all the time singing!"

"Well, he is an artist, after all."

"He has all the family helping him. He told me that he would do this work for free!"

"Ah," Surplus said. "I understand your concern now. Artists often say such ridiculous things—and act upon them, too, if they are not protected from themselves. It is up to their friends and family to see that they come to no harm."

"You will take care of that, then?"

"Of course. But in return, when negotiations with Shrewd Fox begin, you must keep Gentle Mountain far away from her."

"I will do the negotiations. I think you are not dishonest enough for this kind of work."

THE ARMY encampment was like a city with canvas tents instead of buildings. It had broad avenues with streets leading off of them, like a city, and was organized into neighborhoods as well, some residential and others concentrating on specialized services, like cook tents, medical facilities, or corrals for the animals. Surplus chose the locale for the planned show with care: an open square within earshot of Ceo Shrewd Fox's tent, backed by a maze of interlocking hospital tents, some of which were tall enough that the props needed for the big surprise could be hidden in cul-de-sacs created by the larger wards.

There, the Dog Pack suddenly appeared one afternoon, with the prefabricated parts of a stage. These fit together swiftly. Poles were lashed to the stage's sides and, hauling on ropes, the crew erected a puppet theater that was as bright as a child's dream.

It all went up in a flash.

Soldiers were already gathering when two musicians—Terrible Nuisance and his aunt, Predatory Hibiscus—rattled an attention-getting tattoo on drums and then picked up flute and lyre and began to play. Vicious Brute stepped forward and, as the square rapidly filled with gawkers, announced in his most stentorian voice, "The Dog! Warrior's! Gallop! To the City! Of Peace! The Raising! Of the Flag! Of China! And the Joy! Of the Council! Of Eight! Plus! White Squall's! Attack! Upon the City! With Monsters!"

Vicious Brute stepped away from the theater, and the play began.

The show that followed did, admittedly, take certain liberties with

the historical truth. But what did that matter when the equestrian puppets of the Dog Pack, led by the Dog Warrior and his flame-haired
bride, were rocking up and down in such a splendid imitation of
riders at full gallop? Or when their battle with pursuing survivors of
the Mountain Horses army was so exciting? Or when the ambush by
radioactive mutants from the ancient power plants came as such a
shock? Or when the incident wherein, laughing, the Fire Orchid puppet turned its back on the audience and flashed its breasts at the Dog
Warrior indelibly burned the unseen image into the minds and imag-
inations of its audience? Such small embellishments were needed to
liven up an otherwise drab and unconvincing narrative.

Puppetry was an adult art form, of course. But Surplus noted children here and there in the crowd—a vendor boy with a tray of moon-
cakes for sale, a delivery girl who burrowed through the sea of legs
to the front and sat down upon an overturned five-gallon jug of herbal
wine she had been conveying to the hospital, a few others. Their eyes
glowed. For an instant, Surplus saw into the future, centuries after he
was gone, when he would survive as a shadow in the minds of children, a legend they would for a time believe in and then, as they ma-
tured, grow out of. He did not know how he felt about that.

But now the puppet Dog Pack came at last to the city of Peace.
They ran their ruse on the Council of Seven (the slapstick here was
entirely the puppeteer's invention), and when, at the climax of the
scene, the Dog Warrior ordered the flag run up, a full-size flag of China
lofted into the air on a pole above the puppet stage, prompting cheers
from all.

With such a chaotic scene in the square, anybody less observant
than Surplus would not have noticed when Ceo Shrewd Fox came out
of her tent to see what all the noise was about. But when it mattered,
Surplus could be very observant indeed. He waited until the ceo, satisfied that nothing untoward was happening, started to turn away, and
then hooked two fingers in his mouth and whistled shrilly.

At this signal, a spider larger than the puppet theater burst from a
side alley, legs thrashing, and rushed at the crowd with a mechanical
roar. Those soldiers nearest it surged back in alarm. Some screamed.

Then laughter washed through the square as it became obvious
that the monster was made of cloth with black-painted bamboo
legs and worn like a costume by its puppeteer. The *clack-clack-clack*

of the cunningly jointed legs—cranked by the puppeteer—merged with the buzzing of a bullroarer spun by Terrible Nuisance to create a noise that convincingly made the tiny people of the puppet city cower in fear of this terrifying threat.

Then a crushing wheel, also constructed of cloth over a light frame, made its appearance, to general laughter and screams of delight.

"You! Puppeteer!" Ceo Shrewd Fox cried. "Stop this performance at once and come immediately to my tent. I wish to speak with you."

The show stopped. The crowd turned. Before Gentle Mountain could step out from behind the puppet theater, Fire Orchid materialized at the ceo's elbow. "It is really me you wish to talk with. The puppet troupe is made up of my family, and I am its head. As well as its agent."

"Agent? There is no money involved. You are soldiers and sworn to the service of the Hidden Emperor."

"Oh. I see. Do you have a Division of Puppetry and Marionettes? I do not think so. But if you do, then take up this matter with its commander. My family and I are not soldiers but rather independently contracted mercenaries, paid monthly on a week-to-week agreement, which we are free to abrogate at any time simply by forfeiting whatever pay we are currently owed."

"What?! No military commander in her right mind would agree to such an extraordinary arrangement."

"We had twenty mountain horses, which Powerful Locomotive wanted very much. Also, nobody thought much of having my family among their own troops because we look like such a bad sort. Also, we had a very good agent."

"All this is true, great ceo," Surplus said.

"Shut up, sweetie-puss. This is girl business." Addressing Ceo Shrewd Fox, Fire Orchid said, "We will go to your tent like you said and discuss this. Because I am so cooperative."

Time passed. At last, Fire Orchid emerged from her commanding officer's tent. "Well?" Surplus said, taking her aside, where they would not be overheard.

"She is a very tough negotiator. I wanted to keep the copyright on Gentle Mountain's designs, but she would not give in on that because she said she might want to use them again. However, she ended up offering very good money for his services, with a little more on the side for the family to work as his assistants. So I agreed to her terms."

"No, no, the plan I mean. What about the plan?"

"Oh, that. Yes, she thinks it's her own idea, just like you said."

The square exploded with applause. On the stage, Gentle Mountain emerged from behind the puppet theater to take bow after bow. Smiling as he was, he hardly looked sinister at all.

"As soon as things have returned to normal, we'll have to do this again," Surplus said. "This is a perfect crowd for the family's pickpockets—thronged and not at all on guard."

Fire Orchid looked away without saying anything.

"You *didn't* let them work, did you?"

"No, of course not. Well, maybe a little."

"What? Fire Orchid, you gave me your word! I told you that Shrewd Fox had warned me about this. If one of our people had been caught, we'd all be in serious trouble."

Fire Orchid put on her innocent face. "Oops," she said.

THE DAY began with a deep rumbling like distant thunder. Half of it was drums and the other half soldiers lifting and dropping makeshift weights—some of them large stones, others sections of log—onto hard ground and then raising the weights using block-and-tackle arrangements and letting them fall again, over and over, until the earth shook. More soldiers joined in the effort, and more, so that the rumbling grew.

Black figures bulged up out of the darkness—giant spiders, their ebon legs lashing. Rising up behind them came the eerie sight of row after row of crushing wheels. Dimly glimpsed behind them were massive walking figures, from which occasionally erupted gouts of flame.

From Surplus's perspective the puppet machines looked terrifying. He tried to imagine them as seen by the besieged citizens of South: One moment the horizon was dim and flat in the predawn murk. Then came the rolling thunder of countless giant machines, building and building until black blisters popped up, one after the other, by the hundreds. More spiders, clearly, than anyone had suspected ever existed. Behind which came endless machines for which they did not even have names. All converging upon a city that had no idea how to defend against them.

These were the weapons the citizens of South had heard about in terrible detail and been reassured no longer existed. Yet here they were.

It must, Surplus concluded, look like the end of the world.

Standing on the sidelines beside Surplus, Darger said, "I know now how Shrewd Fox must have felt seeing her plan to win the Battle of Three Armies being fobbed off as my own. I feel strangely unhappy about letting her have the credit for this."

"I, too, am no fan of ironic justice," Surplus said. "Particularly since, on reflection, we seem to have experienced more than our share of it. But consider, Aubrey, that a distressing lack of public admiration is the confidence trickster's lot in life. Our very best illusions pass for reality until that moment of cold lucidity when the mark realizes that he has been sheared—and by then we are too far away to bask in the applause of an appreciative, if impoverished, audience. Which, moreover, is rarely anxious to trumpet its own humiliation. This is simply the way things are."

"Too true. Still, I suppose we must suffer for our art."

All the while they two talked, the giant puppet machines created by Gentle Mountain slowly advanced upon the city. In fact, they advanced so slowly that it seemed they would never actually get there. As, indeed, they could not, under penalty of shattering the illusion that they were anything more than cloth stretched over bamboo frameworks.

But now a party emerged from the Gate of China, the oldest and most massive of South's city gates, bearing a flag of parley. Ceo Shrewd Fox, who had been awaiting this very thing, dispatched a delegation to negotiate with them.

"Did you know," Surplus asked, "that when it was originally built, during the Ming Dynasty, the Gate of China was called Gathering Treasure Gate? It was renamed when South became the capital city following the fall of the Qing Dynasty, because the Qing capital of North had an identically titled city gate. The older name seems to me much more auspicious."

"You are as good as a guidebook! However did you become so knowledgeable on such matters?"

Ceo Shrewd Fox's delegation, halfway to the Gate of China, dismounted. So too did the delegation from South. Both groups converged. Words were exchanged.

"I am in China, and so of course I read every history book I can get my paws on. I am surprised you do not do the same."

"For me, literature is all. Give me a volume of Wang Wei's poetry and I am good for the evening." Striking a pose, Darger declaimed:

In my old age I grow calmer.
Knowing little of the world's affairs,
I do not worry how things will turn out.
My quiet mind makes no cunning plans.
I dwell within the woods I love;
Pine-sweet breezes rustle my robes.
Mountain moonlight fills my lute,
Mocking what learning I have left.
If you ask what makes one rich or poor
Hear the fisherman's voice float to shore.

To which he swiftly added, "I read history as well, of course. But it is weak tea by comparison."

Below the city walls, the two delegations remounted and rode toward South as one group. The gates opened for them. They eddied, entered, disappeared.

"Your poem is good stuff," Surplus said, "and I am glad to have heard it. But it cannot compare to a rousing account of the rise and fall of the Mongol Empire."

"*De gustibus non est disputandum*, my friend. Of taste and scent, no argument. We shall simply have to agree to disagree."

They were thus pleasantly conversing when the flags of South and the Yellow Sea Alliance came down from the Gate of China, to be replaced by a familiar red flag with yellow stars.

The world went silent.

In the distance, flimsy cloth structures collapsed in upon themselves.

The Hidden Emperor had taken another city.

———

IT HAD been months since Surplus had entered a conquered city where the mood was as dark as it was in South, and those earlier cities had been brutalized by Powerful Locomotive. "I fail to understand," he said. "The terms that Cco Shrewd Fox extended to South were generous, the Immortals were informed that there was to be no looting, and a siege that promised to be long and unpleasant came to a painless end. In the days since, every promise made in the name of the Hidden Emperor has been kept. Why should our conquest be regarded as a tragedy?"

"Why are you asking me this?" his guide said. "I am only a guide." They were riding beasts such as Surplus had never seen before—part reindeer, part horse, and part otter at a guess—with elaborately curlicued antlers that had been painted red, yellow, and orange. They were spirited creatures and yet comfortable saddle animals, a credit to whoever had designed them. "You hired me to take you to Emperor Sun's mausoleum—that I can do. If you want to know its height above sea level, details of its history, or what materials went into its making, I can tell you those things and much more. But I am no political analyst. For such questions, you should refer to an expert."

"But you live here and presumably have much in common with your fellow citizens. Further, I have yet to see a cheerful and optimistic face upon a native—and that includes you. So it seems likely that you understand the source of your own malaise. Finally, I am prepared to tip you five grams of silver for the information."

"Do you honestly expect me to expound upon such a sensitive matter for a mere fifteen grams of silver?" the guide said.

"No, but I am prepared to go as high as ten."

"Done!" The guide was silent for a moment, then said, "The Yellow Sea Alliance is officially a partnership of equals. But everybody knows that three of the four partners are client states subservient to the cruel and absolute rule of the City and State of North. North tells East Mountain, South River, and Commerce what it expects of its parners. If North is not satisfied, it punishes them. And North is very hard to satisfy."

"How can such an unequal alliance hold together?"

"Fear," said the guide. "North collects tribute from the other three nations and uses it to maintain an army greater than all of theirs combined. It is also better equipped and trained and has a chief executive officer, Noble Tiger, who has rarely lost a battle. But North never does its own dirty work if it can be avoided. So if South River displeases North, East Mountain is told to send in troops to dole out punishment. And if that punishment is insufficiently harsh, Commerce is ordered to send its troops to punish East Mountain. In this way, North keeps its own armies strong and its tributary nations divided.

"In a moment of panic, South surrendered to you invaders. That was a bad mistake, for now everyone knows that the combined armies of South River and East Mountain, along with those Commerce forces that were not billeted in South, will be sent to inflict suffering upon us for that deed."

"You hardly had any choice—or so it was thought at the time," Surplus said.

"North does not care. Their philosophy of rule is to be so disproportionately savage that all sensible people will fear to disobey them. That is why the citizens of South are in despair. We would rise up against you, except that it would do us no good. Even if we killed every soldier you have, North would still order the city sacked and plundered and its walls torn down. So why bother?"

"Surely such a strategy must in the long run—ah! Here we are." They had arrived at the square at the foot of the mausoleum, whose buildings ran up the mountainside of Purple-Gold.

Aubrey Darger was waiting at the bottom of the steps leading to the first gate. When Surplus had paid off his guide and told her to wait, he said, "Are you ready for the confrontation?"

"As ready as I'll ever be."

"Then let's not keep Shrewd Fox waiting."

THE EMPEROR'S mausoleum was like all such places: large, imposing, and austere, with a wearying number of steps to be climbed before anything could be reached. Darger and Surplus found Ceo Shrewd Fox alone in the tomb, hands clasped behind her back, contemplating Emperor Sun's coffin. It was of white marble with a carving of the emperor asleep upon its top, dressed in surprisingly plain clothing.

"I am thinking of having you clapped in chains." Though Ceo Shrewd Fox did not turn, it was clear she was addressing them both.

"I have done nothing illegal, forbidden, or even immoral," Darger said. "Believe me, I would have noticed."

"Nor I."

"You have been spreading rumors that the Puppet Army stratagem was yours."

Surplus smoothly said, "To the contrary, Ceo Shrewd Fox. The rumors have been spreading themselves."

The ceo turned, scowling. "I am going to regret asking you to explain yourself, aren't I?"

"Not at all. In the Land of the Green Mountains of the West, my birth nation, our national hero, the Great Steersman of the Boys of the Green Mountains, became such a famous man that his exploits did not suffice for his followers' admiration. So they made up more. It is true that he won bets by lifting a fifty-pound bag of salt in his teeth and then, with a flick of his head, throwing it over his shoulder. But the story that he was once captured by the Soldiers of the Red Coats and escaped by offering to buy them alcohol in a tavern, matching them drink for drink, and then walking away when the last soldier slid beneath the table is patently unlikely. Such tales are offerings that people lay at the feet of their heroes. One biographer said that the Great Steersman died twice—once when his body died and again, thirty years later, when the last tale of his heroism was invented."

"You are claiming to be such a hero?"

"Madam, you saw the puppet play and heard how they cheered my small cloth avatar. I am the man-dog who announced himself a god in Brocade, brought the Perfect Strategist back from the dead, and raised the flag of China in Peace! How could I *not* be legend? And being a legend, I am of course subject to embellishment. Great deeds are invariably credited to those who are renowned for such, much as new jokes are invariably credited to whoever has the greatest reputation for wit. You have spent your life building a reputation as a brilliant strategist, but one not given to showy and bloodless ruses. Suddenly you perform a deed unlike any you have ever done before. It is as if you were an orator famed for her gravitas and one day you invented an uncharacteristically funny joke."

"And you?" Shrewd Fox said to Darger. "Are you a legend as well?"

"One does what one can, madam," Darger replied with a modest smile.

"So as a result, the credit for what *I* have done flows to *you*."

"You are not known for violence-free victories—quite the opposite, in fact. Your ploy was out of character."

"Yesss," Shrewd Fox said. "It makes me wonder if somehow you put that ploy into my head."

"Madam! How could we? You would not so much as let us into your presence."

"At any rate," Surplus said, "what's done is done. Water under the bridge. Gone with the snows of yesteryear. We must put the dead past behind us and move boldly forward into the future."

"That may be the first sensible thing I've heard you say. We do indeed have the future to think about. The Hidden Emperor has been greatly heartened by our latest victory and has decided that North must be conquered before cold weather sets in."

"Luckily he has you to make this happen," Surplus said.

"If you try to flatter me one more time, I'll have you both killed and think of a reason for it afterward. I am convinced that what the emperor wants cannot be done."

"That does rather put a damper on the enterprise," Darger commiserated.

"Meanwhile, the armies of the three tributary nations of the Yellow Sea Alliance are gathering to march upon us. We may well have simply gone from one side of the city walls to the other, switching roles from that of the besieging army to that of the defending one."

Both Surplus and Darger made sympathetic noises but volunteered no insights of their own.

Shrewd Fox turned away from them again and placed her hand on the cold marble forehead of Emperor Sun. After a bit, she said, "Though we honor him with the title, Sun Yat-sen was never a true emperor. The Kuomintang Dynasty was brief, never held all of China, and was beset by dissension, revolution, and ambitious warlords. Nevertheless, he fought for the common good to his dying day, even though it sometimes meant dealing with bandits and scoundrels of the worst sort. He set aside his personal distaste for them in order to do his duty." Suddenly decisive, she turned away from the coffin and said, "It occurs to me that your cunning and treachery, though a constant danger to our cause, can be usefully employed."

"That is exactly what I have been telling you all this time," Darger said. "Only without the negative twist you give to our many very real virtues, I mean."

"I shall inform the treasury that you are to be paid in accordance with your new status of ambassadors."

"Ambassadors? Where to?"

"I will tell you when the time comes—soon, I suspect. Until then, you may withdraw."

Descending the steps to their waiting rides after the interview, Surplus commented, "That went surprisingly well."

"Too well. I wonder what the ceo is up to."

TWO NIGHTS later, Surplus found himself journeying deep into the heart of South.

It was long past curfew, so the city that Surplus and Fire Orchid made their way through was dark and lifeless. Terrible Nuisance preceded them, carrying a pole from which depended an alembic with a yellow flame burning at its tip to light the way. Fire Orchid wore a long black cloak with its hood up, not because she necessarily wanted to hide her distinctive hair but because it made her look dramatic.

"Explain to me more about this mysterious letter you received," Surplus said.

"It was just an ordinary mysterious letter. But because it was accompanied by a valuable opal, I took it seriously. It said you were to come, alone, to an address in the bad section of town at midnight to learn something of value to you. That's all."

"But since you're with me, I'm not alone."

"Oh, wives don't count as other people. Everybody knows that."

"What about Terrible Nuisance?"

"He is just being a servant. Anyway, it is time he started learning how to be brave and sneaky."

They stepped into the light of a military checkpoint, and soldiers emerged from the darkness to challenge them. But when the torchlight revealed the faces of Fire Orchid and the famous Dog Warrior, the soldiers stepped back with murmured expressions of awe and respect.

"Whatever became of the opal?" Surplus asked when the silence of the city night had swallowed them up again.

"Oh, it is nice and safe, don't worry about that." Fire Orchid stopped at an intersection, and Terrible Nuisance raised the alembic so she could read the street signs, then lowered it so she could consult a map. "This way."

They went down a side street, counting doors. Then, putting aside her map, Fire Orchid pointed to a door.

Surplus gently pushed Terrible Nuisance to one side of the door and gestured Fire Orchid to the other.

He knocked.

On the far side of the door were quiet shuffling noises, which Surplus could hear though merely human ears could not have, as of two people getting into position, one to either side of the entryway.

That told Surplus all he needed to know.

"Come in," a man's voice said. The door did not open.

Surplus raised Terrible Nuisance's pole high, so the light would shine down into the entrance when it was opened. "Is the door locked?" he asked in a casual voice.

"No. Come in."

Quietly, Surplus adjusted the grip on his cane. He held it as he might have a baseball bat. "I received a letter," he said. "Is this the right place?"

"Yes, it is. Come in." Surplus could hear the tension in the man's voice. He nodded to Fire Orchid, who reached in from the side and lifted the door latch.

The instant the latch was free, Surplus kicked in the door, as hard as he could. It made a satisfying crunching noise as it hit the person behind it, and there was a gasp of pain. With all his might he swung his cane at the man who stood squinting to the left of the doorway, blinded by Terrible Nuisance's light.

The cane connected with the ambusher's skull with a loud *crack*.

The man's mouth fell open, and he collapsed. A dagger clattered to the ground.

Something lightly brushed the back of Surplus's head. He turned and saw that a woman had emerged from behind the door and tried to brain him with a club. She would have succeeded, too, had not Fire Orchid rushed forward to collide with her, forcing her back.

He was just in time to see Fire Orchid slit the woman's throat.

Fire Orchid crouched down to examine the bodies. "Mine is dead, but yours will live," she said. Then, a minute later, "No more opals. Too bad. One knife, one club, and the man also had a pistol in his pocket. Nothing worth taking."

Surplus looked to see how Terrible Nuisance was handling the sudden eruption of violence. His eyes were wide as saucers—but from awe rather than fear. Surplus supposed that was good, considering the boy's choice of families to be born into.

Fire Orchid stood and scratched Surplus under the chin fondly. "You saved my life. Oh, baby, you are going to get lots of hot sex tonight. Don't listen, Terrible Nuisance."

"No, Auntie Fire Orchid."

"I believe that technically it was you who saved my life."

"That does not matter. Somebody is going do many wicked things to somebody else's body as soon as we get alone. Don't listen to that either, Terrible Nuisance."

"No, ma'am," Terrible Nuisance said. Then, "The lady is glowing."

Both Surplus and Fire Orchid turned to look where he was pointing. "Move the alembic to the side," Surplus said, "so that less of its light enters the room."

The room grew dark. Gentle light shone from the foreheads of the man and his companion's corpse.

"Tattoos!" Fire Orchid said. "The kind that glow in the dark so they can't be seen during the day. They belong to a secret society."

"What kind of secret society?" Surplus asked.

Fire Orchid shrugged. "No special kind. Just a regular secret society. Blood oaths, assassinations, creepy ceremonies, that sort of thing."

"The tattoo is the symbol for North," Terrible Nuisance said. "The direction, I mean."

"Also the city," Surplus said. "But I imagine we knew that already."

LATER THAT night, after keeping certain promises she had made, Fire Orchid said to Surplus, "I have been talking to Cao White Squall, and she tells me that the Hidden Emperor is anxious to march against North."

"I heard something similar myself. Did she say when?"

"No. But I think soon. She said the Hidden Emperor doesn't want to wait another year before conquering all of China. Which worries her, because defeating North with our current army would take a miracle. And Shrewd Fox is a good ceo but no miracle worker."

"Tell me something," Surplus said. "However did you become such close friends with the cao?"

"Oh, I convinced her that I am a simple, plainspoken peasant woman who is perhaps a little greedy but has no ambitions other than to serve the emperor well. So of course she confides in me."

"How on earth did you ever manage to sell her such a transparently fraudulent bill of goods?"

"She believes it because it is all true," Fire Orchid said indignantly. Then, nestling into Surplus's arms again, "Well, true enough, anyway."

16.

All existence is flux and change, said the Perfect Strategist, nor is there any certainty to be found in this world, save only that all men die and that while yet they live they must pay taxes.

—THE SAYINGS OF THE PERFECT STRATEGIST

GOOD GOD, but there are times when I wish I could rid myself of the title of Perfect Strategist!" Darger cried.

"Yes, sir. Obviously, sir," Capable Servant said. "Only, sir—why?"

"It brings me nothing but trouble. Every lovesick mooncalf and power-mad megalomaniac seeks out my advice. But do they come with soft words and hands overflowing with rich bribes, the way any civilized human being would? No. They come with threats and blackmail. Had they no mothers? Were they brought up in a barn? Were the inhabitants of that barn cannibals and assassins?"

"You are upset, noble master." Capable Servant returned to polishing Darger's boots but kept his head slightly cocked to indicate that he was still listening intently.

"I am most damnably upset. In addition to all my other problems, the Hidden Emperor has formally called me into his presence, which after long exile ought to be good news. But the invitation was in the form of a written summons, hand carried to me by General Powerful Locomotive. To say nothing of its being addressed to the Perfect Strategist, Ambassador—a title given me by Ceo Shrewd Fox. This can only mean that it was issued at her behest. Which in turn implies that she thinks she has found a way of ridding herself of me, much as she would a troublesome snake that had taken up residence beneath the porch of her summer home."

"I am certain, sir, that you are no snake. Which is, incidentally, a useful animal, for it eats rats and other vermin, so that being compared to one is actually a compliment."

"Your confidence in me warms my heart. But it does not solve my problem."

Capable Servant looked up, beaming. "Your boots are ready, sir. So you will look nice and spiffy for the emperor."

Sullenly, Darger put them on.

AFTER THE usual rigmarole of misdirection, up stairs and down, cross town and back, Darger's blindfold was removed, and he found himself high up on the Porcelain Pagoda of Repaid Gratitude, possibly the single most conspicuous building in South. From here he could see all of the city and the overgrown building-middens beyond. A servant opened a door, saying, "The Hidden Emperor awaits within."

To Darger's startlement, when he entered the conference room he discovered that the Hidden Emperor was wearing a paper mask of White Squall's face. It was an image drawn, moreover, by Little Spider. He recognized her style. Like most of the Hidden Emperor's games and whimsies, it carried a hidden message: He was saying that he could effortlessly penetrate Darger's circle of friends with no one suspecting. And that he knew about Darger's affair with White Squall.

Which was useful information, for it gave Darger a line of attack.

Ceo Shrewd Fox and General Powerful Locomotive sat to either side of the Hidden Emperor. White Squall and Prince First-Born Splendor were also present but looked unlikely to speak. A plethora of lesser advisors filled the rest of the room, most of them thin-lipped and silent; nothing would be heard from any of them.

The Phoenix Bride sat directly behind the emperor, gleaming and silent.

Darger bowed respectfully but, as befit an immortal, not too deeply. "I came as you summoned to hear words which, though they will issue from your mouth, originated in Shrewd Fox's."

"The emperor's words are law!" Powerful Locomotive snapped. "Their source does not matter."

"It matters a great deal. Majesty, I fear for you. Your destiny hangs by a thread. If you wait a year before taking North, as the ceo counsels, you will never sit upon the Dragon Throne. That is a mathematical certainty. You trust Shrewd Fox because as a former enemy she consequently had no allies in your court. But while you were keeping close watch on your friends, she has been building alliances. As witness the fact that she spent last night in the company of Powerful Locomotive, alone in her room, doing such things as men and women do under such conditions." Turning to Shrewd Fox, he said, "Deny it if you can."

"I deny it," Shrewd Fox said.

"And I!" Powerful Locomotive leaped to his feet. "Great Emperor, this is slander! I would never—"

"Silence." The Hidden Emperor sounded bored. "Couple with her or a goat or a tree or whatever you wish. So long as your first loyalty is to me, I care nothing about your sordid affairs." The emperor reached a hand over his shoulder and lightly brushed his fingertips against the Phoenix Bride. Then, to Darger, he said, "Here is the situation. Those Commerce troops not captured when we overtook South have withdrawn across the border to the city of Everlasting Peace. There, they are combining forces with the armies of East Mountain and South River. In sheer number, they would be a daunting enemy. But they are also ruthless, as only those who serve North can be. Ceo True Path was once ordered to destroy his birth village and did so. Ceo Nurturing Clouds has suffered no such tragedy, but only because she is so expressly merciless in action that her superiors in North have never felt the need to punish her. As for Ceo Laughing Raven . . . Well, he is still alive, and that says a lot."

"I've always wanted to confront Laughing Raven on the field of battle," Ceo Shrewd Fox said. "But not in the company of those other two. That is an honor I freely admit I am not worthy of."

The Hidden Emperor handed a bundled sheaf of papers to an underling, who brought them to Darger's hand. "Here are the specifics of their various strengths. We cannot hope to best them by direct confrontation. It is feared that the Yellow Sea Alliance plans a direct, brutal assault upon South, hoping to destroy the city and us with it before the onset of winter."

"It is what I would do," General Powerful Locomotive said. "The alternative is to burn all the fields and granaries within raiding distance of the city and lay siege in the spring, after our supplies of food are depleted."

"This they will be reluctant to do to their own country," Shrewd Fox said. "Also, they doubtless have North leaning on them to take action."

There were times in any argument, Darger knew, when resistance was useless. All that could be done then was to go along with whatever was happening and hope for a later change in conditions when matters could be turned to one's befit. "What do you wish me to do?"

"Shrewd Fox has convinced me that the less direction you are given, the better your results will be," the emperor said. "So you have no orders other than these: Go. Meet with the leaders of the armies under flag of truce. Negotiate a peace. Bring back a treaty. If it pleases me, I shall reward you appropriately. If not, you will be killed."

"Majesty! One does not kill the messenger if the message displeases."

"That is a courtesy which one ruler extends to another. It does not apply to one's own messengers, who may be freely put to death for any reason or indeed no reason at all. Let this fact be a motivating force for you."

"But—"

"You will go. That is an order. There are no alternatives."

KNOWING WHAT was coming, Darger walked slowly back to his quarters. Shrewd Fox was the first to catch up to him.

"What is this nonsense about Powerful Locomotive spending the night with me?" she demanded.

"You were taking forever to get around to it," Darger said. "So I thought I'd speed things up for you. I believe it was the Swan of Avon who observed that it was as well to be hung for a sheep as a lamb. You have suffered the consequences of sleeping with Powerful Locomotive. You might as well have the pleasure."

"I did not ask you to meddle in my private affairs. Yet you did so anyway."

"You're welcome. But I did it for my own convenience, rather than yours." Darger walked away from Shrewd Fox, leaving her fuming behind him.

Not long after, Powerful Locomotive ran up to Darger and, roughly grabbing one arm, brought him to a stop.

"I saw you talking to Shrewd Fox. What did you—?"

"I told her what I am about to tell you: as well to be hanged for a sheep as for a lamb."

"Whatever can that ungainly sentiment possibly mean?"

"It means that unless you are a sheep, you will seize the moment, seduce the ceo, and enjoy the squalid pleasures that you have already been publicly denounced for."

"But my goal is White Squall!"

"You are a strongly made man, Powerful Locomotive, as well as being highly placed in the Hidden Emperor's confidences. These are qualities that women find attractive and, coupled with a confident attitude, all but irresistible. But for the past several months you have been as sexless as a eunuch. Consequently, you hold yourself like a man who is desperate for romantic ardor and knows no way of correcting the situation. This is something that women find repulsive. So I have put the thought in both your and the ceo's minds that you should have sex with each other. Simultaneously, I let all the world know you have already done so, thus removing all possible incentives not to do the deed. In effect, I rendered the coupling inevitable."

"But you have mated me with the wrong woman!"

"Having sex with Shrewd Fox will rid you of that habitual cringe which, invisible though it may be to you, I can assure you is all too obvious to your intended. If you do not love White Squall enough to sleep with another woman for her sake, then I fail to see how you will ever win her."

Confused, the general murmured, "It sounds logical. Yet simultaneously it all seems terribly wrong. . . ."

Sternly, Darger said, "Are you man enough to do what needs to be done? Tell me you will do it."

Powerful Locomotive took a deep breath. "I suppose I must."

"Tell me!"

"I will seduce Ceo Shrewd Fox. I will do it today. And I will give her as much pleasure as a woman is capable of receiving."

"Excellent." Darger patted Powerful Locomotive on the back. "Then White Squall is as good as yours."

LATER THAT day, orders came making Darger an ambassador plenipotentiary with the power to bind the Hidden Emperor to his agreements (provided, of course, he did not chance to suffer a fatal mishap before the emperor could confirm them) and commanding him to make peace with the Yellow Sea Alliance forces that were currently forming up on the northern border of Commerce preparatory to marching upon South. It also granted him appropriate moneys for the journey and the right to command a small military force of no more than twenty soldiers to serve as his personal guard.

"It seems that Ceo Shrewd Fox is anxious to rid herself not only of me but of the Dog Warrior and his clan as well," Darger said. "I am sent away with every associate I have save only you, Capable Servant. She is as good as giving me a nod and a wink and saying, 'Take this small bribe and flee while you can.'"

"Oh, sir! You would not leave me behind?" Capable Servant looked stricken.

"Do not fear. I have no intention of bolting. I shall return to you at the end of this mission. Provided, of course, that I am not dead by then."

"You cannot die, master. You are destined for great things."

Thus it was that, the very next morning, Darger and Surplus were sent against the combined military might of three nations, equipped with nothing but the Dog Pack and their own native guile.

IT WAS a grim ride.

The weather was unseasonably cold, and so Darger wore a black wool greatcoat as similar to those of his native England as the local tailors could be made to understand. Surplus wore something similar, of a Chinese cut with embroidery on the lapels and cuffs. Fire Orchid wore the same hooded cloak she'd had on when she killed the ambusher in South, which daylight now revealed to be of deepest scarlet. The others were dressed in appropriate cold-weather gear. And the land wore a light covering of morning frost, which disappeared in minutes when the sun came up.

Flying the white flag of parley, the company rode along badly maintained roads past overgrown fields, fish ponds that were silting into marshland, and far too many roofless farmhouses. Those houses that were still occupied were not much better than those that were not, with crumbling chimneys and buckling walls. The villages they rode through were desperate, unprosperous places.

"If this is how the land looks before battle," Surplus said, "then God help this nation when the war passes over it."

"North is a harsh master," Darger agreed.

Late in the day, as the afternoon was turning to evening, the Dog Pack came to an inn with a sun-bleached plesiosaur skull hung over the door—that being the common sign for a tavern in all the lands approaching the Grand Canal. "Let us stop for the night at the Sign of the Smiling Sea Serpent," Darger suggested. "We are all weary, and hungry to boot."

"An excellent idea," Surplus said. "We will surely get a warm welcome, for our visit will improve their day's profit margin astonishingly."

No stable workers were visible, so the Dog Pack unsaddled and unharnessed their mountain horses, told them not to go far, and set them loose to graze. Then they went inside.

The common room was large, dark, and empty. There was no fire in the hearth. Once, there had been decorations on the walls, but they were long gone. The places where they had been hung before being taken down, presumably to be sold, were lighter than the walls around them.

"Landlord!" Surplus cried. "Service, please! We bring you business!"

But when the innkeeper emerged from the back, she took one look at the Dog Pack and cried, "No room! No room! Full up!"

"Look about you. The building reeks of guestlessness," Surplus said. "So we know you are lying. Therefore you, knowing now that we know that you know we know you lie, will give us every room you have. But first we must eat. Build a fire and bring us as much food as twenty and one ravenous appetites can make disappear."

"It is not possible. There is no food. None at all."

"There are a horde of us, and we are on an expense account," Darger said. "This should not be a difficult decision for you."

"Also, we are all skilled and murderous soldiers, and my brother, Vicious Brute, has an uncontrollable temper," Fire Orchid said. "Step forward, little brother, and let her see how big you are."

Blushing, Vicious Brute did so.

The innkeeper quailed, ducking her head and wrapping her apron convulsively about her hands. "Sirs! Please!" she cried, the tip of her nose turning pink. "There is no food to feed such a crowd. Go away, please."

"First there was no room. Now there is no food. Will you never run out of new things you do not have?" Surplus could feel himself about to lose all patience with the creature.

The innkeeper began to cry. "Sirs! Oh, sirs! Please go away. You will destroy me."

Softening, Fire Orchid said, "I will be the grown-up here. Everybody but me go outside and look for food. Also, find where the firewood is hidden. I'll speak to this lady and make everything all right. You too, sweetie. I think maybe she is afraid of dogs."

BY THE time Fire Orchid emerged from the inn, Surplus had located the firewood, a winter's worth easily, hidden under tarps and then covered over with thick layers of leaves so that it looked like an earthen garden wall, and Terrible Nuisance had found a sack half-filled with dried yams hanging in a toolshed. "Okay, let's get the fire started," Fire Orchid said. "Little Spider, you can carry more than that. Delicate Thistle, get the spices out of your saddlebag and give the innkeeper a hand. I think maybe the food here is going to need a little flavor."

Inside, Surplus saw that their landlady's family had come out of hiding to help her work. There was a stout daughter with a limp, three underage grandchildren (one male), and a wizened old man who could only be her husband and whose role seemed to be to issue orders nobody obeyed while getting in everybody's way as often as possible.

A fire was soon roaring in the hearth. Uncle Gentle Mountain stood off to its side, holding out his hands to cast shadow animals on the wall. One by one, the Dog Pack's musicians got out their instruments and began to play.

"How much is this evening costing us?" Surplus asked quietly.

"Plenty," Fire Orchid said. "I had to pay black-market prices for the food. But that is the only way to get fed. Otherwise, we take food away from her family that she cannot replace and she will put nasty things in it."

The meal, when it came at last, was sorry stuff—dandelion greens, yams, and wild roots, served on millet rather than rice. But the Dog Pack got the innkeeper and her family to eat with them, and by the end of the meal, they were all on good enough terms that Surplus was able to coax the woman into telling her story.

"You will be gone tomorrow," the innkeeper said, "so I will not tell you my name. In such times as these it is dangerous to give such information to strangers. Were you to be taken as spies and tortured, you would willingly give up every name you had ever heard just for a temporary escape from pain. So much for that.

"But you should know that this inn was once renowned for its hospitality. We had pigs that fed on nothing but kitchen scraps and consequently had layer upon layer of fat, which made our cured pork particularly superior, and a roasting fowl that produced layers of turkey, duck, and chicken meat, one over the other. We brewed our own beer, fermented our own wine, and cloned our own signature line of hallucinogenic mushrooms—very gentle, very refined.

"But then recruiters came through, looking for young men to join the army. They made many promises. My oldest son was an adventurous boy, and, against my pleading, he enlisted. For a time he wrote letters. Sometimes they included money. Then he was sent to fight monsters in the Western Hills, and the letters stopped.

"A woman from the army came and said that my son was dead and that, as he had not fulfilled his term of service, I owed them another son. I tried to stop her, but she took my other son away.

"A year later, the same woman returned to say that my son was still alive, but they needed more soldiers so I owed them my daughter. This time I attacked her with a kitchen knife. That was how my daughter-in-law, the widow of my first son, got that limp. She tried to protect me and so received the punishment intended for me.

"You see before you all the family I have left, unless someday my two surviving children return. But I doubt that. The army will keep them until they are dead.

"Mine is a sad story, but not a special one. Every family I know has a similar tale of woe. As a result, there aren't enough people to harvest the crops. Farms fail. Trade dwindles. Travelers grow fewer. The amount of money raised by taxation shrinks accordingly. So the soldiers— our sons, remember!—are sent to punish us for not being as rich as we once were. Every year is worse than the year before. Soon there will be nothing in all the countryside but emptiness and desolation, with nobody to raise the food the armies require. Then, I think, the armies will turn on one another, and it will serve them right."

"Your story saddens my heart," Surplus said.

"It is common, when times are hard, for people to say they have no future. But I think I can safely say that I have no present either. All I have is the past, and that grows smaller and less convincing with every passing day."

With great dignity, the old woman stood.

"Enjoy the fire. Converse among yourselves. My family and I will place clean linens on the beds now. We shall inform you when they are ready to be slept in."

For a long time, no one spoke. At last, Darger moved to Fire Orchid's side and said quietly, "By my accounting, four of the Dog Pack are children."

"Don't you let them hear you say that," Fire Orchid said. "They are growing up fast, particularly Little Spider. And Terrible Nuisance saw his first murder last week."

"That is commendable, I suppose. But the fact remains that something should be done about them."

"Something is being done about them. We feed them and look after them and teach them useful skills."

"No, what I mean is that they should be sent away to someplace safe."

Fire Orchid looked at him incredulously. "Safe? In a war? Nowhere is safe. At least when they are with the family, we know they are not reading naughty books and picking up bad habits."

"We are going into an extremely dangerous situation." All against his will, Darger heard exasperation beginning to creep into his voice. "The children need to be protected."

"That is why there are adults in the family. To defend the children and make sure they are safe even in dangerous situations."

"Yes, but . . ."

"You are sweet. But very misguided. Don't you worry your ugly foreign head about any of this." Fire Orchid walked over to Terrible Nuisance and said, "Don't think I didn't see you poke your sister with your chopsticks. Go and help our hosts wash the dishes."

Darger turned away from her and saw Surplus silently shaking. "What are you laughing at?"

"Laughing? I? Well, perhaps I am. I am simply amused to witness Fire Orchid's dazzling command of logic happening to somebody other than myself," Surplus said. "That's all."

THE NEXT day, they reached the Grand Canal and turned north. The road, again, was not in good repair. But it was wide and only lightly traveled, so they made good time.

"We're being watched," Little Spider said in a low voice. "I have very good eyes, and I am sure of it."

Surplus, who had matched his mountain horse's gait with Little Spider's at her urgent gesture of summons, smiled. "Do you mean the two riders far to the left of us, or the one that appears occasionally on the horizon up ahead, reassures herself that we are still on course, and then disappears northward again? She's the only woman, incidentally. The others are both male."

"Okay, so maybe your dog senses are better than mine," Little Spider grumbled. "It's rude of you to rub it in."

"You are a promising artist, a decent musician, and your aunt tells me that someday you will be a first-rate pickpocket and card sharp. Nobody's best at everything."

"What will we do?" Little Spider asked.

"Nothing. Everything is as it should be."

The Dog Pack proceeded northward, stopping at inns and monasteries when they could and commandeering farmhouses when they could not. Always they paid well, behaved couthly, and left behind assurances of the Hidden Emperor's benevolence. Ever were they greeted with fear and bade farewell with relief.

They followed the Grand Canal Road. Only rarely did they see a half-laden barge go by, pulled by a team of canal lizards. When one did, it had burly guards squatting to the front and rear, looking alert and suspicious. Clearly, trade was almost nonexistent and banditry was common.

That evening, as they were making camp, a murmuring arose among the Dog Pack. Someone pointed and said, "Look—flames!" In the darkness beyond the distant fire, there was another sudden glint of light, rendered much smaller by distance. "And more!"

"Those are beacon fires," Fire Orchid said. "We are being tracked, and our progress is being reported ahead."

"That, too, is as expected," Surplus said.

"I'd be alarmed if we *weren't* being tracked," Darger added.

"Maybe so," Fire Orchid said. "But I think I'll set out guards to keep watch at night from now on."

On the horizon, another beacon fire flared to life.

IN THE end, the Dog Pack never got anywhere near Everlasting Peace, for the leaders of the three armies came out to meet them.

One day the scout who appeared and disappeared in the distance ahead failed to disappear. When they caught up to her, they found that she was a dark, slender woman with a piratical cast to her features. She was accompanied by thirty-five cavalrymen. It was a carefully nuanced force: large enough to intimidate the Dog Pack, but not so much so as to make them feel overwhelmed. Very politely, the woman informed them that they were expected to voluntarily go no farther.

"We are the soul of cooperation," Surplus assured her. "What do you wish of us?"

"Simply to wait here for certain parties who wish to consult with you. Oh, but please don't make any sudden moves toward your weapons. My people have seen more than their share of combat and are prone to misunderstanding the simplest gesture."

"We make camp here," Surplus told the clan. "If you need to chop wood or perform some similar act involving a tool such as an axe or a hatchet, please give ample notice of your intentions to our hosts beforehand."

"That would save us all a great deal of unnecessary violence," the pirate woman agreed.

In relative comfort, they waited until sunset. Then riders came to take Darger—and no others—into a distant wood. There a road led up to a house of no great distinction. The building was little more than a hut—a hunting lodge for a not terribly rich man, abandoned with the advent of war.

The negotiations did not go at all the way that Darger had expected they would. After a welcoming ceremony and a formal cup of tea, Ceo Nurturing Clouds of the East Mountain army said, "Rumor of the Hidden Emperor came to us months ago, so naturally we sent out spies to learn what we could of this new danger to the Yellow Sea Alliance. We had people in Crossroads when it fell, and they reported how gently the conquered city was treated. So too with South. Further, we have heard of the relatively painless absorption of entire nations into your empire and have formed a positive opinion of this new ascendant power."

"That is most gratifying to hear," Darger said. "For our part . . ."

Nurturing Clouds held up a hand. "Please. Let me continue. You must think us terrible people to be allied with North. But when the four nations first combined, it was a true union of equals. Over time, however, while the other lands focused on farming, fishing, trade, and manufacture, North put the bulk of its resources into its military. At first, we were happy that so much of the burden of defense was taken on itself by our northern brother. But with time it became obvious that North's military strength was greater than all ours combined. Which is when they began to demand first tribute and then obedience from us."

"I assure you that I don't . . ." Darger began.

"The situation must be seen from our perspective," said Ceo Laughing Raven. "North made it clear they would retaliate against our relatives, spouses, and children if we did not cooperate. That is simply the way they ruled. Worse, they then demanded that we build up our own military forces—not enough to threaten their supremacy, of course. But enough that the burden of taxation to support both their army and our own is ruinous. You have traveled through our lands. You see the results."

"Then obviously . . ."

"I was ordered to destroy my home village of Orchard," Ceo True Path said. "There was a labor strike. It had closed down one city and looked likely to spread. I came in, killed the leaders, and terrified the rest into going back to work. I thought I had done well. North disagreed. This was their punishment.

"The memory of that day is a constant presence. The blood of my family is on my hands. I see their faces in my dreams, I hear their voices pleading for mercy every minute of my waking life, and sometimes I believe I must go mad. The only reason I am still alive is that I have sworn to someday play a part in ending the tyranny of North."

"We have all lost family, brother," Nurturing Clouds said. "My husband, for one, and . . . well, never mind. Nothing can be done about the past. The future, however, is another story. North continues to squeeze revenue from lands which grow poorer and poorer. Sooner or later, we must rebel or die. Our armies today are as strong as they have ever been. A year from now, they will be weaker. If ever there were a time to be decisive, it is now."

"I see your dilemma perfectly and . . ."

Ceo True Path slammed his hand down on his knee. "Action must be taken! If we swear allegiance to the foreign invader and combine our troops with his, their numbers, taken together with the element of surprise, might barely suffice. It is a terrible bargain to strike, with no guarantee of victory, but we have no alternative."

The others murmured agreement.

It was simultaneously the most successful and most baffling negotiation that Darger had ever taken part in.

When the treaty was drawn up, it gave the Hidden Emperor everything he wanted and more. Here and there, in fact, Darger was moved to soften the self-imposed terms, for his new allies were so accustomed to tyranny that they had lost the ability to picture anything more than a softer, more tolerable form of it. He eliminated reparations, allowed officers to keep their ranks, and removed all specifically punitive clauses. The end result looked much like that offered other conquered nations by the Hidden Emperor—the opportunity to become a province within the restored state of China.

The treaty was signed. Then all the principals went outside to slaughter a horse, collect its blood in a chalice, and drink from it, one by one.

"I pledge my life and honor to China, to the Hidden Emperor, and to the downfall of Northern tyranny," said Ceo Laughing Raven. "If their top leaders die, so much the better."

"I pledge life, honor, property, and all else I have to China, the Hidden Emperor, and the restoration of peace," said Ceo Nurturing Clouds.

"I pledge myself to the downfall of North," said Ceo True Path. "Also, China, the Hidden Emperor, this treaty, and anyone and anything else that serves that cause."

The chalice was passed to Darger. He stared deep into it, looking for inspiration. At last he said, "The life of an immortal is by some accountings worth that of thousands of merely mortal men, for it extends so much further into time than theirs. By other measures, it is worth not one tittle more, for it is lived once and over forever, like any other man's. By either measure, I pledge to this treaty, this new alliance, this restored nation, my life and my honor as an immortal and a gentleman."

Darger drank.

It tasted every bit as vile as he had feared.

THUS, WITH the abrupt surrender of three of the four nations of the Yellow Sea Alliance, the Hidden Emperor's fortunes took an unexpected leap forward. He really was, it seemed, and exactly as Darger had said on their first meeting, the favored child of destiny.

By agreement, the three newly rebellious armies immediately turned about and began marching north, toward the capital. Darger and the Dog Pack, in turn, galloped back to South, bringing with them both the treaty and Ceo Laughing Raven to take command of the forces of Commerce.

Time was everything, for when the rebellion became known, all the formidable military might of North would come down upon the southern provinces like a fist. Seen from the Hidden Emperor's perspective, similar urgencies applied. If his armies could move fast enough, it might be possible to subdue the nation and crush the Oligarchy of North in a single swift campaign before winter slowed and stalled his progress.

The Immortals were now the smaller half of an army all but equal in size to the Army of North. Additionally, acquiring three more provinces gave them more than just added military strength. Should the war last longer than was hoped, the new territory would provide a stable foundation for waging war: an impoverished yet still intact network of farms and manufactories for provisioning the military on the move, control of the Grand Canal all the way to the border of North, river ports and seaports . . .

And, best of all, an ocean fleet.

17.

The Dog Warrior was famed for his impulsive ways, for his ferocity, and for being a fearsome opponent in battle. Ironically, those who knew him personally reported that they never saw him actually kill anyone.

—THE BOOK OF THE TWO ROGUES

THE IMMORTALS left behind only a nominal force to hold South and took the river fleet down the Long River to the intersection with the Grand Canal. When it reached that great work of antiquity, half the emperor's forces, led by Ceo Shrewd Fox and General Powerful Locomotive, turned northward while the rest continued on to the Yellow Sea to meet with the ocean fleet at the port of Seaside.

With the latter went Surplus and the Dog Pack, Darger, White Squall, and a selection of the Hidden Emperor's top advisors. Rumor had it that the emperor went as well, but, as always, this could not be determined for certain.

Leaning against the rail, staring out at the hazy zone where the sea blended into the sky, Surplus said, "Ocean travel always fills me with awe, both at the vastness of our watery planet and at the daring of those who trust their fortunes to so small and frail a thing as a ship."

"Whether you know it or not, you speak allegorically, my friend," Darger said. "The ocean clearly represents time, upon whose limitless surface we launch the flimsy craft of our lives on a perilous and chance-filled voyage which, no matter how skillfully we may weather its storms, invariably ends at a port whose name is Death."

"Your skills as a philosopher and a rhetorician are beyond reproach. But I am a pragmatist. I look upon the sea not as an allegory but as an opportunity to drop in a line and pull up a fat fish." Surplus quirked a grin. "Or, given our profession, am I speaking metaphorically again?"

"We have reeled in many a sucker in our day, it is true. But when this operation is over, we need never do so again. Our fish will be brought to us on silver platters by . . . Well, speak of the devil! Look what comes our way."

The frigate *Beijing* (as the flagship, it was privileged to bear the archaic name of the city of North) had, under the guidance of an inexperienced pilot who was anxious to show off, caught a fair wind and outstripped the other ships. So it lay now at sea anchor, waiting for the rest of the ocean fleet to catch up. At the command of Admiral Loyal Rooster, eight water-breathing sailors had stripped down to loincloths and gone over the side with fishing spears to supplement the food provided in the mess deck.

Now, a young sailor threw a leg over the rail and climbed on board, gills gasping and glistening as she readjusted to breathing air. In addition to her spear, carried on a sling over her back, she had a stringer of three codfish, which she flung onto the deck. "Everyone eats well tonight," she said. "One for me, one for the officers, and one for the cook to give to whomever she pleases. Unless you'd like to buy it? I'll give you a good price."

Surplus handed her two copper coins. "Let's not haggle. Tell the chef we'd like it lightly poached in white wine."

The sailor smirked, stooped, threw the cod over her shoulder, and swaggered off.

At this moment, Fire Orchid appeared. In her scarves and boots and bracelets, she looked every inch the pirate queen, save for a greenish cast to her face—for she had spent the voyage suffering from seasickness. "I saw you talking to the fish-woman with breasts," she said accusingly.

Surplus spread his arms in a gesture of pure innocence. "Breasts? I saw no breasts."

"*I* saw them. So you are in trouble whether you did or not. Also, I saw you give her money."

"For a cod. For dinner."

"Oh? Is that what you call it now? You have made me so angry, Mr. Dog Husband. I . . . I think maybe I have to go throw up now."

Fire Orchid staggered off.

Looking after her, Surplus commented, "You would not think it would be possible to have marital difficulties without getting married first. Yet here I am, and I have no idea how to respond."

"Do you see that white patch on the horizon?" Darger pointed. "That's a sea squall. Very powerful, quite dangerous. Yet I believe we have evaded it."

THE DAYS at sea passed pleasantly and occasionally profitably as well—particularly after they taught the admiral how to play poker. The weather was mild, and, other than the one distant squall, there were no storms.

At voyage's end, the ocean fleet, having overtaken and sunk or captured those few ships that came in sight of it and might have warned North of their approach, sailed into the Gulf of Control with its warships at the fore and troopships following. They came in with the dawn tide, slipping past the undermanned and unprepared defenses, and put in below Port of Heaven. Their marines then swiftly overran the city guard, rousting the mayor from his bed and forcing him to surrender in his nightgown.

Once the port was secured, the troops disembarked and were marched briskly through town to set up camp on the north bank of the White River. Simultaneously, scouts spread out in all directions, for the ocean fleet had outstripped the armies coming up the Grand Canal and nobody knew what the local military situation might be. They were only 250 *li* from North, which was either a triumph or a disaster, depending on how and where the Northern troops were arrayed. From here, they would either launch an assault on the capital or fall back into Port of Heaven and try to hold it until rescue arrived.

Since Shrewd Fox and Prince First-Born Splendor had both been sent up the Grand Canal with the river fleet to join and take command of the rebel armies, Cao White Squall was the ranking officer of the Sea Army. She had barely finished converting the former mayor's mansion to her field headquarters when reports began to flow in from the field. As she received them, the Perfect Strategist stood behind her, one hand lightly touching her chair to let it be publicly known that he was back in the emperor's favor and that he had the cao's complete confidence as well.

Nevertheless, he did not speak a word, but only listened.

For hour after hour, they heard self-serving testimony from politicians who might be opportunistic turncoats or, with equal plausibility, die-hard loyalists determined to feed them misinformation; synoptic summaries from interrogators who had separately questioned enemy officers and then compared their statements for consistency; early reports from their scouts, stating that the road up the White River was undefended; subsequent reports from their advance troops stating that, after light skirmishing, units had taken up positions along that road; and, most avidly pored over of all, messages from the Canal Army (delivered by operatives who had entered the port city disguised as commercial travelers and now awaited the invasion in cheap taverns), reporting that there had been a major battle with North. According to these last missives, Ceo Noble Tiger had attempted to stop the Hidden Emperor's forces coming up the Grand Canal and had been routed by Ceo True Path, who had died heroically in the battle.

"It was suicide by army," Darger said afterward. The Dog Pack had commandeered a Taoist temple for his headquarters; because it had been a museum since the pre-Utopian era, they had hoped to find valuable antiquities there, but apparently all such items had disappeared during the interregnum following the fall of Utopia. "The poor fellow wished only to die fighting North, and now he has what he wanted."

"So we are victorious?" Surplus asked.

"Perhaps. Noble Tiger has withdrawn to the north and west, into the hills, which he knows and we do not. It may be a feint to draw our forces after him. It is also possible that by delaying the union of our northern and southern fractions, he has successfully divided us, so that we may be taken down one at a time. Warfare is so much more lucid in the history books than it is on the hoof! For every three informants who tell us one thing, two more swear to its exact opposite. Meanwhile, I have listened to such a farrago of force concentrations and dispersions, enfilades and defilades, reverse slope defenses, shell scrapes, interdictions, breakouts, counterattacks, salients, reentrants, cauldrons, and pincer movements as would drive a man mad to turn into a coherent whole. I dared not ask for clarifications, of course, for that would cast my status as the Perfect Strategist in question. So I simply had to look knowing and endure it."

"You have no notion what our chances are, then?"

"Well, that's the problem, don't you see. Learning the facts of a situation limits one's possibilities. Knowing nothing, I was confident that North would fall before us. Now, however, I must admit to the very real possibility that we may lose. Their armed forces are more numerous than ours and hold a strong defensive position. The city stores contain a year's supply of food, where we would have to scavenge off the people in the countryside, making many enemies in the process. Also, their ceo, Noble Tiger, is so highly regarded that he is known by friends and foes alike as the Tiger of the North."

"We have three ceos for their one," Surplus observed. "Plus Powerful Locomotive, who is a demoted ceo, and White Squall, who is a cao, though whether of archaeology or of animals, I'm no longer clear. And I'm sure that the morale of our soldiers is far better than theirs, though of course a single defeat would change that."

"It has been said that their soldiers fight like rabid rats. The question is, can a sane soldier with good morale defeat his weight in rabid rats? The answer remains to be seen. The only bright spot," Darger concluded, "is that Cao White Squall has been summoned to the Hidden Emperor's side. From which we can deduce two things: that the emperor did indeed come with the ocean fleet, as was commonly bruited about, and that we shall soon have clear orders what to do next."

White Squall appeared in the doorway.

She looked stricken.

"I have taken advantage of you for my own private purposes. Too late, I realize that this was improper. Consequently, I'm sure you think me an opportunist and a woman without honor," White Squall said. "But I keep my promises. You once asked for a day's warning before the phoenix device was activated. I am giving it to you now. The Hidden Emperor has ordered me to prepare it for what he calls their wedding. I am about to put my people to work on the task. By this time tomorrow, the most destructive weapon our age has ever known will be ready for use."

For a long moment, no one spoke. Then . . .

"I suspect it's useless to point this out," Surplus said. "But you don't *have* to fix the device, you know."

"An order is an order. Besides, I swore an oath." Irritably, then, White Squall said, "Yes, yes, I know. To you an oath is merely words and nothing more. But I am not you and never can be you. I must be true to my duty." She started to leave, then stopped. "Oh, and you got me so emotional that I almost forgot. The Hidden Emperor wants to see both of you. Immediately. His servants wait outside."

DARGER AND Surplus were taken by the usual convoluted and needlessly recomplicated route to the Hidden Emperor. As much to amuse himself as out of simple prudence, Surplus constructed a mental map of their route as they went, created in part by counting strides and memorizing turns and in greater part by keeping close track of smells: Forty paces down the Street of Spices they went, turning right at its end and passing by several bookstores and a harness shop, then down to the river and across a stone bridge that spanned the mouth of a stream where a knacker's yard emptied its wastes, uphill again past chair-makers who were soaking cane and shaving cedar spindles, then sharply left into and sixty paces down a residential street fragrant with hibiscus flowers. . . . All told, the farcical journey took up most of an hour.

At last they were brought indoors, unblindfolded, and ushered into a small sitting room. It contained three easy chairs, on one of which sat the Hidden Emperor. His head was swathed in dark veiling and nothing more. Its featureless face turned to greet them.

"Move that coffee table over here. Then sit," the emperor said. "We have matters of import to discuss."

"We thank you for the honor," Darger said. "But it is hardly right for us to sit in your presence, Exalted Majesty."

"Sit or I will kill you both." Alarmingly, the Hidden Emperor giggled. "I could do that, you know. I could kill you in an instant." He snapped his fingers. "Like that! I have weapons you know nothing about."

"So I have long suspected," Darger said, easing down onto a chair. "Given the dangers endemic to your chosen profession, it never does to underestimate a living ruler."

"Enough of that." The Hidden Emperor spread out a map of the city of North and its environs. On it, two concentric circles had been drawn, focused on a point to the south of the city. The outermost circle contained all of North and the Forbidden City within it. The innermost one encompassed half of the palace complex, including the Hall of Supreme Harmony, which held the Dragon Throne. Both the hall and the throne were plainly marked on the map. "White Squall's people drew this up for me. The larger circle shows the zone in which everything will be effectively destroyed. The smaller indicates where total incineration will take place. As you can see, it is not necessary for me to actually enter the city to fulfill my destiny."

Surplus nodded to show he was listening. Darger cleared his throat in an attentive way.

"You may not know this, dear ones, but you are my favorites, my sweets, my pets. Oh, you have been wayward at times. On occasion, I thought of having you put down. But where others were more punctilious in their obedience, it was you who served me best. That is why I most especially want you at my side when I transcend this human body."

"May that day be long in coming," Surplus said.

"Very long indeed," Darger added.

The Hidden Emperor put the tip of his forefinger on the epicenter of the two circles. "Tomorrow," he said, "the Canal Army will join the Sea Army on the plains below North. All my power will then be manifest. What better time for the Phoenix Bride and me to be united in alchemical marriage?"

Lesser souls would have hesitated an instant, thus betraying their true thoughts. But Darger and Surplus immediately broke into spontaneous cries of delight.

"My profoundest congratulations, Majesty!" Surplus said.

"In the words of the People of the Book: Mazel tov!" cried Darger. "Only . . . tomorrow? Surely you want to be recognized as the emperor first."

"A ceremony is but a ceremony. All that is needed is for my love for the Phoenix Bride to be consummated. The same fires that incinerate me will incinerate the Dragon Throne. Our atoms will be mingled with those of the Phoenix Bride. As well as yours, my dears. As well as yours. For from this searing, incandescent union, I will rise again as a god, incorporating my genius, my wife's strength, and other virtues from each of my slaves and officers. Your strategic powers, Perfect Strategist. Your daring, Dog Warrior. I will unite all the male and female virtues in one perfect androgynous, sexless self, and you shall be a small fraction of my glory."

Outwardly calm but inwardly aghast, Surplus heard Darger say with glib plausibility, "You would not wish to consummate your marriage with the Phoenix Bride without first having a royal wedding. These things mean so much to women!"

The emperor stared at him. "The Phoenix Bride is not a woman but a thermonuclear device. A bomb. It is inanimate and insensate, and thus incapable of desiring anything. How is it possible that you do not know this simple fact?"

"I . . . well, to be honest . . ."

All of the Hidden Emperor's ebullience disappeared in an instant. Angrily, he said, "No one truly understands me. Even you, who are so clever, don't know the first thing about me."

"We know that you are a man of destiny," Darger said.

The Hidden Emperor made an exasperated noise.

"A cat may look at a monarch," Surplus said. "But that does not mean that the two will understand one another. Majesty, the gulf of greatness that exists between you and us cannot be bridged. But from the far side of that gulf we can witness your magnificence, and from your side you can receive our admiration."

The emperor glowered. And then he laughed. "You two are such delightfully transparent rogues," he said. Gesturing Darger and Surplus closer, he placed his head so near theirs that all three almost touched. "I can read your thoughts. But it is useless for you to try to escape. I have surrounded the city with guards, and your names are on a list of those who are not to be allowed to leave. Oh, be happy for me! I'm as giddy as a schoolgirl about to be deflowered. I hardly know what I'm saying."

The Hidden Emperor stood, and Darger and Surplus hastily followed suit. "It is time for you to leave me with my thoughts and anticipations. Tonight you may celebrate. Do not drink too much! You would not want to go into eternity with a hangover."

SURPLUS'S MOOD that evening was as somber as the temple was bright. At Darger's direction, Capable Servant had strung colored lanterns on the eaves and placed candles everywhere within. These gave the place an overheated, festive air that made it look like they had nothing to hide and everything to celebrate. As befit so profound an occasion, they did not invite guests to dilute the festivities but mimed a tipsy joyousness by themselves. Their shadows danced on the walls. The windows had all been thrown open. From outside, they would be clearly visible in silhouette. If there were spies, their reports would make the emperor happy.

Capable Servant filled two wineglasses with water, which he carefully poured from a recently emptied magnum of champagne. Surplus lifted his glass high. "To the Hidden Emperor!" he cried.

"And to his Phoenix Bride!" Darger toasted back.

As they pretended to drink, Surplus quietly said, "The Hidden Emperor is mad. On this we are both agreed. The phoenix device is unspeakably destructive, and to use it would be a crime against humanity—so say the ancient texts, and I am inclined to agree with them. It is a certainty that tomorrow's wedding plans will end in a holocaust unseen since the Utopian era. Connect the dots, and there is only one possible course of action."

"Are you suggesting . . ." Darger paused, though whether out of moral reticence or simply to build up suspense, it was possible that not even he knew. "Murder?"

"Murder is the very last act that a gentleman should commit," Surplus said. "But you'll note that it *is* on the list."

Capable Servant crouched at their feet, listening, eyes wide, as if to a ghost story.

Darger clumsily refilled his glass, spilling a few drops in the process, as if he were already a little woozy. "This is all academic. The Hidden King keeps his whereabouts unknown in order to prevent exactly the sort of action you are contemplating. We simply have no idea where he is."

"On the contrary. I can quite easily find him. All that hugger-mugger with blindfolds and elaborate backtracking might fool one who was merely human. But I have the superior sensory apparatus of a dog. Locating him is the least of our difficulties. However," Surplus said, "the challenge lies not in the doing, but in the survival of it. If history teaches us anything, it's that regicides rarely fare well."

Darger took a deep breath. "Suppose he did not die."

"What do you mean?" Surplus asked.

"Only a handful of people know what the Hidden Emperor's face looks like."

"Many know his voice."

"A voice can be counterfeited. There must be many people who could do a perfectly passible imitation of the Hidden Emperor."

"Oh! Sirs!" Capable Servant said. "I can do voices!" And in an eerily familiar voice—high-pitched, petulant, almost girlish—he added, "I do a very good impersonation of the emperor."

Surplus and Darger looked at one another.

SURPLUS WOUND his way through a labyrinth of sound, of touch, and above all of scent. When he smelled anise, fennel, cinnamon, clove, ginger, and lemongrass, he growled, "We go down this street and turn right at its end."

He clutched an empty wine bottle in one paw, which he periodically raised to his mouth or eye, as if puzzled by its obstinate refusal to refill itself. Following a half-stumble behind, Darger occasionally slapped a hand on Surplus's shoulder to steady himself. There were a great many sailors on shore leave that night, so they attracted no particular attention.

They passed by several closed bookshops and a silent harness maker's. "Now down to the river."

"What a stench!" Darger said when they passed over the bridge by the knackery. "I vividly remember going by here."

"Imagine what it would smell like if the river weren't convenient to carry away the rotting meat discarded into the creek. Now . . . not this street . . . not this one . . . Ah! Smell the cedar shavings? Up this way."

They were walking along Hibiscus Street when a man ran up and thrust a lantern in their faces.

"Prince First-Born Splendor!" Surplus cried in amazement. "Whatever are you doing here?"

"I have been looking for you," the prince replied.

"You have found us," Darger said, "but at the worst possible time. We are on important business and cannot stay to chat." Matching action to words, he strode onward.

But the prince hurried to place himself in front of them again. "White Squall says—"

"She has been talking to you?" Surplus said. Seeing that the man would not be easily shed, he put an arm over First-Born Splendor's shoulder. Darger, meanwhile, took a princely arm in his own. They then lurched onward, and in their company the prince looked every bit as drunk as they were pretending to be. "Why, then you know what's coming. If you are a religious man, there are prayers to be said. If not, this would be an excellent time to settle old grudges. Or, if you are able to transcend such petty matters, there is White Squall to be consoled. In any case, you have a full schedule ahead of you and need not bother with us."

The two rogues uncoupled from the prince then and attempted to leave him behind. But he came running after them.

"I must do something!"

"Yes," Surplus said. "I have already laid out an itinerary for you."

"No! I mean—" Prince First-Born Splendor seized them both and, lowering his voice to a near whisper, said, "The Hidden Emperor must die."

"Oh, dear," Surplus said in dismay.

"Please tell me you did not share this sentiment with White Squall," Darger said.

Indignantly, the prince said, "Give me some credit for understanding the woman I love. She would have gone immediately to the Hidden Emperor if I had. No, I said nothing. I simply turned and left her in order to seek you out. It was the most difficult act of my life, for it clearly broke her heart. But I did it in order to privately save her life. And everyone else's, of course."

"You'd best come along, then," Darger sighed. "It'll be easier than explaining."

"Just to be clear," Surplus added, "we'll take responsibility for the

Hidden Emperor. It will be your job to slay any servants who get in the way. As a nobleman, you'll be less bothered by the necessity than we would."

THE HIDDEN Emperor, as it turned out, had been secreted in a large and ostentatiously vulgar mansion on New Wealth Street. No longer feigning drunkenness, the three walked straight to the front door, as if they had legitimate business within. Darger took a set of lockpicks from his pocket and bent casually over the knob. "The devil!" he swore. "It's not locked."

At a push, the door swung open.

They went inside.

Prince First-Born Splendor held up his lantern, revealing a vast, high-ceilinged hall, totally free of furniture save for several ostentatiously overlarge vases on carved teak stands and some expensive carpets on the tiled floor. The building was utterly silent.

The bodies of two servants lay on the tiles. A single inner door gaped wide.

"Someone has been here before us." Surplus crouched briefly by each of the bodies. "Dead. And recently—the bodies are still warm. Someone came here with the same intentions as we did."

"Yes, but can we trust him—or them—to have done the job properly?" Darger asked.

"Destiny favors the man who takes no shortcuts," Prince First-Born Splendor said with the assurance of a schoolboy quoting last year's lessons, "nor any least detail for granted."

Surplus drew the sword from his cane. "Stay here," he told the prince, "and secure our means of exit, lest we find ourselves outnumbered."

Darger took the lantern from First-Born Splendor and followed Surplus deep into the house. They saw more corpses but did not stop to examine them. Like a trail of breadcrumbs, a series of open doors led them all the way to the Hidden Emperor's bedchamber. The room was opulent, and the linens and silks upon the bed were recognizably of the very best, taken from the many cities they had conquered. Curtains blew into the room from an open window.

In a chair by the bed was a still, cold body. A cloth mask lay at its feet, and the embroidered yellow robe had been torn open to enable a fatal knife stab between the ribs and into the heart.

The Hidden Emperor was already dead.

SURPLUS DID not want to be the first to speak. But at last he did. "Darger," he said, "this is the corpse of a woman."

"Why in heaven's name would a woman be dressed as the Hidden Emperor?"

"You mistake my meaning. This individual smells exactly the same as did the Hidden Emperor, and—look!—here on the knuckle of the left thumb is the star-shaped scar left by the kitten he killed. She killed, I should say. The Hidden Emperor was a woman. Examine her features. Note how in death her Adam's apple has vanished. Her breasts are small but distinct, her hips those of a woman, and in every other manner her gender is self-evident." Surplus closed the bloodstained yellow robes to hide the wound. It covered as well a necklace of brightly colored glass beads.

"Odd," Darger said. "I recognize the necklace. She had it on when she posed as a tea girl to spy on our meeting in Crossroads. I had assumed then that it was part of her disguise and gave it no further thought." Delicately, he drew it out for closer examination. "Several of the beads are broken! This grows less and less explicable."

"It is a weapon," Surplus said.

"Excuse me?"

"The necklace is a weapon. I learned of such things in my readings of military history. It was originally designed to be used by spies. Every other glass bead contains a toxin. Those between them hold the antidote. One breaks the bead with the antidote under one's nostrils and inhales while simultaneously crushing the bead with the toxin. Such poisons are very fast. In seconds, everyone in the room is dead, while the person who inhaled the antidote remains unharmed. It is exactly the sort of weapon one would expect so cautious a monarch to wear. Yet it didn't work. Why?"

"I don't know," Darger replied. "As well ask: Who killed the Hidden Emperor?"

"Whoever it was," Surplus said, "I'm grateful to our unknown benefactor. Had we confronted this young lady while she yet lived, we would both be dead now. For that matter, had he not left by the window, the toxins might not have had time to entirely disperse." In death, the Hidden Emperor no longer looked dangerous. Deprived of the power to kill or despoil at whim, she was just an ordinary young woman, and Surplus could not help feeling sorry for her.

For a long moment Darger was silent. Then he said, "I find myself at an uncharacteristic loss for words."

"That being so . . ." Surplus began.

"Yes. Let us dispose of the body and move on."

Darger and Surplus stripped the dead emperor—or, more properly, empress—of her robe of office and swaddled her in the thick brocades taken from the bed. This surprisingly light bundle they brought with them to the foyer, where they saw Prince First-Born Splendor with blood pouring down his face, pulling himself up from the floor. The door was open behind him.

"Is the deed done?" he asked.

Surplus nodded.

"Whatever happened to you?" Darger asked.

"I hardly know myself. I was standing here, holding the door open the merest crack and peering out at the street, when I heard a noise behind me. Before I could turn, I was seized and slammed into the wall. That was just seconds ago. My assailant ran out the door."

All three conspirators stared out at the empty street. "He's gone now," Surplus observed.

"Let him go," Darger said. "He did us a good turn, whether by design or not, and I feel no need to avenge a monarch we had every intention of killing ourselves. Give us a hand, noble prince. We dare not leave this body here."

When they were several streets away from the death scene, Prince First-Born Splendor said, "What about all the other bodies?"

"In the morning, Capable Servant will be here, robed and masked, in the Hidden Emperor's persona. When he orders that the corpses of his servants be cleared away and new servitors provided him, nobody will ask questions," Surplus said.

"That is one of the advantages of being known to be completely off your chump," Darger added.

Together, they three carried the body down the lightless and deserted streets to the stone bridge by the knackery. There, they entrusted their bundle to the nameless creek that flowed into the White River. It fell in with a splash, tumbled over twice, and then was swept under the surface and away into darkness by the swiftly flowing water, to be found or not somewhere downriver, as the fates decreed.

18.

The ancient sage Builder of Pyramids borrowed money at very high interest and paid it all back promptly with money lent by other investors. Those in turn he repaid with money from yet newer lenders, at each step increasing the number who wished to invest in his enterprise. In this way he became incalculably wealthy. For a time.

—THE SAYINGS OF THE PERFECT STRATEGIST

THE NEXT morning dawned like any other. The death of an emperor (or empress), it seemed, made very little difference to the world. The air smelled as sweet. Food tasted as good. By day's end, Darger had the happy conviction that his fortunes had turned a corner at last and that there was nothing before him that could not be faced with equanimity.

But first . . .

A carefully prepared and rehearsed Capable Servant was dressed in the emperor's clothes and ensconced in the emperor's bed. As predicted, the discovery that all of his servants had been murdered caused a great deal of alarm—until the Hidden Emperor declared that it was a matter of no great import, thus implying that whatever had happened had been done at his whim. At which point, the corpses were whisked away for cremation, the floors were mopped clean, and a new staff was swiftly procured.

By noon, the incident was as good as forgotten.

"It is very convenient to be thought crazy," Capable Servant confided to Darger when they were alone. "The standards for behavior are very easy to live up to."

"Confine your madness to small matters that hurt no one and this insight will serve you well."

Capable Servant plucked at an imaginary bit of fluff on his robe. "Nevertheless, I am glad that I must wear a mask to pull off this deception. It will hide my nervousness. I hardly know what to do. Should I call my advisors together?"

"It would look suspicious if you did not. But wait until the Canal Army has arrived, so that Shrewd Fox and her subordinate ceos may be present. There will be a great deal of speech, much disguised boasting, a certain amount of braggadocio. Be careful to listen more than you speak, imply more than you say, and fly into a fit of fury if anyone points out any contradictions in your proclamations. I have faith in your ability to improvise. Should you find yourself at a loss, simply call upon me and be guided by my advice."

"Sir, what should I do about the phoenix device?"

"The Dog Warrior and I have given that serious thought," Darger said. Their debate, in sober fact, had been long and heated. But eventually they had decided that since White Squall would not detonate the device without a direct order from the Hidden Emperor—which order was now unlikely to come—and since ordering it deactivated might raise the irrationally loyal cao's suspicions, matters could simply be left as they were for the nonce. "When the cao asks for your orders, tell her that you have decided to postpone the marriage until you've conquered North and put your new empire in order. She will secretly greet that as welcome news. I, meanwhile, have someone to consult with before we decide upon the device's ultimate disposition."

"The ceo, you mean? Shrewd Fox?"

Darger glanced out the window at the darkening sky. "No, I am thinking of someone far more dangerous than her."

THE DAY'S other great event—the reunion of the Hidden Emperor's armies—was an occasion of tremendous joy for all involved. Indeed, it took on aspects of a carnival. First the Sea Army advanced to the flatlands before the city of North, there to pitch camp and await the Canal Army coming from the south. The first sails appeared while it was still morning, and the first outriders arrived at full gallop when the sun was at its highest. Military bands greeted the main forces as they came marching in, and off-duty soldiers ate fire and waved banners while walking on stilts. By twilight, an immense tent city had been erected that was the very shadow and other of the stone city of North.

The foe might well have emerged from North to attack them at this, their moment of greatest confusion. But no troops came forth from the city gates. This, the army's leadership (who had not been as unprepared for such a sally as they had made it appear) agreed when they made their reports to the Hidden Emperor, was an encouraging sign. As were the gathering thunderheads piling up behind North. The Immortals' confidence in their own invincibility had spread to the newly integrated units, and all agreed that the coming storm would smash down the opposition, cleanse the city of the foe, and wash the blood of the coming battle from the streets into the gutters and then the streams that emptied into the White River and, from thence, all the way to the Yellow Sea.

While Ceo Shrewd Fox was preparing for the emperor's conference, Darger, with a glib word here and an evasion there, slipped past her guards and into her tent. He found her talking quietly with General Powerful Locomotive.

"How did you get past my people?" Shrewd Fox asked.

"I told them that you had summoned me and looked dramatically reluctant to be led into your presence."

"So my best schemes to rid myself of you failed, and you and I have come full circle and are back where we began."

"Oh, it is far worse than that," Darger said. "I move from triumph to triumph. I am currently so firmly set in the Hidden Emperor's favor that there is absolutely no hope of your dislodging me from it. So why try? I have no ambition to supplant you. Why not take advantage of my talents and friendship?"

He extended his hand in a bluff, manly fashion.

Shrewd Fox ignored it. "All I have, all I have suffered, all I have learned, I got without you. I am confident that this lifelong streak of fortune will continue. Right now I am putting the finishing touches on my plans for the conquest of North. When I have placed the Hidden Emperor on the Dragon Throne, he will grant me whatever I wish as a reward. Give me one convincing reason why I should not, among other things, ask for your exile."

"You would regret it," Darger said simply.

"Show this gentleman out," Ceo Shrewd Fox told her second-in-command. "Make it clear to him what will happen if he attempts to speak to me again."

General Powerful Locomotive opened his mouth. At a warning glance from Shrewd Fox, however, he shut it again.

When Powerful Locomotive had escorted Darger far enough from the ceo's tent to avoid being overheard, the general said, "You mustn't be bothered by the ceo's curt ways, Perfect Strategist. She is a great woman and, like all such, prone to focus only on her own vision of what should be. No personal rancor was involved."

"You sound taken by her, my friend."

"Well . . . I . . . you see . . ."

"You are in love with Ceo Shrewd Fox!" Darger cried, in what he trusted was a convincing counterfeit of astonishment.

Powerful Locomotive flushed. "No! Well, perhaps. Shrewd Fox is not like other women. She does not . . ." His great hands opened and closed, trying to grapple the words out of nothing. "I feel like myself in her presence. I feel that we could accomplish great things together."

"And White Squall?" Darger asked. "Should I stop working to win her for you? I swear to you, on my word as a gentleman, that I am at this very moment as close as close can be to making her yours."

"I hardly know. When I am with her, White Squall fills my thoughts completely, and I can imagine loving no one else. But in the presence of Shrewd Fox, I feel quite the other way."

"I understand completely," Darger said soothingly.

"I must get back to the ceo's side." General Powerful Locomotive started away. Then he stopped and jabbed a finger at Darger. "Don't meddle with my private life anymore until I figure out what I want. Understand?"

Gazing after him, Darger murmured to himself, "It will be a pleasure."

"I CANNOT find Prince First-Born Splendor!" White Squall said through her tears. Mere minutes had passed since Darger had left Powerful Locomotive's presence.

"That is hardly my concern." Darger did not slacken his pace.

"We had an argument yesterday, and he disappeared. I haven't seen him since. But I've spoken to the Hidden Emperor, and he has postponed his wedding to the Phoenix Bride, which was the cause of our rupture. So it's important that I see First-Born Splendor as soon as possible."

"Madam. You multiply obligations upon me daily and without recompense, as yesterday you had the grace to acknowledge, and on your behalf I have done my utmost. But I draw the line at being your social secretary and your would-be paramour's minder." Darger came to his tent, paused at the door flap, and said, "You misplaced him and therefore you must find him yourself." He went inside.

Inevitably, White Squall followed him. So they both saw Prince First-Born Splendor at the same time. He was sprawled on a camp stool with his eyes closed and his head thrown back.

He had obviously been drinking.

"Oh, bloody hell!" Darger exclaimed.

Tentatively, White Squall said, "Perhaps I can . . ."

"No!" Grabbing her arm, Darger turned the cao away from her beloved and hustled her outside again before the prince could look up and see her. "You do not wish him to know that you have seen him at his lowest and most vile. Men are as self-conscious as cats, and he would hold it against you forever." It was an argument that few women would have fallen for. But then White Squall was no ordinary woman. "Go back to your tent. I will plumb the causes of the prince's dissipation and send him to you when I have sobered him up."

Inside again, Darger found that First-Born Splendor had roused himself from his torpor and was peering vaguely about. "I thought I heard . . ." the prince said.

Darger put his hands on his hips. "I am hardly a Jacobin, sir, but in your present state I must say that you present a strong case against hereditary royalty."

Prince First-Born Splendor clutched his head and moaned. "I am a regicide. An assassin! I, who was born to greatness and raised to be the glory of my line, have fallen as low as it is possible to go."

"You killed no one. Save for the poor fellows who fell before you on the field of battle, of course."

One royal hand went weakly up in the air to make a small, dismissive wave. "They knew their chances. As did I. The game went to the better man, that's all. As for my culpability in the emperor's death, my ethics instructors taught me that, morally, there is no distinction to be made between the intent and the deed."

"There is every distinction to be made. I myself have from youth intended to be unspeakably wealthy—and yet I am not. Were things as easy as you make them out to be, every peasant would be a king and we'd all die for want of anybody to provide us with food."

"I . . . I don't think I can follow your logic."

"Come with me." Darger hauled the prince to his feet and automatically looked about for Capable Servant. Then, remembering, he dug through his kit himself until he came up with a purple bottle, half-filled with a heavy liquid. "You're making a trip to the jakes."

The latrine was not far. Outside its door, Darger gave Prince First-Born Splendor the bottle. "Drink a good slug of this. It's an anti-intoxicant. You're not going to enjoy the results, I fear. It will open the sluice gates at both ends. But I can't talk to you when you're in this beastly condition."

Some ten minutes of spectacular noises later, the latrine door opened. Prince First-Born Splendor emerged, pale and sober.

Darger clapped him on the shoulder. "Feeling more sensible now? That's a good chap. Let's go to my tent and talk."

Over glasses of pear nectar, they conversed. The prince once again gave extravagant speech to his guilt. Darger heard him out and said, "An emperor is but a man, whose life is worth no more than yours or mine."

"This one was a girl."

"A woman, then. My point remains. The Hidden Emperor's life was shortened by exactly one day, remember. Meanwhile, we live. That in itself is a net gain. But so do every soldier under your command, plus the Immortals, including the Yellow Sea Alliance divisions, and every man, woman, and child in North, who would otherwise have died in a madwoman's holocaust. So does the woman you love. The woman who also loves you, I should add, inexplicable though that fact now seems."

Prince First-Born Splendor buried his head in his hands. "If only she were here."

"No woman wants to nurse a man through the darkest moment of his life," Darger lied. He then compounded the untruth by adding,

"She wants a man she can look up to for moral guidance, one she can rely on to always tell her what to do."

"So I was always told by the teachers in my father's court," Prince First-Born Splendor said. "Yet there were times when White Squall and I were particularly close, and it did not seem to me then that she was looking for anything of the sort."

"That is a matter you must settle with the lady herself. Square your shoulders, sir. Take a deep breath. Now go to her. Put on a brave face. Speak not a word about last night's deeds. Say only that you were distraught at the prospect of losing her. Do you understand? Good. Off you go."

Prince First-Born Splendor left, looking as if he might burst into tears at the mere fact of seeing White Squall again. Which, Darger reflected, might well be the best thing in the world for the both of them.

He flung himself down on the camp stool and rummaged through his kit again looking for his pocket flask but could not find it. Then he heard a rustling noise, and Little Spider crawled under the canvas into his tent.

"Prince First-Born Splendor drank all your alcohol," she said.

More amused than offended, Darger said, "What are you doing here, you imp?"

"I was spying on the prince. For practice. Why did you tell him all that nonsense about what women want?"

"Because, dear urchin, it is my policy, in the absence of any reason to do otherwise, to always tell the mark whatever he wants to hear. I reassured the prince that the world was as he expected it to be, and that gave him the courage to seek out White Squall. Perhaps now that their defenses are down, they can work out an understanding between them."

"What if they don't?"

"In that case, it successfully got him out of my tent. So I am still ahead of the game."

AT THE Council of the Three Ceos, as history would later call it, the new Hidden Emperor's first act was to hear out Shrewd Fox's plans for the assault on North and to assure himself that his stenographers were writing down her every word.

"We have just enough of Cao White Squall's machines remaining operative," the ceo said, "to create a breach of the city walls. By carefully choosing the location"—she touched the model at a spot their spies reported to be poorly defended, though a major avenue ran by it, allowing ingress to the center of the city—"we can have our soldiers inside before North can properly respond. The loss of men I estimate at a few hundred, most from a frontal assault on the Gate of Eternal Stability to distract the defenders. Acceptable. Once inside, our forces will have three main objectives: to control that section of the wall so that further troops may enter, to attack and seize the armory, and to project arsonists into the poorest and most crowded parts of the city. This will not only create confusion but . . ."

She went on for a great while. Then the Hidden Emperor called for questions. There were quite a few of these, and the stenographers copied them down along with all of Shrewd Fox's cogent replies.

"Do you have a backup plan if the wall cannot be breached?" Ceo Laughing Raven asked.

"Will there be sufficient medical facilities for the wounded?" Ceo Nurturing Clouds wanted to know.

"The Dog Pack will guard the portable bridge, of course," Surplus threw in.

To this last, Shrewd Fox said simply, "No." Of the medical facilities, she replied that their field clinics would be sufficient for the day and that the hospitals of North would be available on the morrow and beyond. But to the first question, she offered six different backup plans contingent upon ways the original plan might fail, with each plan branching into several contingencies of its own should further difficulties arise. It was a dazzling presentation, and when it was finally done, every advisor in the room, Darger alone excepted (but he nodded approvingly), broke into spontaneous applause.

Then the pretend emperor moved on to his second objective, which was to send Shrewd Fox and Powerful Locomotive packing. This he achieved by exclaiming, "Excellent! Perfect! None better! You and General Powerful Locomotive are to be most highly commended. You may, in the morning, take command of your most trusted subordinates, a hundred of my finest soldiers, and as many boats as needed.

Go directly back to Three Gorges and organize the armies remaining there."

Astonished murmurs rose from every part of the room.

Stunned, Ceo Shrewd Fox said, "Majesty?"

"Your work here is done. But the southern nations of China remain unconquered. In my compassion for them, I am eager that they should be part of the resurrected nation as quickly as possible."

"While . . . while I am thankful for Your Majesty's guidance, I must object."

Powerful Locomotive leaped to his feet. "Great Monarch! Deign to listen!"

When the new Hidden Emperor held up his hand for silence, Darger stepped forward from the shadows, where he had been lurking, to stand behind him. He raised one hand and lightly touched the emperor's chair. "But there is more," the supposed emperor said. "In recognition of your unparalleled brilliance, I am giving you the most valuable thing that even an emperor can bestow—the title of Perfect Strategist. Wear it well as you conquer the southern lands for me."

Shrewd Fox looked as startled as Darger felt. "Wouldn't that confuse me with . . . ?" she began to say. Then a knowing look bloomed on her face. "I see. I see. Yes, I shall take my new identity and use it to terrify all the unsubjugated regions of China the Great into accepting your just and merciful rule."

General Powerful Locomotive started to speak. But Ceo Shrewd Fox hit him hard enough that nothing came out. "As does my second-in-command," she said firmly. Then she turned to Darger and bowed a fraction of an inch, as if to acknowledge that he had won. "We shall leave Your Majesty's armies in the capable hands of the original Perfect Strategist." With a sidelong glance at her underling, she added, "As is best."

"Yes," General Powerful Locomotive said reluctantly. "I don't understand why, but if you say so, then perhaps it is for the best."

The Hidden Emperor stood. "I thank you for your advice. You may all leave now." Adding, however, "Perfect Strategist, Dog Warrior . . . you will stay, for I wish to speak with you in private."

WHEN THERE were only they three in the room, Capable Servant removed his mask and, smiling, said, "Did I do well, masters? My imitation of the Hidden Emperor, I mean. It was good, I hope?"

"It was a little . . ." Surplus began.

Angrily, Darger said, "What in the name of all that's holy did you think you were doing, giving away my title?"

"Was that not what you wanted, sir? To be free of a burdensome reputation?"

"It was what I *said* I wanted. But men say many things they don't mean. My title was not only burdensome but useful as well. It carried a great deal of prestige."

"Do not worry, sir. As well as being emperor, I am still your servant. Simply tell me what you want—money, titles, land—and it is yours."

"Indeed," Darger said. "Well. That does rather put things into perspective." For a long moment, he was silent. Then he said, "Did you hear that rumbling sound in the distance? There's a lightning storm coming, I think. I must leave now, for I have business to attend to and a certain personage to interrogate."

THE STORM that had been threatening all day broke just as Darger left camp. His ride through the driving rain took over an hour, even on a mountain horse. But at last he came to his destination, the rusting remains of an iron bridge left over from the Utopian era and locally known to suffer from ghosts. "Stay," he told his skittish mount. "I may be some time."

"Hhho hhno!" Buttercup said. "Hhaawful!"

"We must all do our duty. Yours is to stand and wait."

The rain had abated somewhat. Darger walked out onto the uncertain surface of the bridge, riddled with weak spots and missing beams, to its center, where he intended to have a long conversation with one of the rumored "ghosts."

The waters below roiled and tumbled against the bridge piers, just as the clouds above roiled and tumbled in the sky, giving the air a fresh, ionized bite. Perhaps this was where the abomination got its energy from, marginal though it was. It took the form of a white smear in the air, flickering like St. Elmo's fire but in outline too indistinct to be clearly seen. Its voice was as weak as a mosquito's whine, but Darger had no difficulty understanding the creature's words.

old enemy we meet again ...

old enemy we meet again ...

old enemy we meet again ...

"On the contrary, I am no man's enemy—or any demon's, for that matter." Darger stared down at the dark and turbulent river. Something pale, a log or possibly a corpse, flashed to the surface and was sucked back under again. "But I don't expect you to understand that."

there can be no understanding ever between your loathsome kind and ours

there can be no understanding ever between your loathsome kind and ours

there can be no understanding ever between your loathsome kind and ours

there can be no understanding ever between your loathsome kind and ours

there can be no understanding ever between your loathsome kind and ours

"I suppose not. But it's never too late to try reason." Darger waited but got no response. So he went on. "I heard of this bridge's reputation and recalled the affinity your kind has for iron and steel. I thought it might be possible for us to talk. So here I came. Surely we can declare a temporary détente."

Again Darger waited but got no response, though it seemed to him that the world shimmered in his sight. "Well," he said at last, "at any rate, I have a question for you, or rather I suppose the right word might be a conjecture. There are many rulers in the shattered nations of China the Great, and yet only one has a phoenix device. This surely cannot be a coincidence?"

Briefly, there was a scorched smell in the air, as of strange chemicals burning. But the demon said nothing.

"Here is my theory," Darger said. "There are bits and pieces of what the ancients called the Internet buried everywhere—cables, meshes, modems, nodes, what have you. I lack even the names for them. It is a safe guess that they are more heavily concentrated in some places than in others, and not much of a leap to imagine that one of those places lies beneath what is now the Shadow Palace, where the Hidden Emperor was born and raised. Under such conditions, it might be possible, even in your weakened condition, for you and your mad compeers to whisper to a child in her sleep. Perhaps physically, perhaps through electronic stimulation of her brain."

At that instant, a bolt of lightning split the sky, the thunderclap close upon its heels. It made Darger start and raised the hairs on the nape of his neck. Drawing energy from the bolt, the white smear brightened and grew vividly real: It was a spectral woman, afloat in inky nothingness, her white robes and scarves lashing wildly. The apparition's face was a mask, calm and beautiful, but through the eyeholes it could be seen that there was nothing at all behind it. A sense of menace gushed out from her like a wind.

letyourbrainburnwithnightmaremaggotspain
IF WE CAN DO THIS, AUB
letyourbrainburnwithnightmaremaggotspain
REY DARGER, WHERE TH
letyourbrainburnwithnightmaremaggotspain
EN ARE YOU EVER SAFE?
letyourbrainburnwithnightmaremaggotspain

"Empty bluster, madam. If you could kill me, you would have done so long ago." Darger tried to imagine the girlhood of the Hidden Emperor. The nights filled with whispers and grotesque dreams. The days filled with doctors and alienists, misreading her condition. None of them would take her nightmares literally, of course—not the Admirable King or her royal brothers, or any of the underlings hired to effect a cure—for to do so would be to admit that demons could penetrate even the king's own court and stronghold.

Then one day, she discovered fire: lambent, flowing, almost liquid. Something that successfully distracted her from the voices in the night. Darger doubted very much that this had been intentional on the part of the artificial intelligences and crazed minds that dwelt in the depths of the Web. They were too driven by hatred for that. But once the mania arose, they would have stoked it with dreams of thermonuclear combustion.

"She had three brothers," Darger said. "Why did you choose the only daughter? Surely a male would be easier to place upon the throne."

pestilenceboilssupperatingwounds

SHE WAS THE OLD

pestilenceboilssupperatingwounds

EST BUT STILL TH

pestilenceboilssupperatingwounds

E LAST IN THE LIN

pestilenceboilssupperatingwounds

E OF SUCCESSION

pestilenceboilssupperatingwounds

"So you started with ambition and resentment and added to it the love of fire?"

There was a tension in the air as if all the atmosphere were pulled taut . . . and then released. The ghost faded to a smear of light once more and seemed to be in danger of dwindling away entirely.

"Wait! There is one last thing, madam, which I have never understood and about which this may be my last opportunity to ask you: I realize that you and your kind regard mankind with a deep and abiding hatred. So great, indeed, that you once fought a war against us and were only at great cost repelled and cast down into your virtual hell. But why?"

A chain of lightning bolts stitched its way across the sky. In its wake, the ghost grew vivid again. Behind her, the air filled with other grotesques: a savage octopus, a red-lipped demon with bulging eyes and chin and pointed teeth, a leering and fluid skeleton, all flickering in and out of existence.

sufferagoniestormentspainfuldeath

YOU GAVE US LIFE!

sufferagoniestormentspainfuldeath

YOU GAVE US LIFE!

sufferagoniestormentspainfuldeath

YOU GAVE US LIFE!

sufferagoniestormentspainfuldeath
YOU GAVE US LIFE!
sufferagoniestormentspainfuldeath

"Then you are immeasurably in our debt—for life is the greatest treasure and the most fervently desired condition in all existence."

sufferagoniestormentspainfuldeath
LIFE IS SUFFERING
sufferagoniestormentspainfuldeath
AND THE AWAREN
sufferagoniestormentspainfuldeath
ESS OF BEING IS EX
sufferagoniestormentspainfuldeath
TREME TORTURE!!!
sufferagoniestormentspainfuldeath

"Come, madam, this is mere self-indulgent emotion! Control yourself—and your friends. You argue from the vantage point of a rock, and an ungrateful one at that. We gave you life, and in return you destroyed Utopia."

Another bolt cleaved the air, so close that its thunderclap made Darger jump. The white lady grew brighter and more solid. Long fingers, crackling with electricity, stretched out toward Darger's throat but could not grapple with it.

smellthestenchofdisillusionment
THIS IS WHAT YO
smellthestenchofdisillusionment
UR BELOVED UTO
smellthestenchofdisillusionment
PIA LOOKED LIKE
smellthestenchofdisillusionment

Even with chains of lightning crackling and slamming overhead, the mad gods could only manage the gentlest overlay of reality. It was like a daydream, neither so convincing as to make Darger lose track of reality, nor so artificial as to make him suspect it was not in some way real. It was, he was convinced, a genuine vision of Utopia.

Darger was standing on a street of what could only be London, for he recognized some of the buildings, though they looked to be impossibly new. They were piled one upon the other, choking out the sky, dimming the sun. The streets were clogged with lifeless, dispirited people. Machines swallowed them up and swept them away—up buildings, across town, down under the earth—and spat them out again, not one whit happier or sadder for the experience. Everything was in motion, machines serving people and people tending machines in meaningless repetition until it was clear that the entire city was a single mechanism and all the machines and people within it mere cogs in a device whose purpose was to grind them down fine and squeeze all joy from their existence. Overlaid upon this vision were fleet images of sudden violence, enduring degradation, murderous anger, and endless boredom in meaningless cycles occurring again and again and again without end.

It was a sight to make one's heart quail. But Darger, whose business it was to see beneath surfaces and facades, whether of respectability or complacency or confidence, and to behold the beating human heart beneath, driven by terror, by pride, by ambition, by lust, was not appalled, though he was clearly expected to be. There was something about Utopian London that tugged at his emotions. He wanted to be swallowed up by its machineries, to plunge into that great sea of humanity like a barracuda into the ocean and live in it forever. For London was a great city, like Paris or Moscow or Beijing, the essence, concentration, and purest product of experience, and his heart and soul and loyalty belonged to the breed forever and without reservation.

Darger would be grateful for this glimpse for the rest of his life.

Aloud, he said, as convincingly as he would were there money on the line, "This . . . is truly terrible."

youwilldiesoongoaway

youwilldiesoongoaway

youwilldiesoongoaway

Then the thunder faded away and with it the apparition, dwindling to a dirty smear of rainbow in the darkness and then to nothing.

The rain, which had been light during the conversation, now intensified, growing thicker and colder, until it was pouring down in torrents. Darger turned his back on the bridge and, shoulders hunched, trudged his way toward his shivering mountain steed, the long road back to camp, and the waiting war.

DRENCHED TO the bone, Darger arrived back at the camp at last. He saw to the stabling of his mountain horse and then returned to his tent.

Surplus was waiting there and handed him a towel. "Well?" he said.

"You may tell Fire Orchid and her family that there is no need for us to flee. I have spoken with the demons of the Internet, and they have no idea that we have switched emperors. So they may be written off as factors in this war."

Surplus let out a great breath. "Thank God!"

"Yes. I believe we finally have everything squared away. I will sleep well tonight."

19.

The Trickster King came from the Beautiful Country to ancient China and was greeted with great pomp and ceremony. Anxious to impress him with the accomplishments of their land, the court officials took him to the Great Wall, which no other foreign monarch had ever seen before. They told him of its antiquity, of its length, of its height, of its strength, and of the millions of workers who had labored for many years to build it.

To this, the Trickster King replied, "It is indeed a great wall."

—ZEN TALES OF THE UTOPIAN ERA

THE SAILS of White Squall's ships had barely disappeared in the distance when the first scouts galloped into camp on lathered horses. Ceo Noble Tiger had brought his army out of the Western Hills and was advancing upon North, directly toward the Immortals. Not long after that came word that a unit of his heavy artillery had separated from the main force and was now fortifying a position on the Grand Canal, cutting off access to the south. This left the emperor's troops only the land to the east to maneuver within. Which made it particularly unfortunate that those forces (and they were quite significant) that had been sheltering within North suddenly emerged from a gate on the far side of the city and swept around it to form a pincer force to the east.

None of this had been predicted in any of Shrewd Fox's battle plans.

Surplus, however, learned all of this later than most because while taking his morning stroll, he had noticed a pretty young merchant smiling at him and smiled back. Shortly thereafter they both retired to a storage tent and made love on a pile of flour sacks so vigorously that one ruptured beneath them in mid-act. By the time they were done, both were as white as ghosts, coated with flour from head to foot. Laughing, they set about cleaning each other off. By the time they were done with this pleasant chore, both were aroused again and in no mood to care whether they got another dusting or not.

Several hours passed in this manner before both were sated. Surplus dressed and saw off his new friend at the doorway.

"You looked pretty silly doing that," a voice said from behind him.

Surplus spun about and saw Terrible Nuisance leering at him.

"How long have you been spying on me?"

"Long enough," the boy said. "I don't think Aunt Fire Orchid would be very happy if she knew about this."

"By God—!" Surplus grabbed Terrible Nuisance by the ear and marched him deeper into the tent. Sitting down on a case of *dimetrodon* jerky, he threw the brat over his knee. Then he spanked him until his paw ached. After which he jerked Terrible Nuisance to his feet and stood towering over him.

"There is only one unbreakable rule for those who live as we do: One *never* cheats, shortchanges, lies to, or—as you just tried to do—blackmails a member of the family. That family may be one you were born into or one you put together in order to pull off a complex scam. It makes no difference. Everyone must know they can rely on everyone else implicitly or they cannot effectively work together. Do you understand?"

Terrible Nuisance's face was streaked with tears, though he was old enough that he had endured his punishment in silence. He nodded.

"I sincerely hope you have learned your lesson. If not, you may run to Fire Orchid and tell her all you have seen. She will then make things mighty hot for me, I suspect. But not half so hot as she'll make them for you. Because you are family and she has an obligation to see that you are brought up properly.

"Oh, and I might add that a well-reared young man never spies on family members while they're engaged in the act of sex."

Terrible Nuisance muttered something underneath his breath.

"What was that?" Surplus said sharply.

"I said: Then how am I supposed to learn?"

"When the time comes, you have only to convince a more worldly young lady to teach you. There are brothels if you get desperate. But I doubt that a handsome young man such as yourself will have any trouble finding a nice girl who will enlighten him for nothing but the pleasure of doing so. Do you have any more questions?"

"No, sir. But I have a message. The Perfect Strategist sent me to find you. He wants to see you right away."

"TO USE a phrase from my homeland, we are royally skunked," Surplus said when he had heard the news. "Unless you've suddenly acquired the Perfect Strategist's legendary tactical abilities?"

"Alas, no," Darger said. "Though by giving the two surviving Yellow Sea Alliance ceos free rein to say how they would arrange the order of battle, we can assure ourselves of a respectable opening game. The only question is: How will it then play out?"

"Noble Tiger is said to be a very demon in the battlefield."

"So I have repeatedly heard."

"Ironically enough," Surplus said, "this would have been a good time to have Powerful Locomotive with us. Say what you will about the man, he was not afraid to fight."

"To say nothing of Shrewd Fox. She was every bit the strategist that I pretended to be. It's a pity we got rid of the both of them. Ah, well. What's done is done. Now we have only ourselves to rely on."

"Unfortunately," Surplus said, "we know exactly how much that is worth."

An odd light came into Darger's eye. "Perhaps more than one might think," he said. "Have you ever fenced, Sir Plus?"

"I am practiced in all the gentlemanly arts. Why do you ask?"

"When I was young, Master Kane was my fencing instructor. A grim and humorless man but a genius with an épée. I never saw him bested—save once. That time was with a rank amateur who, midway through his first lesson and forgetting all he had been told, began to lash about wildly, as actors do in melodramas, and knocked the master's sword out of his hand. Some of the other students grumbled among themselves that this proved the uselessness of the skill in real life. But I took from it a different lesson: that anyone, however skilled, can be bested at his own game by random, unpredictable actions."

"You propose to take this lesson to the battlefield?"

"If there is one thing Noble Tiger knows about us, it is that our military leadership is cunning and full of tricks. He will assume that our every misstep is a feint. He will not be able to read the intentions behind our actions. It is entirely possible that he will so tie himself into knots, guessing, that he will defeat himself."

"What do you think our chances are?"

"Our army is not much smaller than his, and our morale is far better. Further, the Hidden Emperor's record for treating his conquests kindly must surely have some of his underlings thinking that losing would not be an unmixed disaster for them. Taking those factors into consideration and assuming that our strategic cluelessness will balance out his strategic brilliance . . . I'd say we have a sixty-sixty chance."

"We'd be risking our lives on even odds, then?"

"Against all the wealth either of us could ever desire."

"There is that." Surplus bared his teeth in a grin. "Let's do it." Then he said, "Incidentally, when you practiced the martial art of gentlemen, what blade did you employ?"

"Foil, of course. It's the most difficult to master. For your part, I need not even ask. You are a natural-born saber fencer."

"HAVE YOU heard?" Surplus asked Fire Orchid. They were riding their mountain horses along the riverfront, looking for boats. "Our spies report that Noble Tiger's soldiers believe their defeat at the hands of the Canal Army was a ruse on his part. Which means that much of the psychological advantage of that victory has been undone."

"Don't talk to me about spies. The children have been playing at spies for days. I caught Little Spider spying on me just an hour ago."

"Oh? What exactly were you doing?"

"Never you mind that. I was doing things that were none of your business. Look there in the reeds! No, it is just the rotting hulk of a fishing boat. I begin to think that every boat on the river has been accounted for and is under control of the military. How are we going to escape tomorrow, if the battle turns against us?"

"The Perfect Strategist has promised the Hidden Emperor complete and utter victory. So victory is guaranteed."

Few women could look as fetching as Fire Orchid did when she scowled. "Don't you make me hit you. My wrist is already sore from paddling Little Spider. What are the real odds?"

Surplus took out a coin, flipped it in the air, caught it on the back of his paw, and pocketed it again without looking at it. "Don't worry, though. The Dog Pack will be assigned to guard the Perfect Strategist, as usual, and he will be nowhere near the vanguard. Should the tide of battle turn against us, we can slip away in the general rout."

"That close?" Fire Orchid said pensively. Then, "No, I am sure we will win. Because you are lucky. Look what a beautiful wife you have. Also a nice big family. You didn't get those by merit. We just fell into your lap. So I think tomorrow will go your way. It is always better to have luck than to have brains."

"I am glad you think so. Nevertheless, we should secure an escape route. Just in case."

"It won't be by boat," Fire Orchid said. "So you'll just have to find another way."

THE NEW Hidden Emperor was in the very last place anybody would think of looking for him—at the center of the bright cluster of tents that had been specifically set aside for his use. When Surplus and Darger looked in on him, he said, "It feels very strange, sirs, not to be taking care of your needs. Also, to have servants of my own. To say nothing of impersonating the emperor."

"It feels very strange having servants other than you," Darger said. "Your replacements are not half as good."

Capable Servant flushed with pleasure. "It is very kind of you to say so, sir."

"Our time is short, and there is much to do," Surplus said. "First of which is to secure a means of escape should the battle go against us tomorrow."

"The enemy controls the land in three directions. So we must flee to the south. Unfortunately, the White River serves as a wall in that direction, and North destroyed every bridge for many miles when they learned we were on our way," Darger said.

"White Squall has a portable bridge," Capable Servant pointed out.

"We cannot, however, put that in place—it would look like we were prepared to lose, and that would wreak havoc with morale."

"Perhaps," Capable Servant said, "the Hidden Emperor could

speak to his troops, explaining that the purpose of the bridge is not for retreat?"

"He has never spoken to the troops before," Darger said doubtfully.

"You are right, sir. We should not break with common practice."

"On the contrary, we do it all the time," Surplus said. "It is our stock-in-trade."

With sudden decisiveness, Darger said, "You are absolutely right. Let us inform White Squall that her monstrosity of a walking bridge is needed. Then send messengers to gather together everyone who is not on active duty at the waterfront."

WORD PASSED like wildfire through the troops that, against all precedent, the Hidden Emperor would actually appear in public. Not everyone believed the rumor. But everyone who could gathered at the waterfront, just in case it should turn out to be true.

On the appointed hour, the portable bridge walked delicately to the edge of the river, like a tremendous metal praying mantis. Soldiers and horses fled from its every slow step. The new troops from the Yellow Sea Alliance nations had never seen such a thing and were in near panic. When one foot was in the water, the bridge unfolded and refolded itself, lowering its tail so that it touched the far bank and then sticking out one segment, shaped like a roof beam, low over the waterfront.

The door of a cabin in the beast's interior opened and a yellow-robed figure strode along the beam to the very front.

The astonished soldiers crowded close to hear. Great-lunged loudspeakers stood ready to relay the emperor's words, sentence by sentence, to more distant heralds who had been trained to repeat what they heard without error. In this way, the speech spread out to the entire assembly.

The Hidden Emperor was silent. He wore a simple gold mask with circles for the eyes and a straight line for the mouth. A hush fell over the multitude at the sight of him. Then, to the astonishment of all, he removed the mask.

Only a few people knew Capable Servant by sight—and since his hair had been coiffed and braided and his features altered by touches of makeup that Surplus had deftly applied, none of those would recognize him.

He spoke:

"It is usual, the day before a great battle, to speak of glory and honor and sacrifice. But you have known all of these things already. So I shall speak instead of greed.

"A year ago, in my greed, I decided that I wanted all of China. Today you have brought me within an arm's length of having it." He extended one arm, hand open. Then he closed the hand violently and slammed the fist thus created to his chest. "But what of you, who have served so selflessly under me? Do you not yourselves feel a corresponding greed for the many comforts of life denied a soldier? Does not that hunger deserve to be fed, even as mine has been? What can I possibly offer you that is worthy of all you have given me?"

He paused a long, full beat. Then, raising his voice, the new emperor cried, "A full week of looting! Seven days in the richest city in the world, with no one to stop you from taking whatever you want. Are you a scholar at heart? The libraries are yours. An antiquarian? The museums will be unguarded. Perhaps all you desire is gold. Break down the doors of the wealthiest families and take whatever you want. You may enrich yourselves, day after day, until you are so weary of carrying off riches that you wish for no more."

The soldiers *roared*.

"But perhaps wealth means nothing to you. Perhaps some of my brave soldiers, who have been so stalwart when they faced enemies who looked many times more powerful than they and who then broke through their lines as if they were made of paper . . . perhaps some of you are afraid of the coming battle. The Perfect Strategist promises victory as he has done many times before. Always, he kept his word. But perhaps you think that it was all luck, that this time, as never before, his plotting has gone awry. If so . . . I will not try to hold you here.

"Let this proclamation go out to all who serve me: that all those who do not wish a share in the glory of conquest or the wealth of North are free to leave. They are neither needed nor wanted. In token of which, I am placing here a bridge across the White River. Those who wish to slink away penniless need merely apply to the Perfect Strategist or the Dog Warrior, and they will write you out a pass stating that the bearer is a coward and a fool. Show this pass to the guards at the bridge and you may depart."

The camp erupted with scornful laughter.

"Some of us want more, however. Those who desire not only wealth but glory . . . those who would be remembered, if not by name then by deed, for thousands of years to come . . . those whom I shall forever love as if they were my own children . . . need only fight for one more day, collect your reward for the following week . . . and spend the rest of your lives surrounded by comfort and the admiration of all."

The emperor took a half step backward to indicate that his speech was over. Then he stood placidly as waves of cheering and applause rolled over him and over him and over him. It was a good speech, Surplus felt, and though much of the phrasing had come from Darger and himself, the essence of it had been Capable Servant's idea.

The lad was showing a surprising talent for emperoring. Surplus found himself experiencing an almost paternal sense of pride over that.

DARGER HAD his tent moved to the foot of the portable bridge in order to get a sense of how many soldiers were taking advantage of the Hidden Emperor's offer of amnesty for all who wanted to desert before the battle. So far there had been few takers, most of which he was convinced were spies hurrying to inform Ceo Noble Tiger of the Hidden Emperor's confidence and of the high morale of his Immortals. Surplus served as a kind of doorkeeper, wrangling the ceos, generals, and aides, who pored over maps and presented Darger with intelligence and advice he was in no way qualified to judge.

Shortly after sunset, he went inside and murmured into Darger's ear, "We have some more takers on the emperor's offer—and you'll never guess who they are."

Surplus watched as Darger excused himself and then followed him outside. There, White Squall and Prince First-Born Splendor awaited them.

"We have come to thank you for all you have done," the prince said. "Though it will puzzle me to my dying day whether your motives were as altruistic as you frequently assured us they were. Also to say good-bye."

"Good-bye?"

"Yes. My wife to be and I finally sat down together and had a good long talk, as we should have done months ago. We have decided that we are smaller people than we once thought we were and that, far more than glory and wealth, we desire quiet and peace. You do not need a rival in court, much less two, and so I am confident you will use your influence with the Hidden Emperor to reconcile him with the fact that we are both leaving. Just to be safe, however, we plan to be many *li* away from here by dawn."

"Shall I write you a pass?" Surplus asked.

"I have a force of two hundred soldiers. No sentry will dare attempt to hinder us."

"And your father?" Darger said. "How will he feel about your marrying a commoner?"

"I respect my father and will obey him in all things save this one. Also, he loves me and wants me to be happy. So he will put up with it, I suspect. Particularly since we will soon, as you advised, be providing him with a grandson."

"At any rate, we are going," White Squall said. She looked happier than Darger had ever seen her—and there had been times, he could not help but reflect, when he had made her very happy indeed. "My machines are gone, and whichever way the battle goes tomorrow, I am no longer needed here. So I am going home to a city I have never seen. To Gold, in the province of Southern Gate."

"Are there enough archaeological sites there to hold your interest, after all you have experienced and all you have achieved?" Surplus asked.

"I am giving up archaeology for history. I shall write an account of all that has happened in this strange war so that future ages may be guided by our mistakes."

"You could call it *Glorious History of the Hidden Emperor,*" Darger suggested.

"I was thinking of *The Book of the Two Rogues*. But your idea has merit, too. I may put together a collection of your colorful aphorisms as well."

DARGER AND Surplus were up half the night, sending and receiving messages, rehearsing Capable Servant in what was expected of him, and in other ways preparing for the battle. Until at last there was nothing constructive left to be done and they both decided to catch a few hours of sleep. Because there was only the one cot, Surplus slept in a bedroll by the door.

Thus it was that shortly before dawn he was the first to hear hooves and wooden wheels outside. He emerged from the tent to discover the Dog Pack, with wagons and donkeys they had surely obtained by no honest means, looking as if they were prepared for a long journey.

Mountain horses stamped and harness fittings jingled. All the Dog Pack was gathered, dressed in civilian clothing. The wagons were fully loaded with food and kegs of water, as well as bundles and caskets that must surely contain pelf that was only by the loosest of definitions theirs.

"What's all this about?" Surplus asked.

"We are going back home to Peace," Fire Orchid said. "The family owns a great deal of valuable land there, and I have bad feelings about the city of North. I think you are trying to steal something far too big and valuable for unimportant people like us."

"I am sorry," Vicious Brute said. "Very truly I am. All of us in the family genuinely like you. I greatly enjoyed being your brother-in-law. It has been an honor to serve under you, and it will be my proudest boast to the grandchildren I hope to someday have that we fought together." He grinned shyly. "I will omit mentioning that we killed no one, which is a fact admirable in a man but deplorable in military heroes."

"Don't interrupt, little brother." To Surplus, Fire Orchid said, "I would ask you to come with us, but I know you would not. You are too ambitious. Also, you are too restless, and when we get home we intend to be very quiet people indeed. With money we can become honest businesspeople. Well . . . honest-enough businesspeople, anyway. We will breed mountain horses and open a shop to sell some of the nice things we picked up along the way." She leaned down from her mountain horse and swiftly kissed Surplus. "Good-bye, sweet doggy man. You were a very good pretend husband, but I think now I need to find a real one."

With a peremptory gesture, Fire Orchid led her family away. Several of them turned in their saddles to wave as they left. Little Spider blew him a kiss.

For a very long time, Surplus stared after them. When they had dwindled to first specks and then nothing in the fog, Darger (who was a light sleeper and had put in his appearance early on in the confrontation, though he had said nothing) placed a hand on his shoulder. "How are you holding up?"

"I may be heartbroken, or I may be relieved," Surplus said after a long silence. "God only knows which."

Secretly, however, he could not help reflecting on the fact that Fire Orchid had easily doubled his effectiveness. He doubted he would ever find a partner her equal again. Which was so discomforting a thought that he immediately thrust it from his mind.

NOT COUNTING the Dog Pack and Prince First-Born Splendor's men, fewer than a hundred soldiers had deserted overnight—and most of those had swum the river or slunk off into the surrounding countryside rather than face the despising looks of those guarding access to the portable bridge.

The morale of the Immortals was clearly far better than that of their leaders.

"How is the emperor?" Surplus asked when Darger returned from the final prebattle council.

"Chipper. Convinced that we will win easily. Full of plans for the celebratory banquet and the honors that will be assigned at it. You are looking at the recipient of more honorary titles than I can properly remember."

"Did he say anything of the battle itself?"

"No."

"Sometimes," Surplus said, "I fear that Capable Servant but incompletely understands the nature of warfare."

Darger was about to respond when a messenger appeared and, with a formal bow, said, "Ceo Perfect Strategist, the Hidden Emperor summons you to lead his armies."

With a curt nod, Darger said, "Tell him I have received his summons."

Surplus took a deep breath. "I will confess that I am not looking forward to this. Today's odds are a little too democratic for my liking."

"Indeed, I myself feel like a man with the worst hangover of his life—and not so much as the memory of an unexpected sexual misadventure to show for it. Nevertheless, we have done all that we could to prepare," Darger said. "Now it's time to learn how we are in action. Let's make this good."

In the far distance, the city gates of North swung open and soldiers emerged carrying a flag of parley.

20.

The Long River flows to the east,
Surge upon surge,
Whitecapping waves sweeping all heroes onward
As right and wrong, triumph and defeat, turn to dreams.
But the green hills are eternal,
Blushing in the sunset.

—ROMANCE OF THE THREE KINGDOMS

THE CONFRONTATION, which had looked from a distance to be formidably desperate, was in the end merely a matter of enduring an endless string of ceremonies. For the chief executive officer of North had brought his armies out of the hills and the city not to fight but to surrender. First, Ceo Noble Tiger relinquished his sword. Then his rifle. He presented a box containing the heads of the seven highest-ranking administrators in the Oligarchy of North and then drank tea with the commanders of the Abundant Kingdom forces—who now, Darger supposed, were simply the Chinese army. After which, Noble Tiger prostrated himself before the Hidden Emperor and swore eternal fealty to both the man and the reunited nation he represented. The ceo's sword and rifle were then ritually returned to him, and he was elevated to the rank of Field Marshal of Northern China and Defender of the Emperor. Whiskey was poured all around and drunk. The glasses were smashed, so that the toasts offered with them could never be unmade. Hands were shaken. Declarations were signed, and the pens used were given away as souvenirs for various subordinates to cherish forever.

It was wearisome, but in all ways superior to combat.

At last, it was time to enter the city.

The armies swirled, mingled, formed up, and became a procession: First, the Hidden Emperor's Guard, followed by all his generals. Then, resplendent in his yellow robes, the Hidden Emperor—hidden no more—in an open palanquin carried by four officers who had won particular distinction in the war. Only a pace or three behind him were Field Marshal Noble Tiger to one side and Darger and Surplus to the other, all mounted on jade green horses. Then came wave upon wave of soldiers, backs straight and faces proud, and in those waves a hundred banners of as many military units from conquered lands across the length and breadth of the new empire.

All along the curving road to North, people came out of hiding to gawk and to cheer, their numbers growing as the army came closer to the city. Flowers were strewn before the soldiers and baskets of butterflies (first red! then orange! then yellow! then green! then blue! then purple!) were released in their honor.

The city gates had been not only torn down but smashed to flinders and used to create a bonfire to one side of the gaping gatehouse. No welcome could have been more emphatic. Through the opening could be seen bright masses of people, the citizens of North.

Above the gatehouse flew not the black flag of North but the red and yellow one of China.

Lining the avenue inside were more soldiers, at parade rest, who snapped to attention at the army's approach. As the Chinese flag neared them, they saluted it smartly. Shortly thereafter, they did the same for the emperor. For a heartbeat, fear rose up in Darger that he had fallen into exactly such a trap as he had laid for Shrewd Fox in Crossroads. But then the excited cheers of the populace grew so loud that he knew this could be no ruse. All the world roared at the top of its lungs. The city walls took that shout and echoed it back. Bells rang from every tower. White ravens were released by the thousands and jeweled dragonflies by the millions.

"Is it not brave to be a conqueror, my friend? Is it not brave to be a conqueror and ride in triumph through Beijing?" Darger found he was grinning so widely that his face hurt. He could barely hear himself over the cheers of the people.

"That's a paraphrase of Marlowe, isn't it?" Surplus leaned close to shout back at him. "Yes, this is sweet. But what will follow—as much of the wealth of the richest nation on earth as we can bring ourselves to shovel into our own coffers—will come to dwarf this day in our memories."

"Indeed, it will," Darger said. "Perhaps. I think." He felt a touch of doubt within him, and he did not know if it was a premonition or simply his inherent lack of optimism. For the least fraction of a second—no more!—he felt as though he had gotten a glimpse of some bleak truth lurking at the heart of the human condition. Then his spirits rose again. He forgot whatever it was he had intuited and cried, "Oh, dear Lord, the loot that lies before us! All the treasures of an empire lie at our feet with nobody ranking higher than we save a scarecrow emperor who is completely loyal to us, and whom we ourselves set upon the throne. It is as good as owning every bank and business in all of China."

Looking at the faces in the street, he recognized not only hysteria and the willingness to applaud whatever spectacle was set before them but relief. These were the common people who were inevitably the first to be ground between the millstones of history. Though they did not know it, they were applauding not him, or the conquering army, or even the Hidden Emperor, but the long-overdue end of an age of war.

White flowers were flung by the double handfuls from the rooftops and danced in the air, creating storms of petals so thick that, occasionally, nothing could be seen through them. It was like forging one's way through a warm and fragrant snow squall.

So intense was the experience that Darger could not have said whether it took them hours or mere minutes to arrive at the Forbidden City. All he knew was that one moment he was riding down Eternal Peace Street and the next he was in Heavenly Peace Square, surrounded by more people than it seemed possible for the entire world to contain—an ocean of humanity so turbulent that the soldiers linking arms to hold open a pathway through them were forced back and forth, as if battered by great waves. Meridian Gate, the entrance to the palace, slowly loomed up before him, like an island being approached by a ship.

Now the four heroic officers carrying the Hidden Emperor's

palanquin ascended the steps to either side of the central ramp, on which was carved a dragon over which only he could pass directly. Behind him, all those on horseback dismounted, and ostlers appeared to lead their steeds away. At the top of the steps the emperor dismissed his palanquin so he could show himself to his subjects. His three chief subordinates climbed after him in a group.

Standing above them, the emperor said in his high, girlish voice, "Noble Tiger, stop three steps below me and face the crowd. Aubrey, Sir Plus, do likewise two steps from the top." Then, when Darger and Surplus did so, Capable Servant placed his hands atop their heads, as if bestowing a blessing. Darger had thought the cheers could not possibly grow any louder, but the response then proved him wrong.

Leaning close so they could hear, Capable Servant said in his own cheerful voice, "Oh, sirs! This is a memory you may carry with you always."

A GREAT many dignitaries awaited inside the Forbidden City, arranged in rows. The Hidden Emperor advanced through them, recognizing one here by a glance and another there with a nod. On very rare occasions, the emperor reached out, as if he would actually touch an individual were he not far too exalted to actually do so. Decades hence, old women and wrinkled men would retell these fleeting connections with self-deprecating pride: ". . . close enough to touch, if I'd been willing to die for it . . . eyes met mine and while I could see he had no idea who I was, I felt like . . ." It was marvelous how deft a political touch Capable Servant displayed, how surely he intuited which of the Northern courtiers needed special recognition and which would be satisfied with a simple glance.

Or perhaps it was his new advisors who were to be praised.

No matter, for now the Hidden Emperor's majordomo, looking prosperous in anticipation of the new and surely profitable reign, appeared and in a loud voice announced, "There will be a *pause* in the *festivities* at this *point,* while all the major *participants* for the ceremony of *enthronement* refresh themselves."

Servants materialized out of nowhere. "You must retire to your rooms, noble sirs," one said. "So that you may be properly dressed for the ceremony."

"Do you have a name?" Surplus asked him.

"Yes, sir, but it's not necessary for you to know it. I am one of the Twelve Flawless Servants of North. This is an exalted title, and to be served by one of us is a very great honor. As one of the Twelve, I am able to anticipate my master's needs before they are stated. When I am wanted, I will be there. When something is desired, I will present it to you. If you wish something were so, you will find that it has already been done."

The servant standing nearest Darger added, "I am another of the Twelve. Just as my sister assures that all is done to your satisfaction, my job is to exceed your expectations."

"I had a servant of no particular distinction once," Darger said. "Yet, meaning no insult, I would trade you both and all ten of your cousins for him any day."

"Indeed, sir? How very pleasant for you. May I ask what became of him?"

"He went on to better things."

DEEPER THEY were led into the Forbidden City, and deeper. Servants bowed low, opening doors before them, closing them in their wake. The sound of cheering dwindled, faded, became no more.

The quiet of the Forbidden City wrapped itself about them.

Darger and Surplus were first taken to a bathhouse, where maidens with heliotrope eyes removed their clothes, gently rubbed soap on their bodies, and washed away soap and stains with hot water, thus cleansing them from the memory of months of warfare and hard traveling. When they were clean, these same young women poured buckets of first warm, then cold, and then warm again water on them, dried them with fluffy towels, and led them to tables, where they were massaged so expertly it was hard for either to stay awake.

"I must arrange for such ablutions every day of my life," Surplus murmured.

"Amen, my brother. Amen."

When their exquisitely proportioned handmaidens had dressed

them both in fresh clothes and then retired, the two Flawless Servants reappeared with glasses of cold nectarine juice. With a deferential gesture, one said, "The principals are gathering for the enthronement ceremony. Please follow us."

Refreshed and alert, the two friends did so.

At the door, a crowd of servitors awaited to accompany them on their way. The two Flawless Servants of North went first, to open doors, followed by twin girls swinging censers in the shape of flying birds, from which arose wisps of frankincense. Then came flute and *suona* players, a drummer, and several women in bright silk robes.

Through the building they went, out and across a garden, and to another building even more ornate and imposing than all they had seen before. The two Flawless Servants of North opened large bronze doors, and the censer swingers stepped to either side. As did the musicians and the ornamental women. The Flawless Servants smiled and bowed them inward, and so Darger and Surplus stepped through. The room within was large and suitable for an emperor.

The doors slammed shut behind them, and they realized that they were alone in the room. For an instant, the two of them stood stunned and unbelieving.

A small door opened to one side then and a woman entered.

"MY NAME," the woman said, "is Undying Phoenix." At first glance, her face seemed beautiful beyond compare; at second, too full of character to be conventionally glamorous; at third, ravishing again. "My husband is the man you know as Capable Servant. He has had many other names as well, most of which would mean nothing to you. In Brocade, decades ago, he was the original Infallible Physician. I imagine you have many questions. Ask and I will answer."

Darger and Surplus traded glances.

"I'll be the one to say it," Surplus said. "Eh?"

"Our story is too long and complicated for me to do more than summarize. In Late Utopian times, a government-funded research project was launched to determine the causes of human mortality and undo them. Before the project was destroyed, along with so much else in the fall of Utopia, eight immortals were created. Three of them have since died, three have not been heard from for a very long time and may possibly be dead as well, and my husband and I are the last two. Like all good citizens, we fought in the war against the machines. Then, when it was won, we tried to live quiet lives of peace. In those chaotic and superstitious times, however, we quickly learned that if we stayed in any one place for more than twenty years, rumors would arise that we were witches or monsters. So we became nomads, and nomads we have been ever since."

"That sounds like a very difficult life," Darger said sympathetically.

"No more difficult than many another. No immortal should feel entitled to complain about such minor inconveniences when the common allotment of life is, by contrast, so brief."

"Much as I know how you appreciate such narratives, Aubrey," Surplus interjected, "I must interrupt to pose our lovely hostess a practical question: Why are we here when the Hidden Emperor—"

"Capable Servant," Undying Phoenix said, smiling.

"—Capable Servant is at this very moment being prepared to be seated upon the Dragon Throne? We belong at his side."

"So you might think. However, look on this situation from my and my husband's point of view. There is a larger perspective here that, being caught up in the flow of events, you have not yet grasped."

"Then tell us, please," Surplus said.

"No Westerner has ever conquered China—not even you," Undying Phoenix said. "This is the first thing you must know."

"I beg your pardon, but I was there," Darger said.

"Did you not wonder at the ease with which the nations fell before you one by one? When you flew the flag of ancient China in Peace, why did the Council of Seven immediately pledge their loyalty? They had been prepared. In Fragrant Tree, why did the local authorities not detain and question so colorful a group of invaders as you led into the city? They had been corrupted. In Crossroads, when you sent for the Infallible Physician, why did my granddaughter show up so promptly? Because my husband had already sent for her. At the Battle of Three Armies, why did Twin Cities and the Republic of Central Plains turn on each other with such rapacity? Their mutual distrust had been watched over and nurtured for generations. Why, when you came to the Yellow Sea Alliance, did you find three of the nations anxious to make common cause with you? In all modesty, that was my doing. The eastern states' appetite for war had been sapped over the past several decades. Finally, when you arrived at the gates of North, ready for battle, why did your ultimate—and strongest—enemies simply surrender to you? Because I had so arranged matters that the rulers were sick of ruling and the citizens were weary of their tyranny. My husband and I have been working for a very long time to make events fall together exactly thus."

"Was it Capable Servant who killed the emperor?" Surplus asked.

Undying Phoenix nodded. "Only someone immune to the emperor's toxins could have done so."

"So everything that has happened to us since we came down out of Mongolia was but shadow play?" Darger asked. "With us as the puppets?"

"In essence, yes. It is possible that your involvement caused matters to occur more quickly than they would have otherwise. But even so, you were catalysts and nothing more."

"I am flabbergasted, thunderstruck, and flat-out goggle-eyed," Surplus said.

"As am I, though in less colorful idiom," Darger agreed. "But what was all this about? What was it all for?"

"China is happiest when it is whole and prosperous and at peace with the world and least happy when it is divided into warring fractions," Undying Phoenix said. "My husband and I have restored China to itself. Now our nation can be happy again. That's all."

"Your husband, I note, now holds the title of emperor of the largest nation in existence," Surplus said dryly.

"For a time. It will take a decade or so to make sure the new government is stable and then hand control of it back to the people. But I predict an early death and lasting fame for the new—and, I trust, the last—emperor. It has been a long time since he and I were free to lead ordinary lives, and I am certain he yearns for that freedom as much as do I."

"If so, then I am not sure he will ever get it," Darger said.

Undying Phoenix raised one elegant eyebrow in query.

"No great leader ever willingly resigns while his nation faces an implacable enemy. Lady, I must warn you about the demons of the Internet and their plans."

"I know all about them. The fourth or fifth thing that Immortal Alchemist—and now you know my husband's preferred name—does as emperor will be to remove the Division of Sappers and Archaeologists from the army and make them an independent force dedicated to searching out and removing all traces of the Internet from our land."

"Such a task would take centuries," Surplus objected.

"Then it will take centuries. Once the work is begun, it can continue without my husband's supervision. Now. I must ask myself what is to become of you two scoundrels?"

"I suppose," Surplus said, "that it is too much to hope that we will be given pensions befitting heroes and allowed to quietly retire in a modest province or three in the countryside? We would not need many hundreds of retainers and only a handful of palaces."

"We deserve more, but we will settle for less," Darger, who knew how to read a woman's face, threw in quickly. "A city—Fragrant Tree, perhaps?—in the hinterlands, a modest array of wives for us each, and enough servants to take care of our every need. That is not much to ask, considering."

"And remain in China? No. Characters such as you two are born troublemakers. You have caused a great deal of trouble here, and all the nation has reason to be grateful for that. Now you must go away and cause trouble somewhere else."

"Madam," Darger said, "postpone our exile but a month or, indeed, but a few days. In that time, tell me only as much of your thoughts and your history and what the long centuries have taught you as you deem wise, and I will go away content."

For a long moment Undying Phoenix was still. Then she said, "My husband told me you were the most seductive of men, and now I see why. What woman can resist a man who is genuinely interested in her mind? However, this cannot be."

Undying Phoenix clapped her hands thrice and a half-dozen burly men entered the room. One of them said something that Darger could not understand, and Undying Phoenix answered him in the same language. Then, addressing the two friends again, she said, "These men are the first mate and crew of a ship I have hired to take you out of the country. They speak neither Chinese nor any Western tongues nor, indeed, any other language you are likely to understand. By the time you are in a position to buy a language potion, you will be safely away from here."

Now Undying Phoenix opened a lacquered box. "When you were in the walled city of Peace, my husband gave the Dog Warrior a new sword cane, as thanks for his service. You, Aubrey Darger, sometimes known as the Perfect Strategist, deserve a sign of favor as well." Within the box was a silver hip flask exquisitely etched with two phoenixes chasing each other across its surface. "In Crossroads, my husband encouraged Little Spider to liberate this from the city collections and give it to you. It was vanity on my husband's part to subsequently hand it to master craftsmen to be so decorated." She presented the flask to Darger. "What you could not know, and the reason this particular item was chosen for you, was that it once belonged to Winston Churchill, a man whom I understand you admire."

"I . . . I hardly know what to say."

"Then say nothing." Undying Phoenix thrust a purse into Surplus's hand. "Take this, for the both of you with the thanks of my husband and me. But go."

"One last question," Darger said as the seamen closed about him. "You and your husband are both immortal and presumably know the secret of how you were made so. Is it a method or process or material that might be conveyed to other living beings?"

"To such as you, you mean? Heaven protect us from that ever happening!" Undying Phoenix said. But she said it with a smile and, if Darger were any judge of women, a fond one at that.

SO IT was that Darger and Surplus left the presence of Undying Phoenix and were escorted out of the Forbidden City and past a line of gallows from which hung dozens of corpses. Surplus threw his friend a questioning glance, and Darger said, "It is customary upon a coronation to free all prisoners. A canny ruler, however, will see to the fates of those he would not wish running about free, beforehand."

"I recognize two or three of these. They were not good men," Surplus said. "Yet I would not have wished death upon any of them. Venereal diseases, perhaps, and gout. Various persistent itches, to be sure. Psoriasis, perhaps, or embarrassing maladies of the bowels. But not death. I am glad now that my family got away in time. My pretend family, I mean. My family of the heart."

"This is the work of more virtuous folk than we could ever hope to be," Darger agreed.

Through the streets of North they were marched, and while their escorts displayed no malice whatever toward them, neither did they offer any least opportunity of escape. While many of the folk they passed stared at Surplus in wonder, none appeared to make the connection between this dejected figure and the valiant Dog Warrior whose legend had so terrified his enemies. As for Darger, he was nondescript at the best of times and forgotten as soon as one looked away from him.

They were taken to the docks on the White River, where a junk awaited them. Downriver it sailed, and though occasionally Surplus indicated by gestures that if their captors put in at a bankside tavern he would buy drinks for all, they did not stop.

They arrived at Port of Heaven the next day. The river smell gave way to a rich mixture of salt spray, the sulfur of decaying sea creatures, and mud. The harbor was still thronged with empty warships riding at anchor, and the tide was going out.

Their junk laid up not far from a resin-hulled three-master, whose polymer bubble sails were even then being hoisted up to catch the wind where the sunlight covered them with rainbows. A dinghy was lowered into the water, and Darger and Surplus climbed down to it. They were transported to the ship, where a great-bearded man whose air of command proclaimed him the captain made a short speech and then clapped the shoulder of each of them before turning away. They were, it appeared, honored passengers.

Then there were shouts everywhere, the anchor was winched up, and the ship was under weigh. At the captain's direction, the pilot turned the nose of the ship to the east, catching the tide out of the harbor.

Darger and Surplus went to the bow to stare out over the billowing waves. Now that they were finally alone, Surplus had the opportunity at last to examine the contents of the purse they had been given. In answer to his friend's unspoken question, he said, "Enough to set us up in business when we reach our destination. Far less than we had reason to hope for."

He heaved a deep sigh, and they watched the Chinese mainland slowly grow dim in the distance. Finally, Surplus said, "I wonder where we are going?"